Malice

LIZ CROKIN

Printed by CreateSpace, Scotts Valley, California
An Amazon.com Company.

ISBN: 978-150776566-1

Printed in the United States

First Paperback Edition

DEDICATION

To Mom & Dad

Thanks for your unconditional love, support, faith and pledge
to stop reading at this page.

ACKNOWLEDGMENTS

Mike Davis deserves to be recognized first. He's a best friend, an amazing lawyer and a marketing genius. He's believed in me when I wasn't even sure if I still believed in myself. He's the most generous person I know; I'm so grateful to have him in my life.

I'm so blessed to have a brother who not only has my back, but he also happens to be an amazing artist. Pat Crokin has influenced this book in so many ways starting with the title *Malice*.

My boyfriend David Hennessey came into my life when I had hit rock bottom. He taught me the true meaning of unconditional love. He has spent days reading and editing my book. He's given me invaluable advice, support and always pushes me to be great. I'm a better person with him in my life.

This book would not have happened without the help from the sharp minds and editing skills of Meaghan Murphy and Danelle McCafferty. These ladies kept me motivated. I want to give a special shout out to Richard Roeper for all his wisdom on book publishing. Much gratitude to Kelly Springer, Tasos Katopodis and Marisa Sullivan for their expertise and support. Also, a huge thanks to the Breaking into Hollywood team for their hard work and industry insight.

I want to thank Shaun Murphy, Detective Shawn Murphy and Alan Jackson for all the countless hours they've worked to help me get the justice I deserve. They've offered me their legal eye during my writing process, and they've all lent me a shoulder to cry on at some point. I owe them all new shirts.

A big thanks to Dr. Jeffery Geohas, Dr. Barry Unger, Dr. Gary Richwald, Mrs. Homan and my Reiki healer extraordinaire Joey Cuellar. These professionals have provided me with some of the best healthcare in the world. They've also advised me on the medical aspects in this book. A big hug to my comfort dog, Oscar, too. There's nothing more therapeutic and healing than the unconditional love of a dog.

Maxine Page, Suzy McCoppin, Laura Argintar and Joana Pizzirusso not only supported me, but they also gave me a voice when others tried to silence me. I will always be grateful for these strong women.

Thanks to all my family and friends who have stood by me through my darkest days when I was not always an easy person to be around. I also want to thank my supporters who took the time to give me suggestions and encouragement for *Malice* via social media.

Finally, I want to thank all the men and women who have survived a crime, overcome an illness or risen above a disability. Many of you have reached out to me and you continue to inspire me every day.

Malice

CHAPTER 1

"What about Jennifer Aniston – did you guys see those photos of her walking on the beach the photo department sent over last night?" Ari Davidson asked as he scanned his office, which was tightly filled with a mix of a dozen reporters and editors.

It was our weekly Wednesday morning meeting. All the weekly gossip magazines close on Monday nights. We take Tuesdays off since we usually work well into the night on Monday. On Wednesday the process starts all over again with a pitch meeting discussing the stories we have on tap for the next issue.

"She looks fuller," Ari continued.

"Yeah, I did notice that," Mick Madden, a British twenty-year veteran at the magazine, chimed in. "How about a 'Pregnant with Twins' cover?"

I shook my head and sighed loudly. I noticed two female reporters shake their heads. One rolled her eyes. I had recently left *Celebrity Weekly* to work at the *L.A. Post*. It took Ari, the editor-in-chief, months to convince me to jump ship.

He seduced me with a fancy dinner at the posh members-only Soho Club in West Hollywood. You can expect to see an A-list movie star there any night of the week. He also offered me a salary worth fifty thousand dollars more per year. I had previously made ninety thousand dollars a year as an editor at *Celebrity Weekly*. The new income put me in a whole new tax bracket – I couldn't resist the extra cash flow. However, Ari also promised to assign me all the big stories, and he assured me that the *L.A. Post* still valued grassroots reporting unlike the other rags.

I attended journalism school because I love getting my hands wet in the field on a good story. However, I quickly learned that I wasn't going to win a Pulitzer working for a tabloid. I had been working at the *L.A. Post* for a few weeks now. I also quickly discovered that – contrary to what Ari had said before I accepted the job – the powers that be at the *L.A. Post* embellish stories just as grossly and recklessly as the editors at *Celebrity Weekly* and all the other weekly magazines.

"What is it, Lana?" Ari asked.

"It's just that the *L.A. Post* has done 'Jennifer Aniston Pregnant' stories on at least thirty different covers already! None of them turned out to be true," I said. "Come on, guys, we all know she's not pregnant."

"But she does look like she's gained weight," Mick said.

"She's probably bloated from her period or ate a carb for once – please!" I said.

"Well, it's a slow week, Lana. You know we have to get creative when there's not a big breaking story to cover," Ari said as he leaned back in his chair. "Unless you have any better ideas…"

I pursed my lips and racked my brain. My publicist friend, Carrie Hennessey, had texted me that morning. She said she had a big story for me about Daniel Vega, a movie star who made it big in the nineties and continues to remain relevant, but she wouldn't tell me any details. I was reluctant to mention in the meeting that I had a potential lead coming in about Daniel Vega, because if it turned out to be a bad lead it would just make me look stupid. Random sources and even experienced publicists call all the time claiming to have a great story, and more likely than not their tip ends up having no news value whatsoever.

"How about we revisit the 'Gavin Rossdale Secret Gay Life' story?" Mick asked.

"Ugh that's an even worse idea!" I said with a laugh. "Really, Mick?"

"Oh, Lana, you're just protecting Gavin because you're friends with Gwen Stefani," Mick said as he playfully slapped my right shoulder with his left hand.

"I didn't know you were friends with her," Ari said as he perked up from behind his desk and sipped coffee from his *L.A. Post* coffee mug.

"We're friendly. I've partied with both Gavin and Gwen a few times. Trust me, Gavin likes women."

"Lana, a tranny did a full interview about how they had a serious relationship and Gavin even admitted to it," Mick said.

"Yeah but that was years ago – way before he married Gwen," I said.

I had been at many parties where I've witnessed celebrities who claim to be straight hit on people of the same sex. The lines of sexuality are totally blurred in Hollywood. I've interviewed Angelina Jolie's former lesbian lover and done countless stories on Will and Jada Smith's swinger parties.

"I wouldn't be so sure about that," Mick said. "I'm sorry but if you fuck a dude – even if it's just once – you're gay."

"Maybe everywhere else in the world but we live in Hollyweird," I said as my phone vibrated in my hand. I looked on the caller ID. It was the call I had been waiting for all morning from Carrie.

"Hey, Ari, do you mind if I go into my office and take this? It's a publicist who claims to have a big story for me."

"By all means, please, go, Lana," Ari said. "Don't come back until you've got me a page one because as of now we've got nothing for next week."

"OK thanks," I said as I rushed out of his office.

I went into my office, closed the door, and had a five-minute conversation with Carrie. Carrie represents Lizzie Jefferson. Lizzie was married to the famous nineties actor, Conrad Jefferson, who famously co-starred along with Daniel Vega in the 1992 classic flick *Lightning*. Conrad tragically died in 2012 from a drug overdose. Lizzie claims to have notarized suicide letters and diary entries from Conrad where he made bombshell accusations against Daniel. Carrie said Lizzie was interested in selling the diary entries and suicide letters to the *L.A. Post* for publication. In Conrad's writings, one of his shocking claims detailed how Daniel molested him one night. Conrad also described many of Daniel's affairs with men that included some powerful Hollywood players. In one section of his diary, Conrad described how Daniel used the casting couch to his advantage. He scored many of his biggest roles by sucking dick. He sucked cock to score his first lead movie role in *Lightning*. I knew this could be *L.A. Post*'s big page one for next week, so I asked Carrie if she and Lizzie would meet me at Joan's on Third Street for lunch in an hour. She said yes. I fired off several e-mails before I rushed out of the office to meet them.

As I cruised down Fairfax Avenue in my black BMW X5, my phone rang. It was a 317 area code, which I didn't recognize. I usually never answer numbers I don't know. To score some cover stories, I've had to give my phone number to some pretty shady sources including criminals, a drug dealer, a pimp and even a homeless person. But today, for some reason, I felt compelled to pick up the phone.

"Hello," I said with curiosity.

"Hey, Lana, it's Ben," an energetic voice said.

"Who?" I asked with confusion.

"Ben Joseph from the Super Bowl."

"Oh, Ben -- how are you?"

I had totally forgotten that I had given this man I met at a Super Bowl party in Indianapolis my business card. Ben, along with a dozen party-hungry men, had welcomed my famous billionaire friend Tony Townsend and me into his modern Indiana home at four in the morning. Tony was one of my longtime high-profile friends who I met at the Cannes Film Festival years ago. He invited a bunch of his friends to his red carpet Super Bowl party, and we needed a place to keep the party going. At eight in the morning, we were still at Ben's house partying with athletes and C-list celebrities, drinking vodka straight from the bottle and dancing on his kitchen countertops. A lot of my non-industry friends envy my lifestyle because I get paid to party with celebrities and schmooze with VIPs.

"I'm great," Ben said. "I just wanted to touch base and tell you how great it was to meet you and Tony Townsend. I had such a blast at his Super Bowl party, and I was so happy to host you guys at my house for the late-night party."

"Oh, that's so sweet of you," I replied sincerely. "Thanks so much for opening your home to our wild crew. We all had a great time!"

"That party was something else. My kids are so jealous that I got to see Rihanna perform."

Tony spares no expense at his parties even if that requires dropping six or seven figures to book a hot musician.

"Yes, she was amazing," I said, wondering why Ben was calling.

I thought he was a nice guy, but I had no interest in dating someone who lives in Indiana.

"Anyway, I recently found your card in my wallet. I wanted to call you and say how wonderful it was to get to know you. I think you're a real cool girl. I'm really impressed with how smart you are and how much you've accomplished as a journalist."

Ben's compliment was flattering, but he needed to get to the point. I had an important lunch meeting. "Ben, you're too kind. I'm glad we met," I said trying to speed up the pace of our conversation. "I've been to many Super Bowls, but this one was definitely the best."

"Yes, it was. There's actually a reason why I'm calling."

"Really – what's that?" Finally he was getting to the point.

"Well, I never usually do this. I have to tell you I hate setting people up. I actually try to avoid it. If you set two people up, and it doesn't work out, you just get stuck in the middle and…it's just so awkward."

I was piecing everything together – Ben wants to play matchmaker?

"But anyway, I have a good friend out there in California who I'm going to say…I just see you guys hitting it off."

It was a nice gesture, but I did not have time for a relationship with my new job. I was focused on making a name for myself at the *L.A. Post.*

"Really...you know I'm single, but I'm really not looking to get into a relationship right now," I explained.

"I hear you," Ben said. "I just think at the least you guys will be good friends. I totally see you guys hitting it off."

I softened. "Does he live in L.A.?"

"He lives in Newport Beach, but he also has a house in San Francisco and homes in a few other places. He's a divorced single dad. The guy is kind of all over the place."

I decided to humor Ben. "Interesting. So what is he like?"

"He's a total thrill seeker. This guy flies planes, cliff dives, rides motorcycles – he's crazy! He thinks he's James Bond."

"James Bond? Oh jeez, he's one of those types. Does he surf?" Nothing turns me on more than a guy on a board.

"Yes, surf, ski, you name it. He does everything! He loves to travel, party and have fun."

"Well, like I said, I'm not looking to get involved with anyone right now, but you've got my attention. I'm intrigued. I do work a lot, so I don't have too much time to date. I'm actually heading to a meeting right now, but it might be fun to at least meet him. What's his name?"

"Malden Murphy."

"I have never met a guy named Malden before."

"Yeah, well, he certainly is one of a kind. Look, I'll have him send you a friend request on Facebook and you guys can start chatting. If it works out, great."

"Sounds good to me. Thanks for thinking of me. If you're ever in L.A., you better hit me up."

"Will do – now you take care, Lana."

I arrived to my lunch a fashionable fifteen minutes late, which is pretty punctual by L.A. standards. Carrie and Lizzie were already sitting at a corner table. They both had iced teas sitting in front of them. I apologized for my tardiness and quickly ordered a Diet Coke.

Lizzie, a skinny woman in her thirties with bleached blonde hair and pink highlights, wasted no time talking about Conrad. Lizzie's ex-husband had many failed rehab attempts – including several stints on *Dr. Duke's Star Rehab*. I could tell she still had a lot of raw emotion over Conrad's tragic death.

"I know this is hard for you to talk about, but why don't you begin by explaining Conrad's relationship with Daniel Vega," I said as sensitively as possible.

"Oh they were great friends at first," Lizzie said, smiling. "They adored each other. They became best friends on the set of *Lightning*, and that friendship lasted a really long time. They spent a lot of time together and always hung out at each other's houses."

"And we want to emphasize their strong friendship," Carrie quickly interjected like the good publicist she is. Carrie is the most down-to-earth publicist I know in Hollywood. She's a single mom of two, she has beautiful emerald green eyes, and long, sun-kissed dirty blonde hair. She's always in a great mood, and—unlike most publicists—I find her to be a pleasure to work with.

"Conrad truly cherished their friendship for years, and that's why what happened is so upsetting," Carrie said diplomatically.

"I get it," I said. "So did Conrad know about Daniel's gay tendencies?"

"Oh yes," Lizzie said with confidence. "He knew long ago. That's how he got many of his roles."

"So...you're saying he slept his way to the top?"

"Yes. He got his role in *Lightning* because he slept with

one of the producers."

"And you're talking about a male producer I take it?"
"Yes."

"So he knew Daniel Vega was gay, but did Conrad ever hook up with men?"

"Oh God no," Lizzie shrieked. "Conrad was as straight as they come. He's not homophobic. He knew Daniel was a closet gay man, and he didn't care."

"And...I take it Daniel knew Conrad was straight?"

"Yes, absolutely."

"So, tell me about the night Daniel tried to seduce Conrad."

"Conrad was at Daniel's house," Lizzie explained. "They had a party there that night. They were drinking and partying pretty hard, and Conrad ended up passing out. He used to spend the night at Daniel's a lot if he got too drunk, so he wouldn't have to worry about driving under the influence. He would just sleep in a guest bedroom."

"Did he sleep in a guest bedroom that night?"

"Yes," explained Lizzie. "He went in the guest bedroom and went to bed. Then, in the early hours of the morning, he woke up to Daniel sucking his dick."

Tears began to stream down Lizzie's face. At first, I was finding it hard not to laugh at this crazy story, but when I saw how painful this was for Lizzie to talk about, I felt terrible for her. Even though Conrad was a grown man when this happened he truly was a victim, and Daniel Vega – big Hollywood actor or not – was nothing but a sexual predator.

"OK take a deep breath," I said as I placed my hand on hers. "When Conrad woke up to Daniel performing oral sex on him – what did he do?"

"He told him to stop," she said with anger. "He said, 'Daniel what are you doing – get off me!'"

"And what was Daniel's reaction?"

"Daniel got real angry. He said if he didn't engage in sex with him then he would destroy his reputation in Hollywood and pull the plug on a cop show they were doing a pilot for at the time. Conrad continued to refuse Daniel, and Conrad left his house. It destroyed their friendship. Daniel trashed him in Hollywood, and he had their TV show canceled."

Lizzie handed me a notebook.

"Here's the notarized diary entry where Conrad wrote about the incident. He got a notary of the public to notarize it before his death."

I looked at the blue Mead notebook filled with dozens of pages of fragmented thoughts, written in what appeared to be the handwriting of a ten-year-old child.

I flipped through to the first dog-eared page, which read: "I woke up and Daniel Vega was sucking my dick. He sucked my dick and would not stop. I told him no, no, no!"

I was shocked at the disturbing diary entries.

"So, why did Conrad get this notarized?" I asked with skepticism. It was a little suspicious that he notarized diary entries with accusations that could be valuable to a publication such as the *L.A. Post*. It made me question if the accusations were true or if Lizzie was pulling a fast one on me to make a quick buck.

"Conrad wanted this to come out," Lizzie pleaded. "He wanted the truth to come out about Daniel Vega and all the couch casting that goes on in Hollywood. He got it notarized because he wanted me to go public with this info if he died. It was his last dying wish."

I looked deep into her eyes. I believed her. I had known

for years about Daniel Vega's true sexuality. He was notorious for perusing gyms and massage parlors all over Southern California for men. He even hit on one of my former bosses in the steam room of the West Hollywood Equinox. Daniel Vega's flaw is not that he's gay. His problem is that his ego has gotten so big that he doesn't seem to think there's anything wrong with sexually assaulting a man who refuses his sexual advances.

The *Post* had already published several stories on at least a half dozen massage therapists he had made unwanted sexual advances toward. All of them had passed polygraph tests and they all had similar stories: If they refused Daniel Vega's sexual advances, he'd get violent and threaten them.

I found Daniel's sense of entitlement disturbing and grotesque. He was a true sexual predator; however, a perfect subject for the *Post*. I told Lizzie that the *Post* would definitely be interested in purchasing the story from her. However, I would have to call Ari to find out how much money I could offer her in exchange for a full interview with excerpts from the diary entries and suicide letters. Most tabloids pay money for stories. Fortunately, the *Post* pays more than any of its competitors. It's always easier to nail down a story when I can throw money at a source. On the flip side, I have to be extra careful with the sources I pay. I have to make sure that they're not fabricating a story just to make money. It's a double-edged sword.

We all ordered salads for lunch. I told Lizzie that I would have a number that I could offer her by the end of the day and paid our lunch bill. I always pick up the bill. Fortunately, I can expense all source meetings. It's one of the many perks that come with the job.

When I got back to my office, I logged onto my computer and noticed that I had a new friend request notification on my Facebook profile from Malden Murphy. I accepted. He messaged me seconds later.

Malden Murphy: "Hello, Lana, how do you know Ben Joseph?"

Before I responded, I quickly went through his photos. The man was gorgeous! In some photos he looked like JFK Jr., but cuter. He had a perfect white smile, thick brown hair, deep blue eyes, and what appeared to be an amazing body. But he was older. In some photos he appeared to be in his early forties and in others he looked to be in his early fifties. However, in every photo, he certainly looked dashing – and yes – a little like James Bond, too. There were photos of Malden flying planes, riding motorcycles and even one of him jumping off a cliff into the ocean with a breathtaking sunset in the background. Oh my God! I could not respond to his Facebook IM quickly enough.

I took a deep breath and fired away.

Lana Burke: "Hey Malden! We met through Tony Townsend at his Super Bowl party in Indy. We all ended up at Ben's house for a late-night party that was super fun! Ben told me great things about you and said we should meet. How often do you come to L.A.?"

Malden Murphy: "How fun. I'm in OC at my house overlooking the ocean 80% of the time, an easy drive to L.A. from Newport Beach. I can buzz up on the motorcycle anytime. What's your cell number? I'll call when you have time to chat. I just got back from my place in Tahoe with my sons... Ever been? My place is in Meeks Bay, West Shore. How is your week going?"

This guy was something. He strategically mentioned that he has an Orange County house with an ocean view and a Tahoe home. Maybe your average L.A. gold digger would be moved by this play, but I wasn't impressed. I deal with rich people at my job every day. It takes more than money to move me.

Lana Burke: "Good. I went to a Clippers game the other night with a friend who was in town. He's doing a cross-country road trip from Chicago. We stayed out a little later than I had planned, but it was worth it.

I ignored the fact that he asked me for my number. I wasn't ready to dish it out just yet.

Malden Murphy: "I once did a two-week cross country road trip with my sons, and it was great! This past weekend I partied at the beach and had dinner with our chairman at his house. I'm giving my liver a 'pep talk' this week."

Lana Burke: "My liver needs a pep talk, too!"

Malden Murphy: "I hit it hard Monday evening and had a stinger Tuesday morning. I hurled before and after a big meeting at First Bank!"

Lana Burke: "OMG that's classic! I like your spirit!"

After I wrote my last IM to Malden, I thought about what he had just written. After a crazy night of drinking, he vomited both before and after a business meeting, and this man is middle-aged with kids? Why is a grown man with children drinking like a frat guy? Or was this an isolated incident? As if he read my mind, he wrote back.

Malden Murphy: "I'm a ten-year-old on the inside."

Lana Burke: "I was going to guess seven. What do you do for work?"

Malden Murphy: "Ha! You're funny. I work at a mortgage lending company in Irvine. Are you free to go out this weekend?"

This guy moves fast, I thought. At least he has a good job and I do like a man who gets straight to the point.

Lana Burke: "I have a wedding. Next week is better."

Malden Murphy: "What day?"

Lana Burke: "How about Thursday?"

Malden Murphy: "OK. Do you want to come down here?"

Lana Burke: "I usually get stuck working at the office late, so I'd prefer it if you'd come up here."

Malden Murphy: "No problem. I'll zip up there on my motorcycle."

Lana Burke: "Sounds like a plan."

I spent the rest of the afternoon negotiating a number to buy Lizzie's story. Carrie asked for twenty-five thousand. Ari told me I could offer five thousand. We met in the middle and agreed on ten thousand dollars. Ari approves all source fees before I'm allowed to draft a contract. I drafted the contract after we all came to an agreement. I scanned it and then e-mailed a copy to Carrie. I told her I needed it returned with Lizzie's signature on it by the end of the next business day. I was feeling good. I had a date with a hot successful man and another cover story in the works.

CHAPTER 2

The next few days flew by. I spent a lot of time with Lizzie. I interviewed her several more times before I wrote the first draft of the cover story on Conrad's sexual encounter with Daniel. It took me days to go through all of Conrad's suicide notes and diary entries. The only break I took from working on the story over the weekend was to attend a girlfriend's wedding in Beverly Hills. I completed the final draft of the story on Monday evening as the magazine went to press. The headline read "Conrad Jefferson's Suicide Letters: 'Daniel Vega Molested Me!'" I was happy with the story, and I was relieved to have a cover story under my belt within the first few weeks at my new job. Ari was pleased too, especially since Daniel's publicist or lawyer didn't challenge our story. We contacted Daniel's high-profile rep before the story went to press for a comment. This is standard protocol for all stories especially the more salacious ones, but she never got back to us. It didn't surprise me. There have been so many stories published about Daniel's gay affairs that his team doesn't even respond to any of them anymore. Radio silence from a publicist can be a good indicator of the validity of a story. Fame and money only go so far. The truth is the only real protection a person has in a lawsuit. Celebrities are well aware of this. Also, if a celebrity does file a lawsuit against a magazine over a story, they know that the publication has the legal rights to subpoena their e-mails and phone records including text messages. So you'll often see a celebrity publicly claim that they're going to sue a publication. Some of them will even send out a legal letter. However, at the end of the day, if a publication prints a scandalous story that is in fact true, you'll rarely ever see that star actually follow through with filing a lawsuit. David Beckham is notorious for this. He threatened to sue a magazine I worked for years ago that broke a cover story about an affair he had. He claimed he was going to sue the publication. His lawyer sent the magazine a legal letter; however, David never filed the lawsuit, and that's because the magazine had the facts and the evidence on its side.

It was Thursday evening before I knew it. I had my big date with Mr. JFK Jr., and I found myself at the office late again. When I got home, I tore through my closet like a hurricane, desperately looking for a hot outfit to wear. I was running at least twenty minutes behind, so I had to act fast to put myself together. I threw on a pair of dark blue denim skinny jeans, the highest shiny black heels I could find and a black blouse. I wore a long gold necklace to spice up my outfit. I sprayed dry shampoo into my hair and touched up my makeup. I gave my eyes a sexy, smoky look. I topped off my outfit with a black leather jacket. I was going for a biker look since Malden said he was picking me up on his motorcycle.

At 7:00 p.m. on the dot, my doorman called to let me know Malden was there. When I walked outside, I spotted Malden right away. He was leaning up against the entrance gate of my building holding a silver motorcycle helmet. He was wearing designer jeans over black boots, a light blue Polo shirt, and his hair was a little windblown from the trek up. Malden did look a bit older than some of the photos on his Facebook page, especially with his salt-and-pepper colored hair, but he was still gorgeous!

Malden grinned as soon as he laid eyes on me and scanned me up and down a few times. I could tell that he liked what he saw. "You're losing points," he shouted at me with a tough guy look on his face.

"Excuse me?" I questioned him.

"You're five minutes late."

"Oh really?" I said with a laugh. "Not so fast, hot shot. It's seven-oh-four, and I walked out as soon as my doorman called me."

"Get over here – I have something for you."

"Gifts already?"

"Not exactly," he said as he handed me a black helmet. "Put this on."

I strapped on the helmet and hopped onto the back of his black BMW motorcycle. I wrapped my arms around his torso and couldn't believe how strong this guy was. I instantly thought about what he looked like naked. As he handled the bike with finesse, I wondered how he would handle me in bed.

"Where to?" he asked.

"There's a good gastro pub called Churchill a few blocks west on Third Street," I suggested.

"Churchill it is. Are you ready for the adventure of your life, Lana?" he asked with a wicked smile.

"Ha! We'll see about that," I said flirtatiously. "I think the real question is – are you ready for the adventure of your life? I know you're a little old, with probably a lot of life experience, but I bet you've never met a girl like me."

Malden let out a loud infectious laugh. "We'll see about that!"

We were off. Malden sped down Third Street like a superhero. His need for speed didn't impress me. It just made me nervous. I tried really hard not to let it show. I happily clung on to him with a tight grip. Malden squeezed into a spot on the street next to a Porsche. He helped me off the motorcycle and we removed our helmets. We walked into the Churchill together, each holding onto our helmets with our right hands.

Before I even blinked, I spotted some of my colleagues at a table right by the entrance. I was mortified. Not exactly the group of people I wanted to run into on a first date. I felt particularly awkward because my date was probably around twenty years older than me. One particular colleague, Ted Thomas, who used to be one of my bosses at the *Post* before he moved to another magazine at our company, had given me grief about dating older men, and Malden's age was a stretch even for me.

"Lana!" Ted shouted with a slur as I walked in. I could tell he was buzzed. Ted was a hard partying cokehead in his forties. He grew up in Malibu and fell into the business by attending Hollywood parties. "What are you doing here?"

"Hey!" I said uncomfortably. "I'm here with my friend Malden. Malden, meet Ted and my colleagues Joe and Sandra. Malden's friends with some of the guys I went to the Super

Bowl with this year."

I was trying to play my date off as a casual thing in the hopes of dealing with less abuse from Ted at the office the next day. They smiled and all politely said hi. Malden and I headed to a table upstairs – far away from my co-workers. I could relax. I attempted to explain to Malden why it was so awkward running into colleagues.

"What do you mean awkward?" Malden asked with confusion. "You just rode up in a BMW motorcycle and walked in with this cool biker guy. You look like a badass in front of your peers."

He was so cocky. It was annoying, but also it turned me on. Malden asked if I was hungry and suggested a flatbread pizza and the spinach artichoke dip. Those were the two items I was already eyeing. He also ordered a fifty-dollar bottle of pinot noir from Napa Valley. We were off to a good start.

"So what exactly is it you do?" Malden asked.

"I'm a reporter for the *Los Angeles Post*," I said. "I've been covering celebrities for years. I've uncovered salacious stories on everyone from big movie stars like Ben Aflleck to reality stars such as Tori Spelling. I just finished a huge cover story about Conrad Jefferson's diary entries. In them, he claims that Daniel Vega molested him."

"Wow! So the rumors are true about Daniel Vega? Is he really gay?"

"Oh yeah."

"Really?"

"Does a bear shit in the woods?"

"I knew it! You know, it's funny because, his wife, Avery Vega, is one of my ex-girlfriends. I dated her years ago, before she got together with Daniel."

That's ironic, I thought as I tried to factor in how old he was based on that fact. I cringed because he had to be in his early fifties. "How long did you guys date for?"

"We dated for a year and lived together in an apartment in Pacific Palisades. I had just graduated from Berkeley. I was working as a waiter at Gladstone's. My mom hated her. I brought her home once, and my mom did not approve. She always told me she was an opportunist and not the girl for me. I later found out she was cheating on me with some fat director. She slept around with anyone she thought would help land her a film role."

"That doesn't surprise me," I said as I shook my head. "It sounds like Mr. and Mrs. Vega are two birds of a feather."

The waitress came over and poured wine into our glasses. We toasted to new friends. I noticed the red wine was going down quickly for both of us. I was a little nervous and intimidated by this man. I usually stay away from guys who are this good looking, because they're typically bad news.

Regardless as we ate, I entertained Malden with my travels as a journalist. I told him about how I recently went to the Galapagos Islands to cover the newly engaged Angelina Jolie and Brad Pitt because we suspected they were planning a secret wedding there that never happened. I explained how I befriended all the islanders there within a few days. He laughed when I told him that I had left my mark on the island by teaching the locals how to air guitar. Whenever I cracked a joke – especially a dirty joke – Malden would pause, making me question if I had stepped over the line, and then let out a roaring, boisterous laugh. I quickly fell in love with his laugh.

I slowly turned the conversation a little more serious. I had questions. "So, if you don't mind me asking, how many kids do you have?"

"I have five."

I reached for the bottle of wine and quickly poured myself another glass of pinot. Five fucking kids? What the hell is this *The Brady Bunch*? I've dated older men before, but never a man with kids – let alone five! I like children, but I'm not looking to be a step-mom–especially to so many kids. I couldn't help but cringe a little and Malden picked up on my reaction that I had tried so hard to hide.

"I know what you're thinking. That's a lot of kids, but all my kids are teenagers and self-sufficient except for one. The youngest doesn't even live here so I rarely see him. I see my other kids about every other weekend and they're great. You'll love them!"

"So they're not all from the same marriage?"

"Well, I have four from my only marriage, and the fifth was a scud missile," Malden said as he poured himself his third glass of wine.

"A scud missile? What does that mean?"

"It's a long story. An ex-girlfriend set me up. She was in San Francisco the same weekend I was there visiting my children. She claimed she was there on a girl's trip with her sister. Turns out, her sister wasn't even there. We met for a drink and one thing lead to another and we had sex. She told me she was on birth control at the time. Not only was she not on birth control, she was ovulating and she had plotted to get pregnant. She was hoping that I would get back together with her if she got pregnant. I couldn't believe she did this to me. I didn't even believe it was my child at first. I got a court order for a paternity test."

And here come the red flags. They were blowing right in my face, but I tried to ignore them. I was too distracted by the gorgeous man sitting across from me.

"Wow, no offense, but you've certainly got some baggage," I said with a frown. This revelation was certainly a turn-off. No woman wakes up and says they can't wait to meet a man with kids from two baby mamas!

Malden flashed his big JFK Jr. smile – wait, what turn-off? "It's a blessing in disguise. He's a great kid, and my other children adore him."

Despite all the baggage, I found Malden to be extremely fun and attractive. I knew that he could sense that I was a little cautious – and I knew that only made me more attractive to him. We continued to talk about politics, current events, books, movies and religion. I couldn't believe how much we had in common. We both come from Irish Catholic families. We are both diehard Republicans. We also share the same values, religious beliefs, sense of humor – we seemed to see eye to eye on almost everything. I was very attracted to him, and I could tell he felt the same way about me. Two hours passed, and we were on our third bottle of wine. Malden had made his way to my side of the table. He squeezed next to me in the booth and put his arm around me. He took me by surprise next by moving in for a kiss. Already? I hate PDA! But, I didn't pull back. It felt right. He put his strong, muscular arm around me and pulled me close.

I hadn't gotten laid in a while, and I could feel my nude lace Victoria's Secret thong instantly get wet. I wanted nothing more than to rip off my motorcycle-inspired outfit and ride him like a horse in this Hollywood bar filled with wannabe actors and cheesy hipsters. The waitress interrupted our immature make-out session with our check. Malden pulled out a credit card and gave it to the waitress without even looking at the bill.

"There's one more place I'd like to take you, if you're up for it," I said to him with a slight buzz.

"If I get to hang out with you longer, I'm up for anything," Malden said with a wide smile. "But if I have any more drinks, I won't be able to ride my motorcycle back down to Orange County."

I certainly knew where this was going. "Oh, are we getting a little presumptuous?" I asked with a flirty smile. "If you want to crash on my couch, you're more than welcome to – if you think you can behave yourself. I would feel terrible if anything happened to you if you attempted to ride your bike all the way home after all the wine we've had."

"Yes, I do want to crash on your couch, and no I don't think I can control myself," he said with his dangerous boyish smile.

Malden and I left Churchill and I dragged him for one more drink to a sports bar right next door called Goal. I always pop in there for a drink if I'm in the neighborhood because Leonardo DiCaprio and several of his celebrity friends frequent the dive. It's one of Hollywood's best-kept secrets, and I usually walk out of the bar with a story I can publish. Plus, I can expense my drinks to the company, so it's always a win-win.

Malden ordered a Stella, and I ordered a glass of cheap red wine. There were less than a dozen people in the bar, and we barely talked. We just continued to make out like two kids in high school. I hadn't even taken one sip of my wine before Malden stopped me.

"Forget the wine, Lana, let's go back to your place. I have a couple bottles of red in the storage compartment of my motorcycle, if you want to drink more."

He keeps wine in his motorcycle?

"OK, but wait, there's one thing we have to do before we leave," I said as I whipped out my iPhone and told Malden to smile as I kissed him on his left cheek. I snapped a selfie of us, and it was priceless. I looked beautiful, and he looked handsome as hell —despite the fact we were three sheets to the wind. We looked way too comfortable with each other in the picture - like a couple who have weathered many years together.

"I'm going to text the photo to Ben," I said.

"Good idea," Malden said. "He'll be so happy that we're hanging out."

I sent the photo to our matchmaker, and I didn't even write a caption. As we walked out of Goal, Ben responded.

Ben Joseph: "Perfect."

The ride on Malden's motorcycle back to my apartment was a blur. We both stumbled through the garage and into the elevator. By the time we made it to my apartment door on the second floor, Malden had already ripped off my leather jacket and was rubbing his massive, masculine hands up and down my chest. I flung the door open, and he asked where my bathroom was. I pointed toward my bedroom.

As Malden raced toward the bathroom, I made a mad dash for the huge mirror in my living room. As I suspected, my black eyeliner was smeared under both my eyes, and my Mac lip-gloss was smeared all over my upper lip. I quickly fixed my makeup and poured two glasses of wine from the bottle I had snagged from Malden's motorcycle. I turned on my iPod. The first song that played was *Start Me Up* by the Rolling Stones. It was the right song for the right moment.

Malden came out of the bathroom. I handed him a glass

of wine, and we headed out to my balcony overlooking the Spanish-style courtyard. We had a view of a huge cement fountain, but the sound of the water was faded by the rock n' roll music in the background. We both took a seat on one of the two wicker chairs and continued to drink.

Without saying a word, I leaped out of my chair straight into Malden's lap. I ripped off my shirt, and with only my bra on, I continued to make out with this grown man in full view of my neighbors' apartments. We somehow made it into my bedroom and into my bed. I wasn't sure how. I was buzzed, feeling fearless and wearing nothing but a thong.

Malden was on top of me, still fully clothed. I ripped off his shirt and quickly flipped him over. Straddling my legs, I climbed on top of him. My arms ran down his bare biceps and forearms, and I once again marveled at how strong his arms were and how soft and smooth his skin was. Malden had the skin of a guy in his twenties. I slowly began to kiss him on his broad chest. I took my time working my tongue down to his naval. I didn't waste any time unbuttoning the top button on his jeans. I looked at him seductively as he unzipped his pants. I aggressively ripped his jeans off his legs. He was wearing blue plaid boxers. I ripped those off next. His cock was hard and perfect. It had good width, and it was big—but not too big. It appeared to be eight to ten inches long. I could feel liquid dripping out of my pussy. I had not had sex in months. I could not control myself. I was so attracted to Malden.

Just as Malden began to thrust the tip of his cock into my wet, waxed vagina, I put my hand over his mouth and told him to hold on. I shifted across the bed and reached for my nightstand drawer. I shuffled through sex toys, batteries and bottles of lube for a few seconds looking for a condom. I couldn't find one. Shit!

"What are you doing, sexy girl?" Malden asked with anticipation. "You've got me all worked up."

"I'm trying to find a condom, but I think I'm out," I said, out of breath.

"Are you on birth control?" he asked.

"Yes, I'm on the NuvaRing, but I can't have unprotected sex with someone I've just met!" I explained.

"I'm clean, and I'll pull out so you don't have to worry," he said.

I evaluated the situation in my drunken head quickly. "OK," I relented. "What the hell."

I couldn't resist the temptation. The good girl in me said: "Don't do it!" The devil pleaded a better case. I convinced myself that even though I liked him, he was too old for me. Plus, I didn't want to date a guy with five kids. I told myself that it would be no loss if he didn't ask me out on a second date because I gave it up on the first one. Malden had way more baggage than I wanted to take on. He was absolutely not the kind of person I wanted to get involved with, even though I found him completely irresistible sexually.

I got back on top of him and thrust myself into his hard cock. An electric rush went through my body. He lowered his head as I rocked back and forth on top of him. He sucked and bit my small, hard nipples. Eventually he flipped me over and got on top. He gazed at me with his ocean blue eyes as he thrust his hard cock deep into my throbbing pussy. I put my arms around his shoulders and inhaled his masculine, musky cologne. I never wanted to forget that smell.

As Malden approached a climax, he squinted his eyes, opened his mouth, and clenched his teeth like a horse chewing on a bit. I was blown away at how much his facial expression turned me on. I let out an enormous moan and came so hard that I felt the room spin. Almost in perfect unison, he slipped his dick out and came all over my tits. Malden lay on top of me and began to shake uncontrollably for several minutes. I found the shaking strange and hot. Why was he shaking? I wrapped my arms around him as he shook and held him close. Neither of us could catch our breath.

Just when I thought he was done getting off, he started shaking all over again. I couldn't believe how intense and dramatic his orgasm was. It was like a huge earthquake–with several aftershocks, every minute or so. I had never slept with a man who reacted that way. After several minutes passed, Malden lifted himself off me. He spread out next to me so that we were lying side by side. Both of us faced the ceiling, still breathing hard. He gently grabbed my hand.

"You're amazing Lana," he whispered. "I like you."

I looked at him and smiled. I then turned over so that my back was against his chest. He quickly reached his right arm around me and held me tight. Within seconds, I was sound asleep in his arms.

The next morning, when I opened my eyes, I saw that my alarm clock read 7:00 a.m. I was in the exact same position that I had fallen asleep in, and Malden's arm was still tightly wrapped around me. Even though I had a virtual stranger in my bed, I had never felt so safe and at home. I felt like I was in bed with someone whom I had woken up next to for years. I remembered the hot sex we had, and I could feel myself getting wet again. I grabbed Malden's right hand with mine and lowered it into my pussy. He instantly started rubbing my clitoris.

"Well, good morning," he said as he kissed my right ear. "You're a very horny girl, aren't you?"

"Don't stop," I panted back.

He fingered me for about twenty minutes and then moved his right hand up to my hard right nipple. He began to pull and twist it as hard as possible. It hurt like a bitch! Just when I thought I couldn't take it any longer, I shouted at him, "Harder! He continued to twist my right nipple harder for five more minutes as he continued to rub my wet pussy. Then he moved on to my left nipple. Both my nipples were throbbing in pain, but I enjoyed it. I had never been into masochistic sex before, but this felt different. We continued to have sex for another hour. This time he flipped me over on my stomach and fucked me from behind. He came all over my back and shook vigorously, yet, again. I couldn't believe that a man his age could come twice in such a short period of time. I wondered if he was taking performance enhancement drugs, but I didn't dare ask. However, I couldn't resist asking his age.

"OK, now that you've gotten to know me – how old are you exactly?"

"Fifty-five," Malden reluctantly said under his breath.

"What?" I said in shock. "You have the stamina of a teenager!"

"I told you, Lana – I'm a kid at heart," he said as he flashed his dashing smile. He really did look like JFK, Jr.

I climbed out of bed and went to the kitchen to get a much-needed glass of ice water. I had a headache from all the wine, and I was pretty certain that I might still be a little drunk. As I gulped almost the entire glass, I surveyed the damage in my tiny – but swanky – Hollywood apartment. Holy shit! I couldn't believe my eyes. There was one shoe in the kitchen, one in the dining area, my jeans were on the couch, and when I looked over on the balcony–I found my bra hanging over the ledge and a broken wine glass shattered on the ground. I knew

I had shown Malden a good time, but I didn't remember showing him that good of a time!

I walked back into my bedroom where Malden was still snuggled under my light blue Calvin Klein floral comforter. I asked him about the broken wineglass.

"You don't remember that?" Malden questioned me with a laugh. "You knocked over the glass as you were kissing me. I asked you if you wanted me to clean it up, and you said, 'don't fucking worry about it.'"

"Wow, I did?" I asked as I blushed in total embarrassment. "What can I say—you got me all worked up."

Malden grabbed my arm and tried to convince me to get back into bed.

"I would love to, but I need to get to work," I said sternly. "I have a lot going on."

"Come on, Lana," he begged.

"Unless you want to pay my rent, I can't risk losing my job to have sex with you all day."

"Well, then I'll be taking a rain check," he said with confidence.

"We'll see about that," I said, winking at him.

After we got dressed, we left my apartment together. He kissed me on the lips and promised me that he would call before we parted ways. I was certain he would, but I told myself that if he didn't, I didn't care – because he was absolutely way too old for me and there was no way I'd get involved with someone more than twenty years older than I was – and who had five children.

I realized during the walk up to my office that I was in a tremendous amount of pain. My crotch and my legs were sore. I could barely walk. I was certain that I smelled like a vineyard from the wine that was oozing out of my pores. I walked at a faster pace. I wanted to get to my office as quickly as possible. I was relieved that Ari worked from his home office at his Palm Desert vacation house on random weeks and this was one of those weeks. I'm especially grateful of his absence on my less productive days at work thanks to the frequent red carpet Hollywood events I regularly attend sometimes into the early hours of the morning. I prayed Ted wouldn't be in yet. Even though he didn't work for my publication any longer, we still had offices right next door to each other that shared a thin wall. As I got closer to Ted's office, I saw that the lights were off and his chair was empty. Ah, relief. I knew Ted probably got more blitzed than I did last night and would most likely roll in late like he so often does when he's hung over. When I got into my office, I immediately closed the door so I could hibernate. I prayed no one would be able to tell that I was extremely hung over.

Someone knocked on my door.

"Come in," I said.

Nigel Thomas, our flamboyant office manager, sauntered in. Nigel wears more hot pink and sparkles in one day than I do in an entire year. I found this ironic and hilarious since his name is a masculine English name. He had a sly look on his face, and he wasted no time prying.

"Lana, why are you walking funny?" he asked with a big smile.

"You're kidding me – are you being serious?"

"Yes, I'm serious," he said in a bratty, exaggerated tone.

"There's no way I'm obviously walking funny."

"Maybe not obvious to others, but obvious to me."

Nigel paused for a moment, then his eyes widened. "Wait a minute, was last night your big date with Mr. Malden?" he asked excitedly.

I blushed. I had made the mistake of telling Nigel about my date with Malden the other afternoon when I had found myself momentarily bored and hungry for gossip at work.

"Close the door," I said. Nigel quickly closed the door and sat on the chair across from my desk.

"Yes, it was," I confessed. "We had wild sex all night, and now I'm in a ton of pain."

"Lana! You didn't! On the first date?"

"I know, I know," I said in embarrassment. "But it's fine. He was amazing in bed, but he's fifty-five. I mean, let's be real, I'm not going to seriously date this guy, so if he never calls me again I couldn't care less. Plus, he has five kids. Five! I'm not looking to be the next star of *The Real Housewives of Orange County*!"

"Lana, you're full of shit," Nigel called me out. "The guy owns five homes, and he is gorgeous. Who cares about the kids? I'm sure he has a nanny or two."

"Well, after the performance I put on for him last night, I'm sure he'll be crawling back for more. I'm not worried about it."

"What kind of performance was that?"

"Let's just say I found an article of clothing I wore last night in each room in my apartment," I said with a grimace.

"Oh, Lana, I have a feeling you'll be getting a ring from this one," he said with a wink as he headed for my office door. He turned around as he opened the door. "Before I forget, please fill out your insurance forms and get them to me as soon as possible so we can get your cute little sore butt on health insurance," he said.

I looked over at the stack of health insurance forms with the thick packet of information regarding the company's healthcare policy that I had been avoiding. It gave me an instant headache.

"Right, of course," I said. "I'll get it done when I have a second."

Nigel flashed me a skeptical look and sauntered out the door. We had only known each other for a few weeks, but he knew me well enough to know that I'm not very good with paperwork.

I found it difficult to get work done. I had several stories to edit, and I needed to come up with a follow-up story on Daniel Vega. My cover on Daniel's affair with Conrad Jefferson sold very well. Ari was very pleased, so he asked me to come up with a follow-up in the hopes of riding off the wave of the success of last week's front-page bombshell story. Every time I tried to focus on work, however, visions of my crazy, sex-charged night with Malden came rushing back. I couldn't resist perusing his Facebook page. I went through hundreds of Malden's pictures. I kept fantasizing about him naked and shaking on top of me. I found some photos of him in a bathing suit on the beach in Newport Beach. I felt my thong get wet again. He was so yummy! This guy had turned me on like no one ever had in my entire thirty-two years of living. I thought the day would never end.

By mid-afternoon I was stone sober. I began to regret my actions from the night before. My nipples stung like a bitch. With my office door still closed, I looked down my shirt. I had rug burns all over my nipples! I even noticed a little dry blood on the inside of my nude lace Victoria's Secret bra. What in the hell have I done? I never sleep with a guy on the first date. Malden will certainly think I'm a whore! I knew deep down inside that I may have blown it with him. I tried to tell myself I didn't care, but I did care. I laid my head in my hands in defeat on my desk. A moment later, my phone beeped.

Malden Murphy: "When can I see you again?"

Phew! That was a close one. I breathed a huge sigh of relief and smiled. He was smitten.

CHAPTER 3

It was 11:00 a.m. on Saturday morning. I was at the Nine Zero One salon in West Hollywood for a haircut with my regular stylist, Hailey. The salon was having a media day with free hair services, spray tans and cocktails for the MTV Movie Awards that were scheduled for the next afternoon. My time with Hailey was always spent gossiping–usually about guys.

"So what's new with you?" Hailey asked as she combed through my clean, wet hair. "Any new guys in your life?"

"Actually, yes," I said. "I'm kind of in a dilemma. I have this handsome Brazilian guy I met in the Galapagos Islands meeting me here in thirty minutes. He's traveling around the world for a year. He's in town now for a week or so, and he wants me to go out clubbing with him tonight."

"Well, that's not a bad problem to have," Hailey said, with a quizzical look on her face. "So, what's the dilemma?"

"So the dilemma is this: I went on a date with this gorgeous man the other night, and he keeps texting me to hang out with him again. He asked me out last night, but I was too wiped from work. So now he's asking me to go down to his

Newport Beach house for dinner. I was really looking forward to hanging out with the Brazilian, but I'm crazy about this new guy."

"Wow! That's exciting," Hailey said. "What's his name?"

"Malden."

"Malden? That's a strange name," Hailey said as she trimmed the ends of my hair.

"I know it is, and I think it's just as sexy as he is. Thursday night was our first date and I swear it was the best first date I've ever had!"

"It sounds like you really like this guy."

"I do, but..."

"But what?"

"Well, he's a lot older."

"How old?"

"He's fifty-five. It makes me a little uncomfortable."

Hailey shrugged, "Lana, this is Hollywood. That's not too crazy of an age difference. You're thirty-two, right?"

"Yes, but it's not just his age. He has five kids. Four of them are from his ex-wife, and he says the fifth was an accident from some girl that he had a fling with. I like kids, but let's be honest, no woman wakes up and says their dream guy will have five kids from two baby mamas. It's a lot of baggage to take on."

"That is a lot, but I've never seen you so giddy," Hailey said with a smile. "You're falling in love. You need to go hang out with Malden tonight. You wouldn't date a guy who lives in Brazil anyway–even if he is drop dead gorgeous. Plus, you look amazing, and your hair will be done. Malden has got to see you tonight."

"You're right, but I don't know if I'm falling in love," I said, blushing. "I'll head down to Newport Beach later tonight to have dinner with Malden."

I reached in my pocket and whipped out my iPhone. I shot Malden a text responding to the message he sent me that morning asking me to drive down to his place for dinner.

Lana Burke: "I'll be there around six. Text me your address."

His response was almost instant.

Malden Murphy: "Yay!"

I sat back in my chair and smiled. Maybe I *was* falling in love. Just minutes after Hailey finished blow drying my hair, Leandro, my Brazilian friend, walked in. He looked just as cute as I remembered him. I met him on a small beach in Santa Cruz Island. It was like a scene from a movie. He was walking out of the ocean when he first caught my eye. He had strong biceps, a dark, rich tan, sun-bleached dirty blonde hair and a big bright white smile. I asked him if he'd take a picture of me on the beach since I was there alone. After we chatted for fifteen minutes, he asked me to meet him for drinks at the local hot spot, Club Bongo. We had a blast doing shots and dancing the night away. We made out in the club, but I went home alone. I wondered at the time if that was a mistake.

"Leandro!" I screeched. I ran over and gave him a big hug.

"Hi, Lana," he said with his sexy Brazilian accent.

"Welcome to the U.S.," I said with a laugh.

"Thank you, thank you," he said, grinning ear-to-ear.

"Let's go in the other room and get you a drink. That's where the bar is," I said as I grabbed his hand and took him in the other room.

We each got a glass of champagne and toasted to our

stateside reunion. Leandro filled me in on his recent adventures. He said he had visited other islands in the Galapagos before he headed to the United States. His first stop was San Diego. He spent his days hitting the beaches and his nights clubbing. As he told me stories from his San Diego trip, I debated in my head how I was going to break the news to him that I wouldn't be able to hang out with him tonight.

"So...I have some good news and bad news for you," I explained.

"Oh you do," he said as he sipped champagne. "Tell me the good news first."

"There's a cocktail party we can go to this afternoon for the MTV Movie Awards," I said in an attempt to entice him. "There will be an open bar, live music and celebrities."

"That sounds like a blast!" he said with excitement. "So what's the catch?"

"Well, the bad news is that something came up, and I can't go out clubbing with you tonight." I sighed with guilt. "I need to head down to Newport Beach at four for a dinner."

"That's OK Lana," he said with ease. "I have other friends who live here. I'm just glad we're hanging out now."

I exhaled a deep sigh of relief. I didn't owe Leandro anything, but he was such a nice guy. I hated disappointing people. Plus, we had been Facebooking about getting together in Los Angeles since I met him a couple months ago, and he'd been very eager to hit the L.A. nightclub circuit.

Leandro and I left the salon and headed to the cocktail party. It was held in the backyard of a big, white mansion in a gated community in Hancock Park. A local rock band performed live music on a stage behind the Olympic-sized swimming pool. There was a full bar and publicists gifting reporters and celebrities various products from companies ranging from electronics to clothes and jewelry.

I introduced Leandro to some of my reporter friends, after which he took full advantage of the open bar. By late afternoon, I could tell Leandro had a serious buzz going. He was dancing with a brunette girl who looked about nineteen with big, fake tits. I didn't want to kill his game, but I was beyond eager to get in my car and drive down to Malden's home. I knew it would take me at least an hour and a half to get there.

"Excuse me," I said to Leandro, tapping him on the shoulder as he was grinding his new female friend.

"Lana!" he slurred. "This is a blast! Meet Daisy."

"Hi Daisy," I said, forcing a smile. "I need to borrow him for one quick second."

"Leandro, I have to head out now so I'm not late for my dinner. Are you OK to stay here alone?"

"No, Lana! Don't leave," he pleaded.

"Leandro I can't stay. I told you I have a dinner."

"But when will I be able to see you again?"

"Why don't we hang out later in the week? You'll be here for a week, right?"

"Yes," Leandro slurred. "Then it's Vegas, baby! Come to Vegas with me!"

"I'll think about Vegas. Do you need me to give you a number for a cab company? Are you cool?"

"No, no," he protested. "Daisy said she'd give me a ride. She's going to go clubbing with me tonight."

"Are you sure?"

"Yes. Thank you, Lana, for everything," Leandro said as he planted a drunken wet kiss on my cheek.

I raced to the valet. It took five minutes for the attendant to pull up my X5. The minutes felt like hours. Once inside my

SUV, I put the address Malden sent me into my GPS. My estimated arrival time was an hour and forty-five minutes, which should place me at Malden's a little before six. I was very eager to see this beach house he boasted about with its sweeping ocean views. I threw on a Muse CD for the drive. I took the I-10 West and headed toward the 405 South. I prayed there would be no traffic. By some miracle, there wasn't. This was very rare in L.A., but it was Saturday. The weekends are usually the safest bets in terms of traffic. I drove past Manhattan Beach, Redondo Beach, Huntington Beach, and Seal Beach—all the beach towns. It felt like the drive would never end. As I approached my exit, my phone beeped.

Malden Murphy: "Meet me down at the private beach. The guard at the gate will tell you how to get there. We'll watch the sunset and drink wine."

Lana Burke: "Sounds good."

I had been to most of the beach cities, but never Newport Beach. As I pulled onto MacArthur Boulevard and headed west, I rolled down my window. I couldn't see the Pacific Ocean yet, but I could smell it as if I was standing in the sand. The air was so crisp and fresh. I had to be close. Within minutes I pulled over a small hill, and I could see the entire ocean. It was a breathtaking view. The ocean looked majestic. There wasn't one cloud in the sky. The sun was due to set in about an hour, and the sky was the most beautiful shades of red, pink and purple.

When I arrived at the gate, I was a little confused because it was on the east side of the road. The guard explained that I would take two right turns, go under a bridge, and then I'd be at the private beach. I slowly pulled my car through the winding roads in the upscale community. The houses were all enormous and beautiful. They were all perched on hills, and most featured huge floor-to-ceiling windows facing the ocean. Almost every house I passed had some kind of a custom golf cart in the driveway. As I got closer to the private beach, I passed a few families headed in the opposite direction in their golf carts. Some were loaded with scuba gear and surfboards. I couldn't believe that people lived like this year round. I was in paradise.

I parked my car at a spot close to the beach. There was a playground with a couple of swings and a jungle gym next to several wooden picnic tables. Barbecue grills lined the beach, and there were about a dozen people enjoying this perfect summer night. One family sat at a table, eating burgers. Another couple strolled hand-in-hand by the water. A father and son played Frisbee. Then, there was Malden. He was on the south end by a cove.

As I approached, waves crashed against huge boulder-sized rocks. Malden sat in a lawn chair sporting a white T-shirt and blue swim trunks. Black sunglasses obscured his eyes as he caressed a glass of white wine in his hand. He was looking out toward the ocean and didn't see me coming. When I was within feet of him, he turned his head to the right and spotted me. He smiled. I smiled back as I approached him.

"There's my beautiful girl!" he said, putting his wineglass down as he stood up.

"Hi!" I said as I ran toward him.

"You found me," Malden said as he opened his arms toward me. I hugged him, and in response, he lifted me in the air and twirled me around. Leaning in for a kiss, he asked, "Do you want a glass of wine?"

"Yes," I cooed as Malden sat back on his chair. I

immediately followed by sitting on his lap, even though he had set up a lawn chair for me. I wrapped my arms around him and kissed him again on the lips. I couldn't control myself. We made out for minutes like high school kids. Finally, Malden poured me a glass of wine.

"Cheers," he said.

"Wait," I responded. "What are we toasting to?"

"To your first of many nights in Newport," he said as he flashed his JFK Jr. smile. I melted.

"I like that," I said as I nodded my head.

"Lana—look," Malden said as he pointed to the ocean. There was a pod of at least five dolphins just a few hundred feet out from the shoreline swimming by.

"Oh my God!" I yelped. "I love dolphins. This is amazing!"

"See what you're missing? You've got to hang out with me more often down here."

I blushed. We watched the sun set as the dolphins swam by. I wanted to pinch myself. The evening was magical, and it had just begun. Once it started to get dark, we headed back to our cars. Malden had taken his vintage VW bus down to the beach. He said he used his bus for the beach since it was big enough to hold his surfboard, paddleboard and scuba diving equipment. Malden instructed me to follow him back to his house.

Although Malden's house was only a few blocks away, the roads were narrow with a few sharp curves, so we drove slowly. He stopped the classic bus at a light-blue colored home with a two-car garage. It appeared modest in the front. However, once I walked inside I realized it was anything but conservative.

"Here it is—this is home," Malden announced as he raised

his arms in the air as we walked into his great room. The room was enormous, with floor-to-ceiling windows and sweeping ocean views.

"Not too shabby," I said as my eyes widened. I looked the other way, trying hard not to seem too impressed.

"It's difficult to see now that the sun has set, but do you see that long, dark shadow?" Malden asked as he pointed straight ahead.

"Yes, what is that?"

"That's Catalina Island."

"No way!"

"See the starboard and port lights from that boat coming in?"

"Yes."

"That's the Catalina Express," Malden said. "It comes in at the same time every day."

"I've always wanted to go to Catalina Island."

"Then we'll go!" Malden said as he winked at me.

He then pointed out lights on the far north end of the shoreline.

"That's the *Queen Mary*," Malden explained. "That's how far you can see from my view. And if you look south--see all those flashing white lights?"

"That's a factory that's been there since I was a child. I actually lived close to that factory when I was a boy. I could see the lights out my window as I lay in bed at night. The monsters," he said under his breath.

"The what?" I asked with confusion.

"The monsters," Malden said as he stared out the window almost in a trance. "The monsters would haunt me at night."

"I don't understand—what do you mean?"

"When I was a kid, I used to think they were monsters,"

Malden said, walking into the open kitchen that fed into his living room and dining room space.

There was something about the way his voice changed when he talked about the "monsters," but I couldn't put my finger on it.

"Are you OK with steak for dinner?" Malden brightened as he took out two filets from the fridge.

"You're talking to a meat and potatoes kind of girl from Chicago. Of course I'm OK with steak!"

"That's my girl." Malden smiled.

As Malden grilled our steaks on his vast deck overlooking the ocean, I walked around with a glass of red wine in my hand, inspecting his home. A framed Miami Dolphins football jersey hung on the wall, above a mahogany pool table covered in red felt. A huge flat screen TV dominated his great room. The deck boasted a hot tub, a massive built-in grill and a wooden table with six matching chairs. This place was definitely a bachelor pad. We sat outside and ate our steaks with an assortment of grilled vegetables. The meal was as delicious as he was.

"Do you like your steak?" Malden asked as he poured more red wine into my glass.

"Yes, it's perfect. I'm impressed. You're a good cook," I said.

"I appreciate that," he said as he looked at me intently. "You know, my ex-wife, Bethenny never let me cook. I love cooking, and she would always tell me the kitchen was her territory. It really hurt me. I enjoy cooking for my kids and entertaining my friends. It's a good way for me to relax."

"Well, honey, you can cook for me anytime you want. I don't cook. I'm really bad at it, and I do not enjoy it."

"I doubt you're that bad."

"Malden, I tried to make a frozen pizza once in the oven, and when I took it out it had curled up into a U-shape. I didn't even know it was scientifically possible for pizza to defy gravity like that—that's how bad I am!"

Malden let out his roaring and boisterous laugh. It made me laugh. His laugh never failed to put a smile on my face. When we finished dinner, I dutifully brought our dirty dishes into the kitchen, rinsed them off and put them in the dishwasher. I figured it was the least I could do since he had cooked such a perfect meal. As I finished putting the last plate in the dishwasher, Malden crept up behind me and wrapped his big arms around me. I put my hands on his. I stared down at his hands. They were huge, thick—and so masculine.

"You've got such strong hands," I said as I stroked them with my nails.

"Bear paws," Malden said.

"They *are* like big bear paws," I said with a laugh.

"Come here—I want to show you something," Malden said as he took my hand and led me into the living room. He walked over to the sand fireplace, turned a metal knob on the right side and lit a match. He slowly lit twelve uniform flames in the gas-powered fireplace.

"What do you think of that," Malden said proudly as he pulled me on to his brown leather wraparound couch.

"I think you're quite the Casanova," I said slyly.

Before I could blink, Malden was ripping off all my clothes and heading straight for my crotch. He swirled his tongue around my G spot like a true expert, going down on me for at least an hour. Malden clearly knew what he was doing when he pleased me. His age and experience showed. After he got me off, he eased his perfect cock into my drenched vagina. I'm pretty sure there was a pool of my cum on the brown leather couch beneath me, but I didn't have a care in the world. Malden got off in minutes, and again, I found his sweaty body shaking uncontrollably on top of me. If I didn't know better, I'd think he was having a seizure or a heart attack. We didn't speak, and with his big cock still inside me, we fell asleep. I could hear the waves crashing on the rocks in the distance, and the fire crackling a few feet away from me. Malden slept with his arms wrapped around me, and the sound of his deep, rhythmic breathing was music to my ears. I was in heaven. With that, I drifted off to sleep.

"Baby," Malden whispered in my ear. I slowly opened my eyes. "It's three in the morning. I'm taking you to bed."

Malden picked up my naked body like a child and carried me into his bedroom. We both snuggled up in his king-sized bed, and we were fast asleep again within minutes.

I woke up to the smell of eggs and bacon. Malden was not in bed next to me, but I could hear sounds of activity in the kitchen. I went to the bathroom and surveyed the damage to my face. My hair was a mess, and I had raccoon eyes from smeared mascara. I washed my face quickly, and put my hair in a ponytail. Then, I went into Malden's closet and threw on a gray Berkeley T-shirt.

"Good morning, gorgeous," Malden said as I walked into the kitchen. He was standing by the stove cooking our eggs. He paused to give me a kiss on the cheek. "Did you sleep well?"

"Yes," I said. "It's so peaceful here."

"Yes, it is," Malden agreed. "This house was very therapeutic for me while I was going through my divorce."

"I'm sure it was," I replied, quickly changing the subject. "Where is the sun today?"

"It will be out by noon. It's only overcast because of the

marine layer—but don't you worry, I've got big plans for us," Malden said as he flashed that sexy smile.

"Oh, do you," I said with skepticism. "I thought I was joining you for dinner last night—not the entire weekend."

"Lana, I'd like you to stay as long as possible," Malden said.

"Well, what if I have plans?"

Malden's face dropped. "What are your plans?"

"I'm supposed to have dinner later with my friend Giselle and her husband," I said.

"Well, that's easy," Malden said with confidence. "Have them come here. I'll cook for everyone."

"I'll think about it," I said with a warm smile. "So where do you want to take me today?"

"I'm going to take you on an adventure to the top of a mountain," Malden said proudly. "On my motorcycle. There, you will see your sun."

"What mountain?" I asked with excitement.

"Mount Baldy—I used to spend the summers there with my family as a kid."

I had heard Mount Baldy was beautiful, and I had been itching to visit it. Not on a motorcycle, though.

"How far away is that?" I anxiously asked.

"If I drive fast, we can be there in ninety minutes."

My stomach dropped. I cringed. I was not comfortable with the idea of riding Malden's motorcycle. I did not feel ready for such a long trek.

"Will we have to take a highway to get there?" I asked.

"Of course." Malden laughed. "What's the problem?"

"I'm just not totally comfortable with your bike quite yet," I said with embarrassment.

"You're tough," Malden said. "You'll be fine. It will be

great!"

Before we headed on our mountain adventure, I shot Giselle Sprint a text asking if she and French Rocker would like to head down to Malden's for dinner. I had told Giselle all about my new man and said I was very eager for her to meet him.

Lana Burke: "Hey! Do you guys want to come down to Malden's Newport Beach home for dinner tonight? His place is amazing with ocean views."

We headed to Malden's garage where he put me in a long-sleeved jacket and gave me a motorcycle helmet.

Before I knew it, I was on the back of Malden's bike. We were flying east on the 10. My heart was pounding in my chest. I clenched Malden's torso with all my strength. I could barely see because of the wind blowing in my face. My eyes were filled with tears from the dust and grime. Malden kept screaming back to me to relax. This ride could not end soon enough. After an hour of what felt like torture, we were off the highway. I eased my hold on Malden, sat back in his bike and breathed a deep sigh of relief.

We were at the bottom of Mount Baldy, turning on to Mount Baldy Road. Malden switched on the radio and stopped at the station playing the weekly *Breakfast with the Beatles* show. We raced his motorcycle through the winding road up the mountain. We were flying higher and higher in elevation with the sun and blue skies beaming down on us.

"I told you we'd find the sun," Malden said as he reached his arm back and rubbed my right leg up and down.

Here Comes the Sun came on the radio.

"It's beautiful up here," I shouted.

"And what an appropriate song for our trip up the

mountain." Malden laughed.

"The flowers are in full bloom," Malden said, pointing to daisies and a beautiful row of purple milk thistle flowers. "I love the smell of the flowers here. It reminds me of my childhood."

We passed several cyclists and encountered dozens of motorcyclists heading the opposite direction. Malden would stick out two fingers each time another motorcyclist passed us. The other rider would do the same. It was some kind of motorcycle code I was unfamiliar with. Malden was such a masculine guy.

When we got to the top of the mountain, Malden parked his bike. There was a tiny wooden lodge and a functioning chairlift to the top of the mountain. Malden explained that there was a restaurant called Top of the Notch at the highest peak, where we could go to for lunch.

We took the rickety chairlift to the top. The views were breathtaking. It was a beautiful and perfect day.

"Are you hungry?" Malden asked.

"Not quite," I said. "We just had breakfast not too long ago."

"I'm not either; let's grab a drink," Malden said eagerly. "What do you want?"

"I'll take a Blue Moon," I said, with a little reluctance to start drinking before noon. However, it was Sunday fun day.

"Good choice." We went inside, and Malden ordered two Blue Moons, which we carried to an outdoor deck where there were wooden tables. Malden pointed out the different hiking trails that he used to explore as a child. "Isn't this fun?" Malden asked.

"Yes!" I said. "I've always wanted to come here. I was actually telling Giselle that the other day."

"See, if you weren't with me right now on this cool adventure, you'd probably be at some douche-y brunch place in Hollywood with some douche-y guy wearing skinny jeans," Malden said with a smirk.

I smiled. "I don't know about that, Mr. Murphy," I quipped. "However, I will say, you certainly picked a fantastic spot, and I couldn't be happier that I'm with a guy who wouldn't be caught dead in skinny jeans!"

With that, Malden let out his roaring laugh. We finished our beers, took a few photos of the majestic view, and headed down the chairlift.

When we got down the mountain Malden said, "I'm going to show you the cabin that we used to stay in when I was a kid."

We got back on Malden's bike and he zipped over to another inn, Mount Baldy Lodge, located at a lower peak. As I got off his motorcycle, I felt my iPhone buzzing in my purse. I looked at it as we walked in. I had a text from Giselle.

Giselle Sprint: "That sounds like fun! What's his address, and what time?"

I wanted to jump for joy. My best friend and her hubby were going to meet my new beau. I had been friends with Giselle since my first day in college at the University of Iowa. She scared me a little at first because she was so wild and loud. However, after our first night sneaking into a bar and having a great time, I knew we'd be friends forever. She always could make me laugh.

"Giselle and her husband said they can join us for dinner," I informed Malden as we walked to the bar.

"Two Blue Moons," Malden said to the bartender as he flashed two fingers on his right hand. "That's great. Tell them to come at six."

I texted Giselle the information. Malden and I sat at the bar and sipped our beers. I looked around the restaurant. There were stuffed deer and moose heads all over the place, and at least two stone fireplaces that I could see. Malden told me stories about the summers he would spend here. He noted that there were a few summers his dad was absent since he was overseas fighting in World War II. He explained that his dad fought at Iwo Jima. He idolized his war hero father. He said he and his siblings would hike, fish, swim and explore the mountain during theirs stays here. He took me outside to the back of the restaurant where we could see dozens of wooden cabins in a field behind the kitchen. In the middle of the scattered cabins, there was a community swimming pool and a park.

"We would stay in one of these cabins," Malden said. "They're over fifty years old. Come on, let's peek inside one."

We both looked through the dirty window of the nearest cabin. The inside featured wooden floors, antique furniture and a stone fireplace in the living room. It was adorable.

"We'll come here for the night sometime," Malden said. "Maybe in the winter."

I envisioned Malden and me cozying up next to each other in one of the cabins on a cold and snowy winter night. I could see us sitting by the roaring fireplace drinking red wine. I loved the fantasy.

Malden and I spent a couple more hours at Mount Baldy before heading back to his beach house. We made it back by four o'clock, and sure enough, the sun was out with no clouds in the sky. Malden's home looked even more impressive in the daylight. The wraparound views of the Pacific Ocean were incredible. I couldn't help but envision myself living in this beautiful beach home with Malden. I could get used to this lifestyle.

CHAPTER 4

I decided to take a shower before Giselle and French Rocker arrived. Meanwhile, Malden went to Ralph's grocery store to pick up our dinner. I threw on a new outfit. I had brought an extra set of clothing that I had left in my car. I didn't want to walk into Malden's house with an overnight bag and scare the shit out of him. However, I had a feeling I might need a second outfit. Sure enough, my instincts were right. Just when I finished blow drying my hair, Malden returned.

"I hope you're up for eating steak again," Malden shouted as he walked through the door. He headed straight to the kitchen. I followed behind him and helped him unload the groceries. As Malden went out to the patio to fire up the grille, the doorbell rang. I raced to the front door to greet Giselle and French Rocker.

"Hey," Giselle said as she walked in with French Rocker following behind. French Rocker held a bottle of pinot noir. I hugged them both.

"Hi, guys," I said beaming. "Are you ready for Sunday fun day?"

"Hell, yeah!" Giselle shouted.

"Thanks for making the trip down. Did you hit any traffic?"

"No, we got real lucky actually," French Rocker said.

Making their way to the great room, Giselle and French Rocker were clearly impressed.

"Wow," Giselle said. "This view is unbelievable!"

"Is that Catalina Island?" French Rocker asked.

"Yes, it is," I confirmed as if I owned the place. I pointed out the *Queen Mary* and the other highlights Malden had told me about the night before. Feeling quite comfortable, I walked around his place like I was his wife.

"So where is this mystery man I've heard so much about?" Giselle asked with a cryptic smile.

"He's grilling our steaks--follow me," I instructed as we walked out on Malden's expansive deck. The sun was close to setting, and the sky looked like a rainbow of red, pink and purple.

"Malden," I shouted as we approached him from behind. "This is my best friend from college, Giselle, and her husband, Jameson Sprint. However, we call him French Rocker."

"Ha!" Malden laughed loudly as he reached out his right hand to shake hands with Jameson. "French Rocker–I like that. You must be in a band."

I was a little apprehensive about how my middle-aged white-collared Republican boyfriend would react to my wild Hollywood friends who were covered in tattoos. However, after Malden shook French Rocker's hand with a friendly laugh; I knew we'd have a great night. French Rocker had moved to L.A. from France years ago, but he still has a thick French accent. He plays the guitar in a local band that plays weekly gigs at different venues on the Sunset Strip. I coined the nickname French Rocker on a Sunday afternoon watching football at Red Rock bar. It's our favorite dive on the Sunset Strip. The name stuck. It's become so popular that most people don't even know his real name.

We dined on the patio again as the sun slowly crept under the expansive ocean blanket. Malden, being a wine connoisseur, boasted about the Merlot we were drinking from his friend's vineyard in Santa Barbara.

"I'll take you to my friend's vineyard soon, Lana," Malden said with a smile.

"There certainly are a lot of places you want to take me," I said as I smiled back at him. "It's going to be a busy summer."

"Lana, remember when we went wine tasting with all those Asian tourists in Australia a few years ago?" Giselle asked with a laugh.

Malden was pouring wine into my glass.

"Oh my God!" I shrieked. I tapped Malden excitedly on his right shoulder. I was on the edge of my chair–I couldn't wait to tell him the story.

To my surprise, Malden whipped his head around and glared at me with a dark look. Aggressively, he shrugged his right arm back. I gasped in disbelief. I gently pulled my arm back and put my hand on my lap.

"Don't you ever touch me while I'm pouring a glass of wine!" he roared. "What were you thinking?"

Humiliated and speechless, a dark feeling came over me. A little voice inside of me screamed, "This man is a wife beater!" I was in shock. I put my head down in retreat like a guilty dog.

There was an awkward pause at the table. I couldn't even bring myself to look at Giselle and French Rocker.

"I was in Australia back when I was a pilot for Pan Am," Malden continued as if nothing had just happened. I couldn't believe it. I sat there in silence. I was shocked. "It's the best place in the world to go hang gliding," Malden carried on.

I looked over at Giselle and French Rocker. They didn't look me in the eye. I was certain the way Malden snapped at me was totally out of line. Or was I wrong? Could I be overreacting? I had a boyfriend who got physically abusive with me one night years ago. I swore when Malden shrugged my finger off his shoulder, I saw the same devil inside him that I saw in my ex. I was too distracted by my racing inner thoughts to pay attention to Malden bragging about his hang gliding experiences.

After we finished dinner, I did the dishes and Malden went to his wine cellar, yet again, to get another bottle of wine. We all reconvened in the living area. Malden lit another fire in his sand gas fireplace, and he threw on a The Who CD. Giselle asked me where the bathroom was.

"I'll show you," I said as I grabbed her hand. I could not get her in the bathroom alone with me quickly enough. I needed to know what she thought of Malden's outburst.

"Your new boyfriend is quite the character," Giselle said as she pulled down her skinny jeans and began to pee in the toilet.

"Did you see how he snapped at me at dinner?" I asked with a sense of urgency.

"When did he snap at you?" Giselle asked with a slur. We were both buzzed from several glasses of wine.

"When I tapped him on the shoulder as he poured wine into my glass. Did you see him shrug his shoulder at me? He scolded me for touching him while he poured wine. Isn't that psycho?"

"Oh yeah – sorry, I didn't really think twice about it," Giselle said as she wiped her crotch with toilet paper.

"I was really taken aback by it. It makes me think he could get physically violent with me. Or, am I just being paranoid?" I questioned as I put my hand over my mouth with concern.

"Lana, just because you had one bad experience with a guy doesn't mean that they're all wife beaters," Giselle said in a motherly tone. "I like Malden. It's obvious he's crazy about you. I think you need to relax."

I conceded. Giselle and I walked back to the living room where French Rocker was animatedly discussing music with Malden. I tried to shake the dark feeling I had about Malden when he snapped at me, but I couldn't. My blood was boiling and I had consumed too many glasses of wine. It was a perfect storm for an explosion.

"Excuse me, I need to talk to you," I said in a grave voice to Malden as he was chatting with French Rocker.

"What's wrong?" Malden asked.

Without hesitation, I unleashed the tiger inside of me on him.

"You know, I didn't appreciate the way you snapped at me earlier when I tapped you on the shoulder as you poured wine," I said. "You got very aggressive with me. That's not how a real man talks to a lady. I already dated one wife beater -- I refuse to date another one!"

"Whoa," Malden said as he innocently raised both hands in the air. "Where is this coming from?"

"Lana... Stop," Giselle interjected.

"No, Giselle, this is important," I countered. "Malden, I do not appreciate the way you talked to me."

"Look, Malden, Lana is a little sensitive because she had a bad experience with an ex-boyfriend," Giselle explained, as she reached up to sit me down. "He hurt her."

"What!" Malden exclaimed. "Where does the bastard live? I will personally go kick his ass!"

"You can't," I said. "He doesn't live here anymore. That's not the issue. This is about you. I do not appreciate the way you snapped at me. I won't tolerate that kind of abuse."

"OK," Giselle said calmly in a further attempt to diffuse the situation. "Look, guys, it's getting late, and we have a long drive ahead of us. We're going to head out."

"No, Giselle, please stay," I pleaded.

"We really do need to get back," French Rocker chimed in. "We had a wonderful time. Malden, you have a great place here. Thanks so much for everything."

I hugged both Giselle and French Rocker goodbye. In my drunken haze I remember giving Malden a piece of my mind after they left. He told me that he couldn't deal with my drama and said he was going to sleep in a different bedroom. I woke up at seven the next morning with a pit in my stomach. I was alone in his bed, feeling terrible for reaming him out. I still had my clothes on from the night before. I quickly went to the bathroom and brushed my teeth before searching the other four bedrooms before I found Malden sound asleep in a guest room. I crept in bed next to him, kissed him on the cheek and wrapped my arms around him. He hugged me back. My tail was between my legs.

"I'm so sorry about last night," I sincerely apologized.

"That was a little bit too much," Malden said as his eyes slowly opened.

"Look, I was in a really bad relationship several years ago, so I'm very sensitive," I said. "I did not mean to lash out at you like that. However, I didn't like the way you snapped at me. It frightened me."

"Lana, I didn't mean to scare you," Malden said as he rubbed my back. "What happened with your ex?"

"It's a long story, but he basically beat the shit out of me." I closed my eyes remembering. "He gave me a black eye...punched out a tooth...it was horrible. Six police officers broke down my door to save me. If they hadn't come when they did–he would've killed me. He had just taken out a knife as they were walking in." I shuddered at the painful memory.

"That's terrible," Malden said. "I told you I would take care of him."

"That's not necessary. He doesn't live in the U.S. and he's not allowed to come back."

Malden softened. "Lana, you don't have to worry about me–I would never hurt you," he said seriously as he looked me in the eye. "I have really strong feelings for you, but I can't deal with drama. My relationship with Bethenny was very tumultuous."

"I understand," I said sadly.

I was scared. I really liked Malden. I wondered if I had just completely blown it. We had had such a perfect weekend until our drunken fight. My head spun. Then, Malden slowly began to strip off all my clothes. We began to make out like wild animals. After our first fight, I was more attracted to him than ever. I felt like I needed to lure him back in with my sexuality. I climbed on top of him and removed his boxers. I started licking his belly button and then slowly made my way with my tongue down to his cock. I licked his growing dick delicately. I then moved on to his testicles. I lathered them up with as much saliva as possible. Malden moaned repeatedly. I gracefully flipped my body around him so my crotch was in his face, and I continued to thrust his cock deep into my mouth. He returned the favor by lathering his tongue all over my wet pussy. I put in my best effort and gave him the deepest blowjob I could withstand without throwing up. I knew I needed to wipe away his memory of our drunken fight by pleasing him the best way I knew how. After I sucked his hard cock for a good twenty minutes, I turned around and straddled him. I slowly inserted his dick into my pussy and aggressively began to fuck him as if our entire relationship depended on it. I rode him like a sexy cowgirl for another twenty minutes until I reached orgasm. I screamed and collapsed on him. I couldn't catch my breath. I breathed heavily. I was unable to move.

"Are you OK?" I asked as soon as I caught my breath.

"I'm great." Malden smiled back and kissed me.

"But you didn't come," I said with concern.

"Oh we're not done yet," he said as he flashed the JFK Jr. smile.

"Oh really," I said as I raised my eyebrows.

Malden slowly lifted me off him. I lay next to him on my stomach and felt him climb onto my back. He straddled my perfectly toned ass from my diligent daily cardio workouts. I could feel his amazing hard cock slip between my wet pussy lips. I got aroused at the thought of him doing me from behind. He slowly rubbed the tip of his cock up and down my clit. I moaned in ecstasy. I could feel another orgasm building. This man was a sexual god. Right before I was about to come again, I felt his penis slowly slide toward my anus. Oh no. What is going on? I raised my ass slowly to direct him back toward my pussy. He must not have known he was about to enter the wrong hole.

"Relax," he whispered in my ear. "Don't tense up."

Malden slowly slid the tip of his penis in my butt hole. I cringed and tightened the muscles in my ass as much as possible. Please, God, no! This can't be happening.

"Wait, I'm not sure about this," I said to Malden as he was still on top of me.

"Just relax Lana," Malden said gently. "I'm going to give you the best orgasm you've ever had."

"But - but," I stuttered. "I've never had anal sex before. I'm not sure about this."

"Do you trust me?" Malden asked.

"Yes, but-" I stammered.

"No buts," Malden said. "Just relax your butt."

"Very funny." I gave in. I knew I had to use my sex goddess skills to make this man forget about our first drunken fight. If there was one way to do that—anal sex was the answer. I reached my hands and grabbed onto his headboard and braced myself for the ride. I slowly felt Malden's wet penis enter my ass.

"Oh, fuck!" I screamed. "That hurts! I don't know about this."

"Don't tighten up," Malden instructed.

"I'm scared -- this feels really uncomfortable," I pleaded.

"Hold on," Malden said as he pulled himself off me and rushed out of the room. He was back in two minutes holding a bottle of K-Y lubricant. He got back on the bed, and I could hear him squeeze the bottle into his hand. He rubbed the cool lube all over my ass. I looked back, and he squeezed more lube onto his right fingers. He slowly slid the fingers dripping with lube into my anus. It felt awkward and sexually gratifying at the same time.

"This feels so strange," I said as I took a deep breath. I tried to relax. I could feel Malden gently glide his hard cock back in. He slowly rocked it in and out. It felt so uncomfortable and surreal. Malden moaned really loud – louder than I had ever heard him moan. It made me relax a little knowing that I was pleasing him so greatly.

"Oh that feels so good!" Malden exclaimed. "You are so tight. You have no idea how amazing you feel."

I was speechless. I clenched my teeth and tried to relax.

"Touch yourself," Malden commanded.

"What?"

"Reach down and touch yourself."

Like a subservient housewife, I reached my right hand down to my clit. My vagina was drenched. I slowly began to masturbate. I moaned. I relaxed a little more and began to enjoy the strange sensation.

"Stick your finger in your pussy," Malden said. I did.

"Wow!" I said.

"Can you feel my hard cock inside you?" Malden questioned. I could. It was such a strange sensation to feel his big cock poking the inner walls of my vagina from my back end. Malden breathed heavily.

"I'm going to come," Malden shouted. "Oh, oh, oh, my God. Oh yeah!"

I could feel Malden's body begin to shake as he was still inside me from behind. I masturbated faster and felt myself explode. I let out a huge roar as Malden collapsed on my back and began to shake uncontrollably. I was blown away. I had just had anal sex!

"You're amazing," Malden said after he finally stopped shaking. "Come on—let's jump in the shower."

We both got in the shower to rinse off. Malden took it upon himself to shampoo my hair. It was sweet and tender. We made out in the shower. We could not keep our hands off each other. When I got out of the shower, I climbed back into bed. It was eight-thirty in the morning. My stomach was in knots from the anal sex, and I had a pounding headache from a hangover. I was due to be in my office by nine in the morning, and I had at least a ninety-minute drive ahead of me. I was screwed. Malden walked out of the bathroom with a towel wrapped around his waist.

"Are you going back to sleep?" Malden asked.

"I feel awful," I said. "I drank way too much last night."

"Then stay here and relax," Malden insisted.

"I'm supposed to be at work in thirty minutes," I said.

"Take the day off," Malden said.

I hadn't taken a day off since I started my new job. I caved. I shot Ari an e-mail and told him I had come down with a bad case of food poisoning. It was a white lie. I figured a small white lie never hurt anyone.

"I can play hooky today, too!" Malden said cheerfully.

"I need to sleep for a couple hours," I said as my eyes started to close. My stomach was in pain and my ass felt sore. I was still in shock that I had just allowed someone to penetrate me anally. My ass throbbed as I slowly dozed off.

"I'll wake you up in a few hours, and we can experiment more with anal sex," Malden said as he kissed me on the cheek and headed to the kitchen.

My eyes abruptly opened. I panicked. He wanted to have another round of anal sex on the same day? The room spun as I pondered what the hell I had signed myself up for.

CHAPTER 5

"Lana, are you feeling better?" Ari asked intently after he called me into his corner office. "Food poisoning is not fun."

"Yes, I am, thank you," I innocently replied.

"Very good. We have a story for you and it's a big one," Ari announced.

He had a stern look on his face – but with a splash of boyish excitement – as he rocked back and forth in his worn-out black leather chair. Ari tapped his fingers together like an evil villain.

Ari's fifteenth floor office boasted a perfect view of the Hollywood sign – and when he said that he had a story for me that was "a big one," I knew that this was my moment. My eyes grew big like a sex addict in a strip club. I could feel my mouth salivating. My appetite for a big story rivals a tiger that hasn't laid eyes on fresh meat for days. This is the opportunity I've been waiting for, I thought. The only better rush I get from an assignment of a huge story is the gratification I get from seeing my page ones on a newsstand. There is no better fulfillment for me than seeing my hard work pay off on the cover of a publication.

"It's about a politician – a huge one!" Ari continued.

My eyes grew even bigger. I'd been yearning to cover a powerful politician for years. My journalism career began in Washington, D.C. I interned with the White House press corps and loved it. I had been itching for some time to get back to my political roots. Somehow, my career path had brought me to Tinseltown and pushed me further and further away from the political scene. The other magazines I've worked for in Hollywood never cover politicians.

"It's about the Republican presidential nominee, Gov. Prescott Richards. We believe he's been having an affair with a hooker for a couple of years now. This story could change the election. History, really, if you think about it."

I could feel the blood rush to my face and sweat start to form on the palm of my hands. The brim of my forehead beaded with sweat. I instinctively grabbed the fourteen-carat gold Republican elephant charm on my necklace and slowly pulled it around the chain so it was hidden under the back of my blouse under my neck. Panic began to set in. Does he not know I'm part of the Silent Majority? Although I don't advertise this to my liberal media counterparts, but not only am I a conservative, I worked for President George W. Bush during his first term in the White House. My suspicious nature as a journalist even had me contemplate if this was some sort of a setup. Why would Ari ask the one conservative Republican reporter at the entire company to take down the Republican presidential nominee? Or – my thoughts racing – maybe he really doesn't know.

"We got tipped off two years ago about this story," Ari said as he pushed his glasses to the top of his nose. "Gov. Richards, of course, wasn't the presidential nominee then, so we didn't put much effort into pursuing the story. Since he became the nominee, the value of the story has obviously gone up. The kind of publicity we could potentially get for breaking a bombshell story like this could be worth millions. We've put two reporters on this story in the past on separate occasions. They both tried to get the hooker to crack, and she wouldn't budge. She claimed she's never met Gov. Richards or had any contact with him. Not surprising. We know there's some sort of connection, though, and we know you're the perfect person for the job. We actually had you in mind for this story when we hired you. We'd love to break the story the week of the Republican National Convention. Do you think you're up for it?"

"Um, well...yes," I stuttered nervously as I fidgeted in the chair across from his desk. "Of course I am. Why wouldn't I be?"

"Good," Ari said as he shuffled papers on his desk. "The first step is that you need to track her down. Find out what city she's residing in now, and we'll send you there. The last place we found her was in Salt Lake City. She was escorting for an agency called Satin Dolls. Her name is Celeste Homan. I'll write it down so you have the correct spelling."

A rainbow of emotions went through my head. I was excited, anxious, nervous and conflicted.

"So who is this tipster, and is he or she credible?" I asked in an urgent tone as I tried to gather my thoughts.

"The tipster is one of her longtime johns," Ari said, as he looked me straight in the eyes.

"A john? OK So clearly he's not credible. Does he want money?"

"Yes, of course. He's signed a contract with us for twenty thousand dollars upon publication of the story."

"OK. So the john has a monetary incentive and if he's sleeping with hookers he's clearly a sketchy dude," I said in disbelief. "I mean, come on, do you really think there is any truth to this story? Gov. Richards is a family man, he governs the conservative state of Utah and he's a devout Mormon with a squeaky clean reputation. It doesn't seem to add up."

"Lana, I've been in this business for twenty years," Ari said in a serious tone. "I wouldn't put anything past any politician – especially after the Senator Jonathan Miller scandal."

The *Post* broke the Jonathan Miller mistress and love child stories. He had an affair as his wife was dying of cancer. It took the mainstream media a full year to pick up on the story after the *Post* first broke the scandal.

"I certainly thought I had seen it all until that story," Ari said dramatically. "Nothing shocks me anymore. Nothing."

When I walked out of Ari's office, I knew I was embarking on the story of my career – as well as the inner moral battle of my life. In a business oversaturated with so many left-leaning journalists, how did the one conservative end up with the story that ultimately could take down the Republican nominee–and possibly ruin the election for him?

I had been a diehard Republican my entire life. I believed that a second term victory for President Muhammad Oyama, with his left-wing socialistic agenda, could potentially do irreversible damage to our country. How in God's name could I help him win the election? In fact, I even campaigned for John McCain in 2008.

But, then again, it was the story I'd been praying to come across. My entire life, I've yearned for the opportunity to cover that one big story that would thrust me in the national spotlight as a journalist. This could put me on the map as an investigative journalist and take my career to the next level. I've spent the past several years covering one train wreck celebrity after another. I've done cover story after cover story on celebrity affairs, divorces, weddings, but I've found it all to be meaningless trash. I deeply craved the opportunity to cover a story that could actually have an impact on the world. In fact, the reason I recently took the job at the *Post* was because I hoped to cover more political and hard news stories. The *Post* features more hard-lined stories than its competitors.

With my new gig working as a journalist for the *L.A. Post*, I finally felt like I was in good company. My colleagues were now real journalists with actual journalism degrees and years of field experience under their belts. My mentor, Mick Madden, is the one who took down Sen. Jonathan Miller. He also traveled to Afghanistan where he managed to infiltrate Al-Qaeda. Due to his excellent reporting, the *Post* broke more front-page terrorism stories following 9/11 than any of the top newspapers in the country. Some of the seasoned veterans I work alongside now are nothing like the amateur wannabe reporters I used to work with at the glossy magazines. The majority of those "journalists" not only lacked a journalism degree, they had a hard time stringing a sentence together. AP style might as well be a fashion trend, as far as they knew.

For now, I figured I had to go about the story in the most objective way possible and pray that our tipster simply had been misinformed. After all, I couldn't turn down the assignment. It was my first huge assignment at the *Post*, and I couldn't afford to lose my job. All I could do was hope for the best.

I walked back into my office and plowed into the story as if I was covering a politician I loathed. I immediately put in a LexisNexis request to the research department for an auto track on Celeste. An auto track provides legal and public information such as criminal records, property and financial records and even personal cell phone numbers on any U.S. resident including celebrities and politicians. Most major media companies and law firms have LexisNexis accounts.

I dived into the social media world digging for info on Celeste. I looked up profiles for her on MySpace, Twitter, LinkedIn, but I had the most luck with Facebook. I friended Celeste under my fake Facebook account. I use the alias Ruby Ghostfire on it, and I show photos of myself that are discreet - shadowy profile photos or pictures of just a body part such as my legs - so you can't make out at all that it's me. By the time I had gone through two years' worth of posts on her Facebook account, a research assistant had sent me Celeste's auto track. The auto track attached her to residences in Salt Lake City, Winnemucca, Nevada, and Centralia, Washington. Her page did not list her current address. However, she recently posted a photo of a car she captioned with: "My new car!"

In the background, I caught an address for a house. The house number was 711. I looked up her parents' address, and it was 707 Echo Lane in Winnemucca. Bingo! Judging by that piece of evidence and other recent pictures she had posted of herself with her family, it appeared that she was currently living in Winnemucca, and possibly at her parents' house. I printed out the evidence on the printer in my office and walked back into Ari's office.

Ari was on the computer and smoking a cigar. I announced that I believed Celeste was currently living in Winnemucca, Nevada.

"Great news!" Ari said with a big smile. "We'll send you out on a flight first thing tomorrow morning,"

It was almost five o'clock, and I had some errands to run

and had hoped to squeeze in a workout.

"Sounds good," I replied. "I'll call the travel department and have them book my flight, hotel and a rental car. Then I'm going to head out for the evening."

"Good plan," he said as he typed up an e-mail.

I walked out of Ari's office, and I began to get a nauseated feeling. Could I, Lana Burke, lifelong Republican, personally be the one person who takes down potentially the next President of the United States? I knew I would have to keep my involvement with this story a secret for now to my conservative friends and especially my parents. They all would disown me.

"Oh, Lana," Ari shouted when I was already a few feet out of his office.

"Yes," I said as I popped my head back in.

"Good luck," he said with a confident smile.

I headed to spin class at SoulCycle in West Hollywood after work to burn off some of my anxiety over the assignment. I ran my errands and packed a carry-on with enough clothes to last me no more than five days. I charged my phone, laptop and iPad as I was getting ready for bed. Before I went to sleep, I called Malden and told him I was leaving town in the morning to cover the story on Gov. Richards. He was shocked at the allegations surrounding Richards, but he was more concerned with my leaving. He sighed and told me he wished I would've told him earlier I was leaving town so he could've driven up to spend the night with me and drive me to the airport in the morning. I was flattered. I thanked him and promised we'd get together as soon as I returned. I had a 10:00 a.m. flight out of LAX the next morning landing me in Winnemucca an hour later if all went as planned, which was nice, because I wouldn't have to wake up too early. I booked the mid-morning flight on purpose. I had never been a morning person. Before I went to bed, I popped a Xanax to help me sleep but still found myself tossing and turning all night.

After a stress-free morning of travel, I found myself driving to Celeste's parents' house. I've traveled to a lot of crappy small towns for work, but this one took the cake. In Winnemucca there's one main road called Winnemucca Boulevard. The main strip boasted brothels, dive casinos and dollar stores. It's in the middle of the desert, frequented by mostly truck drivers who take a break from the road for a blowjob at one of the skeezy brothels. This town disturbed me.

As I got closer to Celeste's parents' address, the environment looked more like a normal suburb. I passed a school, parks, and baseball fields. The outskirts of the town made it look better. When I pulled onto the 700 block of Echo Lane, I was pleasantly surprised. I was staring at a fairly large brick home, probably with four or five bedrooms. It had a perfectly landscaped front yard and an open two-car garage. There was a Ford Explorer in the driveway and an older model Porsche in the garage. The home appeared to be too nice to be owned by the parents of a hooker. But, then again, these were the first parents of a hooker whom I had ever met.

I parked in the street one house away – just to be safe. If they did not act pleasantly toward me, my car did not need to be close enough for them to catch a license plate number or details. I touched up my makeup, using the rearview mirror in the car. I've learned that the better I look the more information I'm prone to get, no matter who the source.

I already prepared in my head what I was going to say, regardless of who answered the door. I rang the doorbell, and within a minute a beautiful blonde woman in her fifties answered the door. She had fake boobs, full makeup on and a magenta-colored blouse. Behind her stood a good-looking man, about the same age, with dirty blonde hair and striking blue eyes. He actually was pretty hot, to my surprise.

"Can I help you?" the woman asked.

"Hi, I'm looking for Celeste," I said with a friendly smile.

"And you are?" the woman asked with caution. Not the response I was hoping for. I didn't want to waste any time playing games – so I got straight to the point.

"I'm actually a journalist. I work for National Publishing, and there's an important story I'm working on that involves Celeste. I've been trying to contact her." I made a point to say National Publishing as opposed to the *Los Angeles Post*. National Publishing owns the *Post* along with several other publications. The *Post* is known for breaking scandalous stories, so I usually tell people I work for National Publishing so I don't scare them off. Then I ease them into the fact that the story I'm working on will most likely go into that publication, as opposed to the other publications owned by the company with less-worse tabloid-y stigmas.

"Well, can you tell me what the story is about?"

"I'm sorry, but I don't want to give away too much information because it's a very sensitive story," I explained to the woman I believed to be Celeste's mom.

"OK, I understand. She's not here. I can relay a message to her, but I can't promise that she'll actually call you."

"That would be great. I would appreciate it so much. I'll give you my business card that has my cell number and e-mail on it."

"I'll be sure to give it to her," she said, eyeing the National Publishing logo on the card as she closed the door slowly. I was grateful Ari was smart enough to issue the staff business cards that did not include the *Post* on them.

"Oh and one more thing," I said before the door fully shut. "Can you please tell Celeste that there is money involved if she is willing to cooperate with me?"

"No problem."

With that I was driving the five-minute drive to the Holiday Inn Express where I planned on staying. I knew at this point it was a waiting game. I couldn't go back to the parents' home until at least tomorrow. So I just had to pray that Celeste would get a hold of me at some point that night. I stopped at a little woman's boutique with a Western vibe. I found a cute pair of brown leather cowboy boots with gold studs that I couldn't resist purchasing. I'd been looking for cowboy boots for a while, and this was the first cute pair I had seen that didn't break the bank. Maybe Winnemucca wasn't so bad after all.

I left the store wearing my boots, daisy dukes and a vintage Lynyrd Skynyrd tee. After I checked into the motel, I got a text from Malden.

Malden Murphy: "How's the trip?"

Lana Burke: "Not so bad. I already talked to the hooker's parents. She wasn't home, but I left my business card. And I got these cute cowboy boots."

I snapped a pic of my right leg crossed over on my left leg as I lay on my bed and sent it to him via text. I began to doze off. I didn't realize how exhausted I was until I lay down. It was 101 degrees Fahrenheit that day. The desert heat had knocked me out. I fell asleep for two hours. I woke up a couple hours later to my phone beeping.

Unknown number: "Hey, Lana, I see you have traveled quite a distance. I'm sure I know what this is about, and I still don't know where to go from here. All I ask is my family does not come under fire for my past actions. They, too, know what this is all about."

I couldn't believe it. It was Celeste. I was not expecting her to get in touch with me so quickly. I sat up and gathered my thoughts before shooting her a response.

Lana Burke: "Hi, Celeste, Thanks for getting in touch with me. I totally understand and respect your concerns. Can you please meet with me tonight?"

I quickly saved Celeste's cell phone number into my phone. Within minutes she responded again.

Celeste Homan: "Do you mind meeting up at my house? My husband wants to hear what you have to say too. I filled him in on what this is about. You can bring someone along with you if it'd make you feel safer."

Lana Burke: "Sure, no problem. Shoot me your address and I can be there by eight."

As I traveled down the dark country road, unable to find Celeste's home, my anxiety level began to rise. My GPS kept taking me in circles and I couldn't read many of the addresses on the small run-down houses and trailer homes I passed. I started to get a really bad feeling, and regretted that I agreed to meet Celeste and her latest husband at their home. I knew very little about them except that they both had criminal records and led very seedy lives.

I'm a fit, thirty-two-year-old Cali girl with blonde hair and a golden tan alone in a dumpy Nevada shit town called Winnemucca--a town that doesn't feature much besides tattered casinos and a few twenty-four hour brothels, not exactly a safe, crime-free neighborhood. One wrong word out of my mouth and – who knew, I might not leave Celeste and her new husband's home in one piece. Before even meeting them, I knew I was dealing with scum of the earth people.

Just then, my phone vibrated on the passenger seat.

Celeste Homan: "OK let's meet somewhere else. My husband's being crazy. He's pissed about a lot of things. I can meet you at the Martin."

I could feel the tightness in my chest intensify upon reading Celeste's text. My killer sixth sense has been a huge contributing factor to my success as a journalist, but it's also kept me safe out in the field. My intuition was telling me that going to Celeste's home would be a huge mistake. I sensed turmoil at her home as I drove in the dark, looking for the right place. Sure enough, I was right.

Lana Burke: "OK headed there now! Sorry to hear."

I Googled the Martin's address and punched it into my GPS. Happily, I pulled a U-turn in my rented Prius.

Ugh–my Prius! I had to laugh to myself. I've grown to despise these eco-friendly cars. Not because the vehicles are eco-friendly, but because it seems that every person who drives a Prius in Los Angeles spends more time with their eyes on their smart phone than on the road. And, whenever I see one, it almost always seems to have a President Oyama bumper sticker. Oh, the ironies of this assignment.

Within five minutes of receiving Celeste's last text, I was parking my car at the old Martin Hotel. It was a run-down white hotel with a bar and restaurant with black shutters. It looked a hundred years old and would be a perfect site to shoot a dramatic gun scene for a Western flick.

The Martin was divided into two large rooms: a bar and a dining room. There were several local men in construction clothes sitting at the bar drinking cheap beer. One townie stood out because he was badly slurring his words, and it looked like he was about to fall off his bar stool at any minute. I couldn't help but laugh under my breath and shake my head. I'm a sucker for a good character – especially drunk ones. Most people are annoyed by characters, but I usually find them fascinating and endlessly amusing. I spotted a hostess and asked her to seat me at a table in the dining room. I told her that my female friend would be arriving shortly. I hadn't eaten since my McDonald's breakfast at LAX that morning. I was starved. I sat down at a table in a corner and whipped out my iPhone to text Celeste.

Lana Burke: "I'm the blonde in the dining room at a table in the corner wearing a Lynyrd Skynyrd tee, skinny jeans and cowboy boots. Look forward to meeting you. ☺"

I knew what Celeste looked like from her Facebook photos. She didn't have too many posted that were viewable to non-friends, but I had a pretty good idea of what to expect. A waitress came over and dropped bread and water at my table. I ordered a glass of red wine immediately. I waited for twenty minutes before I heard from Celeste.

Celeste Homan: "I'm in the bar. Meet me in here."

I chugged the last sip of wine in my glass, told my waitress I was going to join my friend in the bar, and paid for my drink. If she wants to sit in the bar as opposed to the dining room, that's fine with me, I thought. After all, she's the boss tonight, and I will do what it takes to score this story.

When I got into the bar, I saw Celeste sitting at a corner table with the town drunk hovering over her. He wobbled as he attempted to stand and talk, but all that came out was drunken gibberish. I sized her up. Celeste was very petite— about five foot two and probably no more than one hundred pounds. She had fake boobs that appeared to be C cups and a full head of long, wild, jet-black hair. She had green eyes and a big beautiful smile like Angelina Jolie. She had more natural beauty than I expected. She was wearing black skinny jeans with holes and an emerald green blouse. She was drinking a Bud Light Lime, and once I started to talk to her, I knew immediately that it wasn't her first beverage of the day.

"Celeste, hi I'm Lana. So nice to meet you," I said as I hung my purse on the back of the chair across from her.

"Hi. This is Bear. Bear, this is my good friend Lana who just got in from out of town," Celeste said as she nodded at Bear and then at me.

"Are you two girls ready to have some shots or what?" Bear said as he hiccupped and almost tipped over, but somehow managed to catch his balance.

"No Bear. Not now. My friend just got here and we have a lot to catch up on, so please just go back to the bar," Celeste said. "We can do shots later."

"I can order some tequila shots right now," Bear slurred.

At that point, the waitress walked up and literally grabbed Bear's hand and walked him back to the bar.

"I'm sorry about that," Celeste apologized. "Bear is a regular here who is over served just about every night."

"I can see that," I said with a smile. "Don't worry about

it."

"You want something to drink?" Celeste motioned to her bottle.

"Sure," I figured, when in Rome…"I'll have a Bud Light Lime too."

Celeste flagged down the waitress and ordered me my beer. She leaned close to me. "So, I know what this is about."

"OK," I said as I straightened up in my seat.

"What publication do you work for now?"

"I work for National Publishing," I explained. "It owns several publications, such as *Hollywood Investigator*, *Glitz* and the *Los Angeles Post*."

"I've been approached by someone from the *L.A. Post* at least one time before. A guy," Celeste said as she sipped her beer.

"Yeah, I know."

"So what exactly is it you want from me?" she asked defensively.

"Well, we've had information on you and a high-profile politician for quite some time now," I said cautiously. "We've uncovered a lot of details, and it looks like we are moving forward with the story. Ideally though, we would like your cooperation with the story."

"And how much money would you be willing to pay me?" she asked without flinching.

I was a little taken aback that she was talking numbers already, but then I reminded myself I was sitting across the table from a hooker.

"Well, that, of course, all depends on what you're willing to reveal," I said, thinking quickly. "Will you go on the record or off? Do you have photos to sell? E-mails? Texts? We want anything that makes the story stronger. The more you have to offer us, the more money we can offer you. I can assure you that you can make a pretty penny off this story."

Celeste looked dubious. I knew I couldn't bullshit her. "I will just get straight to the point," I said firmly. "Here's the key. You can work with us and make a ton of money off your story. Or, you can work against us and have other people make money off your story."

Celeste looked confused and began to tap her long hot pink fake nails.

"I don't understand. How would others make money off my story?" she asked.

"Other people who know information about your story can sell it to us just as freely as you can," I explained. "So anyone else who you've told, or perhaps people at your old agency who were aware of this particular client, could tell the story."

"I got you."

I was feeling confident. I knew I could get Celeste to cooperate.

"So do you know what client I'm interested in?" I finally asked.

"Well, seeing that we are just months away from the election, I'm guessing Gov. Richards," Celeste said as she peeled the label off her beer.

"Yes, Gov. Richards."

"Client Number Eight."

"Excuse me?"

"Client Number Eight. He was my eighth client. I call him Client Number Eight."

"Ohh, interesting. Client Number Eight. Wow!" I said as I took a huge chug out of my Bud Light Lime. I knew it was going to be some night. I wanted to whip out my tape recorder or take notes but I knew that could intimidate her. I refrained and promised myself that I would do my best to commit to memory every word out of her mouth. "So when did you first meet him?"

"It was in 2010," she said as she pulled her left fingers through her long black mane. She sat uncomfortably in her seat and appeared nervous.

"How did you guys meet?" I asked.

"Through my agency. Satin Dolls. I had no idea who he was for a while."

"Wait, you mean you didn't know he was a famous governor running for president?"

"No, I don't watch the news!" she exclaimed. "I figured he was important because there was always security hanging out around him and his hotel room."

"So you would meet him at hotels?"

"Yes."

"Which ones?"

"Usually the Grand America."

"And that's in Salt Lake City?"

"Yes."

"OK," I said. "So when did you figure out who he was?"

"I think it was maybe my third appointment with him. Like I said, whenever we would get together there would always be security in the hallway of his hotel room. And when I looked out the window I would see Secret Service types outside below his room."

My heart skipped a beat. I knew I had hit the jackpot with Celeste. "So did you ever communicate with him? Do you have texts, e-mails or phone records?"

"No, never," she answered. "He was smarter than that. He never called me himself directly. He would have an aide call the agency and request me. They would say that it was Client Number Eight so that's how I knew it was Gov. Richards. I would drop other clients to go see him."

I felt a little faint. I couldn't believe we were talking about Gov. Richards.

"What about photos?" I asked. "Did you ever take pictures with him or of him or even of his room?"

"No. He would not allow me to take my phone out," she responded. "He covers all his tracks. He wouldn't even touch the money he gave me."

"So then how did he give you payment?"

"Every single time I met with him, once I was done, he would say 'Your donation is in the drawer' and he'd point to a drawer."

"Wow, he really did cover his tracks," I said. "I guess I should expect nothing less from a savvy politician and businessman like Richards."

I knew it was time to go in for the kill. I had grown very comfortable with discussing sex with strangers from all the affair stories I'd broken. "So, what was your sexual relationship like?"

Celeste began to fidget in her chair. She chugged the last sip of her beer and flagged over our waitress and ordered another. She hesitantly began to speak.

"We never actually had sex," she said.

"I don't understand – no sex at all?"

"We hooked up, but we never actually had sexual intercourse."

"OK, so you guys would go down on each other?"

"Well, kind of," she said with hesitation. "He gave me oral, but he never really took off his undergarments."

"Excuse me – the what?" I asked with confusion.

"The Temple garments. You know, the underwear people of the Mormon faith wear."

"Whoa—this is news to me," I said. "I don't know much about the Mormon religion, but I didn't realize they had to wear a certain kind of underwear."

"Yes, they're supposed to," she explained. "Client Number Eight never took his off. It's like a white undershirt and long thin cotton boxers. They're supposed to keep them on in front of their spouses—even during sex."

"Wow – that's crazy! I didn't realize this." I didn't know too much about the Mormon faith aside from the fact that they don't drink alcohol.

"Yeah," she said with indifference. "When he has sex with his wife, he keeps them on. There's a hole he can slip his dick out of. He never took them off for me, though."

Her statements were a lot to process. I could envision how the art department would lay out the bombshell exclusive on the pages of the magazine.

"OK, so let me get this straight. You would meet him at hotels. He wouldn't get naked, but you would, and he would just go down on you?"

"Yes."

"Did he get off?"

"I don't know."

"Well, did he get hard? Did he appear to get off?"

"Sometimes, but honestly he didn't get that hard. He seemed more interested in having me do other things."

I could only imagine. I took a deep breath and braced myself. "Like what?"

"He would ask me to do coke in front of him."

"What? Cocaine?"

"Yes."

"OK – let me get this straight. So he would provide cocaine for you?"

"Yes."

"Did he do coke too?"

"Never in front of me."

"Why would he ask you to do cocaine – I don't get it."

My mind raced. What rational person hires a hooker just to watch her blow lines of coke? The political implications for Client Number Eight would be disastrous if Celeste's accusations were true.

"It was like this," she continued. "Client Number Eight has this picture perfect housewife at home. They don't have an exciting sex life. They lead these conservative and religious lives. He wanted me to do all the things that his wife would never do. He wanted to live out his wildest fantasies with me. It aroused him to see me rip a line of cocaine because Mrs. Richards would never do that. All the dirty things he's fantasized about doing but isn't allowed to do with his wife because of their religious beliefs – he did with me."

"I think I get it," I said. "So, you're the antithesis of his wife. All his dirty fantasies he lives out with you. I'm still a little confused, though, about the sex. I don't see the point of hiring a hooker if she's not going to get you off. Did you give him hand jobs or blow jobs?"

"I would rub him down there, but he was more interested in having me do something else to arouse him."

Just when I thought it couldn't get any better. I couldn't wait to hear what she was going to reveal next. "Like what?"

"Honestly, I'm embarrassed to say," she said quietly. "It's degrading."

"Look, Celeste, I've been doing this for many years," I said with a straight face. "I've seen it all, and I've heard it all.

Nothing fazes me these days. You don't have to be embarrassed."

"Um..." she said as she took another big swallow from the fresh beer the waitress had brought over. "He seemed to have an obsession with...I can't say it."

For a hooker, Celeste was very demure. "Anal sex?"

"No, no. Not that."

All of a sudden a wobbly shadow appeared above our heads. "Ladies, I brought you tequila shots," Bear said as his unsteady hands planted three shots on the table. He spilled half of the shots as he placed them down. I was so frustrated -- we were just getting to the good part.

"Thanks, Bear–cheers guys!" I said as fast as I could. I clanged Bear and Celeste's shots and quickly downed the Patron.

"What are you ladies talking about?" Bear said as he hiccupped, yet again, and then laid his arm on the back of my chair for support.

"You know just girl stuff," I said as I stood up and attempted to escort Bear back to the bar. "Bear, look, we're just catching up. Why don't you sit back here at the bar, and when we're done chatting we'll come hang with you. But thank you so much for the shot."

I raced back to our table. "OK what is it," I eagerly asked as I jumped back into my seat. "Does he have some weird fetish where he made you dress up in some crazy leather S and M outfit and whip you or something?"

"No." She laughed, breaking the tension. "He..."

"What?" I questioned, giddy in anticipation.

"Peeing."

I was slightly disgusted, but sadly not too shocked. "Oh! OK, so he likes you to pee on him?" I asked.

"Yes. Kind of," she answered bashfully.

"That's not so bad," I said, wanting to get as many details as possible. "R. Kelly has a pee fetish. I heard Dave Matthews does too. See, I told you I've heard it all before. So how did he ask you to pee on him?"

This was my attempt to make Celeste feel more comfortable by acting like everyone in Hollywood is into golden showers.

"Sometimes we'd get in the bathtub and other times we'd be in the shower."

"And he still would keep the Mormon undergarments on?"

"Yes."

"Wow, what a fucking mess!"

I knew I had to get all the dirty details tonight just in case I never saw her again. I treaded cautiously with my questioning. "So you would go in the shower with him, and he would ask you to pee on his garments?"

"Yes, sometimes it was in the bathtub. He also liked to... Oh, I can't say it."

"Celeste, come on, we've gotten this far." Sources often play this cat and mouse game. It's frustrating, but I've become accustomed to it. I took a deep breath and silently told myself to have patience with her.

"He liked to drink it."

I did not see this coming!

"He liked to drink your piss?"

"Yes."

"So he'd ask you to pee in his mouth?"

"No, not exactly. He was classier than that."

"Oh, right," I said in disbelief that she just used the word "class" while talking about someone who has a sexual fetish for drinking piss. "So, in what classy way did he drink your urine?"

"He would ask me to go in the shower. There'd be a martini glass on the floor of the shower, and he'd have me pee into the martini glass."

I had to hold back my laughter. Now I've heard it all.

"You've got to be fucking kidding me!"

"No. I'm not. I'm so embarrassed. This is so degrading!"

I couldn't hold back any longer. I cracked a small smile.

"Wow. So his poison of choice is a pee-tini! Does he like them shaken or stirred?" I asked as Celeste blushed. "Just kidding, Celeste."

"I know it's so weird," she said incredulously. "But he truly is such a nice man, and I loved him so much. I still love him. I've already told you so much. If I decide to come out and do a story, what kind of money can you offer me?"

It was time to play the numbers game. It's important in this business never to give out a number until you know what the source is willing to reveal on the record. You don't want to set the monetary expectations too high or low.

"We can definitely offer you a significant amount of money. I'd have to talk to my boss before I give you a number, but if you agree to do the story on the record, the number is going to be much higher."

Celeste looked confused. "What do you mean, on the record?"

I forget most people don't know what on the record actually means. "On the record means we quote you directly, and you sign a contract with us saying that everything you told us is what you believe to be the truth," I explained. "So, when the story comes out, you can't turn around and say you never said that. If you choose to do the story off the record, we would quote you anonymously. So we could quote you as a 'friend' or a 'source' close to you. That way you're protected in the sense that readers –and Client Number Eight – don't know that you're the source."

"OK," she said with relief. "I just don't want my family to get dragged into this. I just got married again, and I started to explain to my husband about my past tonight, and he's not happy. When I left the house, tonight, he was screaming at me and throwing things at me as I ran out the door."

Celeste took out her cell phone and started to go through her text messages nervously. "He keeps texting me. He says he is going to hurt me if I don't go home now."

The last thing I wanted was Celeste out of my sight. I still had so many questions to ask her, and I hoped to get her to sign a contract with National Publishing tonight. I know that with sources like her, if you don't get them to sign a contract right away, you may never see the person again. Plus, I had a bad feeling about Celeste's shady husband.

"If you're afraid of him, you can come to my hotel. You'll be safe there."

"Are you sure?"

"Yes, we can pick up some beer, wine, whatever you want at a gas station along the way."

Celeste's face brightened. "OK, let me just run to the bathroom."

I waved down the waitress and asked for the check. Did I just agree to have a sleepover with a hooker? And not just any hooker – the alleged mistress to someone who may be the next President of the United States? I opened my phone and shot Ari a quick text.

Lana Burke: "I am with Celeste. I got her talking. She has started giving me details of her affair with Gov. Richards. Her husband is threatening her, so she's coming back to my hotel with me. I will call you when I can."

Celeste came back from the bathroom, and we headed out the door. She insisted on driving her car, an older, slightly beat-up black Mercedes four-door sedan. Although getting in a car with an intoxicated person is something I usually would never do, Celeste's driving was the least of my concerns at the moment. I also figured my Prius would be safe at the Martin overnight.

Celeste had crap scattered all over her black four-door. The tan leather seats were littered with Tic Tacs, lip gloss and even a used Trojan condom on the floor. Nice touch.

Moving some junk out of the way, I climbed into the passenger seat, and we took off. Celeste drove us down several dark back roads to Winnemucca Boulevard. She asked where I was staying, and I told her the Holiday Inn Express. She pulled into a dumpy-looking gas station called Pump 'n Save. We both got out and walked in.

"Oh, Celeste, fancy seeing you here!" a fat man with a cheesy eighties mustache called out from behind the counter. He was chewing tobacco and wearing denim overalls with no shirt underneath.

"Hey Phil!" she called back as she made a beeline for the cooler.

"What should we get?" Celeste asked me as she opened the fridge filled with beer.

"It doesn't matter to me," I answered. "Do you like Stella or Corona Light?"

"How about Stella?"

"Sounds good to me." I also picked up a bottle of red

wine and bag of Doritos.

We went back into Celeste's car and headed to the Holiday Inn Express. Back in my room, Celeste wasted no time cracking open a Stella, chugging the beer in its entirety within minutes. At that point, I realized she was wasted.

We sat on two salmon pink chairs on each side of a cheap wooden table in front of a window. Our view overlooked the parking lot. I attempted to continue interviewing Celeste.

"So can you tell me more about what Client Number Eight says about his wife?"

Celeste smiled seductively. "Do you like girls, Lana?"

I shook my head in disbelief. I wasn't sure if my ears were playing tricks on me.

"Excuse me?"

"Have you ever hooked up with a girl before?" Celeste asked as she got off her chair and began to take her shirt off. "Have you ever wondered what it's like?"

"I think women are great, but this is not the time," I said uncomfortably. "You don't need to do this, Celeste."

Celeste was now walking around my hotel room with her shirt off. She wore a hot pink lace bra to support her huge fake tits. She walked over to the nightstand in between the two beds and turned on the clock radio. She found a classic rock station and blared *Jane Says* by Jane's Addiction. She proceeded to walk over to me and started dancing.

Oh God, I thought. This is not happening.

"Celeste, I think you're awesome, but you don't have to give me a lap dance," I said with an awkward smile. "I'm not one of your clients."

"You're funny," she snickered as she unsnapped her bra strap and threw it across the room. "I think you're pretty."

I was sitting on the chair with my legs squeezed together.

She took her hands and spread my legs apart. Then she turned around and crawled on my lap and started rubbing her ass into my crotch. At that point I noticed the huge tramp stamp on her lower back. It was some kind of Chinese design, and it spanned her entire lower back. I slowly attempted to push her off my lap. She quickly snapped up, turned around and took her hand and started rubbing my crotch. I immediately got aroused.

"Do you like that?" she asked with a giggle. Her boobs were in my face. She had huge dark nipples, and her chest looked pretty ridiculous for her body type. But she certainly was hot, in a trashy way. She did turn me on a little bit, but she also made me feel dirty. I could see why Gov. Richards liked her. She was very aggressive and sexy. I realized that this was normal for her. Sex was the only way she knew how to communicate. I didn't see myself getting much more information out of her at the moment.

"Celeste, please," I said as I stood up. I wasn't going to let her seduction work with me. However, if I had a dick, I don't think I would have had self-control in that situation, and I'd definitely have a huge boner right about now. I was certain my pussy was wet.

"Lana, will you just please dance with me? Please. Let's have some fun. I just want to have fun."

I couldn't believe that I found myself stuck in a hotel room with a drunken hooker on a mission to molest me, all for a job. I humored her and reluctantly danced for a few songs. I could see her eyes were slowly closing, to my relief. I brought her over to one of the two queen-sized beds and sat her down. I handed her another beer. She took one last big chug and then passed out cold. I turned off all the lights. I quickly opened my laptop, got back in the corner chair where I got my lap dance, and in the total darkness, I began to type out every single detail that Celeste had told me about her affair with the infamous Client Number Eight.

I looked over at topless Celeste passed out in bed. I fantasized about what it would be like if I did have sex with her. I had become so accustomed to having sex regularly with Malden that I craved it all the time. I couldn't get the lap dance Celeste gave me out of my mind. I pictured her gigantic breasts in my face as she rubbed her fingers over the crotch area of my jean shorts. I could tell I was still wet from the encounter. I quietly unzipped my shorts and reached my hand into my pussy. It was still wet. I was so turned on. Gov. Richards's prostitute had just seduced me. I rubbed my clit slowly up and down and moaned as quietly as possible. I masturbated as I creepily stared at Celeste's fake hot tits. I envisioned what it'd be like if she went down on me with her sexy devilish smile. It was too much. I found myself climaxing in the chair within minutes. I felt sexually empowered and dirty at the same time. Earth to Lana – I told myself to snap out of it! I quickly brushed my teeth and washed my face before getting into bed. I fell asleep relaxed and satisfied.

CHAPTER 6

I woke up with my iPhone vibrating in my hand. I looked at my phone–I had twelve missed calls. Wait, twelve missed calls? There were also seven text messages. Before I had a chance to read any of them, I looked up and quickly remembered the sketchy situation I had gotten myself into. Celeste was still sound asleep on the queen-sized bed next to me, topless. It's not every day you wake up next to a topless hooker in a dumpy motel. The irony is that I get paid to do this. I shook my head and let out a quiet laugh.

I quickly opened my messages, and I was shocked at what I read. All seven text messages were from a 775 area code. Eleven of the missed calls were from the same number, and the other missed call was from my boss. I began going through the texts. They were all nasty.

775- 555- 3472: "You're holding my wife hostage!"

I anxiously read another one:

775- 555- 3472: "I'm calling the police."

I read another:

775- 555- 3472: "This is kidnapping!"

Yet, another:

775- 555- 3472: "You fucking bitch–let me talk to my wife."

I gasped as my stomach dropped. It clearly was Celeste's crazy husband. He came off like a total lunatic. This was not good. I immediately got up. I attempted to wake my topless roommate.

"Celeste, Celeste," I said as I gently tapped her bare right shoulder.

She rolled over and slowly opened her eyes. Her huge, dark black nipples were staring right at me. I forgot how big they were! I couldn't help but stare at them.

Focus, Lana, focus.

"Hi," she said as she sat up and shot me a seductive smile. "What time is it?"

"It's eight o'clock and your husband is freaking out!" I anxiously said. "I woke up this morning to several unpleasant messages from him. How did he get my cell phone number?"

"Oh my God!" Celeste said as she bolted up and put both hands over her face. "I'm so sorry. Chad asked for your number before I left last night. I told you he's crazy!"

"Well, you better call him right away–he's threatening to call the police," I sternly instructed.

"OK–I will," Celeste casually said as if this were a normal morning. "I just need to go to the bathroom first."

As Celeste walked into the bathroom, I quickly threw on a

T-shirt, jean shorts and my flip-flops. I needed to call Ari back immediately; however, I didn't want Celeste to listen in on the conversation. I gently tapped on the bathroom door.

"Yeah," Celeste shouted from the other end.

"I'm going to get some breakfast from the buffet," I explained, not mentioning that I was going to call my boss. "Do you want anything?"

"I'm good," Celeste said.

"Don't forget to call your husband please," I requested.

I anxiously made my way to the motel lobby. There was a continental breakfast set up. I scanned the room filled with mostly dirty-looking men--truckers I presumed--enjoying eggs, bagels and bacon. I poured myself a coffee, threw in some sugar and milk, and quickly walked outside. I frantically called my boss.

"Lana," Ari said picking up the phone after one ring. "I read your file. You're doing a great job."

"Thank you," I responded proudly.

"A few things need to happen today," Ari continued.

"OK," I responded.

"One, I need you to get any kind of evidence to link Celeste to Richards. There's got to be e-mails, phone records, text messages, receipts, photos—there must be something."

"That might be tricky," I responded. "I don't think there is a paper or electronic trail. Gov. Richards is smarter than that. Celeste said there are no photos of them together."

"They had to communicate somehow—figure it out."

"Understood," I said obediently.

"Also, we need to get her to sign a contract today. Start discussing money with her. I want you to start with a low number, somewhere around twenty thousand. I will e-mail you a contract after we get off the phone for her to sign. Print it up in the business center of your hotel. You can fill out the number that we end up agreeing upon. Finally, I want you to go to the local police station and courthouse to pull all of her criminal records, divorce papers and anything else you can find. She has a pretty colorful past. This doesn't help us. Her sketchy past makes her a less credible source."

"No problem," I assured him. "I'll take care of all of this today."

I hung up the phone and went back to the room as soon as possible. I feared that if I left Celeste alone for too long she would disappear on me forever. She definitely was a flight risk.

To my relief, when I returned to the room, she was still there. I found her staring out the window, fully clothed. She didn't even flinch when I closed the door. She just stared intently out the window, like a zombie.

"Are you OK?" I asked.

"See that black SUV?" Celeste asked as she pointed to a huge black Suburban with tinted windows in the corner of the parking lot.

"Yeah?" I asked. "What about it?"

"I've seen it before," she continued. "There are two men sitting in it."

"Do you know them?" I asked.

"No," she said calmly. "The car has government license plates."

"How do you know they are government plates?" I asked.

"Because the plates are beige-colored," Celeste said. "Government plates are a different shade than ordinary plates."

"OK, I don't get it," I said anxiously. "What's going on?"

"I think I'm being followed," Celeste said as she slowly turned around and looked me in the eye.

"Seriously?" I asked, raising my eyebrows in concern.

"Yep."

"Because of your ties with Gov. Richards?"

"I don't know, but I need to get out of here," she said as she made her way toward her purse on the desk.

I was flustered. I wasn't sure what to say to her. She grabbed her cheap oversized black shiny purse and began to put her heels on.

"OK I understand," I said with patience. "Were you able to talk to your husband?"

"Yes," she said. "I need to go home and talk to him in person. He is so upset that I didn't come home last night that he didn't go to work today."

"I understand, but I need to get my car," I said swiftly. "Is there any way you could drive me to my car? I'll buy you a coffee somewhere on the way."

"Sure," Celeste said with a smile.

I knew I needed as much time with her as possible to get more information out of her. Plus, I needed to convince her to sign a contract today.

We walked down to the lobby of the motel. As we exited the main entrance, I noticed a clean-cut man with a military haircut in a black business suit–who stuck out like a sore thumb surrounded by truckers in overalls, dirty jeans, T-shirts and trucker hats–lurking by the front desk. He made eye contact with me, then slowly turned around and began speaking with the receptionist. Chills immediately ran up and down my spine.

The second we stepped outside, it felt like we had walked into a dry sauna. The sun was blasting without a cloud in the sky, and the heat felt suffocating. I looked over to the black SUV, and now there was only one man in the vehicle sitting in the driver's seat.

"Celeste, did you see that man by the front desk?" I asked as I nudged her on the arm. "Do you think that's the other guy who was in the SUV? I only see one man in the SUV now."

"Just don't look that direction," she said hurriedly. "Keep walking."

Celeste did not look at the SUV. Once we arrived at her vehicle, she repeatedly rattled her car keys in an attempt to open the door. I looked straight at Celeste, but out of the corner of my eye I watched the man in the business suit exit the motel and climb back into the passenger seat of the SUV.

Finally, Celeste got her door unlocked. We both climbed into her messy car. It looked worse in the daylight. The tan interior had coffee stains and cigarette burn holes all over the place. And there was that condom. I shuddered.

"My car won't start," Celeste said to me with concern. "Did I leave my car lights on last night?"

"No, I would've noticed that." I said.

"I think the battery is dead," she said frantically. "My husband probably came and messed with my car last night."

"How could he know where you were?" I asked with skepticism.

"Lana, there's only a handful of motels in Winnemucca. It wouldn't take him long to find my car."

"What about the men in the SUV—do you think they messed with your car?"

"I don't know," Celeste said as she ran her fingers through her hair in distress.

"Are you sure the battery is the problem?"

"I don't know," she said. "I sure hope that's all it is!"

"OK, look," I calmly said. "Why don't you go next door to that gas station and see if there is a mechanic there who can look at your car." I pointed to the 76 gas station across the street. "I'll go inside the motel and ask if they have any jumper cables."

"OK."

My anxiety level began to rise. I did not know what was happening, but my gut told me I was in danger. I quickly walked to the front desk where a woman with long curly brown hair with bad blonde highlights in a navy business suit was standing. She went through papers with her long, bright orange fingernails.

"Hi," I said quickly. "My friend is having car trouble. We think her battery might be dead. Does the hotel keep a pair of jumper cables handy by any chance?"

"No, I'm sorry we don't," the receptionist politely said. "Do you want me to call AAA for you?"

"Let me talk to my friend first," I said. "She's at the gas station next door trying to get help. Hopefully someone there will be able to assist us."

"Well, just let me know," she said with a smile.

I was almost halfway to the front entrance when I stopped in my tracks. I turned around and walked back to the desk. "You know..." I slowly said to the receptionist, gathering my thoughts. "There was a man in a business suit standing at the front desk a few minutes ago. Is he a guest of the motel?"

"No he's not," she said, unfazed.

"Then what was he doing here?"

"He asked to use the phone," she continued. "But when I handed it to him, he never ended up making a call. He walked away without saying a word. It was a little strange. Why do you ask?"

My stomach dropped. "You know..." I said, quickly coming up with a lie. "He looked like someone I know, but I think I'm mistaken."

She shrugged and picked up her nail file to work on her nails.

When I walked back outside, I found Celeste with two overweight truckers opening the hood of her car. They had jumper cables in their hands, and Celeste had found someone who let her use their car for the jump.

"Has someone been messing with your engine?" one of the trucker's asked.

"I'm not sure," Celeste said.

"Well, the cover of your battery is not on properly," he said as he shook his head. "This engine was not put back together correctly. Whoever last worked on your car did a shoddy job."

As Celeste got into the front seat of her car to rev the engine, I backed off several feet. I immediately thought about the car explosion scene from the movie *Michael Clayton*. Could there be a bomb in her car? Was it insane that I was even thinking this? I couldn't shake the feeling that another shoe was about to drop. As Celeste put the key in the ignition, I backed off a couple more feet. I closed my eyes and cringed as if I was preparing for someone to pull the trigger on a gun pressed against my forehead. I began to sweat. Before I knew it, I heard the sound of an engine. I opened my eyes – Celeste had gotten the engine to start. I wiped the sweat off the brim of my forehead and exhaled a sigh of relief. We thanked the truckers and motel guest for helping us and within minutes we were off.

"Celeste, we need to talk," I said sternly. "I feel like there's more you need to tell me. I'm not sure what exactly is going on, but it's making me extremely uncomfortable. Is there a safe place we can go to talk?"

"OK," she said resignedly. "There's a diner we can go to up the road."

We pulled into a run-down diner that looked like it had been around since the fifties. It was painted a light blue with a big red faded sign with the paint peeling that read: Winnemucca Dine-In. There were about ten people inside, mostly men who looked like—yet again—truckers, sitting at the counter eating breakfast. We grabbed a booth in a corner and quickly ordered two coffees from our waitress.

"You need to tell me more about these people who you think are following you," I said tersely to Celeste as I poured sugar and milk into my coffee.

"There's not much to tell. I don't know who they are." Celeste sighed. "I'm not even sure if I'm being followed."

"Then, who were those guys in the SUV with a government-issued license plate?" I asked, exasperated.

"I have no idea." She shook her head.

"Have the same guys followed you before?" I asked.

"I've had this feeling that I've been followed these past few weeks," she replied between sips of coffee. "But I'm not sure if it was by those men."

"Has anyone from Gov. Richards's team contacted you?"

"No," she resolutely said. "I haven't talked to him in over a year."

"Have there been any other strange things happening?" I quizzed her.

"Yes, there is something I haven't told you," she said.

"Well, what is it?" I perked up in suspense.

"My--my house," she stammered. "My... it... someone broke into my house last week."

"Were you home?"

"No," she said. "My husband and I were out of town for

the weekend. We went camping."

"What was stolen?" I asked. "Jewelry, money, a TV?"

"That's the weird thing. Nothing of value was stolen."

"What do you mean?" I asked with confusion. "So, what was taken?"

"Documents like my birth certificate, my Social Security card, phone bills," she continued. "I have a safe where I keep all these documents. The lock was busted open from a bullet."

Alarm bells were going off in my head. The break-in sounded like a professional hit. My reporter's intuition told me this had everything to do with her affair with Gov. Richards.

"Did you file a police report?"

"Yes, and they couldn't find one fingerprint," she said. "They found almost nothing. There was no evidence left behind except for one item."

"What was that?" I asked on the edge of my seat.

"A white-collared shirt with a five-pointed star on it," she said.

"Was it a pentagram?" I asked.

"What is that?"

"It's a five-pointed star with strokes through the middle. It's usually not shaded in," I clarified.

"I think so," Celeste said hesitantly.

I racked my brain. A pentagram is symbolic to so many different political and religious groups. It was a religious symbol to Babylonian and Pythagoreans in Ancient Greece. The star is also tied to Christianity, most commonly used to represent the five wounds of Jesus, and even Satanism. It's also used as a symbol for the Order of the Eastern Star, an association linked to Freemasonry. Could Gov. Richards be a Free Mason? Then, I quickly remembered that their star was multicolored. Fortunately, I had spent many years researching secret societies—a passionate hobby of mine. I thought I remembered stars on the outside of the Mormon temples near where I grew up in Chicago, but I couldn't be sure. I quickly took out my iPhone and Googled "five-pointed star" and "Mormon Church." I clicked on the first relevant website. I rapidly skimmed the first paragraph. I read in silence.

> The Church of Jesus Christ of Latter-day Saints began using both upright and inverted five-pointed stars in temple architecture, dating from the Nauvoo Illinois Temple, which was dedicated on April 30, 1846. Other temples decorated with five-pointed stars in both orientations include the Salt Lake Temple, and the Logan Utah Temple. These symbols come from the symbolism found in Revelation Chapter Twelve, which says, "And there appeared a great wonder in heaven; a woman clothed with the sun and the moon under her feet and upon her head a crown of twelve stars.

"What are you reading?" Celeste asked, breaking my concentration.

"An e-mail from my boss," I lied, quickly putting my phone back into my purse.

I tried to process what was happening. There were a few possibilities. Either Celeste had a wild imagination, someone was playing a prank on her, or someone from the Mormon Church was trying to harm her. Or, it was even possible that President Oyama's administration was trying to collect evidence on her to link her to Gov. Richards. The scenarios were vast. I certainly had my work cut out for me. I bit my lip and scratched my head nervously.

"So...was there any evidence on the shirt like fingerprints or hairs?" I asked.

"No—nothing." She shook her head. "But they took some other things, too, that I don't understand."

"What do you mean?" I asked, sitting upright. "What else did they take?"

"They took photos of me. I dressed up in a Nazi costume last year for Halloween. They stole a bunch of photos of me in the Nazi uniform. They also took the costume. I had a Confederate flag that they took too. I don't know why anyone would want any of these things. They're worthless!"

My jaw dropped. I couldn't believe how naïve Celeste was. With my background in politics and volunteering on two presidential campaigns, I knew enough about smear campaigns to know that either Gov. Richards's team or the Oyama's administration was behind the break-in. They had stolen any items that would paint Celeste in a horrible light and give her little or zero credibility.

When and if the story of her affair with Gov. Richards broke, Oyama's administration would want to release the fact that not only did Gov. Richards have sexual relations with a hooker, but she was also a hooker who happened to be a white supremacist bigot!

On the other hand, I reasoned, Gov. Richards's team could be collecting as much evidence as possible to discredit Celeste in case her story did come out. They would paint her to be a white supremacist Nazi sympathizer.

I found it also ironic that they took a flag that was covered in five-pointed stars. It started to sink in what a dangerous situation I was in. The stakes were very high for the presidential election, and I knew if I wasn't careful, I could get hurt or even die. If I was a target, Celeste certainly was an even bigger one.

"Celeste, I don't want to scare you, but I think you're in

danger," I explained. "Whoever robbed your home clearly stole anything that would paint you in a bad light and hurt your credibility. If Gov. Richards's people are behind the break-in, they are preparing for a media showdown."

"What do you mean?" she asked.

"It seems like they are preparing for the day that you do come out with your story," I explained. "They're building their defense, and their defense will be that you're a racist hooker with no credibility, so nothing you say has any validity."

"I see," she said as she looked down at her coffee.

"I think your life could be in danger," I continued. "Honestly, the best way to protect yourself is by coming forward with your story. I'm not just saying this because I want to break your story. I won't lie, though—I do want to break your story. However, I'm saying this because you'll be safer once the story is out. No one is going to hurt you after its surfaced. Until then, your life may be in serious jeopardy."

"Do you really believe that?" Celeste questioned, her eyes growing wide with fear.

"Yes," I stated emphatically. "I lived down the street from Chandra Levy when I lived in Washington, D.C. and worked as an intern in the White House for my second semester senior year of college. Do you remember her?"

"Vaguely," she said.

"She was an intern and Gary Condit's mistress," I explained. "Gary represented California's eighteenth congressional district. He had an affair with her for several months. No one knew. Then, he knocked her up, and soon after, she mysteriously disappeared. Eventually, they found her murdered in a park."

"I do remember that," she said. "But didn't they clear Condit and convict the real killer?"

"Yes, but do you really believe Condit had nothing to do with it?" I asked. I had learned a lot of secrets while I worked at the White House such as more dirty details of Monica Lewinsky's affair with President Bill Clinton that still haven't gone public to this day.

"But then who is the man they threw in jail for the murder?" Celeste asked in confusion.

"Celeste," I said patiently. "Have you heard of Occam's razor?"

"No." She shook her head and looked down at her coffee. I knew she most likely didn't even have a GED, so of course I had lost her when I started talking about philosophy.

"It's a theory that in, layman's terms, means that the simplest explanation is probably the right one," I explained.

"I see," Celeste replied.

"But take someone like Monica Lewinsky," I explained. "Her story became public, and I guarantee you that saved her life."

"OK I see what you're saying," Celeste said calmly. I think all the information I was relaying to her sailed right over her head.

"Look, again, I don't want to scare you, but with everything you're telling me, and how much is riding on this election—or any presidential election for that matter—I'm very concerned for your safety," I said. And I meant it. "I do believe I can help you, though. We absolutely want to publish your story, and like I explained last night, we can break it either on or off the record."

"I remember," she said. "Can you tell me how much you think I can get for coming forward?"

"Don't quote me on this, but if you come forward and did the story with us on the record, I could get you more than fifty thousand dollars, maybe even six figures. If you do the story off the record, it would be less than that, most likely somewhere around twenty thousand dollars. You would have to sign a contract. The contract protects both your interests and the interests of my company."

"OK," She said, her eyes growing big. "That's a lot of money."

"I know it's a lot to think about," I said. "You should also know that time is of the essence. The Republican National Convention is just a few weeks away. We would like to have the story locked down by then. Clearly, we need the story before the election–after the election your story is almost worthless. Do you understand?"

"Yes, I do," she said. "I'll need some time to think about this."

"I understand," I conceded. "But there is something else I need from you."

"What's that?"

"I'm going to need some sort of evidence that supports your claim. Do you have any phone records or anything to back up your allegations?"

"I have an old cell phone I used to communicate with Gov. Richards's nephew, Steve Swanson, and attorney, James Garrett. They were my clients too. I didn't communicate with Gov. Richards, but I did communicate with them."

"Wait, hold up, you slept with Gov. Richards's lawyer and nephew too?" I asked in disbelief.

"Yes," she said meekly.

"And you have evidence of phone communication with them?"

"Yes."

"Well, that's a start," I said, shaking my head in disbelief that she had slept with two men who were blood relatives. I kept forgetting that I was dealing with a professional. "Can I see this cell phone?"

"Yeah, I can give it to you," she said.

"So, Gov. Richards's attorney and nephew were your regular clients as well?" I asked.

"Not so much the attorney, but his nephew was a regular," she replied.

"Isn't that weird–that you were working with two family members?" Even though I've seen a lot of wild things through my line of work, Celeste still managed to shock me.

"I don't think they knew they were both using me at first," she said. "I didn't realize Steve was Gov. Richards's nephew for months. I kind of found out by accident."

"Are you still sleeping with Steve?" I asked.

"No," she said. "He actually died in a tragic accident."

This story was sounding more and more like a soap opera. "What kind of an accident?"

"A car accident."

My mind went back to that scene from *Michael Clayton*. Was the car crash really an accident? Things weren't adding up.

"How did you find out?"

"I hadn't heard from him in a few days. I was worried, so I called his phone and his wife answered. I said I was a friend. She said he died in a car accident and asked me to never call again. It's so sad. I was devastated."

The plot thickened. My mind continued to race. I reviewed in my head everything Celeste was telling me: mysterious break-ins, five-pointed stars and a fatal car accident. Could all these events be a string of strange coincidences? I doubted it. My journey in life researching the spiritual and religious worlds had led me to conclude that there is no such thing as a coincidence. I always believed that, and my beliefs were strengthened after I read the *Celestine Prophecy* my freshman year in college. The ancient insights discussed in the book have helped me become a successful journalist -- especially the insight that stresses that there are no coincidences in life.

I wondered if Gov. Richards's camp was behind the fatal car accident. Had he found out that Steve was sleeping with "his" hooker? Did he put a fatal stop to it? I felt ashamed for even thinking such horrible thoughts about a candidate whom I so deeply believed in and supported. It made me sick.

"We should go," Celeste said.

"I'll grab the check," I said, putting down a ten-dollar bill for the coffee.

Celeste took me to the Martin where I picked up my car. She agreed to allow me to follow her back to her place. She said I could wait in my car as she ran into her house to get her old cell phone. My Prius was in the same spot where I had left it the night before. I feared my car wouldn't start–just like Celeste's Mercedes. I breathed a sigh of relief as I pushed the ignition button and all I heard was a soft hum.

In the daylight, Celeste's street looked way less creepy. However, it still was very redneck. Almost every front yard had overgrown lawns covered in junk. We pulled up to a blue trailer with a pebble driveway. Celeste ran out of her car while I waited in mine a couple houses down the street. I knew her crazy husband was most likely home, and I did not want to have a run-in with him. Celeste walked out of the trailer in less than five minutes.

"Here it is," she said, frantically, handing me an old Sprint flip phone as she approached my car window. "My husband went to run some errands. You should leave now before he returns."

"I will." I nodded. "Thank you."

"I couldn't find the charger for that phone and it's dead," she explained. "You're probably going to have to go to Best Buy or somewhere to get a new charger for it."

"That won't be a problem," I said.

I drove away and remembered that there was a Target a few blocks from my hotel. There I managed to find a charger for the ancient cell phone in just a few minutes. I was worried that they no longer made the charger – let alone that one would be available at Target. After I picked up the charger, I raced to the Winnemucca Police Station to follow up on my boss's instruction to get all of Celeste's criminal records.

When I arrived, I identified myself as a reporter with National Publishing and requested Celeste's arrest records. An overweight male police officer, with silver hair, a big nose and a beard slowly made copies of all the police reports. I quickly looked through the stack of papers. I couldn't believe Celeste's checkered past. Police had arrested her for: stalking, driving under the influence, obstruction of justice, resisting arrest, and shoplifting. I shook my head in disappointment. I knew that even with rock-solid evidence proving that Celeste had had an affair with Gov. Richards—and even if she passed a polygraph test—it still would be difficult to have the company lawyers clear the story for publication. With Celeste's criminal record, she had no credibility as a source. That would be highly problematic.

After I left the police station, I headed to the courthouse to search for documents that concerned her two divorces and the custody battles over her three children. In the records room, I found two old ladies sitting behind the desk complaining about the summer heat. There was a brass bell on the counter. I rang it. They hadn't noticed my arrival despite the fact they were both sitting three feet away from me. They informed me that each paper would cost ten cents. There were a total of eighty-seven papers with all of Celeste's dramatic legal proceedings. They handed me a stack of about a dozen papers at a time. I cringed as I scrolled through the papers. The allegations in her divorce papers from both parties were nauseating. There were allegations of drug and alcohol abuse, domestic violence, child neglect and abuse, among other accusations. I discovered that Celeste's parents had custody of her daughter. Then I read that two of her other children lived in Colorado with one of her ex-husbands. However, my eyes got real big when I read that he was a registered sex offender! I thought, how fucked up of a person do you have to be to lose custody of your children to a registered sex offender? I sighed. This was bad. I knew Ari would not be happy with these revelations.

I walked out of the courthouse and headed to my Prius. I suddenly felt uneasy. I did a quick scan of my surroundings and spotted a black SUV parked in an alley two blocks away. I did not react and tried my best to carry on as if I didn't see the SUV. I jumped in my car and raced back to my motel. I looked through my rearview mirror for the entire five-minute drive to the motel. The SUV followed behind me for a few blocks and turned away just two blocks shy of the motel. Was it the same SUV? I wasn't sure if I was becoming paranoid or if my instincts were right.

I rushed back to my room as quickly as possible. When I got there, I opened my door slowly, just in case someone had broken into my room. I searched the closet and the bathroom. All clear.

I knew my anxiety level was extremely high because my heart was racing. I figured a good workout would make me feel better. I dug through my suitcase, looking for a sports bra in the compartment where I kept my lingerie. I was shocked to find that it was almost completely empty. All of my lace Victoria's Secret thongs were gone, as well as a black lace and leopard bra. I continued searching. I definitely had packed a bright yellow bikini too–just in case I had an opportunity to work from the pool–and that was also gone!

"That fucking whore!" I screamed out loud. I knew that Celeste had snagged my lingerie and bikini. Only a hooker would steal underwear! I calculated in my head that the items she stole totaled at least five hundred dollars. I wanted nothing more than to call and ream her out, but I knew I had to keep her on my good side–at least until I got her to sign a contract. My blood boiled.

My phone rang. It was Malden.

"Hi baby! How is the story going? I miss you!" he said cheerfully on the other end.

"I can't believe it–the prostitute stole my brand new lingerie from Victoria's Secret," I fumed. "Oh, and my favorite bikini too!"

"Wait, what?" he asked in shock. "What are you talking about, Lana?"

"It's a long story, but I brought the prostitute back to my hotel room. She ended up getting drunk and passing out in one of the beds."

"No way! Did you get her talking about Richards?"

"Yes, I did."

"That's amazing! Well played, Lana."

"Thanks," I said proudly, momentarily forgetting about my stolen goods. "So, I got a ton of info out of her. But this morning, I left her alone for no more than ten minutes to go call my boss. That must have been when she stole my stuff. I can't believe it!"

"Ha!" Malden laughed. "Well, she *is* a hooker."

"It's not funny," I said still angry, but I couldn't help but laugh. He did have a point. "She claims she's not hooking anymore though since she got married. Anyway, it's been a crazy twenty-four hours. The account of her affair with Gov. Richards is outrageous. She claims he had her piss on him!"

"What," he said, raising his voice as if he had heard me incorrectly.

"I know, crazy right!" I said. "It gets worse. She says that not only does he like her to pee on him, but he loves to drink her piss."

"No way!" Malden said in disbelief. "I don't believe that. Do you?"

"I'm not sure what to think," I said. "She's a tough read. I spent half my morning gathering background information on her criminal history. It isn't pretty. However, she was very quick to give me details of her affair. She seemed to be too quick on her toes to lie. I can't figure her out yet."

"Well, these are very serious accusations—you need to be careful," Malden cautioned.

"I know." I sighed. "There are some other strange things going on."

"What do you mean?"

"She told me her house was broken into last week," I said. "Nothing of value was stolen. The thief only took items that would paint her in a negative light, as well as her Social Security card and some other documents. Then, this morning her car wouldn't start. We got a trucker to jump her battery, but he said it looked like someone had intentionally messed with the engine. On top of that, I think we were being followed by two men in a black SUV with government-issued plates."

"Wow, I don't know what to say," Malden said with concern. "I'm worried about you. This is a dangerous assignment. If the prostitute did have an affair with Gov. Richards, there are people who are going to go to great lengths to silence her–and the messenger. You need to be careful, Lana. You're playing with fire."

"I know," I exhaled. "I don't feel safe here. I have so much anxiety. I'm going to go for a run to calm my nerves."

"Lana, you're not going for a run," Malden instructed.

"Don't worry, I'm going to go for a run at the local gym down the street," I assured him. "The hotel gives guests free passes to the local gym. I'll be safe there."

"Promise me you will not run outside," Malden begged.

"Don't worry," I reassured him. "I won't."

"Do you think you'll be home by the weekend?" Malden asked. I could hear the eagerness in his voice. It made my heart flutter.

"I'm not sure. I got a ton of information from her last night, but I still need to get her to sign a contract. I'm not sure how long that will take. Right now, she's at home, thinking about the offer I made her."

"Well, I want to take you wine tasting in Santa Barbara this weekend at my friend's vineyard," Malden said, changing gears.

I got butterflies in my stomach thinking about spending a romantic weekend with my gorgeous man in wine country. The offer was particularly appealing after spending twenty-four hours in this shit hole of a town.

"That sounds amazing," I said.

"We'll take the Pacific Coast Highway all the way," Malden said.

"Sounds like a plan," I said.

After I got off the phone with Malden, I called Ari to give him an update. He was not happy to hear about Celeste's criminal resume. I headed to the gym in my car. On the way, I found myself looking over my shoulder constantly. I couldn't wait to get on a treadmill to burn off all the anxiety I had accumulated about my current assignment. I parked in a lot next to the tiny gym. I walked inside and gave the teenage girl at the reception desk my guest pass. The treadmills were in front of a panel of windows that didn't have a view of my car. A gnawing feeling came over me. I ran back outside, telling the girl at the desk that I had left something in my car. I quickly pulled it around the corner and parked it on the street right in front the treadmills. I exhaled and went back inside. Now that I could keep an eye on my car during my run, I could relax. I spent the next forty minutes running with Pandora's classic rock station blaring in my earphones. I tried to process the past twenty-four hours. I found it hard to make sense of everything. When I finished my run, I noticed a text from Celeste.

Celeste Homan: "I need the weekend to think about your offer. My husband is very upset with me. He does not want me to do the story. We are going to go away for a few days. I will contact you when I am back."

Fuck! I knew she was a flight risk. I immediately called Celeste. I got her voicemail. It was full, so I couldn't leave her a message. I quickly responded to her text.

Lana Burke: "I understand this is a huge decision that

114

you need to think through carefully. I completely respect that. Is there any way I could take you and your husband to a nice dinner tonight to answer any questions you may have?"

Celeste took less than five minutes to respond. I opened her text as it beeped.

Celeste Homan: "We're already on the road headed out of town. Maybe next week when I'm back."

"Fuck!" I screamed out loud as I threw the phone down. I knew this assignment was going too well to be true. I called Ari and broke the bad news. He calmly told me not to get discouraged because I had made huge headway in twenty-four hours. He approved a flight for me to take home the next morning for the weekend and instructed that I return to Winnemucca on Monday morning. I texted Malden an update.

Lana Burke: "I'm coming home tomorrow morning. I can go to Santa Barbara with you this weekend."

He responded in minutes.

Malden Murphy: "Great news!"

I charged Celeste's phone as I packed my belongings. I threw on a T-shirt and boxer shorts and got into bed with my laptop. I couldn't resist researching more about pentagrams, the Mormon Church and secret societies.

I pulled up information from a conspiracy theory website on an old Mormon secret combination in the Book of Mormon. In the Latter Day Saints movement, a secret combination is a secret society of "people bound together by oaths to carry out the evil purposes of the group."

Secret combinations were first discussed in the Book of Mormon, published in 1830 by Joseph Smith, Jr. The most notable example of a secret combination is the Gadianton robbers, a conspiracy throughout much of the Book of Mormon narrative. According to the Joseph Smith translation of the Bible, Cain also entered a secret combination with Satan and became Master Mahan.

I read further.

The Book of Mormon denounces secret combinations as 'most abominable and wicked above all, in the sight of God.' They are also considered to be one of the signs that a people is ripe for the Lord's vengeance, and according to the Book of Mormon, in the last days will be prevalent on the earth.

On other conspiracy theory sites and Wikipedia I also found information about a modern-day Mormon secret society called the Danites.

The Danites were a fraternal organization founded by Latter Day Saint members in June 1838, in the town of Far West in Caldwell County, Missouri. During their period of organization in Missouri, the Danites operated as a vigilante group and took a central role in the events of the 1838 Mormon War. Whether or not the Danites existed after the 1847 arrival of the LDS in Utah is still debated. However, they remained an important part of Mormon and non-Mormon folklore, polemics, and propaganda for the remainder of the 19th century, waning in ideological prominence after

Utah gained statehood. Notwithstanding public excommunications of Danites leaders by the Church and both public and private statements from Joseph Smith referring to the band as being both evil in nature and a "secret combination" to which he attributed no part of, the nature and scope of the organization, and the degree to which it was officially connected to the Church of Jesus Christ of Latter-day Saints, are a matter of some dispute among historians.

I was fascinated, but also scared. My concentration was broken by a knock on my door. My heart stopped. I quickly ran to the door. I was relieved that I had remembered to use the bolt lock. I looked through the peephole, and I saw a Latina woman carrying a tray.

"Who's there?" I shouted without even cracking the door open.

"Room service," she responded.

"I didn't order anything—you must have the wrong room," I shouted back.

"Oops—sorry," she replied.

I sighed. Was she really a room service waitress? What would've happened if I opened the door? I couldn't be happier that I was leaving this piece of shit town first thing in the morning. I just needed to make it through the night. I got back in my bed and looked at my iPhone. There was his number, President Oyama's mole, Gunnar Smith. I contemplated calling him. I knew he was the one person who could protect me.

CHAPTER 7

"Lana, Lana," Malden said softly as he caressed my forehead.

"The Danites!" I screamed, half-conscious.

"What?"

"The pentagram!" I shouted, opening my eyes wide.

"What in the world are you talking about?" Malden laughed. "It's OK, babe—you were just having a bad dream."

"Oh my God!" I panted, sitting up as I put my hand on my pounding chest. "What time is it?"

"It's three in the afternoon," Malden said.

"How did you get in here?" I asked.

"Your door was unlocked," Malden said nonchalantly. "The security guard at the front gate tried to call you, but you didn't answer your phone."

I slowly gathered my thoughts. I had been up since the crack of dawn, traveling home from Winnemucca. When I got back to my apartment around lunchtime, I lay down on my bed to relax and watch some TV. I must've fallen asleep for a few hours.

"I just had a crazy dream," I said.

"I can tell," Malden said as he raised his voice with each word. "You'll have to tell me about it on the way to Santa Barbara. We should leave soon."

"Yes," I replied, rubbing my eyes like a child. "Just give me an hour. I'm going to take a shower. I need to get some work done too. I'm sure my boss has been trying to get a hold of me."

My concern about my story on Gov. Richards slowly waned in Malden's presence. I had the weekend off. There wasn't much I could do to move it forward until I was back in Winnemucca on Monday, and I was with my gorgeous boyfriend.

"I'll drive–you can work from the car. Just get ready. We have a big weekend ahead of us," Malden said.

"OK," I said, rushing into the bathroom. I turned on the shower. The cool high-pressured water on my back felt like a catharsis. When I got out, Malden was standing in my bedroom, holding up two short-sleeved, collared shirts. One was soft blue the other was lime green with white stripes.

"Which one do you like better?" Malden asked with a smile.

"I think they both would look hot on you," I said as I seductively dropped my towel and stood completely naked in front of him.

"I think I would look hot on you," he said, creeping closer to me.

"Not so fast," I said, pushing him back and bending over to wrap the towel around my wet hair. "We have to get on the road for our romantic weekend wine tasting."

"OK," Malden relented, as he stood in front of me nose-to-nose. "But only because I'll have all weekend to have my way with you. We'll stop at Nobu in Malibu on the way up for a nice dinner on the ocean to watch the sunset."

"Sounds great. I'm going to wear this neon green dress," I said, holding up my most flattering short and tight dress.

"That's hot!" Malden nodded. "Then I'll wear my green shirt, too."

"Oh, so we're going to be that couple," I smirked.

"Why not?" Malden asked.

"It works for me," I said as I winked at him.

We took the Sunset Strip all the way to the Pacific Coast Highway in my X5. Malden drove so that I could work. Ari had emailed me some follow-up questions that he had after reading my file on Gov. Richards's affair with Celeste.

"What's that you got?" Malden said, putting in a Rolling Stones CD from the case he brought with him filled with his entire collection. I had peeked through his CDs when I got into the car – all his CDs were classic rock or rock. My kind of guy.

I had grabbed Celeste's phone out of my purse. "It's the hooker's cell phone," I replied.

"Now, tell me, why do you have her phone?"

"Well... it's not her current phone," I explained. "It's one of her old ones. There's supposed to be some texts in here that link her to some of Gov. Richards's people."

"I see," Malden said. "I can't believe you managed to convince her to give you her phone. How did you do that?"

"I just asked for it."

Malden shook his head in disbelief, "You're good, Lana."

I smiled at Malden.

Last night at the motel, I had briefly looked through Celeste's phone. I saw that there were messages from someone named James Garrett. Allegedly, James was an attorney for Gov. Richards who also used Celeste's services. There were also several messages from Steve Swanson, Gov. Richards's nephew. Like Celeste alleged, he had texted her whenever he wanted to see her.

I typed out the date and time of every message, along with their phone numbers, and e-mailed the document to Ari on my MacBook Air. Malden brought his Mifi so I had wireless Internet in the car. I knew that the company's private investigator could verify if these numbers were definitively attached to a James Garrett and a Steve Swanson. The messages were good evidence, but they weren't as salacious as I hoped. Our company uses a private investigator to help with our bigger stories. Most tabloids use the services of a private investigation firm.

Steve's texts were right to the point. "Are you free for a quickie?"

James, meanwhile, was a little more discreet, "Are you available for a noon appointment?"

Clearly, both men were clients of Celeste. However, it would be easier to prove that Steve had sex with her, based on his text messages. I diligently typed out every message into a Word file on my laptop, as Malden drove my X5 past one huge Beverly Hills mansion after the other. After about a half hour of work, I put my laptop and phone away.

"You get your work done?" Malden asked.

"Yeah, I did actually."

"I'm real glad you're back in town," Malden said with a furrowed brow. "I was worried about you. I don't like this story you're covering. I don't think it's safe."

"I'll be fine," I reassured him. "You don't have to worry about me."

"Do you think that the hooker is telling the truth?"

"I don't know," I replied. I thought about all the years I

had spent in college and in my early twenties campaigning for one Republican candidate after the other. I dreaded the thought of any Republican candidate cavorting with a hooker. "I honestly hope she isn't. I'm such a believer in Gov. Richards. I'll honestly be crushed if it's true."

"I just don't get it."

"You don't get what?"

"Why any man would sleep with a hooker." Malden shrugged.

"Well, I can understand why an ugly man would need to pay for sex," I said as I gathered my thoughts. "But I'm sure a billionaire running for president could find plenty of women who would be more than happy to have sex with him for free."

"Ha!" Malden laughed. "Very true."

Malden changed the subject.

"So, did you like the Holiday Inn Express?"

"It certainly wasn't the Four Seasons, but it was fine." I laughed.

Malden looked wistful. "My sons and I stayed there during our cross-country road trip."

"What?" I responded in disbelief.

"Yeah. We stayed there and in Salt Lake too."

"Oh my God, how did you not tell me that?" I asked in surprise. "I didn't even know anyone else knew that town existed."

"I guess it just slipped my mind. We didn't hang out there. We just crashed for the night."

After a solid hour in the car, we arrived at Nobu. We sat on the outdoor patio overlooking the ocean. We watched the sunset as we ate sushi and drank wine. Anytime I had been to that Nobu I'd seen celebrities there. That night I spotted Kourtney Kardashian and Scott Disick at a table inside and

Cindy Crawford, Rande Gerber and George Clooney at a table with a big group. Malden ordered a few margaritas with extra shots of Casamigos Tequila before he paid our bill. It concerned me.

"Malden are you sure you're going to be OK to drive?" I asked as we walked to the valet.

"Lana, relax, I'm six foot two and I weigh over two hundred pounds," he said with a subtle slur. "Plus, the drinks were all ice!"

"OK," I said. I trusted him. Or did I?

When we got to the valet, Malden seemed more chatty than usual. I offered to drive, but he insisted again that he was perfectly fine to drive. We took the Pacific Coast Highway north. Malden drove the whole ninety minutes to Santa Barbara.

"Check this out," Malden said, smiling. He pressed a button, and the moon roof opened. We could see the full moon perfectly hanging over the Pacific Ocean. I had thrown on a U2 CD from Malden's collection. The ocean air smelled so fresh, and the light from the moon reflected off the ocean. It was magical.

"I can't resist," I said, unsnapping my seatbelt. I pulled myself out the sunroof and raised my arms in the air. It was liberating. I felt like I was flying through space. There were no streetlights and no other cars on the road. It was as if Malden and I were the only two people in the world, and I could not be happier. I was with a man I was falling hard for. I had a great job. I had just left an amazing dinner, and I lived in the most beautiful state in the whole country. I felt so lucky. I looked up at the stars and said a quiet prayer in gratitude of my blessed life.

"Alright, wild child, get back in here before we get pulled

over," Malden said, tugging on my dress. I didn't move at first. Then I felt his right hand slowly creep up my short dress. I instantly got wet.

"You naughty girl," Malden said as he slowly caressed my wet pussy.

"Excuse me?" I said as I flopped back down in my seat.

"You heard me," he said with a smile.

"I'm not naughty," I said with a laugh.

"Oh, yes you are, and that's why I like you." Malden laughed.

"Then why don't you punish me?" I asked with a flirtatious smile.

"Oh, I will when we get to Santa Barbara." Malden laughed.

I leaped over the center counsel and wrapped my arms around Malden. I kissed him on the cheek and then on the mouth as he cruised the PCH.

"I can't wait," I whispered in his ear as I lodged my tongue deep into his ear.

"I'm going to have to pull over," Malden said as I lowered my hand on his crotch and felt his hard cock throbbing.

"OK, I'll behave till we get there," I relented as I sat back in my seat and threw my seatbelt on. He was irresistible. I was tempted to make him pull over and rip all his clothes off on the beach. I restrained myself. As exotic as that sounded, it was chilly, and I yearned to get to our destination.

We were finally in Santa Barbara. Cruising down Coast Village Road, the area looked super familiar to me. I racked my brain. Then I remembered: Kim Kardashian's wedding. I had been down here a couple of years prior to cover the reality-star's faux wedding. I ended up hanging out with talk show host

George Lopez at the bar the entire night. He gave me a ton of info for my feature on the wedding. We had a great time—until I refused to go back to his hotel room with him. We were just blocks away from the Four Seasons. I held my breath. Had Malden booked the Four Seasons Hotel?

"I know where we are," I stated.

"Oh do you," Malden said smoothly.

"Did you get us a room at the Four Seasons?" I asked.

"Not a room," he teased.

"Are we going there for a drink?" I asked, confused.

"A suite, Lana," Malden said.

"Wow, look at you!" I said, giddy with excitement.

"Have you been?" he casually asked.

"Only once, but it was for work."

I was ecstatic that Malden liked me enough to book such a pricey suite at such a special place. He was definitely sweeping me off my feet. Malden seduced me with a gorgeous suite overlooking the ocean. The room was accented with yellow, gold and green hues. There were marble floors and a gold-trimmed fireplace. We had a veranda with huge white French doors. It looked like a room fit for a princess—and I felt like Cinderella.

Malden ordered a bottle of red while I filled our Jacuzzi bathtub with hot water. In true California form, the temperature had dropped significantly after sunset. I wanted to get the chill off. I poured as much body wash into the tub as I could find in an attempt to fill the bathtub with bubbles. I slowly inched into the tub and hoped to have my *Pretty Woman* bathtub moment when Malden walked in. All I was missing was a nineties Walkman and a Prince cassette.

"Whatcha doing in there?" Malden asked as he burst into the bathroom with the bottle of wine and two glasses.

"Deep sea diving!" I excitedly said.

"Sounds like an adventure," Malden said. "Can I join you?"

"I thought you'd never ask."

Malden got naked and hopped in the bathtub. I couldn't help but stare at his cock and his perfect ass. I adored his body. He quickly poured us each a glass of wine. We toasted, took a sip, and then I climbed on top of him. I wrapped my arms around him and we made out. I could not get enough of this man. I sat up, catching my breath and taking another sip of wine. I truly felt like I had died and gone to heaven.

"You know, Lana, I haven't dated anyone seriously in ten years," Malden said as he scrubbed my back with a washcloth.

"Oh," I responded. I wasn't sure what to say to that.

"No woman has met my family since my divorce. That was a little over a decade ago."

"Well, maybe you haven't met the right one," I joked in an attempt to lighten the mood.

"I hadn't... but that's changed now," Malden whispered, wrapping his arms around my chest as we soaked in the warm bath. He cupped each one of my breasts with those big, strong hands. It made me melt instantly. God, how I loved those bear paws.

"I'm telling you this, Lana, because I want you to come with me to my family reunion in a few weeks," he said, continuing to rub my breasts under the water. I froze. I couldn't believe my ears. This man was serious about me, and he was wasting no time. I was speechless.

"Well, what do you think?" Malden asked intently.

"Oh–oh-oh I think," I stammered, "that sounds like fun. I just would need to make sure it doesn't conflict with work. I have to do more traveling for my story on Gov. Richards."

"Well, hopefully you can work around that."

"OK," I complied. I leaned back on Malden's broad chest. This man was too good to be true.

We toweled off and finished our bottle of wine in bed. We talked more about our past relationships and what we both wanted out of life. Malden told me stories of his days working on Wall Street. He told me all about his global travels when he worked as a pilot for Pan Am. Under the covers, I curled up on his chest and fell half-asleep, listening to his tales.

As I lay in the super comfy bed with Egyptian cotton sheets, I felt him slowly crawl out from underneath me. He was straddling my back now. I opened my eyes. I felt his hard dick push up against my ass. Oh no–not again!

He leaned over and whispered in my ear, "Are you ready to have some fun?"

I exhaled and lifted my ass toward his hard cock. I tried to embrace my new hobby. I heard him spit in his hands. He then rubbed his saliva all over my anus. I remained still. I felt his dick slowly go deep into my anus. It went in smoother with his saliva, but I wished we had lube. I moaned out loud. Malden delicately rocked himself back and forth. He didn't use much aggression. He stayed in me for ten minutes before he began to subtly shake.

"I can't control myself," he groaned. "You feel so good!"

I could feel my pussy get wetter with each of his deep groans. It turned me on to hear him so excited.

"Oh God!" he shouted. "I can't hold it anymore. I'm coming!"

He exploded on top of me at the same time I felt an electric bolt go through my body. I quickly reached down to my wet pussy to rub myself a few times as quickly as possible to enhance that final sensation. Malden collapsed on top of me, and within seconds the earthquake aftershocks came. His body shook and trembled again for what seemed like an hour. We fell asleep in each other's arms without even rinsing ourselves off.

Malden woke me up at nine in the morning with eggs and bacon from room service for breakfast in bed. He informed me that we had a big day of wine tasting ahead of us. We started at his friend's vineyard, the Santa Barbara Winery. We met tourists from all over the world. Malden and I both made new friends with ease. People kept asking us how long we'd been married. It made me blush. It was a perfect seventy-five degree day without a cloud in the sky, and I had a slight buzz going on.

After finishing the tour at the Santa Barbara Winery, Malden and I drove to the Deep Sea Tasting Room for lunch. It was right on the ocean and beautiful. We got a table facing one of the floor-to-ceiling windows. As we sat down, a school of dolphins popped up. It was as if Malden had planned the dolphins' appearance to coincide with our arrival. It was magical.

There was just one thing off about what was otherwise a perfect day. Malden's phone kept ringing. He kept saying "thank you" over and over in many of his conversations. I couldn't help but wonder why.

"You're very popular today," I teased when he got off the phone. "Is everything OK?"

"Everything's great!" he said with a smile. "I'm not usually this popular, though. Today is an exception."

"Why's that?"

"Today's my birthday," he said nonchalantly.

"What? Are you joking me?" I said angrily.

"No, Lana," he said calmly. "June twenty-eighth. That's my birthday."

"Oh my God I feel horrible! I had no idea—why didn't you tell me?"

"Once you get to be my age, you don't advertise your birthday."

Then it dawned on me that this man was actually fifty-six not fifty-five! I tried to not let myself get upset about his age. The age gap between us was so great already—what was another year?

"Well, I wish you would've told me. Here you've been spoiling me all weekend long, and it's your birthday we should be celebrating."

"Lana, there's nowhere else in the world I'd rather be than right here with you on my birthday," Malden said with a smile.

"Come on," I blushed.

"No, Lana, I'm serious," Malden said as he looked at me sternly. "I love you, Lana."

I was momentarily paralyzed. What did he just say? I couldn't believe he dropped the L bomb already. I didn't know what to say. I didn't know if I should dance on the table or dive in the ocean and swim as far away as possible. However, the few glasses of wine I had at the winery took over my mouth. I didn't even have a say.

"I love you, too." The words spilled out. Afterwards, I sat there in shock. I couldn't believe I was telling a fifty-six year-old man with five kids who I had only dated for about a month that I loved him! What had gotten into me?

Malden smiled back, leaned in, and kissed me on the mouth. The world stopped. I was in love. I'd fallen fast. I dove in headfirst with my arms behind my back with no protection. I knew there was no turning back now.

CHAPTER 8

Beep, beep.

My eyes popped right open. I sat up in bed quickly realizing that I was having a nightmare and I was back at the crappy Winnemucca Holiday Inn Express. I sighed. The stress from the story had sky rocketed my anxiety level. I clenched my phone in my clammy hand. I couldn't believe that I had been at the Four Seasons in Santa Barbara less than twenty-four hours ago, and now I was back in a tacky motel room possibly risking my life for my job—not to mention that I could potentially take down the one candidate I truly wanted to win the election. Yawning, I shook my head in disbelief at the dichotomy of the past twenty-four hours, unlocked my phone and read the text.

Malden Murphy: "Hey sexy girl! How was your flight?"

I leaned back in bed, and sighed. I reflected on my romantic weekend wine tasting in Santa Barbara with Malden. He was gorgeous, and he was all mine. The man of my dreams was not only my boyfriend—he loved me. I couldn't believe he had asked me to his family reunion. I prayed I'd be home from this dirty assignment in time to make the trip to meet his relatives. I fantasized about meeting his family and children. Would they be my family one-day? Lana Murphy? It had a nice ring to it, I thought, and laughed out loud. The thought got me excited. Slowly, I worked my right hand down to my white cotton boy shorts. I began to touch myself as I envisioned Malden naked on top of me. Then I stopped and looked at my cell again. It was already three in the afternoon, and

Celeste hadn't returned my call. I couldn't waste time masturbating—I had to get to work! After all, this was the biggest story of my career—what was I thinking? I loved Malden, but I didn't want him to distract me from my mission. Mick had flown into town to help me with the story. I want to make sure to be on the top of my game in front of him. After all, he was my mentor, and I did not want to disappoint him. I crafted the perfect text to Celeste.

Lana Burke: "Hi Celeste, I hope you guys had a great trip. I left you a voicemail earlier. I'm back in town with a colleague. We'd love to take you and your husband to your favorite restaurant tonight for dinner and to discuss the story. I know I got on the wrong foot with your hubby, please tell him I want to fix that."

Before I could put my phone down, it beeped again.

Mick Madden: "Any word back from Celeste yet?"

Mick and I had flown out to Winnemucca earlier that morning. Ari had decided it would be more effective to work as a team—good cop, bad cop. I'd be the good cop. Mick loved playing the bad cop. I was certain he got off on it. He brought all his specialized equipment to Winnemucca including a paparazzi-style long lens camera and an HD video recorder. My hotel was completely booked by the time Ari decided to send Mick. The only room left at the Days Inn was an executive suite for three hundred dollars a night. I laughed hysterically when Mick told me about his room. I could not wait to see what a suite in a dive hotel in a shitty desert town looked like.

Lana Burke: "She hasn't called me back yet, but I just shot her a text."

Mick Madden: "Do you still have Numbnuts' number?"

Lana Burke: "Who?"

Mick Madden: "Her husband."

Lana Burke: "Oh yeah, Chad. Yes I do. LOL!"

Mick Madden: "Why don't you shoot Numbnuts a text too. Try to make him feel like he's in control. Let's get this moving."

From a psychological standpoint, that was good advice. If we engaged Chad by making him feel like he was in control, he would feel like the "man" of the household. That's the position we wanted him to be in. He'd be that much more likely to cooperate. Or, at the very least, it would allow Celeste to cooperate with us.

Lana Burke: "OK."

I was relieved to have Mick in town with me. I knew it would be safer with him around. After all, he had survived infiltrating Al-Qaeda. Even if the Danites were onto us, dealing with a secret society would be a walk in the park for a seasoned journalist like Mick.

I spent a couple of minutes deciding what I should write in my text to Chad. I figured a nice, free dinner for a guy like this would be the equivalent to winning the lottery for him. I looked up "steakhouse" and "Winnemucca" on Google. I found a Basque restaurant with great reviews called Ormachea's. Done.

Lana Burke: "Hi, Chad, I wanted to invite you and Celeste out to dinner tonight on me to fill you in on the story we are working on. I'm sorry we got off on the wrong foot. There is a lot of money at stake, and I know Celeste wants you involved with this process. My colleague and I are thinking of going to Ormachea's unless you have a different preference. Please let me know either way."

Next, I shot Malden a quick response to his text.

Lana Burke: "Hi boo! Flight was good. I'm definitely missing our luxury hotel suite as I sit here and stare at the coffee stains on the carpet of my Holiday Inn Express room while I type this, LOL! I miss you too."

My phone beeped.

Mick Madden: "Want to meet for a drink at the Winner's Casino at five while we wait to hear back from Bonnie & Clyde?"

Lana Burke: "A drink at the Winner's Casino? I thought you'd never ask."

Mick Madden: "I'll come pick you up. No point in taking two cars."

I exhaled a sigh of relief. I couldn't be happier that Mick offered to drive. I knew that I would need to drink as much as possible to deal with the stress of this story and the fact that I was in the shittiest town in America.

Lana Burke: "Good point. See you soon."

I took a shower, blow-dried my hair, and put on full makeup. I threw on a sexy, low-cut, red blouse from Bebe, a pair of dark denim jean shorts and a pair of nude high heels. I knew it was an outrageous outfit for this trashy town; however, I needed to step up my game. I planned to play Chad like a fiddle.

At 4:55 p.m., Mick shot me a text that he was in the parking lot. As I made my way through the motel lobby I got another text.

Mick Madden: "I'm in the green Grand Jeep Cherokee."

Grand Jeep Cherokee? I thought, slightly amazed. How did he possibly get a cool rental car?

"Well, you look nice," Mick said, as I climbed into the front seat.

"Thank you. Speaking of nice, how the hell did you score an SUV? The company would only clear a crappy Prius for me."

"I had extra points with Avis," Mick said with a laugh. "I hate those bullshit trendy eco cars too!"

"Well, I'm jealous! You're quite the Winnemucca baller—you with your executive suite and an SUV."

Mick laughed hysterically. "Lana, I don't think it's possible to be a baller in this town."

"Touché."

Five minutes later, we were walking into the casino. I literally gagged as I entered the casino. It smelled like a combination of urine and thick cigarette smoke. The dirty carpet was a deep ugly red color covered with beer stains, and there were tacky brass railings that trimmed the outer part of the casino floor. The lighting was very dim, and there were no more than a few dozen people, either gambling at slot machines or sitting at the bar. Everyone there looked like they had not taken a shower in over a year. I'm pretty sure I saw grease dripping from one overweight middle-aged woman's long gray ponytail. This place was full of pathetic people who were clearly down on their luck hoping for a miracle at the slot machines. It was depressing. I tried to ignore the bad energy.

"Want to sit at the bar?" Mick asked.

"Why not." I shrugged, and then sat on a nasty barstool.

Motioning to the bartender, Mick asked me what I wanted to drink. A bald, elderly man with thick glasses approached us and asked for our drink order. All I wanted was a glass of wine, but I knew that could be dangerous in a place like this. The diva in me won't drink a glass of wine from a bottle that has been open for over twenty-four hours. Unless, of course, I've already had too much of a buzz to notice.

"I'll take a Corona," I said.

"Make that a Corona and a Bud Light," Mick added.

Before we got our drinks, Mick plowed right into our goals for the night. "So I just got off the phone with Ari. He said we must get Celeste to sign a contract tonight, and get her to do an interview on camera."

"OK," I said skeptically.

"Do you think that's possible?"

"It would definitely be possible if it wasn't for Numbnuts. He's cock blocking her."

"Yeah, I know he's been trouble. I went to the courthouse earlier and got criminal records on him today. Neither of them has custody of their children from previous marriages, and Numbnuts is currently trying to get partial custody of his kids."

My phone beeped.

"Is it them?" Mick eagerly asked as the bartender placed our beers in front of us.

"Unfortunately no," I said with a frown. It was Malden.

Malden Murphy: "I miss ya too. I'm horny for ya!"

"Who is it?" Mick asked.

"Just a friend," I said. I had no idea why I lied to him. As Mick dug his hands in the bowl of nuts on the bar, I quickly responded to Malden.

Lana Burke: "Classy."

Malden Murphy: "Oh come on—I'm just having fun."

I quickly put my phone down so Mick couldn't read my texts.

"Cheers to hopefully a productive night," Mick said. We drank our entire beers in less than fifteen minutes. I ordered another round while Mick headed to the bathroom. I whipped out my phone to text Malden again.

Lana Burke: "I'm horny for you, too."

Malden Murphy: "Really?"

Lana Burke: "I touched myself thinking about you today."

Malden Murphy: "You're making me hard. When did you become self-aware?"

I paused. Self-aware? What in the world was he talking about?

Lana Burke: "Huh?"

Malden Murphy: "Were you ten years old?"

Ten years old what? Was that a typo? Mick came back. I started to worry that our dinner with Numbnuts and Celeste was not going to happen. Just as I was about to express my concern to Mick, my phone beeped again.

Chad Homan: "Can you meet us at Ormachea's at six-thirty?"

"They can meet us for dinner!" I screeched, tapping Mick on his right shoulder.

"Perfect," Mick said. "I knew Numbnuts wouldn't pass up a free steak dinner!"

I quickly texted Chad back.

Lana Burke: "Sounds good. We look forward to meeting you."

I secretly read Malden's text one more time before I put my phone down. I racked my brain. What did he mean by self-aware? Was he asking me how old I was when I started masturbating? I turned so that my phone was at an angle that prevented Mick from reading what I was typing.

Lana Burke: "Are you asking me how old I was when I first masturbated?"

Malden Murphy: "Yep."

I froze. I'd been asked a lot of odd things by boyfriends, but this struck me as exceptionally strange. Why did he want to know how old I was when I started masturbating? And why would he throw out the age of ten? I don't even think I knew what sex was at that age let alone self-gratification. My stomach sank–this gave me pause.

"Lana," Mick said.

"Huh?"

"I asked what time they can meet us for dinner."

"Oh, right, yeah he said six-thirty."

"OK great," Mick said. "If all goes as planned, we'll have a contract signed and a videotaped interview done by midnight."

I brushed off Malden's odd question. Instead, for the next hour I asked Mick detailed questions about how he had infiltrated Al-Qaeda. His courage astounded me. I couldn't get enough of his adventures.

"What was it like to go to Afghanistan?" I eagerly asked.

"It wasn't Afghanistan–it was Pakistan," Mick nonchalantly said as he took a sip of his beer.

"How did you infiltrate Al-Qaeda?"

"I infiltrated an Al-Qaeda training camp there. I was there for months."

"How did you do it?" I asked. I could not ask questions quickly enough.

"I flew through Canada to get to Pakistan. I got lucky. I met a great source there who connected me with the right people."

"How did you file your stories?"

"I brought a satellite phone with me. I would call in every few days when I had a break from the camp."

I was in disbelief. "Weren't you terrified? If they caught you—they for sure would've beheaded you or stoned you to death."

"Nah," Mick said calmly.

"Oh, come on, Mick, you weren't even a little scared?"

"There was one time I got myself into a sticky situation there, and I got nervous. Other than that, I wasn't too worried."

"You're my hero. I'd like to think I'm a tough journalist, but I don't know if I could've pulled that off."

"Something tells me you could," Mick said as he flashed me a smile. "So what is your take on Celeste—is she full of shit or what?"

"She's complicated," I said thoughtfully. "She is very quick to answer questions, and she's pretty consistent. Her stories are wild and outrageous, and, I mean, really outrageous!"

"Why?" Mick said as he gulped his beer.

"She claims Gov. Richards drank her piss," I said, attempting to keep a straight face. "That was his thing."

"Wh-a-a-a-t!" Mick sputtered, spraying beer on me. "Sorry about that, but what?"

Smiling, I wiped off Mick's nasty spit and beer from my face, and let out a slight giggle. "No joke—she claims Gov. Richards is not only into golden showers, but he likes pee-tini cocktails."

"A pee-tini?" Mick asked.

"Yes–she told me that he drank her pee out of a martini glass."

Mick shook his head in disbelief. "I have no doubt that Gov. Richards may be having an affair with a hooker, but that's just ridiculous!" he said. "Man oh man, I certainly hope that's not true."

"Why?" I asked with confusion. "It makes for a better story, right?"

"Oh absolutely, but I really like Gov. Richards."

I raised my eyebrows in shock. "Wait–you do?"

"Are you kidding me? I voted for President Oyama four years ago. I really had confidence in him, but the way he has absolutely destroyed our economy, downsized the military and brought our national debt up to six trillion dollars since he took office. He's been an epic failure. I pray to God he isn't reelected."

I couldn't believe it. Mick supported Gov. Richards too! I thought that I was the only Gov. Richards supporter in Hollywood or at least at our company.

"I'm so relieved to hear this," I said. "I'm a big supporter of Gov. Richards, too. I've had a guilty conscience about covering this story because of my strong ties to the Republican Party."

"Well, Lana, you're smart enough to know that most politicians are scumbags regardless of their political party. And quite frankly, even if he is drinking this hooker's piss, I'm still voting for him. I'd rather have a piss drinker who can get the economy back on the right track than some egomaniac who is pissing all over this country."

"That's a very unique way to put it." I said. "I couldn't agree with you more."

We both laughed as we finished the last sips of our beers.

"You know, there is something else she said that's been bothering me," I told Mick.

"What's that?"

"Well..." I said, looking over my shoulder. "The last time I was in Winnemucca I was followed by shady Secret Service types. Also Celeste said that someone broke into her house recently and stole nothing of value. She said that thieves took paperwork and objects that would portray her in a negative light."

"Like what?" Mick asked.

"Photos of her dressed up in a Nazi costume for Halloween," I replied. "She also said that they left behind a white-collared shirt with a pentagram on it, you know, as if some group was trying to leave their mark."

"It sounds like Celeste has quite an imagination," Mick scoffed. He was not amused.

"I don't know about that. She told me she filed a police report. The last time I was in town, I swear someone was following us. It made me really uncomfortable."

"If Celeste filed a police report on the break-in, we should be able to get a copy. We can do that tomorrow. In the meantime, I don't think you have anything to worry about. Celeste sounds like a nut job. I highly doubt anyone broke into her house. Unfortunately, I don't even think her story is true, or at least all of it. However, I did have my doubts about Jonathan Miller so you never know..."

Mick's calm demeanor eased my nerves. Maybe I was paranoid and Celeste was just a nut. I hadn't noticed anyone following me since I got back into town. Mick paid the tab and we headed to Ormachea's.

The restaurant was only a half-mile away. It was across

the street from one of the brothels, which Mick made sure to point out to me. The brothel was a run-down two-story green house with boarded-up windows and a huge gravel parking lot with a view of the freeway. There was a red broken neon sign in the window that read, "Open 24 Hours." The site made me shudder. The restaurant looked much better. It was a homey, medium-sized red brick building with brown awnings. If it weren't for the sign in the window, I wouldn't have known it was a business. It looked like a family home.

We parked, then walked inside and a skinny teenage hostess who wore her long, blonde hair in a ponytail tied with a pink bow greeted us. I cringed at her hairdo. I quickly scanned the bar area for Celeste. There were several overweight townies sitting at one end of the bar, drinking beer. At the other end, a butch, heavyset woman with a red bandana around her head was drinking a Coors Light. No Celeste, no Numbnuts. Mick told the hostess we'd wait at the bar for the rest of our party. I ordered a glass of the house wine and Mick ordered another beer. Their pinot noir tasted surprisingly fantastic.

"There's the guy," Mick said, nudging me as he cocked his head toward a tall man in construction boots who was wearing ripped jeans with a Bud Light cap on.

"What guy?" I asked in confusion.

"He was walking out of the brothel when we drove by. Didn't you see him? He totally knocked one out!"

"Oh my God ew!" I shrieked. "That's disgusting. Good Lord, I can't even look at him."

Mick giggled like a schoolboy, "He knocked one out, and now he's probably going to join his wife and kids for a big steak dinner–ha, ha!"

I was horrified. The man made his way into the dining

room. I had to look in the other direction. I chugged the rest of my wine and ordered another glass. I knew this was going to be a long night. As soon as my second glass arrived, I saw Celeste walk in with a tall, good-looking guy in khakis and a blue-collared shirt. Wait, this is her husband? No way! Could it be a friend? One of her johns? Her pimp?

"Hi, Celeste," I said, as Mick and I rose to our feet. "So good to see you again."

I turned to introduce Mick. "This is my colleague, Mick."

"Hi," Celeste said, flashing her sexy Angelina Jolie smile. She wore a low-cut purple blouse with skinny jeans and a black blazer. She looked amazing. I was surprised at how well she cleaned up. She motioned to the handsome guy. "This is my husband, Chad."

I leaned in to give Celeste a hug before turning to Chad. As I embraced her I couldn't resist sneaking a peek at her gigantic cleavage and that's when I noticed she was wearing my leopard print bra. That bitch! Not only did it look ridiculous for her to wear my B-cup bra on tits that had to be at least Cs or Ds-but it was my new bra! I wanted to rip it off her! I knew I couldn't though. Instead, I smiled and turned to greet Chad.

"Hello," Chad said meekly, as he held out his hand for me to shake.

Wait, this is her abusive psychotic husband? I was expecting a guy with a Mohawk and covered with tattoos to walk in–not an altar boy.

The hostess escorted us to a corner table away from other patrons, as I had requested.

"She's hot!" Mick whispered in my ear as we sat down.

"Yeah she's a hot thief," I whispered back.

"What?"

"That bitch stole my bra, and she's fucking wearing it!"

"No way," Mick whispered back as we pulled our chairs out at a corner table across from them.

I tried to erase the bra scandal out of my mind; I had a mission to accomplish. I started the conversation off with some small talk. I asked Celeste and Chad about their weekend. Celeste fidgeted in her chair and bit her nails. This surprised me. When I first met with her, she was cool as a cucumber. Then, I remembered that she had a buzz going the first time we met. Tonight she appeared to be stone sober. When the waitress arrived, I encouraged them to order drinks. Chad ordered rum and coke and Celeste ordered a beer. Mick warmed Chad up by asking him about his job at the nearby mining company. I charmed Celeste by complimenting her on her clothes and makeup. I almost complimented her on her bra, but I refrained. Mick and I were a good team. By the time Chad and Celeste had almost finished their first drink, I knew it was time to shift the conversation. After all, we were here to talk business.

"So, Chad, I'm so happy you're here tonight, because we have a significant offer to make Celeste, and I know she wants to involve you with her decision," I said with delicacy.

"Yeah, I know," Chad murmured as he slunk back in his chair. "I'm really not comfortable with any of this."

"I understand," I continued. "That's why I'm glad you're here. We want to answer any questions you guys have and make you feel as comfortable as possible about this whole situation."

"Well, what if Celeste doesn't want to do the story?"

"Here's the problem with that," I explained, leaning in from across the table, well aware of the fact that now a significant amount of my cleavage was exposed. "That's fine. That is her right. However, we'll most likely run the story with

144

or without Celeste's cooperation. Other sources have already given us enough information to publish the story. So if Celeste doesn't cooperate with us, the story most likely will come out anyway, and then you guys will miss out on a huge payout. As I explained to Celeste before, if she wants to do the story off the record we can arrange that too, but there will be less money involved."

Mick ordered another round of drinks as I tried to ease Chad into this process. Celeste sat in silence. She was a completely different person with her husband next to her than the vixen who tried to seduce me.

"Here's my main concern," explained Chad. "I'm in a custody battle with my ex-wife for our kids. I'm afraid this will affect my case."

"Look man, I have kids. I feel for you," Mick interjected. "But like Lana said, this story will come out with or without Celeste's cooperation. It would be unethical for a judge to discriminate against you because your wife made a mistake in the past. And if this story does hurt your case, you're going to need money to pay for a good attorney. We can help you with that."

I could see the wheels in Chad's head begin to turn.

"What kind of money are we talking about?"

"We could probably get you fifty thousand for off the record," Mick explained. "However, if she agreed to do an on the record interview, we could offer her one hundred thousand."

I could see Chad's eyes bulge out.

"That's a lot of money," Celeste said, breaking her silence.

The waitress interrupted our discussion to take our order. Mick and Chad ordered the prime rib, I ordered a filet, and Celeste ordered a chicken pasta dish. Mick ordered two bottles of a nice red wine for the table. The dinner was going well. I held my breath.

"So, when would we get the money?" Chad asked.

"We would send the check within two weeks upon publication," I said.

"How can you guarantee that?"

"I can guarantee that because we'll have Celeste sign a contract that will protect her interests and the interests of National Publishing. Her payment will be outlined in the contract."

The mood lightened drastically by the time our main entrees arrived. We were on our second bottle of red. Mick managed to crack a few jokes that got the entire table laughing. By the end of dinner, Celeste and Chad agreed to go back to Mick's suite to do the interview on camera for one hundred thousand dollars. I was so excited, I almost peed in my pants—but I didn't want to jinx it. I knew that nothing was set in stone until her name was signed in ink and we recorded her on video telling her story. I was happy and feeling so buzzed. I didn't have time to think about the repercussions this story could possibly have on myself—and more important, the country.

Mick and I returned to the Days Inn and Celeste and Chad said they'd meet us there. We walked up to his executive suite. It looked like an apartment I had in the nineties while I was attending the University of Iowa. The kitchen had drab off-white cabinets with tacky wooden trim. The living room looked like my grandma's place, with a salmon-colored rug and dated furniture. There was a cheesy ghetto Jacuzzi, also salmon pink, smack in the middle of the master bathroom. I joked to Mick that if we got Celeste drunk enough, maybe we could convince her to do a bathtub photo shoot. While Mick set up his high-tech camera equipment, I ran across the street to the

Chevron to get more alcohol. I stocked up on a case of Bud Light beer and two bottles of Yellow Tail wine. When I arrived back to Mick's suite, he was sitting behind the desk in the living area alone.

"Where are Chad and Celeste?" I frantically asked.

"They're not here yet." He sighed. "I hope they aren't changing their minds."

"No—they can't," I said.

I whipped out my phone and called Celeste. She picked up. "Where are you guys? Is everything OK?"

"Yes, we're in the parking lot. Chad is having a cigarette. He's having second thoughts."

"Just come upstairs and we'll talk it out," I said, slightly panicked. "I got some wine and beer for you guys."

"OK," Celeste said.

I immediately bolted toward the door.

"Where are you going?" Mick asked as I flung the door open.

"To save our story!"

I ran outside and saw Celeste's beat--up Mercedes in the parking lot with the headlights on. She was sitting in the passenger seat. It looked like she was opening the car door. I could see Chad a distance away on the phone smoking a cigarette.

"What's going on?" I asked Celeste as I approached the vehicle.

"Chad's on the phone with his lawyer running things by him."

My stomach sank. No! I have been in this situation in the past, and although a lawyer may have their client's best interest at heart—they don't always end up serving their best interest in situations like this. They have fucked up many big stories for me and my sources before. I told myself to remain calm.

"OK, that's cool," I told Celeste. "He's smart. I'm sure he wants to protect you. Let's go inside and have a drink and wait for him to get off the phone."

Celeste relented. Chad didn't see us sneak into the motel. As soon as we got into the suite, I sat her on the couch and grabbed her a beer. I realized getting her drunk was not entirely ethical; however, it's not like I worked for the *Wall Street Journal*. After all, I am a tabloid journalist.

Mick immediately got the contract out, and he started to explain the terms to Celeste. As he went over each line, I quickly ran to the bathroom. I said a little prayer as I peed. I knew the bombshell story could still slip through my fingers even though we were so close to nailing it.

When I walked out, Chad had arrived. He and Mick were talking.

"My lawyer said this is a huge mistake," Chad said. "He said this would hurt my custody case."

"Of course he's going to say that," Mick responded. "However, he's not the one leaving one-hundred thousand dollars on the table."

My whole body tensed up. Why did Chad have to be here? I knew we'd have the contract signed days ago if it wasn't for him putting a wrench in our deal. Chad paced back and forth. Celeste sipped her beer nervously. Finally, she stood up.

"I'm going to do it," she announced. "We need the money. It's my story, my life, and my mistake. I don't want to hurt your custody hearing, Chad, but that's not for months. The story will blow over by then."

"She has a good point," I quickly interjected. "There will probably be a dozen new women who will come out with similar stories regarding Gov. Richards by then. Remember the

Tiger Woods scandal?"

In my heart, I knew that wouldn't be the case with Celeste's story.

"I don't know," Chad said, shaking his head.

I quickly got him a cold beer. He sat down on the couch next to Celeste and read the contract. After several minutes, he finally looked at her in despair and told her that it was her decision. With that, Mick handed her the pen. I watched her sign the contract for a hundred thousand dollars. The two seconds it took for her to sign that piece of paper felt like eternity. When she was done, I felt the weight of the world off my shoulders.

Mick rushed to get the lighting perfect and positioned Celeste in a corner. I helped her touch up her makeup and assured her that she looked gorgeous. Mick threw out some compliments too—I could tell he had a hard-on for her.

"Now I don't get it," Chad said. "If you guys work for a print publication—why are you videotaping her?"

"Well, for starters, our lawyers want it on video so we can prove that she did actually say what we're going to quote her saying in the magazine. This story is a huge liability, as you can imagine. Also, we may tease snippets of this video on our website to help promote and sell the magazine."

Chad didn't respond. He sat back down on the couch, and he watched the train wreck begin.

"OK, so Celeste can I get you to spell your name slowly?" Mick asked as he videotaped her.

"C-E-L-E-S-T-E," she spelled calmly. "H-O-M-A-N."

"I'm just going to ask you some basic questions to get the straight facts surrounding your relationship with Gov. Richards," Mick explained. Celeste nodded. "When did you first meet Gov. Richards?"

"I met Client Number Eight about two years ago at the Grand America Hotel in Salt Lake City, Utah."

"Why are you calling him Client Number Eight?"

"Because he was my eighth client."

I looked over at Chad. He looked catatonic. He stared at the wall and did not move.

"Tell me about your sexual experiences with Gov. Richards."

"Well, we never had sex. He did give me oral sex, though."

"How did that go down?"

"The first time he went down on me," Celeste explained. It didn't seem to faze her at all that her husband was sitting only a few feet away from her. "He asked me to strip for him first."

At those words, Chad ran into the bathroom. Mick immediately saw this as his chance to go in for the kill knowing he could squeeze more out of her with Chad out of sight.

"So was he good at giving you oral sex?"

"Oh yes. He was amazing! He knew exactly what to do with his tongue and hands. He licked me everywhere down there—even in the ass."

"Wow!" a giddy Mick said.

I shook my head.

"Was there foreplay?"

"We kissed passionately for a while. He then took off my bra and sucked on my nipples forever. He liked my fake breasts. He always talked about how perfect they are. After he got my tits nice and hard, he'd slowly lick his tongue all the way down to my pussy."

"Did he make you wet?"

I sat there in shock. I couldn't believe how calm Celeste

was.

"Oh, so wet! Client Number Eight is so handsome, and his touch is so erotic."

"Did he give you an orgasm?"

"Oh, he gave me the best orgasm of my life! It was like fireworks on the Fourth of July," Celeste said as Chad stormed back into the room.

"That's enough!" a beet red-faced Chad said, storming toward Celeste.

"Chad, please, we just got started," I pleaded, strategically stroking his right bicep. "Why don't we go down to the hotel bar and I'll buy you a drink. There's no need for you to sit through this."

Chad agreed. I managed to get him to sit with me for one more drink at the bar. It bought Mick twenty more minutes with Celeste, and that was all the time he needed to finish the job.

As I paid the tab, Chad went back up to the room to fetch Celeste. I called Ari to give him a quick update. He was ecstatic at our progress. He told me that the final step would be to have Celeste take a lie detector test. He explained that it would need to take place in Los Angeles where the company that conducts all polygraph tests for our sources is located. He asked me to try to convince Celeste to fly there with me tomorrow. I told him I'd try my best.

When I got back to the room, Chad and Celeste were almost out the door. I told Celeste we would need her to take and pass a polygraph test in Los Angeles for us to clear the story with our company lawyers before publication. She told me she understood and assured me that wouldn't be a problem. I explained that we could figure out how to proceed with the poly test tomorrow. With that, they were gone.

"Did you see Chad's face when she was talking about the orgasm Gov. Richards gave her?" Mick asked as he laughed hysterically. "I bet Numbnuts has never given her a real orgasm their entire marriage–what an idiot he is!"

I had to laugh, "You're so bad!"

Mick was almost doubled over with laughter. "I was waiting for him to jump out the window! The poor guy–that's what you get for marrying a hooker!"

I stayed with Mick for one more drink in his room to celebrate our huge coup. He dropped me off at the Holiday Inn Express right around midnight. As I walked into my room, my phone rang. It was Giselle.

"Hey!" I said, picking up the phone. I hadn't talked to her in days. She didn't even know I was working on this salacious story.

"Hi, stranger," she replied. "What have you been up to? I saw on Facebook that you and Malden went wine tasting in Santa Barbara."

"Yes," I acknowledged. "It was so fun."

"So, it sounds like things are getting serious with you guys."

"They kind of are," I admitted. "He dropped the 'L' bomb."

"No way!"

"Yeah–he did. And he wants me to go with him to his family reunion."

"That's amazing, Lana! I'm so happy for you guys."

"Thanks," I answered, changing gears. "Hey–let me ask you a random question. You're a sexual person, so I know you're the right person to ask: Is it weird that he asked me today at what age I started masturbating?"

"I mean, he has a penis so like all men he's a pervert,"

152

Giselle said. "I'm sure he gets off, though, on the fact that you're so much younger than he is."

"Maybe," I answered dubiously. "But he asked me if I started at age ten."

"That's random, but I think you need to save your overanalyzing for your job, not your relationship."

"Good advice." I laughed. "I'm actually out of town for a crazy story right now that I'll fill you in on when I get back. But I have one more relationship question to ask you. Actually, it's more of a sex question."

"OK shoot," Giselle said.

"Well, during sex, after, er, Malden ejaculates," I stammered. "He shakes really bad."

"Nice!" Giselle said. "It sounds like you really turn him on."

"No, you don't understand. He trembles and spasms on and off uncontrollably for minutes as if he's having a seizure."

"Hmm, that is weird," Giselle said. "I've fucked plenty of dudes. Most guys shake during and a little bit after an orgasm but only for a few seconds. How long does it last?"

"I don't know – sometimes ten, fifteen minutes."

"OK that's definitely not normal. He's so much older than you. Is he taking Viagra or Cialis?" Giselle asked.

"I don't know," I said.

"I'd look into that," Giselle said. "Maybe the shaking is a side effect of a sex enhancement drug."

"Yeah, that would make sense," I said.

Giselle and I continued to talk for about a half hour. She and French Rocker were having marital issues. She was the breadwinner in the relationship, and he had been struggling to find a job for months now. After I vented about my relationship woes, she complained to me about their problems.

I suggested they go to marriage counseling. I didn't want to see their marriage fall apart. Despite French Rocker's struggles to find full-time work, I thought his calm demeanor had a positive effect on Giselle's wild nature. Plus, he is such a good husband. I worried because I could tell Giselle was bored with her marriage. Although this was her first marriage, historically whenever she's bored in a relationship she cheats.

When I got off the phone with her, I gave Malden a call. He didn't answer. I figured he was in bed sleeping like a baby. I crawled into bed and prayed that I'd be heading back to L.A. by tomorrow afternoon with Celeste. If that happened, I'd probably get the story wrapped up in enough time to make it to Malden's family reunion. I fell asleep fantasizing about how wonderful it would be to meet Malden's family.

The next morning, I called Celeste and texted her, reiterating that we needed to arrange a poly test as soon as possible. I went to the gym to run on the treadmill. An hour later, I still hadn't heard from her. It made me nervous. I told myself she probably was just sleeping in. While I worked out, Mick went to the police station to get the alleged police report from Celeste's break-in. Mick and I planned to meet at the Martin Inn for lunch at one in the afternoon.

I arrived before he did. I sat in the bar and drank a Diet Coke. My phone beeped. Finally, it was Celeste.

Celeste Homan: "I can't do the poly. My lawyer told me not to."

I instantly felt sick. Mick walked in as I put my phone down on the bar. "You look like you've seen a ghost—what's wrong?"

I shook my head. "The bitch is bailing on the poly!"

"Oh jeez." Mick sighed as he rested his arms on the bar and bowed his head. I noticed the police report in his hand.

"Why won't she take the poly–I don't get it," I said to Mick. "She claims her lawyer instructed her not to, but she's already told us the whole story on video and signed a contract. What is she afraid of–do you think she's lying?"

"Well, yesterday I would've said yes, but check this out," Mick said, handing me the police report.

The Winnemucca Police incident report had the correct address and date for Celeste's alleged burglary. I quickly scanned the document further and noticed that it cited a gun as the tool used to break into her safe. I read the list of stolen items on the police report:

- birth certificate
- personal photos
- Confederate flag
- Social Security card
- phone bills
- Nazi costume
- paperwork

I looked further and read that the point of entry was unknown. Finally, in the summary box I read: "Homeowner claims the intruder left behind a white-collared shirt with a black star on it."

I gasped, put my hand over my mouth and looked at Mick in shock.

"Consistency…maybe she's not making the break-in up!"

"I know," Mick moaned. "I'm surprised, too."

CHAPTER 9

Mick and I spent the next few days unsuccessfully trying to get Celeste to talk to us. We went to her home on several occasions, and I contacted her by phone multiple times. She completely ignored us. It was Thursday morning—one day before Malden's family reunion. Luckily, Ari had approved return flights home for both of us for later in the day. Ari suggested that we to try to get through to Celeste through her parents, and if that did not work, next week we would have to head to Utah to try and track down other possible sources who might know about her affair with Gov. Richards. We all agreed that Chad was stopping Celeste from taking the poly. We didn't think he'd be able to stop her for long. During the meantime, Ari instructed us to pursue other leads.

Mick picked me up at eleven in the morning to drive to Celeste's parents' house. When we arrived, the garage door was open and their cars were in the driveway. I prepped Mick on Celeste's parents during the drive over. I told him that they appeared to be nice down-to-earth people, and they both were very attractive. I rang the doorbell. Celeste's mother answered.

She looked stunning. I could feel Mick's eyes grow big.

"Hi," I said, as she aggressively walked outside with her arms folded and rolled her eyes. "I'm so sorry to bug you again. We're a little desperate. We've negotiated a contract with your daughter for a story, and she's disappeared on us."

"Honey—who's at the door?" a masculine voice shouted from inside. I knew it was Celeste's hot dad.

"It's that reporter," she said with disdain.

Her father walked outside wearing Nike biker shorts, a white T-shirt and cycling shoes. I noticed an expensive speed bike in the driveway. I figured he was a cyclist—he had a body like Lance Armstrong's - muscular, lean and a perfectly bronzed tan.

"What's going on?" he asked, joining his wife.

"Hi, I'm Mick," Mick said, extending his hand.

"Jim," Celeste's dad said as he shook it. I quickly shook his hand and reintroduced myself too.

"I'm Marian," Celeste's mother introduced herself tensely.

"We're just hoping you guys could give us some insight," Mick explained. "We're in a sticky situation."

"Celeste in a sticky situation? Shocking," Jim said. "You have no idea what that girl has put us through."

"I can't imagine," Mick said as he shook his head. "I'm a father too. Parenthood is not easy."

"Tell me about it," Jim said. Marian took a deep breath, inflating her breasts so much that they appeared to double in size. As she exhaled, she looked down at the ground.

"You know we're working on a big story with Celeste," I said. "She signed a contract with us, and now she's disappeared. If she doesn't cooperate with us after signing a contract there can be some major legal repercussions for her."

"Celeste has dealt with a multitude of legal repercussions

157

her entire life, and, quite frankly, I'm sick of bailing her out." Jim sighed. "What story exactly are you working on?"

"It involves Celeste and a high-profile politician," Mick interjected. "Are you familiar with this?"

"I'm not proud of this, but I'm well aware of what kind of business my daughter involved herself in while she lived in Salt Lake City. She's turned a corner though. She's married and a full-time housewife now."

"Do you know which politician we are referring to?" Mick asked.

"Well, if he's tied to Salt Lake City–I have a pretty good idea," he said resignedly.

"Jim, you shouldn't be talking about this," Marian said as she put her right hand on his left bicep.

"Look, we just want to make sure that we're not going to publish anything inaccurate," Mick said. "Do you believe the story is true?"

"You seem like nice people and I know you have a job to do," Jim said emphatically. "This is what I'll tell you. My daughter is a pathological liar, and she's bipolar. You have to take everything she says with a grain of salt."

"We know your daughter has issues," I said sympathetically. "We don't doubt that, but that doesn't necessarily mean she hasn't had some kind of relationship with Gov. Richards. We're just trying to get the facts straight here."

"Do you think it's at all possible that she could've had some kind of affair with Gov. Richards–even if it was just a one-time incident?" Mick asked.

"I don't know." Jim sighed. "It's possible, but like I said, she's a liar. I would be very careful with any information she tells you."

"Understood," Mick said, nodding his head. He reached

into his pocket for his wallet and pulled out his business card.

"Look, I really appreciate you guys chatting with us. Celeste is supposed to do a polygraph test for us per the contract she signed with our company. Hopefully, that will weed out fact from fiction. We have offered her a significant amount of money for her story, but unless she takes the poly, she won't see one red cent of it. When you talk to her please tell her to call us."

"We'll relay the message," Jim said as he read over Mick's card. He smiled and grabbed Marian's arm as he walked back inside.

As we walked to Mick's Jeep, he whispered in my ear, "You know Celeste is daddy's little girl."

"What do you mean?"

"Oh come on–it's obvious. I bet he molested Celeste! Her behavior screams sexual abuse."

I felt a chill go up and down my spine. Could he be right? "Mick–don't say that," I shuddered. "You don't know that."

I took a 4:00 p.m. flight back to LAX that got me back in L.A. by 6:00 p.m. Malden picked me up from the airport. We went for a low-key dinner at my favorite West Hollywood Italian restaurant called Craig's. I filled him in on my time in Winnemucca and the ups and downs Mick and I faced with our story. Malden shook his head in disbelief at every twist and turn.

We went through two bottles of wine, and then headed back to my place. We went to bed early. We had planned on an early start the next morning, driving up to San Francisco for Malden's family reunion. I was exhausted. I just wanted to pass out and get lost in my dreams. I lay in bed on my stomach wearing nothing but Malden's Berkeley T-shirt. Malden scratched my back. I was drifting off to dreamland when I felt him climb on my back. Then I felt his hard cock pressing against my anus. Oh no! Not again! What happened to missionary? Was it that out of style? Is this the new trend—anal sex? I was starting to enjoy it, but not *every time* we had sex. I was half asleep, but too tired to fight him off me. I relented and let him slip his big dick into my ass yet another time. I only moved to reach my hand in my drawer to hand him some K-Y. I did not have the energy for this nor was I in the mood.

"Is everything OK?" Malden whispered in my ear.

"Yes, I'm just tired," I replied.

"Do you want me to stop?"

"No. I want to please you."

"That's my sexy little girl," he darkly whispered in my ear. "You're my little girl."

I tensed up. Little girl? What the fuck was he talking about? I may be twenty years younger than he is, but I'm thirty-two. He aggressively thrust his hard cock further into my ass. It stung like a bitch.

"Ouch!" Oh God, Malden!" I shrieked.

"Shhh," he said as he put his hand on my mouth. "You have to be quiet so the others don't hear you. OK, little girl?"

I froze. I could feel Malden shake and come in my ass. It was hot and disgusting at the same time. I was confused. Why was he calling me his little girl and what "others" was he referring to? We were alone in my one-bedroom apartment! There was no one else here. I felt a shroud of darkness creep over me. Malden went to the bathroom to rinse off, I didn't move.

"Can I ask you a question?" I asked as he climbed back into bed.

"Of course, beautiful." He smiled back at me.

"Why are you calling me your little girl?" I asked, my tone serious.

"Oh, come on, Lana—I'm just being playful and having fun with you. I think it's hot. You're young and beautiful. That's all. Haven't you ever role-played before?"

I exhaled a sigh of relief. This made sense, right? I worried I was coming off like a prude. "Well, yeah, of course I have role-played," I said. It was a total lie. "Who hasn't?"

"All guys have fantasies! I want to be your daddy and take care of you." He laughed innocently.

"Well—if that's what turns you on, you've got it, Daddy," I said with a smile. I was relieved we had this conversation, but I still found it a little strange that he wanted to pretend I was his daughter considering the fact that he had a teenage daughter. I brushed it off—I had much bigger problems to worry about. I was about to meet his family for the first time, and next week I had to go to Utah to find a different way to prove my story—if Celeste continued to refuse to take the poly.

We took my X5 North on Highway 1 all the way to Marin County in San Francisco. I insisted on taking my SUV as opposed to Malden's two-door Jaguar convertible simply because it was more practical. During our drive up to his family reunion, Malden talked nonstop about his ten-year marriage to Bethenny. He told me about the dozens of different fights they had. He said that they even argued the first night of their honeymoon because she didn't approve of the beautiful suite Malden booked for them at a five-star Mexican resort. I didn't say much. I wasn't sure how to react to all his stories. I really didn't need to hear about every fight he got into with his ex-wife. About three hours into his venting about his failed marriage, I put my foot down.

"OK, enough," I sternly said.

"Huh?" Malden responded in total surprise.

"I get it. You had a horrible marriage from day one. You guys fought a lot. I just don't understand why you're telling me all this. I don't need to know about every fight you got into with Bethenny."

"Lana, I'm telling you all this because I'm taking you to my family reunion to meet my family," Malden explained. "I'm telling you this because you are the first girl I've brought home in ten years since my divorce. I want you to know about my past because I'm very serious about you."

My heart stopped. Was he serious? I couldn't believe it. Was he thinking marriage already? I got butterflies in my stomach. I was giddy at the thought.

"OK, I understand," I said softly.

"I've talked your ear off, haven't I?"

"Just a little, but it's OK."

"OK, I'm sorry to vent about my ex-wife. It's therapeutic for me, though. I'm really excited for you to meet my family. We're going to have a great weekend."

"I'm excited too," I said as I gently placed my left hand over his right hand that was tightly gripping the steering wheel.

We arrived in Marin County around five. Malden took me to Piedmont where he used to live with Bethenny. The neighborhood was filled with gorgeous English-style gated mansions on a hillside with beautiful oak trees lining the streets. It reminded me of the neighborhood where I went to high school in Winnetka, Illinois. Malden boasted that no home went for less than five million dollars in Piedmont. Malden pointed out four homes he had owned over the course of his marriage. One was bigger than the next. The final home was white with a Spanish tile roof. The guest home alone was bigger than the house I grew up in.

"Our dining room was built to entertain hundreds," Malden boasted. "We had a huge mahogany dining room table that sat a hundred guests. No matter what I did or bought Bethenny, she was never happy. I love having family and friends over. We had this huge house built for entertaining, and she wouldn't even let my parents stay over."

I was shocked at the stories Malden told me about his ex-wife. I couldn't believe that she was so fortunate to have such a wonderful husband, beautiful children and a home fit for royalty, and yet, she threw it all away. I would be so grateful to have the life she had. I didn't understand how a person could be so unappreciative.

We arrived at Malden's current Piedmont home. He kept it so the children had a place to stay with him when he came to visit. It was a four-bedroom brown manse on top of a hill with a view of the Bay. Enormous oak trees covered the entire property, and Malden had built a tree house in the backyard for the children.

When we got inside the home, Malden instructed me to unpack and get ready as quickly as possible. He said that we had a dinner party to go to at his Uncle Paul's house, explaining that we'd pick up his children the next morning from Bethenny's house for the official family reunion.

Malden took me on a detour on the way to Uncle Paul's. He stopped at a scenic lookout point and parked my car. He insisted on driving everywhere. Even though it was my car, I liked how he took control. He was an alpha male.

"Come on," he said as he grabbed a bottle of Syrah, a wine bottle opener, and got out of the car. I was wearing heels, a blue sweater and black skinny jeans with my black leather jacket–and I was still freezing. I couldn't believe how cold it was in San Francisco in the middle of the summer.

I sat down next to Malden, and we watched the sunset as we drank wine. We were at such a high peak; the clouds in the distance appeared to be at the same level as we were. Even though it was foggy and cloudy, we could still see slivers of sky, and the hues were a beautiful yellow, orange and peach. The fog and clouds made our surroundings look like an enchanted forest. I felt like I was in a fairytale. After sunset, Malden pointed in the opposite direction.

"Stare that way for a few minutes," Malden pointed.

"OK," I said, asking no questions.

Within minutes a huge bright yellow moon rose behind the hills in the opposite direction. It looked surreal. "Wow!" I exclaimed.

"Isn't it breathtaking?"

"It's magical," I said. I quickly remembered why I was dating an older man. No guy my age in Hollywood would ever think to take a girl to a lookout point where you could watch the sun set as the moon ascended.

Malden and I finished the entire bottle of wine and headed over to Uncle Paul's. His home was a humble, gray two-story house with three bedrooms in a middle-class neighborhood. Uncle Paul greeted us at the door. He was a tall, slender man with a baldhead and thick glasses, who wore khakis and a red-checkered shirt.

Paul greeted us with a big hug and a smile. There were about two dozen family members puttering in the home. I quickly met some of Malden's siblings. He had one sister and five brothers. His sister, Melissa, was a sweet, down-to-earth middle-aged woman with brown hair. Malden was the middle child, and his brothers were all handsome men, but Malden was by far the most gorgeous. They were all very kind to me.

Dinner was set up in a buffet style. We dined on roast beef, salad and vegetables. Everyone consumed alcohol. That didn't surprise me. After all, his family is Irish.

Malden particularly idolized his ninety-year-old uncle from Copenhagen. He had just flown in that morning from Europe. Malden explained to me that he used to be a priest. His name was Uncle Gene. I chatted up Uncle Gene and told him about my job. He spoke softly as he slouched over like the hunchback of Notre Dame in a wooden chair by the dining room table. I was pretty sure he had no idea what I was saying, and in return–I had no clue what he was talking about. His soft voice was slurring from the alcohol and it made him impossible to understand. Plus, Malden's sister blasted oldies music in the background. This family sure knew how to party.

Malden sat opposite Uncle Gene and aggressively grabbed his face with his strong right bear paw and pulled Uncle Gene's face toward me.

"Will you still love me when I look like this one day?" Malden asked with a puppy dog look on his face. My heart melted. I stared at the liver spots on Gene's forehead. Not an attractive sight. However, I could envision myself growing old with Malden.

"Yeah, I will," I cooed back at Malden.

"Good!" Malden said.

We headed back to Malden's house shortly after that. We both passed out as soon as our heads hit the pillows. The next morning, a shuffling sound in the bedroom slowly awoke me. Malden was under the covers ripping my underwear off. I was sleeping on my stomach when he pulled my panties off my legs with ease. Before I could grasp what was happening, I felt something wet in my ass. Holy shit he's licking my ass! What the fuck! I tensed up and panicked. What is he doing? This is so disgusting! Why is he licking my ass? Oh my God - what if I'm not clean down there? I was horrified. I didn't know what to do so I didn't move. I just froze.

"You lie so still for me," Malden finally said after licking my ass for a few minutes. "You're such a good girl."

He continued to lick my ass, and I didn't know what to say. Why wouldn't I lie still for him? Not knowing how else to react, I moaned.

"That's it. Relax," Malden coached me. "You're such a good little girl."

I tried to relax. Once I got past how disgusting this was, I let myself go. It did feel good. My nerves eased, and my pussy began to leak. I reminded myself I was in bed with a man whose family I had just met. I'm going to marry this man one day. My pussy got wetter. I was so turned on.

"We're going to try something different, my little girl," Malden said as he flipped me over.

Oh God. I cringed. What now? No, don't be a prude. You're a sex goddess!

"Whatever you say, Daddy," I whispered back. I swore Malden's cock expanded when I called him daddy.

"You're my naughty little girl."

He got out of the bed and pulled me by my legs to the edge. He lifted my legs in the air. What's happening? I tried not to panic.

"You're so beautiful – I want to look at you when I fuck you," he said.

OK, I can do this, I thought. I braced myself. He held tight onto my feet as he slowly moved his hard dick toward my groin. I moaned. He slowly rubbed his cock up and down my wet pussy. It felt amazing even though my legs were uncomfortably defying gravity. He pushed his dick into my ass. Wait, my ass? Oh no! No, no, no! Not again! Did he forget I have a vagina too?

"You're so hot. I love staring at you while I fuck you."

I moaned. Not in ecstasy, but in pain. Anal sex felt more painful in this awkward position. Unlike my teen days as a gymnast, I had zero flexibility as an adult. If our sex life continued like this, I'd have to start taking yoga. Malden continued to moan. It was kind of hot, but I was too uncomfortable to get off in this position. I had to put my foot down. After all, there were two people in this relationship, and I was horny. I must get off.

"Don't come yet," I said.

"Huh?" Malden said as he exhaled another loud moan.

"This isn't comfortable. I want to get on top of you."

"OK," Malden conceded. "Let me just rinse off quickly. I don't want you to get any infections."

Malden was back in two minutes. He slapped my ass as he climbed back into bed. I grabbed his arms and threw him down on the bed. I took a T-shirt and tied it around his head, hiding his eyes. I was horny and pissed. Enough with the anal sex!

"I'm in control now," I said to him after I blindfolded him. He smiled and laughed. I couldn't help but giggle a little too. I got on top of him and slid his cock into my wet pussy. Ahhh, satisfaction–his cock was finally in the right hole. I banged him as hard and fast as I possibly could. I had a ton of frustration over his obsession with anal sex. It was my turn to dominate. I felt sweat dripping out of every pore. It felt amazing. I could tell Malden was turned on, too.

"Yeah, put my big cock inside you underneath your little schoolgirl skirt," Malden yelled.

Wait, schoolgirl skirt? Huh? I wasn't wearing a schoolgirl

skirt. I was confused. What the hell was he talking about? No, stop allowing your mind to wander. I was so close to having an orgasm. I didn't want anything to distract me from my erotic goal.

"Oh, oh, oh God," Malden screeched. "See, see how my cock fits perfectly inside you? See how your pussy opens up for me?"

I paused, why wouldn't his dick fit into my pussy?

"I'm going to come!" Malden shouted.

Hearing that made me wetter. I could feel the muscles in his dick expand inside of me. I looked at his face and saw him clench his teeth. It made me go wild. I let out one huge scream. Malden exploded inside of me and shook uncontrollably. He wrapped his arms around me and held me tight. I lay on top of him for five minutes before I removed his blindfold.

"That was amazing," Malden said as he kissed me on the cheek. "I can't wait for you to meet my kids. Let's get in the shower."

He went back to the bathroom. My head spun. I was turned on and confused. I wasn't sure what to make of Malden's bedroom talk. I shrugged it off and I joined Malden in the shower.

Malden drove us to the ex-wife's home. It was a huge red brick mansion with white shutters. There was a gray stone driveway leading up to the two-car garage and a brick sidewalk feeding into the front door. The front lawn was meticulously kept, with bright colored flowers and perfectly trimmed shrubs. It was obvious that she had shelled out big money for professional landscaping. When Malden got out, I stayed in the car.

"What are you doing?" Malden questioned.

"What do you mean?" I asked.

"Aren't you going to come with me?"

"You want me to go inside with you?" I hesitated.

"Yes," Malden said impatiently.

"Wait, isn't Bethenny home?"

"She should be."

"I'm not prepared to meet Bethenny! I thought I was just going to meet your children."

"Don't be a baby—come on."

"Are you sure?" I asked.

"Yes, I'm sure."

I reluctantly got out of the car. As we walked to the front door I asked, "She knows I'm coming, right?"

"No." Malden shrugged.

"Malden! That's not cool," I snapped back at him.

"It will be great. She'll probably be in her workout clothes and look like shit."

"Oh my God," I said as I shook my head nervously.

Malden flung the door open as if he owned the place. Wait, did he?

"Let's go!" Malden shouted like a drill sergeant as he walked into the foyer.

"Get your stuff boys—Malden's here," a cold woman's voice shouted from the kitchen off to the right. I could see Spanish tile floors, a huge white island with a green granite countertop and matching cabinets. The foyer featured a huge, wraparound staircase. The floor was a dark mahogany color. There was a grand living room to my left filled with an enormous Oriental rug, antiques and what appeared to be very expensive art. Malden just stood in the foyer.

"Well, are you going to introduce me?" I asked Malden as I nodded my head toward the kitchen.

"OK," Malden said as he reluctantly grabbed my hand

and brought me into the kitchen.

"This is Lana," he announced as he entered the kitchen but stopped close to the doorway. I took it upon myself to walk closer to Bethenny.

"Hi, I'm Lana," I said. I was staring at a petite, middle-aged woman with long blonde hair in black Lululemon yoga pants and a matching hoodie, sitting on a stool at the end of the island. She was pretty, but no supermodel.

"Hello," Bethenny said, surprised, as she briefly paused from browsing through a catalogue.

I heard rustling in the opposite corner. I saw another petite blonde searching through a kitchen cabinet–also in Lululemon gear. She had long curly blonde hair. I recognized her from pictures. It was Malden's teenage daughter Hillary.

"You must be Hillary," I said politely, looking toward her. "I'm Lana."

"Hey," she said back with a straight face. I felt Malden's presence behind me. He put his hands on my shoulders.

"Aren't you going to give your pop a hug?" Malden asked Hillary. He walked over and embraced her. She didn't move or even crack a smile. You would think that a serial killer was hugging her. This baffled me. How could she be so cold to her loving father?

"You're my beautiful girl," Malden said as he stroked her hair. I paused. Malden was using the same tone he used with me during sex.

"Come on, Lana, I'll show you the boys' rooms," Malden said, grabbing me by the hand and leading me upstairs. Each boy was in his individual room. There was eleven-year-old Mike, fourteen-year-old Matt and sixteen-year-old Mark. They were all sweet and adorable. They proudly showed me posters, trophies and their video games. I was touched. I could tell they were raised well, despite their parents' divorce.

As Malden led us out the front door to head to the family reunion, I noticed Hillary remained in the kitchen with her mother.

"Wait, Malden, what about Hillary?" I asked.

"Huh?"

"Um, your daughter -- isn't she coming to the family reunion with us?"

"Oh yeah," Malden said as if I had asked him to take out the garbage. "Hillary are you meeting us there?"

"No!" she shouted.

"Hillary, this is your family. Your uncle flew in from Copenhagen for this. Please come."

"You don't care about me!" she barked at him.

My jaw dropped. I couldn't believe she talked to her father this way. I would never dare talk to my parents like that.

"What's that look on your face?" she continued.

Oh no, was she talking to me? I didn't mean to give her a dirty look. I cringed.

"I'm disappointed in you," Malden said.

"Well, I don't feel good," she said as she gave him a dark look.

Malden didn't respond and walked out the door. I followed.

"I don't understand—why does she talk to you like that?" I asked as we walked toward my car. The boys were already in the backseat.

"She's just bitter because of her illness," he explained. "And she's brainwashed by her mother. It's just a phase. She'll grow out of it."

"Wait, hold up—what illness?"

"She has Lyme disease and she's anorexic."

"She has what?" I asked in shock.

"We were hiking in Malibu a few years ago," he said, disinterested. "A tick bit her. She suffers from a ton of neurological problems because of it."

"That's horrible!" I gasped. "Anorexia and Lyme disease—that's so awful! Your poor daughter. I feel so bad for her."

"She's struggled with the disease for years. However, she's so negative about everything. Just like her mother. Do you see how dark they are?"

"I'm not sure what I just saw." I said with concern.

I was so confused. I didn't know Lyme disease even existed in California. I thought it was only prevalent on the East Coast and in the Midwest. There was so much tension in that house. It deeply concerned me. I couldn't quite put my finger on the situation. Malden remained quiet as we drove back to Uncle Paul's.

The boys were silent during the first part of our drive. However, the closer we got to Uncle Paul's home, the more they opened up. They told me about their rugby games and an Alaskan fishing trip they went on with their grandfather. We stopped at a gas station to fill up my car. As soon as Malden got out to pump the tank, they turned the tables on me.

"Why do you like my dad?" Mike, the youngest son, asked.

"I like him because he's very nice to me, and we have a lot of fun together," I explained.

"You know my dad is really weird," Mike said sternly.

I laughed, "That's okay. I'm a little weird too. It's good to be a little weird. Normal is boring."

"Yeah, but he does the weirdest stuff," Mike complained.

"Oh really, like what?" I asked.

"He just disappears sometimes," Mike said as his brothers

played with their iPhones.

"What do you mean he disappears, Mike?" I asked in wonder.

"Like, one time he took me to Home Depot. Right after we got there, I saw him leave the store. I thought he forgot something in the car, but instead he got in and drove away. He didn't come back for over an hour."

"Wait, what! He left you alone in the store all by yourself?"

"Yeah. It was so weird."

"I don't understand–where did he tell you he went?"

"When he came back I asked him and he said, 'Don't worry about it!'"

I was horrified. How could he leave an eleven year old alone in a store for hours?

"Did he forget you were with him?"

"No," Mike shrugged. "He does that. He disappears for a few hours and we never know where he goes."

I shook my head. Was Mike playing me? I didn't know how to respond to this.

"All set!" Malden cheerfully said as he climbed back into the driver's seat.

I cringed and looked at Malden with skepticism. I didn't know what to make of the information Mike had just revealed to me.

"What?" Malden sharply asked me when he saw the stunned look on my face.

"Nothing," I lied. "I'm excited for the family reunion. We're going to have fun, right guys?" I said as joyfully as possible, looking back at the boys as they continued to pound away on their iPhones.

When we arrived at Uncle Paul's house around midafternoon, Malden's relatives were setting up long collapsible tables in the backyard. There were close to a dozen tables, enough room to seat about seventy-five people. There were adults and children scattered all over the three-acre backyard–there was even a creek. The caterers were there setting up all kinds of salads, meat dishes and pasta. Everyone was in a happy mood and there were lots of hugs and kisses exchanged. I felt more comfortable than I did the night before because I had already met several relatives. Everyone gave me a warm greeting.

"Hey, Lana, come here," Malden shouted to me as I saw him pour two glasses of red wine by the bar area that had been set up near the garage. Malden was standing next to his brother Martin. Martin and I have a lot in common--we are both workout fanatics and diehard Republicans.

"What's up?" I asked them as I approached.

Malden handed me a glass of red wine. "Tell Martin about the story you're working on right now."

"Come on, Malden!" I barked.

"Lana, it's my brother, he's not going to tell anyone," Malden pleaded.

"It must be a doozy," Martin said, raising his eyebrows.

"It is." I sighed then turned to Malden. "It's not that I don't trust your brother–I just don't want Martin to hate me. I know he's a big supporter of Gov. Richards."

"I could never hate you, Lana," Martin said with a dashing smile and a wink. I blushed. He was almost as cute as Malden.

"Is that a promise?" I asked.

"Of course it is," Malden interjected. "Now just tell him the story."

"It's about Gov. Richards, and, er, his involvement

with..." I hesitated.

"With what?" Martin asked as he leaned his head closer to me.

"With a hooker!" Malden shouted.

"Malden—tone it down," I snapped.

"No way!" Martin gasped. "I never saw that coming. I mean, is it true?"

"Well, that's what I'm trying to figure out. I hope not for his sake— and for the country's sake."

"Well, don't worry, Lana, your secret is safe with me," Martin said, winking again.

"If anyone can break this story it's Lana," Malden bragged. "She's broken more front-page stories than any journalist in Hollywood."

I blushed. I loved it when Malden talked me up. It felt so good to be with a man who put me on a pedestal.

After we finished dinner, Malden's sister set up a stereo in the garage for an impromptu dance party. The little kids, teenagers and the elderly relatives were all dancing in the garage. It was one big, happy Irish family. It was what I had always dreamed of having for myself. Although I have an amazing Irish family too, it's very small. I remember as a child, my next-door neighbors had a big Irish family like Malden's. They threw a big holiday dinner on Christmas Eve every year. I remember looking at their celebration through the windows of my home and wishing our family were a little bit bigger.

Toward the end of the night, I began to learn more about Malden and his family, and I found some of it surprising. He allowed his fourteen and sixteen-year-old boys to play beer pong, and he even joined in for a few rounds. He explained that he thought it would be hypocritical for him not to allow his boys to drink alcohol. He said that it was safe—as long as he supervised. I also learned from Melissa that their mother was an alcoholic and she had two babies out of wedlock as a teenager that she put up for adoption. This stunned me. Malden raved about his mother. He said she was such a wonderful and strong woman. He said she was a good person who was able to provide for several children while their father was off fighting in World War II. Malden made her out to be a saint; however, the information his sister gave me made her appear to be more of a tortured soul than a saint.

We ended the night by singing songs as Uncle Paul played the piano. It was a warm ending to a beautiful night with a loving family. Malden and I drove back to his house with the boys. They raced into the TV room to play video games, and we headed straight to bed.

Predictably, Malden attempted to rip off all my clothes the second we got into his bedroom. The idea of us having sex when his children-who had just met me-were in the same house made me uncomfortable.

"Hold on," I said, as Malden, kissing me tried to push me on the bed. "Is the door locked?"

"I don't know." Malden shrugged.

"Well, will you please lock it?" I pleaded.

"OK," he said as he walked to the door.

"Thank you. I just don't want one of the kids to walk in on us."

"They won't—don't worry!" Malden insisted.

We had sex in the missionary position upon my insistence. I told Malden to make it quick, because I was nervous about the children. We both came, but we were as quiet as mice. As Malden lay naked on top of me, we heard a knock at the door.

"Go away!" Malden shouted loudly. It made me flinch.

"We can't find Call of Duty," one of the boys whined on the other side of the door.

"What did he say?" Malden whispered to me.

"It's a video game," I replied.

"God damn it!" Malden said, leaping out of bed. I quickly pulled the sheet over my sweaty, naked body.

Malden went straight to the door and whipped it open. "What the hell do you guys want?" he asked. All three boys stood in the doorway, staring at their butt-naked dad. I was shocked. His penis was still erect! The whole situation felt extremely inappropriate to me.

"We can't find some of our games," Mark explained. He didn't even flinch at the sight of his nude father.

"I'll find them," Malden said as he stormed out of the bedroom, stark naked.

I knew Malden was a free spirit, but I was horrified that he didn't take a second to throw his boxers on. My family is more traditional—my parents would never walk around naked in front of me. I grew up in the Midwest with an extremely conservative family. Modern families are so different nowadays – especially in the progressive state of California. I had only been in L.A. for a few years – the California lifestyle was still growing on me. I wrapped my arms around Malden's pillow, and I wondered if I was out of touch as I drifted off to sleep.

CHAPTER 10

As I drove through the desert highway, I tried to decide in my mind what I loathed more. The fact I'm driving a Prius again or the fact that I'm back in fucking Winnemucca for the third time in one month. Ari instructed me to fly into the Reno Airport and drive to Salt Lake City so that I could stop by Celeste's house on the way. I obliged, but I really wanted to punch Ari in the face. That's a six-hour detour, minimum! As much as I was willing to do whatever it took to get Celeste to take the poly, I knew she wouldn't answer the door. Sure enough, I stood outside her run-down trailer knocking on the rickety door for a good twenty minutes. There were no cars in her gravel driveway, and if she was inside, there was no sign of her. The Republican National Convention was only a week away, and regrettably, I knew my story wouldn't be ready for print by then. I was disappointed, but I still had hope that my career-changing bombshell story would pan out before Election Day.

Initially, I resented Ari for my cross-country drive, but after an hour into it, I found it extremely therapeutic. I threw on an Elvis CD that I had bought at a gas station along the way. As I listened to an amazing live version of *Never Been to Spain*, I thought about my life. I was in love with an amazing man, my career was on the up and up, I was happy and healthy–I felt great. The only dark cloud that lurked over my head was the possibility that I could be taking down my favorite presidential candidate, but I knew I had to ignore that minor detail in order to objectively work my story. I compartmentalized the thought for the time being. I drove eighty MPH heading east on I-80, passing one car after the next. I zoomed through breathtaking desert canyons painted with the light of a soft blue sky. I rolled down the window and started to sing along at the top of my lungs. I was moved to celebrate the joy I felt in my life.

My awful singing was quickly interrupted by a buzzing sensation in my crotch. It was my iPhone. I had placed it in between my legs, since I needed it close for the GPS app to get me to Salt Lake City the quickest way possible.

Malden Murphy: "Hi babe! How's the trip going?"

I instantly got giddy when I saw Malden's name appear on my phone. My love for this man was the ultimate aphrodisiac. I had never felt such a high in my entire life. The only time I'd ever felt a natural high as close to this was when I jumped out of an airplane. Skydiving was one of the most exhilarating experiences I've ever had, but my relationship with Malden felt that much better.

I responded by texting him a photo of the brown desert mountains outside my windshield. There wasn't one cloud in the bright blue sky, and you could only see tiny patches of green grass between the sandy yellow dirt. My profile in the rearview mirror with my long blonde hair blowing in the window was in the shot too. I did that on purpose.

Malden Murphy: "Great photo!"

Lana Burke: "I had no luck at the hooker's house, so I'm en route to SLC."

Malden Murphy: "Have you passed the salt flats yet?"

Lana Burke: "The what?"

Malden Murphy: "The Bonneville Salt Flats. It's a vast salt den from a dried-up lake. Very cool natural phenomena. It looks like arctic ice. My boys and I stopped to take photos during our road trip."

Lana Burke: "Sounds beautiful!"

Malden Murphy: "During the Ice Age, Lake Bonneville was as big as your Lake Michigan."

I got goose bumps at how knowledgeable Malden was.

Lana Burke: "That's so fascinating. I might have to stop to take photos, too."

Malden Murphy: "Call me when you get there. Drive safely!"

Lana Burke: "xoxo"

Malden Murphy: "Love you."

Lana Burke: "Love you, too."

After a few hours had passed, I hit the salt flats. The natural beauty of the barren land blew me away. I'd been all over the world hunting down stories in some of the most exotic places, but I'd never seen anything like this. My trip to Ecuador to cover Brangelina was my most recent work trip. I also had been to Alaska and covered Sarah Palin. I lived in the Bahamas for three months covering the birth of late Anna Nicole's daughter, the tragic death of her teenage son and her wedding to her creepy lawyer Howard Stern. I went to Spain for George Clooney and Rande Gerber's restaurant opening; France for the Cannes Film Festival; Africa for the birth of Brad and Angelina's firstborn Shiloh, and Canada to infiltrate the production of the *Twilight* movie to uncover scoop on Kristen Stewart and Robert Pattinson. However, Utah's salt flats were like nothing I had ever seen. It didn't even look like Earth; I felt like I was driving through Mars on NASA's Mars Rover. The sparkling white plains went on for dozens of miles. The dazzling beauty of this seemingly unearthly but breathtaking habitat hypnotized me. Another vibrating sensation in my crotch broke me out of my spell. It was Mick.

Mick Madden: "You almost here?"

Ari had instructed Mick to fly out to Salt Lake City, too. The plan was to approach Gov. Richards's lawyer, other Satin Dolls employees, and anyone else who could possibly help us with our story. We were sticking with our good cop, bad cop strategy. Mick had the luxury of bypassing Winnemucca and flying straight into the Salt Lake City airport. Mick avoided a lot of grunt work. Due to his seniority, I slightly resented him when I found myself banging on Celeste's door this morning, but my unexpected sightseeing bonus with the salt flats had certainly turned my mood around.

Lana Burke: "I'm twenty-five miles away, according to my GPS."

Mick Madden: "Great! Let's meet at eight for dinner. We'll have a strategy session. I have a new development too."

My eyes grew wide when I read that Mick had a new development. I couldn't wait to hear what it was.

Lana Burke: "Sounds good. Where do you want to go?"

Mick Madden: "Meet me in the lobby of the Grand America. We'll go to one of the restaurants in the hotel so we can chat up the staff. Who knows…maybe we'll get more info on Gov. Richards's extracurricular activities there."

Lana Burke: "Good plan. See you soon!"

When I pulled into the Grand America Hotel, I was totally blown away. It was a huge elegant white stone building. There were black chandeliers hanging in the carport under a majestic golden Grand America sign. I pulled my Prius into the brick roundabout driveway. When the valet attendant opened my car door, he said, "Welcome home."

I walked into the hotel and was instantly overwhelmed by the dozens of exotic pink and yellow flowers. The flowers were displayed in a China vase on an elegant glass and gold table in the center of the foyer. There was gold and dark mahogany trim on the walls and Oriental rugs strategically placed throughout the marble lobby. The antique furniture and grand piano in the lounge looked as if it was taken straight off the Titanic before its epic voyage. Everything appeared to be in mint condition. Ancient art, exotic sculptures and timeless pieces of furniture filled the hotel. I even spotted a gold clock that I swear had to be the inspiration for Cogsworth in Disney's *Beauty and the Beast*. I felt like a princess in an enchanted castle–the only thing missing was my prince. The thought of Malden reminded me that I had told him that I'd call him when I arrived. As I waited in line to check in, I typed his number on the screen.

"Hey," Malden said. There was an abundance of noise in the background.

"Hi, I made it to Salt Lake," I said.

"What?" Malden shouted.

"I made it to my hotel," I said, raising my voice. "Where are you?"

"I just stepped out–I'm at a restaurant," Malden quickly responded as the background noise fell dead.

"Oh–OK. Who are you with?"

"Some of the guys from work, but I'm glad you made it there safely," Malden said.

"Yeah," I said with a hint of sadness.

"What's wrong?"

"I don't know. I guess I'm just a little sad that I'm back on the road and won't be able to see you for…who knows how long."

"I miss you too," Malden cooed. "But, honey, I got to go. The guys are waiting inside for me."

"OK." I sighed.

"I'll call you later tonight; I'm going home right after dinner," Malden assured me.

"Sounds good," I said with a smile before hanging up.

I got my room key and declined assistance with my medium-sized suitcase. My room at the five-star hotel was currently going for four hundred dollars a night. One of my favorite perks of my job is that I have to stay at the same hotel as my subjects, as it usually helps with research for the story. For that reason alone, I've stayed at some of the finest hotels on the planet—hotels that I never would've been able to afford if my company wasn't footing the bill. One of my favorite hotels is the Four Seasons in Maui. I went there years ago to cover Lindsay Lohan's alleged engagement to Harry Morton.

My room looked like what I imagined a bedroom at Buckingham Palace would look like. There was a magenta and forest-green-colored carpet and light yellow-and white-striped wallpaper covering every wall. I was immediately drawn to the sliding glass doors framed by golden curtains. I dropped my purse and suitcase and walked toward the doors. I slid one of the doors open with ease and walked out onto the narrow balcony. There were picturesque snow-capped mountains dead ahead of me. A huge castle like church greeted me to my left. I flinched as I caught the church lights flicker on. As the sun set behind me, I noticed a strong bright light coming from the church's majestic clock tower. The place looked like a medieval church, like one you'd find in Europe. It was spectacular—and a little spooky, too. I was in a luxurious place in a stunning natural setting. However, I couldn't help but shake the uneasy feeling that had just come over me. My carefree spirit from my sing along road trip evaporated the moment I walked into my room. I felt a chill and wondered if the A/C was on in my room. The temperature was falling outside, and I knew I'd need to bring a jacket with me to dinner.

I turned on the LDTV in the bathroom. It was an elaborate, marble room. I switched the channel to Rox News and got into the shower. *The Rox Report* was on, and Scott Shepard aired footage from a speech Gov. Richards had made earlier that day.

"If you teach your kids the right values and help them

make the right choices, you know their future will be prosperous and secure," Gov. Richards said, surrounded by supporters at the Iowa State Fair.

I laughed to myself, listening to Gov. Richards talk about family values. I couldn't stop envisioning him asking Celeste to pee in a martini glass in the bathroom of this very hotel—possibly even the very one I was showering in! I cringed. After stepping out of the shower, I blew my hair dry and put on a light amount of makeup. I threw on a white blouse, skinny jeans, my black leather jacket and a dangly, gold necklace. It had been a long day, and I was ready for an excellent meal and a bottle—or two—of wine. I headed down to the Gibson Girl Lounge, per Mick's request.

When I got to the restaurant, I saw Mick sitting at a table in the corner. There was a Steinway grand piano with an East Indian rosewood and walnut finish in a corner, with a pianist playing Coldplay's *Clocks*. Big, wooden chairs and comfy, but elegant, couches surrounded small cocktail tables. When I approached the table, Mick got up and pulled out my chair for me.

"And we meet again." Mick smiled, kissing me on the cheek.

"Yes, good to see you." I beamed. "Quite a different setting than our last adventure!"

"Ha!" Mick laughed. "What...you mean there's not a brothel next door to this five-star hotel?"

"Too funny," I said with a loud laugh. "We certainly find ourselves in interesting situations. I'm relieved, though, it's just the two of us tonight. I don't think I can handle another dinner with Numbnuts and Celeste."

He laughed again as he reached for my wineglass and poured HobNob pinot noir into it. I was impressed that he already had a bottle waiting for me. It was as if he had read my mind.

"Thank you," I said, my mouth salivating as he poured my glass.

"Cheers to our next adventure," he said with a smile.

"And more hotel accommodations like this," I said, clinking his wineglass. I took a sip of the delicious wine. It went down like butter. I reached for my menu. I was starving.

"So...I've been sitting on the edge of my seat all afternoon. What's the new development?" I eagerly asked.

"Steve," he began cryptically, sipping his wine. "He didn't die in a car accident."

"Oh yes, Steve. How could I forget about him? Another one of Celeste's clients," I said, shaking my head. "How did he die then?"

"He didn't," Mick said with a cunning smile.

"He's alive?" I asked in utter shock.

"Yep," he said with a laugh.

"Oh my God!" I said in disbelief. "I don't understand. How did you figure this out?"

"Easy," Mick said with a hint of arrogance. "I auto tracked him and did a simple Google search. He's alive and kicking. His office is right down the street. I called and confirmed that he works there."

"I can't believe this," I said, still in slight shock. "If he's alive then why does Celeste think he's dead? Was she lying to protect him?"

"No," Mick said.

"Then what's the explanation?"

"Think about it, Lana. It's easy. Clearly, his wife found out about Celeste. She told Celeste that he had died to get her out of his life, and it worked. She fell for it. Now I'm sure

Steve just found a new hooker to fuck, but what can you do."

"Wow, okay," I said, processing this new information. "That makes sense. You know, I could tell Celeste had strong feelings for him. I'm sure she'd be interested in knowing this information."

"Exactly," Mick said, his eyes lighting up. "That's why I want you to reach out to her in a few days and bait her with this info. Maybe you can use it as leverage to get her to take the poly."

"Agreed."

"But in the meantime, we will continue to investigate Steve and James over the next few days."

"OK," I said cautiously. "How do you want to go about this?"

"I've been thinking about our approach," Mick began. "I think we should just cut to the chase and go to James and Steve's offices tomorrow."

I paused.

"Undercover?" I asked skeptically.

"No, we'll go and tell them we work for the *L.A. Post*," Mick boldly said. "Fuck it."

I almost spit out my wine. "I don't know about this, Mick," I said nervously. "Why would we want to out ourselves? Especially on our first day here?"

"Because at this point, Lana, the sand is slipping through the hourglass faster than ever. We're running out of time—the convention is next week! With Celeste refusing to take the poly as of right now, we need to get another source to confirm the story in order to get it published before the election. This is our only backup plan. If we had the luxury of time, we'd be able to take our time with the story. But we don't. There's no point in playing games with these chumps."

I knew he was right. I just worried about exposing our identities in a city where Gov. Richards was worshipped as the Second Coming. I knew this would put our safety at risk. However, Mick didn't seem to have a care in the world.

"So if we get one of them face-to-face—what do we say?" I asked, taking a huge swallow of wine.

"We'll play our usual good cop, bad cop game with them," Mick explained. "I'm going to be real harsh, though. Here's the deal: we will make them an offer they can't refuse. We'll tell them we know they've used Celeste's services. We'll threaten to expose them in the magazine and to their wives directly, unless they agree to give us any info that can confirm she also had an affair with Gov. Richards."

It was a sneaky and dirty approach, but I knew it could be effective. "OK," I said, taking a deep breath. "You're the boss. It's your call. I'll follow your lead."

A young waitress with big boobs and long jet-black hair approached our table. She resembled Celeste. I wondered if it was a sign. "Are you guys ready to order?" she asked with a soft voice.

"What's your favorite dish here?" Mick said with a flirtatious smile that was just awkward.

"The Grand Burger is a favorite," she said with a smile. "This is the hotel's more casual restaurant, but our gourmet burgers are made with Angus beef and topped with aged Swiss cheese.

"Is it your favorite?" Mick asked, winking. I rolled my eyes. He never failed to remind me that he had a dick.

"Yeah, it is actually," she said, nodding.

"I'll take your word for it," Mick said. "Medium-rare please."

"OK, then," I interrupted. "I'll start out with a shrimp

cocktail. Mick, we can share that. And I'll do the chicken wings."

"Great choice," the waitress said, before grabbing our menus and walking away.

"You know…she's pretty friendly," I said to Mick, raising my wineglass as the wheels started turning in my head. "I bet she can tell us some info on Gov. Richards. I'm sure she's at least heard about some of his stays here."

"I agree," Mick said. "Let's chat her up when she gets back."

I mauled my food like a champion. I looked like I had just murdered someone, since my hands and mouth were covered with wing sauce.

"Easy there, tiger," Mick said, laughing.

"I'm so embarrassed. I'm just so hungry," I said, dipping my napkin in my water glass to wash off my bloody massacre.

"Lana, take my advice." Mick chuckled. "Never order chicken wings on a first date."

"You jerk!" I said, playfully flicking water on him from my water glass. I was giddy from the wine, and ready to seduce our waitress into giving us info on Gov. Richards.

"Excuse me," I said as she walked by. "I'm thinking we need to order another bottle of red. It's been a long day. Actually, it's been a long month for the both of us."

"I can make that happen," she said.

"I'm sure you can make anything happen for us," I said as I put on the charm. "This hotel is so luxurious. How long have you been working here?"

"Yes, it is a luxurious hotel." she said. "I've actually been here for five years."

"Wow! I'm impressed. That's a long time," Mick said with a smile.

"You must have a lot of stories," I said with exaggerated interest. "I bet a lot of celebrities and high-profile people stay here."

"Oh yes, they do!" she exclaimed. "Aerosmith stayed here recently."

"Shut the front door–what is Steven Tyler like?" I asked eagerly. Once again, I had to laugh at myself. What I really wanted to say to her was that just a few weeks ago I was hanging out with Steven Tyler in his dressing room on the set of *American Idol*. Not only did I know what he was like–his number was on my speed dial. When I'm on assignment covering a celebrity, I often pretend like I'm an innocent tourist who is just a big fan of the subject at hand. Most people fall for the act.

"Oh, he is such a nice guy," she said. "The whole band had dinner here the other night."

"Wow!" Mick stated. "That's so cool."

Now I'm laughing hysterically on the inside. Mick had infiltrated Al-Qaeda. Now that was cool!

"So, what about politicians?" I asked slyly. "Have you met any presidents?"

"Oh, well, Gov. Richards stays here all the time," she said.

"Really?" Mick asked.

"Yeah, he'll rent out entire floors." She smiled. "And he just recently rented out this whole restaurant."

"That's so rad, have you met him?" I asked.

"Yes," she said. "I was disappointed."

"Why is that?" I asked.

"Well, he rented out our entire restaurant for the whole night. It was for him and a group of a dozen people. They didn't even stay the whole night, so I lost a lot of money in tips. Plus, they don't drink, so their bill was really cheap.

And…"

"And what?" Mick asked, leaning in closer to her.

"There's just something off about him. I can't put my finger on it. He just seems real cocky. I don't think he's that nice."

"That's such a shame," I said, disappointed. "Most politicians are total scumbags."

"Have you met Mrs. Richards?" Mick interjected.

"Oh no, she's never been here that I know of," she said.

"Well, that's strange," I said as I perked up. "I wonder why that is?"

"I think he just uses the hotel for business meetings," she continued.

"Oh, I bet he does." Mick smirked.

"I wonder if he cheats on his wife," I pondered out loud. "He seems so family-oriented and religious."

"I'm sure he does," the waitress said.

This was my cue to go in for the kill. "Have you heard of him bringing women around the hotel?"

"No, I haven't, but it wouldn't surprise me," she said.

"Interesting," Mick said as he rocked his head up and down in deep thought.

"I'll go grab you guys that bottle," she said, swiftly walking away.

I looked at Mick.

"You know, if Gov. Richards was fucking Celeste here, you would think that the staff would be all abuzz about it.

"Yes and no," Mick said. "He's smart. He never calls the agency or Celeste himself. She doesn't spend the night. Hell, he won't even touch her 'donation.' He knows what he's doing."

"True," I conceded, gathering my thoughts. I was hoping to pull more info out of our waitress, but I was also happy that we got something out of her on Gov. Richards. At least we confirmed he stayed at the Grand America.

With several glasses of wine in me and little sleep the night before, I was feeling really tipsy. Mick escorted me to the elevator. We were on different floors. He offered to walk me to my room, and I told him I was fine. When I walked out of the elevator, I looked down the long corridor to my room. Chills went up and down my spine, just like they had when I first walked into my room. I had a feeling that I was being watched. I looked over my shoulder as I walked down the hallway. No one was there. I looked down the hallway, and it suddenly dawned on me how incredibly creepy this place was. The lights on the wall flickered, and I noticed the hallway carpeting was a blood red color. I could see dark shadows and got a feeling of multiple presences. The hallway was almost an exact replica from the *The Shining*. I shivered. Could this place be haunted? At the end of the hallway, there was a wooden dining room cabinet. Inside the glass case sat old china pieces. The antique pieces haunted me. I walked hurriedly to my room and quickly shut and locked the door. I checked all the closets before ordering a bottle of wine from room service. I knew I didn't need another glass, but I wanted something to take the edge off.

"Can you throw in some martini glasses too?" I asked.

"Would you like a martini too, Ms. Burke?" the confused male staffer asked on the other line.

"No, just a martini glass," I said with a giggle. I wanted to lighten the night with humor. I was feeling silly.

As I waited for my vino, I went on Facebook. Photos of Neil Diamond popped up on my stream from Malden's account. Wait, Malden's account? I got a sick feeling in my stomach. He had told me he was at dinner with his friends and that he was going straight home after that. I wondered why he hadn't told me he was planning on going to a Neil Diamond concert. I looked at my phone and he still hadn't called as he had promised. I analyzed the comments on his page and all the women who liked his status update. Could he be with another woman? My mind raced. My paranoid thoughts were interrupted by a knock at my door. The room service waiter cracked my bottle of wine for me, and I was sipping my first glass before he even left my room. I grabbed the martini glass he brought for me and headed for the bathroom. I grabbed the yellow body wash from the sink and poured almost all of its contents into the martini glass. Then, I placed it on the floor of the marble shower and snapped a photo. I looked at the photo. The body wash looked like piss—success!

I quickly sent the photo to Mick and Ari with a snappy caption.

Lana Burke: "Pee-tini, anyone?"

I could barely contain my laughter. I'm pretty sure I laugh the hardest at my own jokes—especially by my third bottle of wine.

Ari Davidson: "Hahahahahahahaha! I see you're staying busy in SLC!"

Mick Madden: "You're so bad! Love it!"

Lana Burke: "It should be a cocktail special here, LOL!"

Ari Davidson: "Have you guys made any progress?"

Lana Burke: "We got some info from our waitress at

dinner tonight. She confirmed that Gov. Richards stays here all the time. However, Mrs. Richards never stays here, interestingly enough."

Ari Davidson: "That is interesting! Keep up the good work!"

By my third glass of wine from my new bottle, I was slowly passing out. I was also itching to talk to Malden. I caved and called him. No answer. I didn't leave a message. I figured he'd see my missed call, and would call back before he went to bed. Or would he? With that, I dozed off to sleep.

CHAPTER 11

I woke up to my hotel room phone ringing. "Yeah," I said, picking up the phone half asleep.

"How you feeling?" Mick asked on the other line.

"Um, great," I lied.

"Uh, huh."

"OK, I may be slightly hung over."

"Too many pee-tinis?"

I laughed. "Yes, they get me every time!"

"Can you be ready by ten?"

"Yes," I said, getting out of bed.

"We'll hit up James and Steve's office today like we discussed."

"Sounds good," I said, hanging up.

Mick and I drove up Third Street and headed to Steve's office first. The old buildings and the cleanliness of the city charmed me. As we got closer to Steve's downtown office, we drove under the Eagle Gate monument. The famous landmark is a rusty black arch with green paint peeling through topped with a statute of an eagle. I noticed that the eagle proudly spread his wings while perched atop a box marked with a five-pointed star. I had read about the site in a hotel brochure. It was erected in 1859 to commemorate the entrance of Brigham Young's property. He was the President of The Church of Jesus Christ of Latter-day Saints from 1847 until his death in

1877. It also reminded me how I read that Brigham Young allegedly used the Danites to carry out barbarous acts of murder, rape and theft to anyone who got in the way of the Mormon Church. Driving under the spooky looking arch gave me the creeps. The reality of what I was dealing with began to set in. I thought about everything Celeste had told me. What was the significance of the five-pointed star? We were in the Mormon capital of the United States. Is this a symbol of the Danites? The Free Masons? We passed a red brick Mormon Church with a white steeple. Underneath the steeple, there was a huge circular glass window—decorated with another five-pointed star. Chills went up and down my spine. I almost said something to Mick, but I bit my tongue. I didn't want to appear paranoid. We parked the car at a meter on the street and headed into Steve's office building.

The building was a white building, several stories tall. The lobby was huge, with marble floors. There were a few white benches, plants and black-and-white photographs in the sleek lobby. That was the extent of the décor. The building appeared to be very secure. There were cameras everywhere, and you couldn't get to the elevators without a pass and a photo ID. Mick walked straight up to the front desk.

"Can I help you?" a tall black man in navy slacks asked as we approached.

"Hi, there," Mick said in an exceedingly friendly tone. "We're here to see Steve Swanson."

"Is he expecting you?" he asked in an unfriendly tone.

"I don't think so," Mick said. "Is that your daughter?" he asked, pointing to a photo of a little black girl in braids that was framed on the desk.

"Yes, it is." He smiled.

"She's beautiful," Mick said. "I have a daughter about her

age, too."

"He's not answering his phone," the security guard said.

"We can wait," Mick said with a smile.

"There's a waiting room in his office," he said. "You guys can go up and wait there."

With that, we were in. When we walked into the tenth floor office, we immediately spotted a frumpy, overweight brunette secretary in her forties sitting behind the desk. I wondered if she had sister wives. She looked the part. And after all, we were in Mormon country.

"Hello," she said with a smile.

"Hi," Mick said. "We're here to talk to Steve."

"Oh, he just left for lunch," she cautiously said. "Is he expecting you?"

"I don't think so," Mick said, shaking his head.

"I can leave a message. What is this about?"

"We're journalists. My name is Mick Madden, and this is Lana Burke. We work for the *Los Angeles Post*. We're working on a story involving Steve."

"What is the story about?" The secretary's face dropped.

"I'm sorry, we aren't really at liberty to say; it's a highly sensitive story. We need to talk to Steve."

"OK," she said somewhat skeptically.

"Here are our cards," Mick said, handing our business cards to her. My stomach sank. I knew that within a few hours we'd be outed if Gov. Richards didn't already know we were working on this story.

"I'll give him the message," the secretary coldly said.

When we got back into the elevator, Mick cheerfully asked me what I wanted to eat for lunch.

"Aren't you in the least bit nervous about what might happen?" I anxiously asked him.

197

"What are you talking about, Lana?" Mick replied, confused.

"We just revealed ourselves to the nephew of someone who may potentially be the next President of the United States. Don't you think that puts us in a certain degree of danger?"

"Nah, don't worry about it Lana," Mick said reassuringly. "We're dealing with his idiot nephew. He's not going to want it to get out that he's fucking a hooker. We hold all the cards. You're paranoid."

"Am I?" I took a deep breath and rolled my shoulders back. Was I paranoid? As we walked to the car, my phone rang. It was Malden. I told Mick to hold on for a minute as I stepped aside.

"Hello."

"Hey, babe, how's it going?" a cheery Malden said on the other end.

"Good. We're just hitting the ground today. How are you?"

"I'm good. Just recovering a little bit from last night. I ended up going to hear Neil Diamond."

"Oh," I said with suspicion.

"Yeah, one of the guy's from the office ended up having an extra ticket to the concert."

"That sounds fun," I said flatly. "Yeah, I tried calling you last night when I got home."

"I'm sorry, honey, I must've been passed out cold," Malden tenderly said.

"Was it a good show?"

"It was fantastic!"

"I really like Neil Diamond too," I said with a hint of jealousy.

"Well, do you like Muse and The Who?"

"Yes, of course."

"I have tickets to both those upcoming shows; would you like to be my date?"

"That sounds like a lot of fun," I softened. "I've got to go. Mick is waiting for me. I'll touch base with you later."

"OK, have a good day."

When I hung up the phone, that sinking feeling reappeared in my stomach. Everything seemed off. Malden seemed off. This trip didn't feel right. I believed we had made a mistake exposing our identities to close allies of Gov. Richards. The whole fucking trip–everything felt wrong.

I got back into the car with Mick. We spent the next hour trying to track down James. When we finally found his office, his secretary informed us he was out of town. We left our business cards with her and took a break for lunch. Mick took me to an Italian restaurant on the outskirts of the city. On the way, we drove by home addressees that we had for James and Steve–unfortunately, both were obsolete. LexisNexis is a great resource, but it doesn't always pull up the most current addresses for people. We decided to make one more stop after lunch before calling it a day–a stop at the office of Celeste's old escort agency, Satin Dolls.

When we arrived at the address, which we located through a quick Google search, we found ourselves pulling into a tacky strip mall. The Satin Dolls office appeared to be a low-rent hair salon.

"What do you think?" I asked Mick as we got out of the car. "Do you think this is a cover for the agency? I don't get it."

"I'm not sure," Mick replied, scratching his head.

"Well, it looks like there's an Asian man and woman in there. Let's just ask."

"I'll follow you," Mick said.

I pulled open the glass door, which was covered with a pair of plastic blinds. Several loud, brass bells jingled as I pushed the door open. A petite, hunched-over woman swept hair off the floor, and a bored-looking man sat behind a desk. There were no customers.

"Hi, we're looking for Satin Dolls," I said reluctantly.

"What your name?" the man asked in broken English, his thick black glasses falling to his nose.

"My name's Lana," I continued. "We're looking for Satin Dolls. You know, the escort agency? We need to talk to someone there."

"Ahhh yes, the Satin Dolls," he said with a laugh, revealing a pair of stained buckteeth. I couldn't help but giggle a little.

"Isn't this the address for Satin Dolls?" Mick asked.

"Satin Dolls is upstairs," the man said. "Come—I show you."

The man led us around the corner to a hidden staircase that led to a second floor. At the top of the stairs, we could see one glass door. It appeared dark on the other end. We thanked the man and proceeded. The door was locked. I tried to peek in through cracks in the drawn blinds. I could see a desk and a couple of chairs and one phone. As we stood outside the office, the phone rang.

"I bet no one works from this office," Mick said. "It's a phone and cash business. I'm surprised they even have a storefront."

"Yeah, you do have a point," I said. "There must be a reason, though, why this office exists. I can come back later tonight. I'll do a drive-by just to see if anyone shows up."

"Sounds good," Mick said.

We headed back to the hotel. Mick had to spend the night working on another story. I told him I was going to go through Celeste's phone to find other possible sources. Maybe Celeste's friends or her other clients would have some info. Before Mick drove into the hotel's elaborate porte-cochère, he pulled over and parked at a meter on the street.

"You know what—I found a cell number for James that probably is accurate," Mick offered.

"Really?"

"Yeah, why don't you try calling now?"

"What do you want me to say?"

"Tell him you work for the *Los Angeles Post* and we stopped by his office today—and that it's important we talk to him."

"OK," I said with hesitation. "I can do that."

I dialed his number on my cell phone, but before I hit the last digit I stopped. "Wait, should I block my number?"

"No, why would you do that?"

"I don't know—I guess I'm just a little uncomfortable giving someone like him my number."

"Lana, we already handed over our business cards."

"Right," I exhaled. "I forgot."

I hit the last digit. The phone rang once. Twice. Three times. I was certain I was going to get a voicemail recording by the fourth ring, but someone picked up.

"Hello?" a soft male voice answered on the other end.

"Is this James?" I blurted.

"Who's this?" he snapped back.

"This is Lana," I started cautiously. "I work for the *Los Angeles Post*. My colleague and I stopped by your office today. We need to talk to you about a story involving someone we believe you know, Celeste Homan."

"I have nothing to say."

"James, please just hear us out. We're not interested in your involvement with Celeste. We're interested in Gov. Richards's involvement with her."

"I have no comment."

"Do you know anything about that?"

"I- I'm sorry," he stammered before hanging up.

"Lana, that was fantastic!" Mick said, laughing hysterically. "Did you hear his voice tremble? That idiot is shaking in his boots!"

I looked at him quizzically. My heart was racing. James was not the only person shaking in his boots. I did not feel good about James knowing I was in town working on a story involving his famous client. My phone beeping interrupted my thoughts.

"It's a text from him!" I exclaimed as I jumped up in my seat.

"What does it say?"

I read the text aloud: "'I will have my lawyer contact you.' What should I write back?"

"Hmmm," Mick said. "Tell him that's fine, and then ask who his lawyer is."

I conceded.

Lana Burke: "Thank you. Who is your lawyer?"

James Garrett: "I'll have him contact you in the next day or so."

"That's bullshit," Mick said. "Push him again—tell him you need to know a name so you know the right person is contacting you when they do."

"OK."

Lana Burke: "Who is your lawyer so I know the right person is contacting me."

Mick and I sat in the car for a few more minutes waiting to see if he would text back, but we were met with radio silence.

"That's okay," Mick said. "If he doesn't respond, we'll just keep stopping by his office until he does."

I grimaced.

Mick and I both went to our separate rooms. I went for a run in the gym, and when I got back to my room, I ordered a salad and a truffle fried chicken dish from room service. I turned on Rox News Channel and scrolled through Celeste's phone as I ate. She made my job easy, as she had listed all of her fellow hookers' place of work as Satin Dolls in her phone directory. There were seven Satin Dolls girls in her contacts, and every single number was disconnected. The only phone number that was functioning was for the madame of Satin Dolls, Madame Victoria. I got her voicemail, but I held off on leaving a message. I figured I'd try her a few more times before I would go that route. I contemplated calling Celeste to tell her about Steve's miraculous survival from the car crash, but I decided to hold off on that, too. I didn't want Celeste to ruin my chances of convincing Steve to cooperate with us. I figured that once I broke the news to Celeste that Steve was alive she would contact him. I went on Facebook and saw that Celeste had either blocked me or closed her account. I fell asleep thinking about all the unanswered questions I had with my story—and now in my personal life, too.

Mick and I spent the next few days going back to James and Steve's offices. We were told at Steve's office that they would call the police if we returned one more time. Meanwhile, every time we went to James's office, his secretary kept telling us he still was on vacation. We checked out several homes as potential residences for both men, and nothing panned out. Either that, or we just had the bad luck of showing up when no one was home. We went back to Satin Dolls a few more times, but the office remained empty. Finally, I cracked and left Madame Victoria a message. I was frustrated, exhausted and worn out. My relationship with Malden was not in a great place either. We kept missing each other's phone calls. On top of everything, Mick was leaving me alone in Utah. He had to fly out to work on another story.

It was ten in the morning. I was in bed, with my laptop, researching more about the Danites. I found a conspiracy theory website that explained how the alleged modern-day Danites were also known as the Mormon Secret Police.

"Danites have taken an oath to support the heads of the Mormon Church in all things that they say or do whether it's right or wrong." I softly read aloud.

Knock, knock.

I got out of bed wearing Malden's Berkeley T-shirt and a pair of his boxers. I looked through my peephole and saw Mick on the other end with a suitcase. I unhooked the bolt lock and opened the door.

"Sexy outfit," Mick said with a beaming smile.

"Shut up," I snarled back at him.

"No, I mean it—there's nothing sexier than a girl in a T-shirt," Mick said, still smiling.

"You're just smiling because you get to leave this creepy-ass town, and I hate you for it," I snapped.

"Oh come on, Lana, you'll only be here a few more days. If nothing comes of this trip, we'll regroup back in L.A. and figure out our next move. Don't get discouraged."

"Ugh, I know—I'm just so exhausted."

"Here's an idea. Why don't you only spend a few hours working today and then go to the spa? I'll make sure you can expense any service you want."

"That's really sweet," I said. "Are you sure?"

"Consider it done," Mick said.

I gave Mick a hug and went back to my research. I booked a massage for noon and called down to the front desk to renew my room for three more nights. I prayed I wouldn't need to stay any longer than that.

"Front desk," a young woman's voice answered on the other line.

"Hi this is Lana Burke. I wanted to know if I could renew my room for three more nights."

"Yes, Ms. Burke, that won't be a problem."

"Great – so I can stay in the same room?"

"Of course. We have a wedding tonight, but that still only puts us at almost sixty percent occupancy."

"Great."

"Just make sure to come down to the front desk to get your new key. Your old one has already been deactivated."

"No problem," I said as I noticed my cell phone buzzing on the nightstand. I almost hit the ceiling—it was Madame Victoria!

"Thank you," I said as I quickly hung up the phone.

"Hello," I said, scrambling through my purse for my tape recorder.

"Is this Lana?"

"Yes," I anxiously said.

"I've been meaning to return your call. I've been crazed these past few days," the woman on the other line said apologetically.

"Oh no worries—thanks so much for calling me back," I said breathlessly.

"So, what story are you working on?" She wasted no time getting to the point.

"Well, I've been working on a story involving one of your former employees. She's made some strong allegations against a very high-profile person, and I was wondering if you could offer me any insight."

"Which employee is it?"

"Celeste Homan," I said as if I were asking a question.

"Oh," said Madame Victoria, who laughed uncontrollably. "That crazy bitch!"

"So, you know Celeste?"

"Yes, of course. She's worked on and off at the agency for several years. However, I haven't seen her for at least a year or two."

"Well, I met with her recently, and she told me she had an affair with Gov. Richards while she was working at your agency."

"Oh, did she?" Madame Victoria said cryptically.

"Yes. Do you know anything about this?"

"You know," Madame Victoria paused. "Celeste is a raging lunatic. She is bipolar and totally full of crap. She's had run-ins with the law her entire life, and she doesn't even have custody of her own children."

"Yes, I do know all of this," I said with irritation. "That may make her white trash, but that doesn't mean she didn't sleep with Gov. Richards."

"Lana, she's a pathological liar," Madame Victoria

continued.

"Well, then let me ask you this—do you know about Steve Swanson hiring Celeste?"

"If she claimed that she slept with Steve—it's a lie," Madame Victoria said with confidence.

"That's where you're wrong," I said, feeling empowered. "I have phone records in front of me that prove without a doubt that he was one of her clients."

"Well—I—er," Madame Victoria stammered.

"Look, Madame—I understand you have a business to run and protect. I'm not a cop. I have no interest in hurting you or your business. I just want to know if there's any truth in Celeste's claims about her affair with Gov. Richards. Did she ever mention him?"

"She may have mentioned him once or twice," Madame Victoria said, lowering her voice.

"And did you ever have contact with Gov. Richards or any of his handlers? Don't most clients book their appointments through you?"

"He may have. Honestly, I couldn't tell you. I get cold calls from anonymous men who I never meet. Only my girls have face-to-face contact with them."

"So what did Celeste say to you when she talked about Gov. Richards?" I pried.

"She didn't say much to me," Madame Victoria continued. "I heard about her alleged trysts with him usually through the other girls. Celeste bragged that she slept with him and several Hollywood movie stars. I don't believe much that comes out of her mouth, though."

"Are there any records of Celeste's appointments I could look at?"

"Lana, there's no way I can share that with you. That's

confidential information."

"What if I offered you some cash in exchange for a peek?" I asked in desperation, trying to remember how much money Ari was allowed to wire me from the office's petty cash to pay off a source.

"Lana, that's just not going to happen. I wish you the best with your story, but I have to go."

Madame Victoria hung up before I had a chance to get another word in. I opened my laptop and typed up a file for Ari and Mick outlining everything Madame Victoria told me. I was happy she called me back, but I was left with more questions than I had before. I couldn't decide if Celeste was lying about her affair with Gov. Richards or if she was actually telling the truth. I went back and forth about it the whole time I wrote my file. By the time I finished, it was almost time for my massage. I was about to walk out the door, when my cell phone rang again. It was Madame. My eyes lit up.

"Hello," I quickly answered.

"If you quote me on anything I told you, I will personally sue you, your publication and your entire company," Madame Victoria shouted from the other end.

"Whoa—whoa," I calmly said. "Where is this coming from? We just had a rational conversation a couple hours ago and now you're screaming at me. I don't understand; why are you so upset?"

"Gov. Richards is a good person," Madame Victoria shouted into the phone. "There are good people in this community. You'd be making a huge mistake by publishing a false story on a very well-respected and cherished person."

"Madame, please," I begged. "You need to calm down. I never said we're publishing any story. As of now, we're simply reporting on a lead that we got."

"Celeste is a pathological liar! She's playing you! Steve is a good person. He doesn't deserve you stalking him at his place of work."

"Excuse me?" I said in confusion. "Where did you hear that?"

"I just talked to him!" she shouted back.

"So you do know Steve," I said sharply. "I see what's going on here. I understand he's a good paying customer; now I know why you're so upset."

"Look lady, you're barking up the wrong tree," she warned. "All I'm saying is back off—or else you're going to regret it."

I heard a click and the line dropped. I felt chills go up and down my spine, and that sick feeling returned to my stomach. Her warning haunted me. I tried to shrug off the phone call and headed to my spa appointment.

The spa was elegant but dated. It looked like it hadn't been updated since the seventies. The walls and the carpet were a light pink color, and there was bamboo furniture in the lounge area. I got a fifty-minute Swedish massage. I tried to relax, but I couldn't. My massage therapist even commented about how tense my body felt. When the massage was over, I threw my robe on and took turns sitting in the sauna and the steam room. I was the only person in the spa. I got another eerie feeling. Again, I felt like I was being watched. I heard clicking noises outside the sauna door, but when I checked it out, there was nothing there. I cut my time in the ladies locker room short. After I paid my bill, I headed out to the pool.

I felt much better in the sun. Beautiful flowers and perfectly trimmed shrubs surrounded the pool. There was an outdoor bar and patio. I noticed a big group of young adults boozing it up. I figured they were in town for the wedding.

After a couple of hours in the sun, I trekked to the front desk to get my new key.

"I'm sorry, Ms. Burke, but your room is no longer available," the middle-aged stone-faced woman at the front desk explained.

"There must be a misunderstanding—I extended my stay this morning," I said.

"Yes, I know, but your room is not available," she said as she typed on her computer. "If you'd like to extend your stay; we'll need to transfer you to another room."

"Okay," I said suspiciously. "But why would my room suddenly become unavailable? The hotel isn't even at full capacity."

"I can't say, Ms. Burke," she replied, her face unchanged.

My head spun. The dark feeling I've had since I arrived to the Grand America deepened. My gut told me something was off–real off. Did hotel management find out I was a reporter investigating Gov. Richards's affair with Celeste? But then, why would they move me to a different room? Is the new room bugged?

"Here's a key for your old room. I'll have the bellman come up with your new key and to help you with your stuff," she said.

I thanked her and hurried back to my room. The balcony door was cracked open, and the curtains danced around a gust of wind from outside. My heart started racing. Was someone in my room? I slowly walked to the balcony and peeked outside. No one was there. I quickly packed my bags. I looked for the tape recorder that I could've sworn I left on my nightstand after I taped my conversation with Madame Victoria, but it was nowhere to be found. My breathing got heavy, with anxiety.

Just then, there was a knock on the door.

I rushed to see who it was. I looked through the peephole and saw the bellman on the other side. I slowly opened the door.

"Hi, Ms. Burke–I'm here to help you with your bags," a cheery young man with dark hair and a big smile said.

"Thank you so much," I said skeptically. "I packed all of my stuff, but I can't seem to find a tape recorder I had."

"Do you want me to call lost and found?" he asked.

"I think I just misplaced it. I'll call tomorrow if it doesn't turn up. But I'm pretty sure I never took it out of my room."

"May I ask why you're switching rooms–is there something wrong with this one?"

"No, I would prefer to stay in this one."

"Oh well, then I'm sure there'd be no reason why you can't."

"But they told me I have to transfer."

"That's strange," he said as he scratched his head. "I thought you requested a room change."

"Well, I thought it was strange too," I pried. "They told me you'd bring up a new room key."

"There must be some kind of a misunderstanding–I never got your new room key. I've worked here for five years, and I've never had to transfer someone out of a room–especially with the hotel at barely half capacity. I'll go downstairs and get your new key and find out the reason for the transfer."

"OK I appreciate that," I said with relief.

While the bellman went back downstairs, I tore up my room looking for my tape recorder. I threw the comforter off my bed. I looked under the bed. I looked in the nightstand drawer, behind the curtains, everywhere. It was gone. I went onto the balcony to get a breath of fresh air and I noticed in the courtyard the wedding was taking place. The bride looked gorgeous, and the setting in the grand courtyard was breathtaking. There was a huge, star-shaped brick fountain in the middle of the garden. It wasn't a pentagram, though, as it had seven points. It was a heptagram. I wondered if that had any meaning with the Mormon religion or the Danites. There was also an area on the patio that was made up of checkered bricks, and it looked like a life-sized chessboard.

There was a knock on the door. The bellman was back. I quickly opened the door. "How did it go?" I asked anxiously.

"Fine," he said with no emotion. "I got your new key."

"Well, did you find out why they're switching me?"

"No, I didn't," he said. "It was strange, but my boss told me not to worry about it."

I froze. I knew immediately I was in danger. The bellman grabbed my suitcase and purse and instructed me to follow him down the hallway.

"It's just down the hall," he said as he walked. "We managed to keep you on the same floor, and it's actually a nicer room. It's in the corner so you have a better view."

Just what I needed—to be isolated in the corner where no one can hear me scream, I thought.

"So I'm still confused," I said. "In all your years working here you've never had to switch someone out of their room against their will?"

"I only had to once," he said.

"Why was that?"

"A couple was here celebrating their anniversary. They wanted to stay in the same room they stayed in the night they got engaged. Maybe that's why you're getting transferred. I'm so sorry for the inconvenience."

In my heart I knew that wasn't the reason. Madame Victoria had called me earlier flipping out. Steve and James knew my name and probably my whereabouts. By now, I was sure Gov. Richards had been tipped off about the context of the story I was covering–and to top it off, my tape recorder had just been stolen. I felt like a prisoner on a pirate ship walking the plank to my death. As I got closer and closer to the door, my anxiety level skyrocketed. The doorman showed me around my new room. I tipped him five dollars and called Malden immediately after he left.

"Hi, babe!" a cheery Malden said on the other end.

"Malden, I'm freaking out. I think I'm in trouble!" I said in a panic.

"Whoa, slow down. What do you mean?"

"I think my hotel room was broken into, and the management just insisted I switch rooms, but they wouldn't tell me why. Plus, I got a hold of the hooker's madame, and she basically threatened me. And Richards's lawyer and nephew know who I am now. What if I'm being followed? What if the Danites broke into my room just like they broke into the hooker's house?"

"OK, Lana relax," Malden said coolly. "Who's Danites?"

"It's a secret society I've been researching–it's the Mormon Secret Police," I said.

"OK, Lana, take a deep breath, gather all of your stuff together and check out. Go stay in another hotel."

"OK, but Ari wanted me to stay here to do background reporting, and I don't know if he's going to think I'm crazy if I tell him this."

"Lana, I don't care what he says. Your safety is number one, and if your room was broken into–you're not in a good spot. Tell Ari you're switching hotels, or tell him that you just want to come home."

"OK," I said with relief. "Thank you. I'll let you know

213

what happens."

"I love you, Lana."

"I love you, too."

I raced out of the room with my luggage. I felt sweat dripping between my breasts as I ran down the creepy hallway. There was no one else in the corridor. When I reached the lobby, I didn't even bother to stop at the front desk to cancel my extended stay. I figured it would be safer to call them. I tried to play it cool as I exited the hotel. When I got my Prius, I tore out of the circular hotel driveway as quickly as possible. I drove aimlessly for a half hour, constantly checking my rearview mirror to see if anyone was following me. When I felt safe, I pulled over and called Ari.

"How's it going, Lana?" Ari asked with a smoker's cough. "Your file on Madame Victoria was quite interesting."

"Thank you," I said quickly. "Something happened I need to tell you about."

"Are you OK?"

"Yes, I'm fine. I'm just—I'm a little worried," I stammered. "Madame Victoria called again today and threatened me. I left my room for a while, and when I came back, I noticed that my tape recorder was missing. I know I left it on my nightstand. I think someone stole it. Then the management insisted that they switch my room. It made me very uncomfortable. I feel like I'm being watched or followed."

"Well, I don't want you to feel uncomfortable. Why don't you check out? You can stay somewhere else."

"I already left the hotel. I'll do that, but I don't feel comfortable staying here much longer. Richards's attorney and nephew now have my contact info. They know I'm working on a story involving Richards and a hooker. I swear people are following me. I know it sounds crazy, but I'm very intuitive, and everything inside me is telling me to leave town as soon as possible. I feel like I'm in danger."

"That's not a problem, Lana. Why don't you fly home first thing tomorrow? You and Mick have already exhausted all the leads there. You guys can continue to work the story from L.A."

"Thank you."

"Get a new hotel room, relax and order in a movie or something. If you need anything else, call me."

"Thank you," I said.

I checked into the University Marriott, which was on the other side of town. I made no eye contact with anyone when I was checking in, and afterward went straight to my room—I didn't dare leave. I ordered room service. After a runner delivered my food, I locked and bolted the door—and pushed a desk in front of it for good measure. I could see my car in the parking lot and kept walking to the window to make sure no one was tampering with it. I tried to go to bed at eleven, but I still found myself tossing and turning by one in the morning. I couldn't take it any longer. I knew it was time to contact Gunnar. I quickly typed him a text.

Lana Burke: "Hi, I'm working on a crazy story, and I need your help. I'm afraid I might be in trouble."

Within five minutes, my phone beeped.

Gunnar Smith: "I'm worried—are you OK?"

Lana Burke: "Yeah, I'll be fine. Too much to explain over text."

Gunnar Smith: "I'll be in town tomorrow. I can meet up with you at night to talk."

Lana Burke: "Perfect. I'll hit you up tomorrow."

I felt my nerves calm immediately as if I had just popped a Xanax. I knew Gunnar would protect me–just like he always had in the past.

CHAPTER 12

I drove my X5 East on Third Street through Koreatown. As I passed dollar stores, martial arts studios and countless cheap massage parlors, I could barely contain my excitement to see Gunnar. Earlier that morning, I caught the first flight out of Salt Lake City and got back to L.A. in enough time to join him for happy hour. He instructed me to meet him in his room at the Ritz-Carlton in downtown Los Angeles at L.A. Live. It had been almost a year since I last saw him. I was feeling nostalgic. I never fail to get butterflies in my stomach when I see his smiling face.

We first met in Washington, D.C., when I was an intern at the White House. He's an extremely wealthy entrepreneur with deep-rooted ties in the Capital, mostly with Democrats. In the years since I last saw him, he had developed a very intimate relationship with President Oyama. Gunnar told me he was working on a few business deals with the President but would never elaborate. Most likely because he knew how I truly felt about Oyama. Despite our political differences, our chemistry was off the charts. I fell for him the second I laid eyes on him. We had a steamy love affair during my time in D.C. As much as I loved him, I knew it would never work. He was thirty years older than I was, and shortly after our tryst, he got married and his wife gave birth to his first child. I knew I had an age gap with Malden but I met him at a point in my life where I was way more settled and mature. Nevertheless, Gunnar and I have remained friends over the years. He's always had my back, and I've always had his. I felt fortunate to have such a powerful friend and ally on my side that would do anything to protect me.

When I arrived at the five-star hotel, I told the valet attendant that I'd only be there for a few hours. I had promised Malden that I'd drive to his beach house after my meeting with Gunnar. Conveniently, I didn't tell Malden exactly who Gunnar was. I walked up to the front desk and told the primly dressed, redheaded receptionist that I was headed to Gunnar's room.

"Oh you're here to see Mr. Smith," she said, raising her eyebrows. He was a very well-known figure, earning a spot on the Forbes World's Billionaires list every year. I knew she was questioning why a young, attractive woman would be meeting with him in his suite.

"Yes, I am," I said with a hard smile.

She called his room to tell him I had arrived. "Follow me, I need to type in a code to get you to the penthouse," she said as she led me to the elevators. When the door opened, she punched in a code. She instructed me to go to Penthouse One and left me alone in the elevator.

When I got to the top floor, I found several doors with a sign marked "No. 1." Confused, I knocked on one of them. Within seconds, Gunnar opened the door. He looked dashing. Here came the butterflies along with goose bumps all over my arms and breasts. I had a big smile on my face. He beamed back at me, smiling his perfect smile. Gunnar was wearing a black designer suit with a custom-fitted soft blue shirt. His light brown hair was sun-kissed, and he sported a light tan. I wanted to melt.

"Um, hey…hi," I stuttered. After more than a decade of friendship, I could not believe this man still made me nervous enough to fidget.

"Get over here," he said, pulling me in for a hug. My heart stopped. He smelled fresh and clean. I let out a deep breath. After my Salt Lake City ordeal, this was the first time in days I felt safe. He embraced me for what felt like minutes and wouldn't let go. Despite our inability to be together, we deeply loved each other. I slowly crept my hands down toward his perfectly toned ass. I squeezed it hard and got a rush.

Wait, Lana, no–stop! I thought. You have a boyfriend. Behave. I pulled back and broke our embrace.

"It's so good to see you," I said with a deep exhale.

"It's so good to see you, missy," he said with his billion-dollar smile. "You had me worried–it sounds like you're in trouble."

Gunnar led me toward the end of his suite. It was a huge bedroom with a king-sized bed, modern furniture and a gigantic flat screen TV. It was a nice room, but humble by Gunnar's standards.

"Yeah, I need your help," I explained, easing onto the

bed.

"Lana, what have you got yourself into now?" Gunnar asked, reaching for a door that I assumed connected to a separate suite. I always told him my adventures covering celebrities. He pretended he wasn't fascinated with their lifestyles, but he loved hearing all the dirt.

"Follow me," he said with a devilish smile. "I think you'll like the view there better."

"Really – well okay then." I got off the bed and walked through the doorway. My jaw instantly dropped. "Holy fucking shit!"

I stared at his penthouse living room, dining room, office and family room. It was the presidential suite. There were floor-to-ceiling windows with a view that started with downtown L.A., led to the Hollywood Hills, and finally reached the beach cities. It may have been the most amazing hotel room I'd ever seen.

"You like?" he said nonchalantly, leading me to the southwest corner, which overlooked the 10 Freeway. Looking around, I noticed a cream-colored sectional, a marble coffee table and a bottle of champagne in a silver bucket with ice.

"I thought the first room I walked into was the extent of it," I said. "I was going to ask why you were slumming it!"

"Ha!" he said with that big smile of his. He was still a handsome man, well into his sixties. However, I knew that his money had a lot more to do with his looks than good genes. Regardless of his tune-ups, I always thought he was beautiful inside and out. "So, Lana, talk to me. What crazy situation have you gotten yourself into now?"

"Well…" I tried to decide where to begin. "Jeez, I don't even know where to start," I said, sitting on the couch.

"OK," he replied, opening the bottle of champagne and

pouring two glasses. He handed me one. "Let's start with this–it's good to see my girl!"

"And it's good to see my boy," I returned, with a giddy smile on my face. This man sure knew how to make me feel special.

"OK." I began as he sat down next to me. "So, I'm working on a crazy story, and it involves a high-profile politician. And unfortunately for me–it's not the President."

"Very funny, Lana," Gunnar said with a smile. "What's the story about?"

"It's about someone having an affair with a hooker," I said bluntly.

"So, which Congressman is sleeping around on his wife this week?" He laughed.

"It's not a member of Congress," I said.

"Okay," he said as he set the champagne glass down. "Then who is it?"

I had trouble getting the words out of my mouth and couldn't help but flinch when my mouth finally moved. "It's Gov. Richards."

"What!" Gunnar exclaimed, standing up from the couch as his jaw dropped. "I can't believe this."

"Yep."

"Lana Burke–the biggest Republican Nazi I know–is taking down Gov. Richards," Gunnar said, shaking his head.

I flashed him a dirty look.

"I'm sorry, Lana, but you have to laugh a little bit at the irony," he said with a smile as he giggled like a schoolboy.

I struggled to hold back a smile. Gunnar always knew how to make me smile.

"Okay, maybe it'd be a little easier to smile if I didn't think my life was in jeopardy," I explained to Gunnar with a serious tone. "I just had a few crazy days in Salt Lake City. My hotel room was broken into, and I think people were following me—it really freaked me out. I'm worried that I could be in serious danger."

"Deep breaths, Lana—you're okay now," Gunnar assured me. "Do you think the story is true? It seems like a stretch for Gov. Richards. He's so straight-laced."

"I agree," I said. "I met with the hooker, whose name is Celeste, and I don't know. She's not credible; however, her story has very few holes. Plus, if it weren't true, why would my hotel room get broken into? And why would government vehicles be following me?"

"Wow—I'm in shock," Gunnar said. "Do you want me to talk to the President about this?"

"Well, that's kind of why I wanted to meet with you," I explained. "I know the election will be here soon. I know the President has access to any kind of information and resources he could ever want. I'm just wondering if the President or his team knows about this."

"I haven't heard anything yet, but that doesn't mean it's not true," Gunnar said as he sipped his champagne.

"Celeste said that her house was broken into and there was nothing of value stolen. The only items that were taken were things that painted her in a bad light—a Confederate flag, a Nazi costume, photos of her wearing the costume, a Social Security card, paperwork and a few other items."

"Interesting," Gunnar said, his brow furrowed.

"I figured that either Gov. Richards's people or President Oyama's team were behind the break-in," I explained. "I know the election is creeping up on us, and what an October surprise it would be to expose Gov. Richards's affair with a hooker."

"That would be a bombshell October surprise," Gunnar

calmly said. I could see he was in deep thought.

"So, I'm wondering if the President knows about the affair–and if they're planning on leaking it in October. However, if I can get Celeste to take a poly, then the *Post* will break it."

"Will she take a one?"

"That's the problem," I said, sighing. "She agreed to take it at first, but her husband is cock-blocking her from taking it now. My story is finished. She's already done the interview; I've pulled phone records, talked to other sources. The poly is the only missing link. But if she doesn't take and pass it the lawyers will not approve the story. I can still publish it, but I'll need to get at least one more source to confirm the affair. Regardless, I'd be interested to know what President Oyama knows, and more important, what kind of danger I could be in."

"Okay," Gunnar said, puckering his lips. I could tell he was still deep in thought. "This is what I'm going to do. I'll bring this up to the President as casually as possible. I won't mention your name for your protection. I'll feel him out to find out what he knows and tell him what you've dug up on the story. I'll circle back with you next week or so. Until then, just lay low. However, I don't think you have anything to worry about. If anyone is in trouble, it's Celeste. You're not the one who had an affair with a politician."

"I know, I know. It's just that...I don't know. When I was in Salt Lake City, my gut told me that if I had stayed even one day longer, I would've been in big trouble."

"You're safe, Lana," Gunnar said reassuringly as he rubbed my back. "Now, who is this Malden fool?"

"Excuse me," I said, blushing. "Has someone been creeping on my Facebook page?"

"Me–never," he said with a smile. "Is it serious?"

"Kind of," I said, then paused.

"What does that mean?"

"Well, he told me he loved me, so, I guess yes it is," I said with a smile.

"Wow! That's quick. Didn't you just meet him a couple weeks ago?"

"No it's been several weeks," I said defensively.

"I see. Do you love him?"

"I do," I said.

Gunnar squirmed on the couch. I could tell he was a little jealous. "I'm happy for you."

"Thank you. That means a lot to me. Do you want to see a picture of him?"

"No, no, no–absolutely not," Gunnar said as he threw his hands in the air.

"Why not?"

"I'm not that happy for you," he said, shaking his head.

"You're jealous."

Gunnar remained silent as he looked at me intently.

"It's okay," I said softly. "I understand. Speaking of the devil, I need to head down to Orange County. I haven't seen him in days, and I know he's waiting for me."

"You know I'd like to keep you here for a few more hours," Gunnar said seductively.

"Well, my guess is your wife wouldn't be too happy with that, so I think this is my cue to leave. We both know what happens when we drink more than one bottle of champagne."

Gunnar laughed. The first night we had sex, we destroyed at least six bottles of champagne, probably more. By the end of the night, I found myself in his D.C. penthouse. We were dancing on his dining room table, and he literally poured champagne all over my body. I was drenched, and it was a great excuse for him to rip off all of my clothes. He did. We had sex all night.

I gave Gunnar a big hug, kissed him on the cheek and slapped him on the ass. I couldn't resist touching his cute butt one more time. I thanked him for helping me. I drove on the 10 and headed west to the 405. I tried to shake the high I felt from meeting the only other man I truly loved as much as Malden. I felt grateful that Malden was more age appropriate, and more important, available.

When I got to Malden's beach house, I found him on the back patio drinking a glass of wine and staring out into the ocean.

"Hey there," I said, putting my arms on his shoulders.

"Oh my God Lana," he said, abruptly turning around. "You scared me! Hi, baby!"

"Hi," I said. Malden stood up and wrapped his bear paws around me and kissed me passionately.

"It's so good to see you," he said as he squeezed me and looked into my eyes.

"It's good to see you, too," I said, looking away.

Malden noticed my hesitation. "What is it?" he asked, confused.

"What?" I asked, feigning innocence.

"You made a face," he said. "Is something wrong?"

"It's just that... when I was in Salt Lake City, I felt a disconnect between us," I explained. "Something felt wrong."

"Lana," Malden said as he pulled me closer and thrust his groin toward me. His cock was already hard. "The only thing that's wrong is that I haven't seen my girlfriend in ten long days. I miss you and I love you."

I smiled. "I love you too," I said, burying my face in his chest.

I was home. It felt good.

CHAPTER 13

Summer flew by like a dream and fall had arrived. Ari gave me some time off, since I dedicated so much of my time working on my big story in Winnemucca and Salt Lake City. Malden took me everywhere, and each trip was more incredible than the last. He flew me first class to his house in Port Huron, Michigan. It was Thomas Edison's old estate. I spent my mornings soaking in the summer sun on his private beach on Lake Huron while Malden and his boys landscaped the yard. The only person missing was his daughter. In the afternoons, we swam in the great lake's fresh waters. It was crystal clear, with a hint of Caribbean blue. We biked into town while the boys followed on their skateboards. At night, we barbecued on the expansive deck of the English-style home and stayed up late and played cards and board games. I even convinced the boys to sit through a screening of *The Notebook*. I caught Malden tearing up at the end of my favorite romance flick, which made my own heart flutter.

After the boys were in bed, Malden and I sat and watched the cargo ships crawl by at a snail's pace with the moon reflecting over the water. Malden took me yachting in San Diego, rafting in Tahoe and he even attended one of my best friend's weddings with me in Chicago. Everyone seemed to love him as much as I did–including my family. My father, who had always been a tough critic of all my suitors, fell in love with him too. I thought Malden's age would make my father uncomfortable, but they got along swimmingly. They bonded over their love of the military, our country and their mutual interest in aviation. Both were history buffs and had degrees in economics. They were a match made in heaven, and it was a huge relief for me. With Malden, our summer travels were straight out of a romance novel. In my mind, I was *The Bachelorette* without cameras–and Malden was my only contestant. There was no doubt that I'd be handing him the final rose at the last rose ceremony. Everything was perfect.

Despite my dreamlike holiday, one thing hung over me like a black cloud: Gov. Richards's affair. I never stopped working the story. Once I got home I checked Celeste's Facebook page a dozen times a day, like a crazed Hollywood fan, I became obsessed. I knew time wasn't on my side, and I needed to catch a break soon. Just when I felt like my story was a lost cause, I caught a break. On a rainy afternoon in my office, I finally managed to get a working number for her ex-husband and sex offender Billie Jones. I called him from my office.

"Hello," a meek male voice answered on the other end.

"Is this Billie?"

"Yes–who's this," Billie replied skeptically.

"Hi. My name is Lana Burke. I'm a journalist, and I was hoping you could help me with a story I'm working on. It involves your ex-wife, Celeste."

"You have my attention," he said.

"I'm working on a story involving a relationship she had with a high-profile figure. I know that you and Celeste aren't on the best of terms. If you could help me, I could compensate you financially."

"Okay," he said with hesitation. "But I don't need my name in no magazine."

"I totally understand that," I sympathized. "I can guarantee you complete anonymity."

"What do you need from me?"

"I need to know anything you know about her affair with Gov. Richards. Are you familiar with this?"

"Yes, I am." He sighed.

Jackpot. My heart skipped a beat.

"You know, she allegedly had an intimate relationship with him while you were married to her."

"Yep," he said. I could hear the disdain in his voice.

"Were you aware of this at the time?"

"No, I wasn't," he said sharply.

"So, how did you find out?"

"I had to hire a private investigator to help with the divorce. He uncovered a lot!"

"Really?" I asked, perking up. I quickly typed notes as fast as I could on my desktop computer.

"Yeah, Richards's name was on the report he gave me."

"Excuse me—the PI report?"

"Yes."

I tried to catch my breath. I couldn't contain my excitement. "So his name is in the report? In print?"

"Well, no not his name. It said a high-profile Republican politician. He fit the bill."

229

"Is there any way I could get a copy of this report?"

"You'd have to ask the private investigator."

"Could I get his number?"

"I don't see why not."

"Now, did you ever find any evidence that she was with him?"

"No, I didn't, but I know she bragged to some of her friends that she was fucking him."

"Do you know why the private investigator concluded that she had a connection with Gov. Richards?"

"Ugh—it was so long ago. I'm trying to think. I don't know if it was through phone records or some of the people he interviewed. I'm sorry, I'm not sure. All I know is that he was pretty certain that she had a sexual relationship with him."

I felt like a kid racing to the presents under the tree on Christmas morning. This could be the smoking gun that I needed to ensure my story would see the light of day. Billie gave me the private investigator's phone number. I called his office immediately. No answer. I left a vague message with my work and cell number. I prayed he was the answer I was looking for. Ari was thrilled. I left my office midafternoon to avoid traffic and headed straight to meet Malden at the home of his boss and company chairman, John Jacobson. I hadn't seen Malden in a few days. I couldn't wait to tell him about my new lead.

I approached the gate of John's home in an exclusive section of Newport Beach. There was a security camera and a keypad. Malden had given me the security code, so I punched it in and the gate opened. When I pulled into the long, wooded driveway, I could see breathtaking views of the Pacific Ocean. The solid brick mansion sat on a dramatic ocean side cliff. There was also a sizable guesthouse. I saw Malden's BMW motorcycle parked in the driveway. I smiled in relief and happiness. I couldn't wait to see him.

The front door was cracked open. I entered the house and immediately heard Malden's booming laughter. I loved that Malden had a good friendship with his powerful boss. There was a huge spiral staircase in front of me with an elaborate gold and crystal chandelier hanging above me.

"Hello," I shouted, resting my purse on a chair in the foyer.

"Hi, Lana," Mrs. Jacobson shouted. "We're in the kitchen."

I followed their voices to a huge, country-style kitchen that opened up to a vast family room with an inviting brick fireplace. There was a large wooden table in the open area, and Malden sat in a regal brown leather chair drinking a glass of red wine.

"Hi, baby." Malden beamed and got up to give me a hug. "I missed you."

"I know," I said, hugging him back and giving him a light kiss on the lips. "It feels like we haven't seen each other in years, even though it's only been a few days."

John also greeted me with a big hug, as did his wife. John's friend and colleague, co-chairman, Jeffrey Stern, was also at the gathering. John's teenage children were in the backyard, sitting by the pool. Mrs. Jacobson went back to working in the kitchen, making lasagna, salad, vegetables, and appetizers while I caught up with the men at the table.

"How was work today?" Malden asked, pouring me a glass of wine.

"It was good, actually," I said. "I got a promising lead today on my story."

"Really? What's the lead?" Malden asked.

"Well," I hesitated. I knew John was not only a Republican, but he also was a huge supporter of Gov. Richards. He had recently thrown a fundraiser for him. "I can tell you later."

"Wait, no, it's fine. You're in good company. John, you've got to hear about the story Lana is working on about Gov. Richards."

"If it's bad, I don't want to know," John said, shaking his head. "The country can't afford to lose another election to President Oyama."

"Well, it's not good." I sighed.

"John," Malden interjected. "You know that Lana is a diehard Republican, but she can't control what stories her boss assigns to her. She has to do her job."

"Trust me, John—there's no one who wants him to win more than I do," I assured him.

"I believe that," John said. "That's a rather difficult position you've got yourself into." John stood up and gave us a slight nod. "I'm going to go outside and smoke a cigar before dinner."

After John left the room, Jeff leaned in. "So what's the story about Gov. Richards?" he eagerly asked. "Does it involve a hooker?"

My jaw dropped.

"Why would you ask me that?" I shot back at Jeff. "Did Malden tell you what I was working on?"

"No, not at all," Jeff said. "I've helped raise money for his campaign, and I have some high-powered friends who are based in Salt Lake City. You hear things. I've heard he uses hookers. I thought it was just hearsay or rumors. Is it true?"

"Well, that's what I'm trying to figure out." I sighed.

"Lana has been working on this story for months. She's

been flying all over. She was in Nevada, then Salt Lake–I'm really proud of her. There's a woman– a hooker –who claims that she's slept with Gov. Richards." Malden said.

"Wow!" Jeff said, taking a sip of what looked like whiskey.

"The only thing is that she refuses to take a polygraph." I grunted. "Without that, the story won't see the light of day."

"So what's your new lead?" Malden asked.

"I finally talked to her ex-husband," I explained. "You know, the sex offender. He said that he heard she slept with Gov. Richards."

"No way," Malden said, raising his eyebrows. "How does he know?"

"Well, when they were getting a divorce he hired a private investigator. He said the PI uncovered an affair involving her and a high-profile Republican politician. He said it was even cited in his report. So now I'm trying to get hold of him. I left him a message this afternoon."

"Wow, that's crazy," Jeff said. "I guess I'm not surprised, though."

"Cheers babe," Malden said, raising his wineglass. "I know this has been a difficult story for you to cover, but I want to say I'm really proud of you."

"Thank you," I said, smiling.

I barely paid attention to the dinner conversation the rest of the night. I was in shock that Jeff had heard of Gov. Richards's trysts with hookers. Until tonight, I was beginning to think Celeste was totally full of shit because I still didn't have that smoking gun I needed to break the story. I had been tempted to give up on the story completely, but this was yet another lead. Malden and I stayed for a few more drinks after dinner. At around ten John announced that it was way past his bedtime.

"Before you leave, Lana, there's something I want to give you," John said, turning to walk into another room. "I'll be right back."

I was intrigued. What could the CEO of a billion-dollar company have for me? In less than five minutes, he slowly strolled back into the family room with a blue gift bag in his hands.

"I want you to have this," he said, pressing the bag into my hands.

I smiled at him and quickly looked inside. I pulled out a navy blue baseball cap that read: "Richards 2012."

"I don't know what to say," I said, laughing. "I won't be wearing this to my office, because I think my boss would have a heart attack–but thank you."

"You're welcome, Lana," John said with a smile. "Just because you're covering a story you would prefer not to–it doesn't make you any less of a Republican."

"I appreciate that," I said, offering a slight smile. "And you know what–I'm going to proudly wear this hat around in West Hollywood. I may get beat up for it, but I don't care."

"That's why I like you," he said, giving me a wink.

Malden and I tailgated back to his beach home, which was just down the street. I could not wait to curl up in bed next to him. I hadn't slept well in bed without Malden. I felt attached to Malden, and I didn't like going to bed without him next to me even when he snored loudly. I felt peace just knowing he was there, and that he would do anything to protect me.

When we got to his house, we both immediately went to his master bathroom. I was peeing in his toilet and he was picking at the facial hair he had grown since I last saw him.

"What's with the facial hair?" I asked, grabbing toilet

paper.

"Oh. I play this game with my kids where I grow out my facial hair until they tell me to shave it."

"That's an interesting game," I said sarcastically.

"Yeah, well I get these ingrown hairs that drive me nuts. Do you have a tweezers?"

"Yes, in my makeup bag on the counter."

As I sat on the toilet and watched my boyfriend pick at his ingrown hairs on his face with my tweezers, I wondered if the honeymoon phase of our relationship was over. I couldn't think of anything less sexy than sitting on a toilet and watching my boyfriend pick at his face. I wiped my crotch, walked into Malden's closet to throw on one of his T-shirts, and crawled into bed. Just when I thought we had become that boring couple, Malden was standing above me with a devious look on his face. He crawled on top of me and began to kiss my stomach. He grabbed my cotton boy shorts underwear with his teeth and slowly ripped them off. I was wet by the time my boy shorts were wrapped around my ankles.

"I want to taste you," Malden said as he slowly began to lick my clit.

"And here I thought we were skipping dessert tonight," I joked.

Malden continued to swirl his tongue around my clit. I hated going more than a day without sex with him. I rocked my pelvis back and forth to enhance the sensation. I was so horny for him. An orgasm was long overdue.

"Touch yourself on your clit while I go down on you," Malden instructed, grabbing my right hand and lowering it to my vagina.

I obeyed his orders like I always did. He licked me for what felt like hours and slowly worked his way down to my butt hole. I thought, not this again, but I didn't resist. I loved the dirty ways he touched and licked me. I began to finger myself faster as he licked my ass. I moaned over and over again—each groan louder than the last one, until I exploded. I was shaking all over, just like Malden did after he comes. I couldn't move—I was so out of breath. I felt like I had gotten the wind knocked out of me. As I tried to catch my breath, Malden stood up on his knees—that's when I saw his enormous cock sticking straight up. It was harder than ever. I had no energy, but I knew there was no way I could just roll over and go to sleep with that huge dick in my face.

Malden flipped me over and immediately started to rub his cock up and down my inner butt cheeks. He didn't waste more than a few minutes before he fully penetrated me anally. I knew he'd come quickly since he'd been anticipating a climax for over an hour now. Within minutes, I felt my ass fill up with his warm cum. I figured there was a little extra inside me, since we hadn't had sex for days. Then the aftershocks began. He shook for minutes. I just lay there until he stopped.

As Malden lay still in bed, trying to catch his breath, I went to the bathroom to wash myself off. I peed again, and I could feel his warm cum oozing out of my ass. It was such a strange and dirty sensation. But it was hot, too—in a nasty way. I sat there for minutes waiting for it all to drip out, and that's when a silver wrapper in the garbage can next to the toilet caught my eye.

My heart stopped. No! Could it be?

I swiftly reached my hand into the garbage can, and there it was: A Trojan condom wrapper. My hands literally began to shake, and my heart felt like it was going to burst out of my chest. Malden and I had never once used a condom—why would there be a condom wrapper in the garbage can? I remembered that Malden had told me that he had rented out his beach house to friends while we were away recently. I told myself to remain calm and not to jump to conclusions.

"Malden," I shouted from the bathroom.

"Yeah, babe," Malden shouted back.

"You said that you had renters here while we were away?"

"Yeah, just for a couple of days."

"Well, did your maid come after they left?"

"Yes, she came here two days ago and cleaned the entire house."

Ice ran through my veins. My heart raced faster. I felt sick. My hands were shaking uncontrollably. How could this man who claimed that he loved me cheat on me? I grabbed the condom wrapper and stormed straight into his bedroom. "Then why the fuck is there a condom wrapper in your garbage can?" I screamed at the top of my lungs as I held the condom wrapper in the air.

"What is wrong with you," Malden shouted back. "You're digging through my trash?"

"Fuck you!" I shouted with tears streaming down my face. "I didn't have to dig through your trash to find this, you idiot! It was sitting on top of your open garbage can staring at me. The fucking tin foil was glistening in the light like a fucking neon sign, you asshole!"

"How dare you accuse me of cheating in my very own house!" he yelled.

"How dare you cheat on me?" I yelled back.

"Is this your condom?" I asked as my eyes pierced into his like a laser beam.

He didn't respond. He looked away. Wow, I thought. First he tried to turn it around on me, and now he wouldn't look me in the eye. I knew from my experience as a reporter that defensiveness meant guilt. It was Journalism 101.

"Who is she? Who the fuck is she?" I demanded to know as my skin crawled.

"Lana, it was probably from the friends who stayed at my house," Malden pleaded.

"You just fucking told me the maid cleaned your entire house—you're lying," I screeched, fury exploding from my mouth like fire from a dragon.

"I don't even keep condoms in the house—you can check."

I stormed back into the bathroom and looked into every bathroom cabinet door as quickly as I possible. I slammed each one as loud as possible—each slammed door shook his house like a boom of thunder.

"What are you doing?" Malden yelled from the bedroom.

"Fuck off!" I shouted back. I couldn't find one condom. Then I remembered that early on in our relationship, I noticed that Malden had condoms in his suitcase. I didn't think anything of it at the time, because we had just started dating. We weren't in an exclusive relationship at that point. I raced toward his closet and found his black carry-on suitcase that he brought with him everywhere. There, in a side pocket—I found the same Trojan ultra-thin lubricated condoms. The reporter in me insisted that I "find the lot number" to see if the codes matched up. Sure enough, the lot number on the condoms in the suitcase matched the lot number on the condom wrapper I found in his garbage. The used condom was from the same box of condoms that was in Malden's suitcase. I wanted to die. My fairytale had just crumbled right before my eyes—I was devastated.

I raced back into his bedroom with all the condoms I found and threw them at him.

"The condom has the same lot number as the ones in your suitcase, you asshole!" I shouted, tears streaming down my face. "How could you do this to me? You told me you loved me. I went to your family reunion with you."

"You're crazy," Malden shouted back. "You're a reporter. You're paranoid."

"I'm not paranoid, and I'm also not an idiot!" I shouted as I stormed out. "And P.S., if you're going to cheat—don't date an investigative journalist! Fucking idiot!"

"You should just leave," I could hear him shout from the other room. There's nothing I wanted more than to leave, but I had a ninety-minute drive ahead of me. I was buzzed from the wine at dinner, and I was shaking so badly from shock and experiencing chest pains that I couldn't even stand up any longer. There was no way I could drive home safely.

I collapsed on his living room couch facing his floor-to-ceiling windows. I stared at the moon glistening over the ocean and found it hard to believe that just a month ago—I was lying in bed with Malden, holding hands, head over heels in love and happy, discussing our future together. I thought back to us lying in bed at his Michigan home, staring at the same moon hovering over Lake Huron. Shaken, I sat in the darkness and sobbed uncontrollably. Malden was the one man I had ever truly loved in my whole entire life. I factored him into every decision I made since I met him. I figured that for once in my thirty-two years of living, I deserved to put my personal life first even though I was still working my ass off on my story. I boasted to everyone how lucky I was to find Malden, and even said a prayer to the Lord every night thanking him for bringing him into my life.

I felt ashamed and humiliated. I had spent all summer trying to expose Gov. Richards's affair; meanwhile, my would-be beloved boyfriend was the cheater! I couldn't believe it—the joke was on me.

"What are you doing?" Malden asked, storming into the great room.

"I'm just thinking," I said in a zombie-like state. I knew our relationship was most likely over. How could we move on from this?

"Lana, it's late. I have to leave at six in the morning to go on John's jet for a business meeting in Portland for the day. Let's go to bed, or you should leave."

I slowly got up and strolled back to his bedroom with my back hunched over. I wanted to ask a thousand more questions and yell at him all night, but I felt physically handicapped. My chest hurt so much from the stress I had trouble breathing. I could barely breathe, let alone talk. I got back in his bed as far away from him as possible. I faced the wall and almost fell off the bed because I was so close to the edge. I silently prayed to God to help me get through the night. I begged him to tell me none of this was happening; it had to be one horrendous nightmare that I was due to wake up from at any moment.

At dawn, I woke to the sound of Malden rustling around the bedroom. I waited for him to say something to me. Anything. An apology. A reasonable explanation for the condom wrapper I found. He said nothing. For the first morning since our first sleepover, he left without saying goodbye and kissing me on the cheek. I was shattered. I knew I couldn't stay in his home any longer. The house that was so magical and beautiful to me was now shrouded in deceit and darkness.

I quickly dressed and took the 405 North back to Hollywood. The sun had not yet risen. I didn't even bother to turn on the radio. I drove in silence. Few cars were on the road this early. I was still a zombie. The entire drive home, my thoughts raced about Malden. Who was this man? Did he cheat? Could it have been a condom from a friend? But then—why did the lot number on the condom wrapper match the condoms in his suitcase? My heart said no—it couldn't possibly be true—but my mind said, wake the fuck up, Lana! The reporter in me knew it was true.

I got back to my Weho apartment by seven-thirty in the morning. I headed for my bed and set my alarm to wake me in an hour. I fell back asleep. When I woke up, I took a two-minute shower. I got dressed, and I didn't put any effort into my appearance. I didn't blow dry my hair or put on any makeup. I put on a pair of skinny jeans, sandals and a green blouse. I looked like shit, and I felt worse. The rage was starting to kick in. I cut off at least three people on my way to work and blew through one red light. I stormed straight up to my office and didn't even say hello to the doorman in the lobby of my office building. I don't think I've ever done that.

When I got to my office, I immediately closed the door. I opened my e-mail and tried to bury myself in work, but I couldn't. I couldn't help but wonder who the other woman was. How did Malden have the time to have an affair? We were almost always together. Was it a one-time fling, or was he in a relationship with someone else too? I reminded myself that it couldn't be possible because of all the time I had spent with him and his family.

I quickly went on Malden's Facebook page. I couldn't believe it—he had already posted five photos of him and John on the jet traveling to their business meeting in Portland. In one caption of the two of them on the private plane Malden wrote: "Superiority!"

I instantly felt sick. Not only had Malden just shattered

my heart into a million pieces, but also now he was gloating on Facebook? I was horrified. Who the fuck is this man? Moreover, who does he think I am? I certainly was not a doormat—and I'd be damned if he thought otherwise.

The ring of my office phone broke me out of my angry trance. "Hello," I answered sharply.

"Is this Lana Burke?" A deep male voice asked on the other line.

"Yes—who's this?" I asked with an edge of bitchiness.

"This is Kipp Schmidt, the private investigator, – I believe you called."

"Oh yes, hi," I said, immediately softening my tone. "Thank you so much for calling me back. I'm working on a story that I was hoping you could help me with. One of your clients told me that you had uncovered some information about my subject. I was hoping you could help me."

"I'm sorry, miss, but I sign a confidentiality agreement with all my clients," Kipp explained.

"I understand that completely," I said as I racked my brain. "But what if your client gives you permission to give me the report?"

"I guess I could possibly make an exception."

"It's Billie Jones," I said. "I'm working on a story involving his ex-wife, Celeste and Gov. Richards. He said that you had uncovered some information about their affair."

"Oh, Billie," he said. "Yes, I remember that case. It was so long ago. At least one or two years ago."

"Were you able to prove a connection between Gov. Richards and Celeste?" I eagerly asked.

"I remember some chatter about her and Gov. Richards," he slowly admitted.

"What do you mean chatter—did you find any evidence

242

linking them together? Maybe phone records?"

"I don't recall anything like that." He sighed. "If I recall correctly, some of her hooker friends told me that she bragged of an affair with Gov. Richards. I was able to put them in the same hotel at the same time, but no smoking gun."

I shut my eyes in defeat. I needed concrete proof; a bunch of hookers spreading rumors didn't mean jack shit–especially to the company's lawyers. Opening my eyes, I said, "All right– well, what about the report? Is there any way you could get that to me?"

"I'm not sure," he said reluctantly. "I switched offices a year ago and lost a lot of files."

"OK, how about this–if the client signs off, will you at least consider it?" I begged. "I will compensate you for your time. I'll send you a contract."

"I'll tell you what–I'll think about it. But I don't think what you're looking for will be in the report. Just some interviews with washed-up hooker friends of hers. If I recall correctly, one shot up heroin during my interview with her."

"Good Lord." I sighed. "OK–I appreciate your honesty, but please think about it. I might find something in that report that could help me find what I'm looking for."

I hung up the phone and rubbed the temples of my forehead in frustration due to yet another roadblock with my story. My head pounded and I felt nauseated. Today sucked. I glanced at my computer and noticed that Malden's jet photos had eleven "likes" on Facebook. All of them were from women, except for one. My skin began to crawl. I growled at the computer as I stared at the women who liked his photos. They all looked like overweight homely housewives. Could one of these women be the culprit?

CHAPTER 14

It was dusk on Saturday evening. I lay on the floor of my living room, wearing Malden's Berkeley T-shirt. I wasn't sure why I threw on his T-shirt. I was angry with him, but I also missed him. My emotions were so mixed. I felt like a three-ring circus. I had not left my apartment in twenty-four hours and had popped four Xanax the night before. I had exchanged a few texts with Giselle revealing that Malden had cheated. However, I kept missing her calls. I was passed out cold every time she called me, and when I called her back she didn't answer. My phone rang. It was Giselle. Finally, I was able to answer.

"Hey," I answered in defeat.

"Lana, how are you doing?" she asked with concern. "Have you left your place at all today?"

"Nope." I sighed.

"Ugh, Lana—I'm so sorry," she said.

My eyes began to fill with tears. "I just don't understand how he could do this to me," I cried. "I love him so much!"

"I know you do," Giselle said sympathetically. "Look, I'm

not here to make excuses for him. However, to play devil's advocate, the two of you have only been dating a few months. Do you think you can get past this if he comes clean? You guys aren't engaged or married, you know?"

"I know that if he doesn't come clean, I could never move forward with him. If he owned up to what he did, and it never happens again, I do think I could get past this. Unfortunately, his cheating on me doesn't change the fact that I love him."

"Well, hang in there. He does seem to be Mr. Self-Reflective. I'm sure you'll hear from him in a few days. Do you want me to come over? We can watch bad Lifetime movies all night."

"I appreciate that, but no thanks." I sighed. "I just want to be alone."

I hung up, popped another Xanax, and crawled back into bed. I slept through the entire weekend in a Xanax coma. I felt too ill from heartache to move. Days without talking to Malden felt like an eternity. I was used to talking to him a dozen times a day. Finally, on Monday morning, I got a text from Malden while I was in the office.

Malden Murphy: "I miss you."

Malden sent a photo of the Golden Gate Bridge along with the text. I figured he was in San Francisco visiting the children for the weekend. The second I got his text, all the anger and rage I felt for him evaporated. I caved immediately and texted him back right away.

Lana Burke: "I miss you too."

Within minutes, my phone rang. It was Malden. My heart stopped. I picked up the phone after three rings.

"Hello," I said reluctantly.

"Lana, I-I..." Malden stammered nervously on the other end. I could tell his voice was shaking. "I don't know what to say...I miss you."

"I miss you too," I responded.

"I–I'm so sorry," he said softly.

"I need to know the truth," I said sternly. "Did you cheat on me?"

"Yes," he said hesitantly. "I did."

I composed myself the best I could, and told myself that I needed to handle the situation as maturely as possible.

"Are you dating this person, too?" I asked, sucking in my breath.

"No, of course not. It was a mistake. I am not in love with this person–I love you."

"Who is she?"

"She's a person I've been friends with for several years. She's a single mom who lives in Sacramento. She was in town for business and had no one to hang out with."

"Did she spend the night with you?"

"Yes, but she wasn't supposed to," he said. "We had some drinks, and one thing led to another. Lana, I've been single for ten years–you're the first person I've loved since my ex-wife. I screwed up. Can you find it in your heart to forgive me?"

"All right, here's the deal," I said. "I thought we were in an exclusive relationship, but clearly we weren't on the same page. I'm telling you right now, I'm not interested in an open relationship with you. You've been single for ten years, and you've lived the life of a bachelor the entire time. With that said, maybe you're just not capable of being with one person. If that's the case, that's fine. We can be friends, but I can't date you. I love you too much to share you. However, if you can be with only me, we can try to work this out, but I will not be with a person who's going to cheat on me."

"Lana, I'm so relieved to hear you say that—you have no idea. Of course, I can be with one person; you're the only person I want to be with. I love you."

I exhaled a deep sigh of relief too. The thought of losing Malden was unbearable.

"Look, I'm driving home from San Francisco right now. I need to come back here this weekend. Mark's football team is playing this Friday night. I'd like for you to come with me. Please say yes."

"OK," I whispered.

"I love you," Malden said.

"I love you too," I said and hung up the phone.

I felt a mixture of relief and paranoia. I so badly wanted to believe Malden when he said he'd never cheat again, but I knew damn well especially—considering the nature of my business—that once a cheat, always a cheat.

I muscled through the rest of the day at work with a little more focus now that I had talked with Malden. But I still found my mind wandering and my fingers clicking on his Facebook page. I scrolled through photos of every woman on his friends list. I desperately wanted to find this bitch, but I couldn't find one woman from Sacramento. As if I didn't have enough problems, I found myself scratching my crotch all afternoon and making frequent trips to the bathroom. I could tell I had a urinary tract infection coming on or maybe a yeast infection. Or both.

I booked a doctor's appointment for nine in the morning.

On my way home, I picked up a box of over-the-counter yeast infection medication, hoping it would relieve my symptoms. When I got home, I squeezed the tube of white cream up into my vagina. My vagina was irritated, and even my ass felt raw. Could I have an infection in my ass from the anal sex?

By the next morning, the pain I felt in my crotch had worsened. The medicine did not relieve my symptoms at all. If anything, the cream exacerbated the problem. I got to my doctor's office in a white, high-rise building on the Sunset Strip on time. I was not looking forward to the appointment.

In the exam room, I got naked and threw on a flimsy cotton gown while I waited for my seventy-five-year-old doctor. He entered the room with my chart in hand. He was wearing a traditional doctor's coat and thick glasses. He had wrinkled skin probably from too much time in the California sun.

"Hi Lana." He smiled as he came in. "What brings you in here today?"

"Hi," I responded softly. "I'm concerned I have some kind of a vaginal infection. I thought I might have a yeast infection, but the medicine I bought from the drug store just seems to make it worse."

"What are your symptoms?"

"I have a white discharge," I said, ashamed. I could feel the blood rush to my face. "I'm really itchy down there. I'm peeing frequently. It feels like I have both a yeast infection and a UTI."

"Well, I'm sure that's all it is. You just need something more powerful than over-the-counter medicine."

"Yeah," I said. "But there's something else—I just found out my boyfriend cheated on me. Do you think it's possible I could have an STD?"

"We can certainly give you STD tests," he said calmly.

I instantly remembered that I still had not filled out those damn insurance forms Nigel had been pestering me to complete for months now. I had gotten so wrapped up on my story and relationship with Malden, that it completely slipped my mind. I wanted to kick myself in the ass.

"Well, here's the thing, I switched jobs recently, and my new insurance hasn't kicked in yet. They told me it'd take a few months. How much would that cost me out of pocket?" I didn't want to admit that the fact I didn't have insurance yet was due to my procrastination.

"At least a few hundred dollars," he said. "How about this—I can write you a script for oral antibiotics and a topical cream. That combination will kill any vaginal infection and should kill the UTI. If that doesn't do the trick, come back in a few days, and then we'll test you for everything."

"OK." I sighed. "There's one more thing I want to tell you, but it's really embarrassing."

"Yes," he said as he wrote the script.

I blushed. "My boyfriend and I have a lot of…anal sex." I cringed.

"OK," he said as he looked up from his notepad.

"Well, I feel irritated, you know, in that area too – what does that mean?"

"You could have bacterial vaginosis and it just spread to that region as well, but I can look down there if you want."

I wanted to kill myself. The last thing I wanted was a seventy-five-year-old man looking up my butt hole, but I knew I would feel better if he did. I was becoming paranoid I had some crazy anal disease from all the backdoor sex I was having.

"OK." I sighed as I flipped over.

I could feel his cold and wrinkly hands grab my ass and squeeze apart my butt cheeks. Oh God no–please God, tell me that this is not happening. I cringed as sweat formed on the brim of my forehead. I was mortified. I reminded myself that I needed to find a new doctor who was female!

"Lana, everything looks fine–I think you're going to be just fine," he said, placing my gown back over my butt.

"Really?" I said, flipping back over. I felt relieved–but wait, did I just have this old man look at my asshole for nothing? I felt so humiliated.

I went straight to the drug store after my appointment to pick up my medicine and then headed to work. The doctor had written a script for Bactrim and for a topical cream, MetroGel. I went to the bathroom when I got to my office. I popped a Bactrim and rubbed the cream all over my vagina and ass in a stall. The cream gave me some relief almost instantly.

The rest of the week flew by. Malden called and texted me as if everything was back to normal–but the cheating scandal hung over my head like a big black cloud. On Friday, Malden had planned to pick me up from the office at noon in an attempt to avoid traffic on our way to San Francisco. It was an otherwise mundane morning at work, until I noticed a status pop-up on my Facebook page. It was Celeste, and she had posted a message about getting a divorce. It was the news I had been waiting to hear for a long time.

Celeste Homan: "I have kept my mouth quiet for a long-ass fucking time, but when your loser husband punches you in the face and throws all your shit in the front yard it's time to get a divorce. Asshole!"

I raced into Ari's office giddy with excitement. "Ari—I have a new development on Celeste!" I shouted as I flung his door open. I didn't even bother to knock.

"Yes, Lana," he said as he pushed his glasses to the top of his nose and inspected a mockup of next week's cover story.

"It's Celeste," I said breathlessly. "She's getting a divorce. She just posted it on her Facebook page."

"Really!" Ari said, raising his eyebrows.

"Yes!"

"This is great news! Try calling her and messaging her on Facebook. We should really send you back to Winnemucca tonight, though—are you free this weekend?"

"I'm actually leaving in a few hours to go to San Francisco with my boyfriend," I said reluctantly. I considered canceling, but I knew this weekend was important for Malden and me to rebuild our relationship, so I hesitated.

"You know, Mick is on duty, I can fly him out for the night. We need to get her on a plane to take a poly. Are you back by Monday in case I need you to take her to the polygraph test?"

"Absolutely," I said with a confident smile.

I hurried back into my office and tried calling Celeste from my office phone. Her number was out of order. That didn't shock me. I went to my keyboard and quickly punched out a message to her on Facebook.

Lana Burke: "Hi Celeste! Long time no talk. I'm sorry to hear that you're getting a divorce. Maybe we can talk about finishing the business deal we started together. I'd like to see you get your check."

I knew it was sneaky to throw in a line about the money, but I knew she probably was desperate for cash right now. Mick managed to book an afternoon flight back to Winnemucca. I assured him that I'd be available to help him by phone. Just as I was about to leave the office, I got a text from Gunnar.

Gunnar Smith: "I spoke to the President and his associates a few times about Gov. Richards's affair. I can't get any info. No one seems to know anything about it. I'll keep trying though."

I wasn't sure what to make of Gunnar's text. If the President knew about Gov. Richards's affair–which potentially could be their big October surprise–would they really relay the information to a tabloid journalist?

Lana Burke: "Thanks for all your help."

Noon arrived before I knew it. I promptly turned off my computer and grabbed my Louis Vuitton duffle bag and headed to the parking lot. When I got there, I saw Malden sitting in his navy blue Expedition with the engine running. I got butterflies in my stomach, as I hadn't seen him since our explosive fight. I didn't know what to expect. I threw my bag in the trunk and hopped in the passenger front seat.

"Hi, baby," Malden said quickly, putting the phone down. "Mark's on the phone. He wants to talk to you."

I could tell Malden was anxious to see me. I couldn't help but wonder if he staged the call to his son to create a diversion from the mess in our relationship that he had created. He knew I adored Mark. I shared some small talk with Mark for a minute and told him that we were really excited to watch him play at his football game that night. It was obvious that Mark had no idea that his dad had been found guilty of cheating on me. When I got off with Mark, I forced a smile at Malden as I handed his phone back.

"Come here," Malden said, leaning over and wrapping his arms around me. When he planted a kiss on the top of my head, tears filled my eyes.

"This is so hard," I said as my voice cracked. "You really broke my heart."

"I know," Malden said as he stroked my hair. "I'm so sorry. It really scares me how much I love you. These past few days have been horrible without you. I can't believe how much I missed you. I promise it will never happen again."

I pulled back to wipe away my tears. Malden turned onto Wilshire Boulevard, and we were off. We carried on like we always did during our road trips. I filled Malden in on what was going on with work. I updated him on Celeste's divorce and how Mick was en route to Winnemucca with a goal to finally convince her to take the poly.

"We might have to leave San Francisco early Sunday to take this hooker to dinner Sunday night," I informed Malden.

"Oh really." Malden laughed. "That will make for a great story. You know it's Fleet Weekend in San Francisco this weekend."

"Really?" I said as my face lit up.

"Yeah."

"Oh my God I love watching the Blue Angels. I didn't realize it was this weekend. We have to watch the air show."

"Whatever you want, Lana." Malden smiled.

A few hours passed during our drive north, I began to feel more and more uncomfortable in my crotch area again. I had been on medicine for almost four days now and my vagina still itched like a bitch. I had already taken a Bactrim earlier, but I took another one in the hopes that it would relieve the itching. I couldn't understand why my UTI was lingering. In the past, infections had cleared up within hours of taking my first prescription pill. The unrelenting vaginal pain made me really nervous. My phone beeped, breaking my chain of obsessive thoughts over my pain. We were just an hour outside of San Francisco, and we were headed straight to Mark's football game.

Mick Madden: "Hey Lana–I just landed in Winnemucca. I'm going straight to Celeste's before I check into my hotel. It won't be the same without you."

Lana Burke: "Ha, ha! I can't say I'm too bummed I'm not there with you–sorry, chief. However, if you get lonely, I can recommend a few brothels you can swing by."

Mick Madden: "Very funny. I'll be hitting up Carmachea's for a steak–that's the only meat in this town that won't expose me to a disease, I hope."

Lana Burke: "Gross! Keep me posted on Celeste. Good luck."

I put my phone down and turned on the radio. I found a news channel on the AM dial. "Today's Gallup Poll has Gov. Richards beating President Oyama in a nationwide poll by seven percent with a five percent margin," the female voice announced.

My stomach sank. The election was just around the corner. November was only a few weeks away. My story was becoming a big reality again.

"Why are you so quiet?" Malden asked as he snacked on walnuts that we had picked up at a gas station along the way.

"I'm just thinking about my story and what will happen if it comes out–how it could change the election," I said, gazing out the window as we passed one strip mall after another. Traffic had lightened up a bit.

"Well, Lana, you're just doing your job. It will work out."

"Yeah," I whispered under my breath with uncertainty.

We finally arrived at Mark's high school a little after the game started. We parked on a dark side street and followed the bright stadium lights all the way to the football field. Malden and I grabbed a burger and soft drinks before we made our way into the stands. I kept my eyes peeled for Bethenny, but I saw no sign of her. Malden and I cozied up in-between the parents' of his son's friend, who was the star quarterback. I hadn't been to a high school football game since I was actually in high school. I knew that my Friday nights wouldn't always consist of attending fabulous Hollywood parties, but I never thought that I'd be attending a high school football game to cheer on someone who wasn't my child. My thin leather jacket barely kept me warm against the chill. Malden put his arm around me and kept rubbing my arms to keep me warm. I barely moved I was so cold. I felt my phone vibrating in my back pocket, and I quickly pulled it out to read the message.

Mick Madden: "I found her. She agreed to do the poly. Call me."

I gasped.

"What is it?" Malden asked.

"The hooker–she agreed to take the poly," I screeched.

"Wow!"

"I've got to call Mick," I said, jumping off the steel bench. "I'll be back."

I ran down the steps of the riser and raced toward the

main building of the high school to find a quiet spot. I finally found an open women's bathroom. The mirrors were faded, and the walls were a light discolored yellow. I was alone, though. I quickly called Mick.

"Hey," he said cheerfully.

"Is it true?" I eagerly asked. "Is she really going to take the poly?"

"Yep," Mick said. "I tracked her down at her parents' house. I got her eager to talk to me because I told her Steve never died in the car accident. She seemed shocked by this as we suspected. Anyway, Celeste said she'd fly back to L.A. with me Sunday night. Tomorrow I'm going to take her to dinner and try my best to keep her happy."

"Wow—I can't believe it. I'm in shock. I'm shaking over here," I said as my heart pounded in my chest. "So, this is it? After the poly, the story will be ready to go in time to hit newsstands before the election?"

"Exactly—it looks like our guy Gov. Richards is screwed."

"Ugh, I don't know how I feel about this." I sighed. "I'm going to have a lot of guilt if Gov. Richards loses."

"Well, Lana, what can you do. It's the nature of the business we're in. You just have to roll with it."

"Yeah," I said sadly. "I guess."

"Look, I have to check into my crappy hotel, let's chat tomorrow. I'll keep you posted. Have fun in San Francisco."

"OK. Thanks. Have a good night."

I put my phone in my back pocket, pushed my back up against the wall in the bathroom and fell to the ground like a little kid. The tears began to stream down my face. What had I done? This is it. Gov. Richards could lose the election, and it will be my fault! I crossed my arms over my bent knees and put my head down as I wept. Guilt overcame me like a deadly cancer spreading throughout my body. I slowly pulled my phone out and decided it was finally time to confess my secret to Mary Posas.

Mary was my longtime friend from Chicago who had lived next door to me since I was a newborn. Our family became close with her family. I'm a best friend to her daughter, and Mary is like a second mother to me. I had confessed to my parents about my bombshell story involving Gov. Richards and the hooker, but I hadn't told Mary. Mary and I were like two peas in a pod. We were both obsessed with politics, conspiracy theories–and more important, our shared disdain for President Oyama. We'd sit and drink wine and talk on the phone for hours complaining about all the things he was doing wrong for our country. She was the one person who may have loathed the President more than I did. I loved and adored Mary so much, but I was afraid that she would lose respect for me if she knew that I'd been working on a bombshell exposé on Gov. Richards. I felt compelled to call her and finally confess my secret. I pulled up her number and hit the call button.

"Hi, Lana," a happy Mary answered on the other line. "I haven't heard from you in a while. How are you?"

"Mary," I said as my voice trembled. "I'm not good. There's something I need to tell you that's been sitting on my conscience. I'm worried I did something wrong."

"OK, calm down, Lana. You can talk to me. What is it?"

"It's this story I've been working on all summer," I explained, wiping the snot from my nostrils. "It's about someone I care about. I've been conflicted about doing the story, but I felt like I had no choice but to do it in order to keep my job."

"Well, it can't be that bad," Mary said calmly.

"It's about a politician–someone we support," I said reluctantly.

"What? Is another senator coming out of the closet?" Mary asked with her warm and infectious laugh.

"No, worse–it's about Gov. Richards," I said.

"OK, well–what is the story about?"

"He-he had an affair," I stammered. "With a prostitute."

"Oh, I don't believe that, Lana–Gov. Richards? Come on. I think someone has you going," she said with authority.

"I don't think so. I've worked on it all summer. We just need the prostitute to take a polygraph and pass it. She just agreed to take it. If she passes, then the story comes out before the election. I'm having all these horrible regrets. I don't want to be responsible for him losing the election. It's such an important election for this country. I have so much guilt."

"OK, calm down, Lana–take a deep breath," Mary said soothingly.

I took in the biggest breath I could and exhaled slowly. I noticed my crotch was starting to itch again, but I was too preoccupied to dwell on it.

"Lana, I don't know the details of this story you're working on. I do know that you are a loyal Republican–you want Gov. Richards to win as much as I do. But you also have a job. I know you, and you would not be a journalist if you didn't go after this story like you would any other story."

"I know," I said, tears streaming down my face. "But this is different. What if Gov. Richards loses? What happens then? We're going to turn into a socialist country and lose a lot of the freedoms our Founding Fathers fought for us to have. How can I live with that?"

"You know what my answer to that is?" Mary asked with

an angelic tone.

"What?"

"I've come to realize—you've got to have trust in God," she explained, in an unusually peaceful tone I had never heard in her voice before. "You know, I used to get very worked up about these elections and President Oyama, but I realize it's not worth it. You have to have faith and trust in God. You need to believe he has a plan."

I couldn't believe it. I thought Mary was going to disown me. I had never heard her talk about President Oyama or politics so calmly before. I wasn't sure what had come over her, but something was different about her in a positive way. I was relieved.

"So you don't think I'm a horrible person for doing this story?"

"Of course not." Mary laughed. "Just promise me you'll trust in God."

I promised. Mary and I wrapped up our conversation. I headed back to the game. I felt like hundred-pound weights had been lifted from my chest—I was so relieved that Mary was not upset with me. Her words gave me peace and comfort. I kept repeating in my mind her message with the sound of her voice: "Trust in God."

Mark's team won twenty-one to seven. We quickly congratulated him before heading back to Malden's Piedmont house. We invited Mark to join us, but he wanted to celebrate at a local pizza joint with his teammates instead. By the time we got to Malden's place, it was only eleven at night, but I was beat. I was emotionally exhausted from working the story and traveling all afternoon. Besides, my vagina continued to burn, and I felt drowsy from the antibiotics.

"I can't wait to fall asleep in your arms tonight—it's been

awful sleeping without you," Malden said as we changed out of our clothes and got ready for bed.

"Me too. But look, there's something I've got to tell you," I said nervously. I knew Malden had big plans for us to fuck all night, but the idea of having sex made me want to vomit. My vagina felt so itchy and sore–there was no way I could engage in any kind of sex.

"What's wrong?" Malden asked with a look of concern.

"I think," I slowly mustered. "I think I have a UTI. I'm on medicine for it, and I'm really uncomfortable. I just can't have sex right now."

A look of fear crept into Malden's dark blue eyes. His jaw dropped. "Are you OK?"

"Yeah, I'll be fine. I just don't want to have sex."

"I understand. That's no problem. I'm just happy to cuddle up next to my snuggle bug."

I smiled, crawled into bed and within seconds Malden's bear paws were wrapped around my chest. He kept kissing me on the head and stroking my hair. I felt at peace and at home again. The thoughts of his affair tried to creep back into my mind, but I kept pushing them out. No – we can get past this! - the voice screamed in my mind. This man is my soul mate and this little bump in the road will only make us stronger. It wasn't long before I was sound asleep in Maldenland.

"Mother fucker!" I screamed in agony, grabbing my vagina. It was three in the morning and I was sitting on the toilet. The pain was unbearable. It felt like someone had poured a full bottle of Tabasco sauce in my vagina. I tried to urinate, but nothing would come out. I was in so much pain. I had had some severe UTIs in the past, but nothing like this. Tears rolled down my face. I rocked back and forth on the toilet. I felt so helpless. I didn't know what to do to make myself feel better. I slowly glided my bare ass off the seat and lay down on the freezing cold white marble tiles in Malden's master bathroom in the affluent San Francisco suburb. I still held my crotch. If I put pressure on my vagina, it slightly alleviated the unbearable pain. I lay there, helpless and crying. I couldn't take the pain for one more second.

I crawled back to Malden's bedroom. It was dark, and he was sound asleep cuddled under his brown comforter.

"Malden–wake up!" I said, shaking his shoulder with my right hand. My left hand continued to grab my crotch. He slowly rolled over and opened his eyes.

"What is it?" he asked, bolting up. He turned on the lamp on his nightstand table.

"I need to see a doctor or go to an emergency room–something's really wrong!" Tears were rolling down my face.

"What do you mean–I don't understand."

"My fucking pussy–it's on fire! The pain is unbearable. I can't sleep."

And there it was. That look of fear that I had seen in Malden's eyes just a few hours ago was back. Why? I hopped over to Malden's oak dresser and grabbed my purse. I was walking like an old lady. I could not even stand up straight, and I kept my hand on my crotch. I whipped out my cell phone and immediately Googled twenty-four-hour clinics.

"OK we'll take you to a doctor first thing in the morning," Malden calmly said.

"I don't know if I can wait that long. I'm in so much pain!"

I pulled up several walk-in clinics in the Bay Area on my iPhone. However, none of them were open twenty-four hours.

"God damn it!" I shouted out loud.

"What is it?" Malden asked.

"There are no twenty-four-hour clinics. The earliest one opens is at nine in the morning. It's in Corte Madera," I said in defeat. "Maybe I should go to the emergency room."

"Lana, we can go first thing in the morning. We'll get there before it opens, and we'll be the first people there," Malden said lovingly.

"That's five hours away. I just don't know if I can wait that long."

"If you can't then we'll go to the hospital," Malden said.

I sat on the bed, still holding my crotch. Malden rubbed my back. I slowly leaned back on his pillows and tried to close my eyes. Five hours, Lana, only five hours of your life. You can do this. I sat in bed and prayed to God to get me through the next five hours.

Malden and I were up by eight in the morning. I threw on jeans, Uggs, a white V-neck T-shirt, and a blue Chicago Cubs cap. I put on zero makeup and didn't even bother to brush my hair. Malden and I barely talked all morning. The pain had subsided slightly, but I was still miserable.

When we pulled up at the clinic, there was a Hispanic man waiting outside. We arrived fifteen minutes before it opened. I figured he was another patient with a medical emergency. Malden and I sat in his Expedition until the doors to the clinic opened. It was a small white building that looked like a house in an upper class suburb of San Francisco. There was a strip mall with a Rite Aid across the street.

As soon as the door opened, I got out of Malden's car without saying a word. He slowly followed behind me. Once inside, I noticed an overweight black woman with long, curly black hair and thick, dark glasses sitting at the front desk. Her boobs were so huge they literally rested on the desk.

"How can I help you?" she asked cheerfully when I approached. I was in so much pain; I could barely open my eyes and mouth. I felt like a bus had just hit me. Malden stood a couple of feet behind me and said nothing.

"Hi, I thought I had a UTI. I'm on medicine for it, and last night my infection got so bad I couldn't sleep. I'm in a severe amount of pain." I said.

"OK honey, I'll need your insurance card, and you'll need to fill out this form," she said as she handed me a clipboard.

"Well, I don't have insurance right now. It hasn't kicked in yet at my new job, so I'll be paying out of pocket."

Those insurance forms that were back in L.A. sitting on my desk continued to haunt me wherever I went.

"You know what," Malden said as he approached the counter. "I'm her boyfriend, and I do have insurance. If she has some kind of an STD, I must have it too. Why don't you guys test me instead? Whatever she has, I must have too."

"We can do that," she said as she glared at him with a stink eye. I wondered what she was thinking. I was so embarrassed. "I'll need you both to fill out these forms. When you're done, bring them back, and the doctor will call you in when he's ready."

I slowly walked to a chair in the corner and sat down. Malden lingered at the front desk. He was whispering to the receptionist. I couldn't hear what he was saying. He grabbed his clipboard and sat down in a chair across the room from me. Wait, *across* the room from me? This is a man who can't bear sitting more than a few inches away from me when we are together and now he's sitting across the room from me? It made my heart beat quicker. What was he hiding from me? What in the world was he writing down on those medical forms that he did not want me to see? I wanted to shout at him: "What's wrong with you?" However, I didn't have the energy. I felt so sick, just holding the pen was painful.

The doctor called me close to an hour later. It felt like an eternity. When I went back to the exam room, Malden just sat there. He didn't even look up when I walked out of the waiting room. I couldn't believe he wasn't coming into the room with me. Who was this person I had fallen in love with?

When I got into the exam room, I put my purse on the floor and slowly climbed onto the exam table. I barely could lift my ass up high enough to sit on the elevated table properly. I could hear the paper-lining crinkle as I struggled to get comfortable.

"Hi, Lana–I'm Dr. Phil Nguyen," he said. He was an Asian man. He had a shaved head and thin, clear glasses. He had a friendly presence, which made me feel a little more comfortable. "What brings you here today?"

"Hi, doctor," I said, out of breath from pain. "I've had vaginal symptoms for days. My doctor in L.A.–I'm not from here we're just visiting for the weekend–prescribed me MetroGel and Bactrim. He thought I had a UTI and a yeast infection. However, it's been days, and my infection has gotten way worse. I couldn't sleep last night. I'm in a ton of pain. I'm very worried. My boyfriend, who is also here, just cheated on me. I'm scared he's given me an STD."

"OK–do you have vaginal discharge?"

"Yes. But it's not like the kind you get from a yeast infection. It's thinner. It's almost as thin as water–not thick like yeast."

"And on a scale of one to ten, what is the vaginal burning like?"

"It's about one hundred – I have never felt pain down there like this in my life. I can barely walk."

"OK, here's the deal. If you've been treated with Bactrim and MetroGel—that would've knocked out most vaginal infections and UTIs. I think there are two possibilities here. You either have a UTI that has spread to your kidneys or you have an STD. You're showing symptoms for chlamydia or gonorrhea."

"OK," I said. "So, what do I need to do?"

"I can give you a whole battery of STD tests right now; however, the problem is that those test results will not come back for a week and you don't even live here."

"Doctor, please," I begged. "I need something immediately to put me out of this pain. Plus, I don't have health insurance now, so I don't want to have to pay for a ton of tests."

"This is what I can do. I can give you a Rocephin shot. That will wipe out a UTI that's spread to your kidneys and gonorrhea. I can also write you a script for Lidocaine and Doxycycline. That will wipe out chlamydia. But I need to warn you, the Rocephin shot is intense. You may develop flulike symptoms from it as a result, such as a fever."

"I don't fucking care. I'm willing to do whatever it takes to alleviate the pain. I'm miserable. Is there a painkiller you can give me too?"

"I can write you a script for Vicodin too if that would help you," he said.

"Oh, thank God. Thank you so much."

"I'll be back with the nurse to give you the Rocephin shot. Meanwhile, I'm going to have a chat with your boyfriend. I need to ask him if he has any STDs."

I closed my eyes in humiliation. "OK, thank you."

I felt like a pathetic loser. What happened to my Prince Charming? I went from being on top of the world and in love with a man who I believed was perfect—to sitting in the Marin County Medical Clinic with a boyfriend who wouldn't even escort me into the exam room. My brain felt fried. I couldn't process the situation. I felt out of my body. This wasn't my life. I was watching a Lifetime movie—a really, really bad Lifetime movie.

Minutes passed before the Dr. Nguyen returned with a nurse. It felt like an eternity as I lay on the cold examination table, holding my crotch the entire time.

"OK Lana, we're going to inject the shot into your lower back," the doctor instructed. "Can you stand up please and unzip your pants?"

"But what did my boyfriend say? Did you ask him if he has an STD?"

"He said he doesn't have any STDs that he's aware of and he's asymptomatic."

I felt slightly relieved to hear that, but I was still skeptical. I slowly pushed my body up and placed my feet on the floor. I tried to lower my body off the table, but I almost collapsed.

"Are you OK?" Dr. Nguyen asked as he grabbed my arm.

"Yeah, I'm just a little dizzy," I said, catching my breath. Every small move my body made was a huge challenge. Whenever I tried to move an arm or a muscle, it was like swimming through black tar.

I slowly unzipped my jeans and pulled them down, but kept them high enough so that I wasn't flashing the doc my pussy.

"So, which ass cheek do you want?" I asked.

"Um, er, we can inject the shot into your left side," the doctor said. "You can hold onto the nurse for support. Now I need to warn you, this shot will most likely make you more dizzy and faint. It may sting a little bit too. Also, don't be alarmed if you come down with a fever later today. As I mentioned before, it's known for giving patients flulike symptoms."

"Great," I said sarcastically, suddenly I felt the needle enter my left side. "Just what I fucking need–oh God Jesus Christ! That hurts like a bitch!"

"Almost done, Lana, don't move," Dr. Nguyen said calmly.

"Mother fucker!"

"Done."

The room began to spin again. I felt my knees go weak.

"Lana, sit down," Dr. Nguyen said as he slowly placed me back on the table. "Do you want some water?"

"OK," I whispered, again out of breath. My head was in a fog. I felt nauseated and the room would not stop spinning. I lay down.

"Why don't you lay here for a few minutes," Dr. Nguyen said as he handed me a glass of water. "I'll write up your scripts."

"Vicodin…" I mumbled.

"Excuse me?" Dr. Nguyen said as he swiveled around on his stool with wheels.

"Painkillers. Please don't forget to write me a script for that too." I knew in my heart that I would not be able to get through the day without painkillers. The pain came in waves, but at its peak, it felt unbearable!

After sweating and moaning my way through the pain and dizziness in the exam room, I slowly collected my belongings and walked out to the waiting area. No Malden in sight. Where was he?

"Are you ready to check out, honey?" the receptionist asked sympathetically. I'm sure I looked awful. I had sweat stains on my shirt, and I was certain I smelled.

"Yeah, I guess so," I said. "Is my boyfriend in an exam room getting tests done?"

"No, he walked out a bit ago," she said. "I'm not sure where he is."

"Uh okay," I said in frustration. How could he leave me here?

"It'll be five hundred and twenty-two dollars," she said.

"Five hundred and twenty two dollars!" I said. "Jesus."

"Well, since you don't have insurance…"

"Yeah, yeah, I know," I said sharply. Where the hell was my boyfriend and why the hell wasn't he paying for my visit?

When I walked outside, I saw Malden sitting on a bench. The sun was beaming down on him, and there wasn't a cloud in the sky. The leaves were crisp and had turned to a beautiful burnt orange and red autumn color. The Northern California suburb looked heavenly; yet, I was in hell.

"Wow, that took a long time," Malden said as he rose from the bench with his cell phone in hand.

"Yeah no shit, Sherlock," I said spitefully.

"Well, what happened—are you OK?"

"No, I'm not fucking OK, Malden. I just got a fucking shot injected into my ass to treat me for gonorrhea, and this piece of paper I have here is to get me a prescription for chlamydia. So no, I'm not OK."

"So you have gonorrhea and chlamydia?"

"Possibly."

"Did they test you?"

"No, because I don't have insurance. You were supposed to get tested since you have insurance, remember? Did you get tested?"

"I'm going to get tested in OC. This clinic is a rip-off.

268

My insurance plan wouldn't cover all of their tests."

"Yeah, well I know it's a rip off – I just paid my five-hundred-dollar bill."

Malden awkwardly stared at me like a deer in headlights. "So…" he nervously stammered, "what do you want to do?"

"I want to go to the Rite Aid across the street to get my chlamydia pills and Vicodin. Then I'm going to take as many painkillers as I need to so I don't put a gun to my head."

Silence from Malden. Complete silence.

Malden dropped me off at Rite Aid. I gave the pharmacist my scripts and shopped around the store for any other remedies that would relieve my pain. I bought cranberry juice, AZO cranberry pills and Uristat pills in the case that I simply had a severe UTI.

When the pharmacist called my name for me to pick up the medications, Malden was nowhere in sight yet again. The total for, both prescriptions and over-the-counter medications, was a little over two hundred dollars. I couldn't believe it. In a few hours, I had thrown down almost a thousand dollars for medicine and medical treatment for the potential STD my boyfriend may have given me. Suspiciously, every single time I went to pay–my boyfriend was AWOL.

When I walked outside, I saw Malden standing at a hot dog stand.

"Do you want a hot dog?" Malden asked casually, chewing on his loaded dog. "No, I don't want a fucking hot dog Malden. I feel nauseated. I just took a shot that made me feel worse than I already felt. And by the way, I just charged another two hundred bucks. Let's get out of here."

"You should still try to eat something," Malden said as we walked to the car.

I ignored him.

I got into the passenger seat of his SUV and immediately dove into my plastic Rite Aid bags. I opened the cranberry juice and chugged it as if I hadn't had anything to drink in days. I then popped two Vicodin. I followed that with my prescription for chlamydia, one Uristat pill and then several AZO cranberry pills. Malden drove on the I-80 and headed back to his home.

"The Blue Angels perform in a couple of hours, and then America's Cup is right after that—what do you want to do, Lana?"

"Ugh, I don't know," I said, placing my hands on my face in defeat. "You know I love the Blue Angels. Why don't we go back to your house, I'll lie down for a little bit and if I feel better, we can head down to Golden Gate Park."

"OK," Malden said. "I actually thought we could watch the show from the San Francisco Yacht Club."

"Wherever," I exhaled. "I don't care."

As we wound around the hills of Marin County, we passed thick forests and inlets from the San Francisco Bay. The traffic was getting heavy, most likely due to Fleet Weekend.

When we got back to Malden's, it was one in the afternoon. I lied down and set my alarm for two o'clock. I fell asleep the second I hit my pillow. When I woke up an hour later, I felt groggy, but better. Maybe the medicine was working? I went to the bathroom, and then looked for Malden. I found him in the garage, lying underneath his forest green Harley Davidson. He had a screwdriver in his hand and was attaching a piece back over the rear tire.

"There's my little girl," he said, flashing his JFK Jr. smile, as if he didn't have a care in the world. "How are you feeling?"

"A little better," I said, yawning.

"Should we head down to the yacht club?"

"Um…." I pondered if I was up for navigating through a crowd of thousands. "Yeah, I think I can do it. I feel better, and the painkillers have kicked in."

"Great! The bike is almost ready."

"Wait, the bike?"

"Yeah, the Harley. I was just working on it."

"You want to take the motorcycle?" I asked in confusion.

"Lana, the traffic is horrendous. We'll save ourselves an hour in traffic if we take the bike."

"But," I said, trying to process what was going on. "Malden, my vagina has been burning like a fire in hell for the past twenty-four hours, and now you're asking me to straddle your motorcycle for an afternoon ride?"

"Okay, okay—we can drive then," Malden said as he lifted his bear paws up in the air.

"Forge it—it's fine. We'll take the bike."

I took a quick shower, blow-dried my hair and threw on minimal makeup. I still looked a little peaked, so I threw my Cubs hat back on. After we geared up in our leather jackets, Malden and I got on his motorcycle, and we were off. We zipped down I-80 and headed toward the Golden Gate Bridge. I held onto Malden's broad chest as we weaved in and out of the heavy traffic. I gripped him tighter than usual. I still felt dizzy and woozy. I figured it was from the Rocephin shot.

"Stay centered," Malden shouted as he reached his right bear paw behind and pushed my torso toward the left. "You're swaying off to the right, the bike's not steady."

"I'm trying," I said as I closed my eyes.

"What?" he shouted.

"I'm trying!" I shouted back. "I'm still dizzy."

I opened my eyes and could see the crowd of thousands lined up along the shore waiting for the legendary Blue Angels to take flight. There were hundreds of boats parked all over the bay. The water was a brilliant blue and the sun glistened on the waves. It was in the high seventies – a rare warm day for San Francisco. However, it still felt a little chilly as we drove over the bridge on the bike. When we got to the underground Waldo Tunnel, the line of cars forced Malden to slow down. I was relieved. I could feel myself slowly slipping off his bike, and I didn't feel like I had control over my muscles. It was more difficult to hang on with all the drugs going through my system. We found a spot close to the yacht club. I dismounted the bike and ripped off my helmet. The world started to spin again. I was dizzier than I had been at the clinic. I sat down on the sidewalk as Malden threw his jacket in the storage compartment on the back of his Harley.

"You okay?"

"I'm just really dizzy. I need a second," I panted.

Malden locked up the storage compartment and sat on the pavement next to me. He rubbed my back lovingly. "We can sit here as long as you need."

"OK," I said. "That shot they gave me -- they said it'd make me sick."

"I'm sure your body is just readjusting—you'll be fine."

"Yep," I said reluctantly. Something inside me told me I wasn't going to be fine.

The earth slowly stopped spinning. I got up and told Malden I was ready to walk over. We passed through the mobs of people. There were tents everywhere that different companies had set up—many of them were endorsing America's Cup. People were drinking beer and wine. There was a rock band playing in the park right outside of the club. Everyone appeared to be having the time of his or her lives on this beautiful day, and I was struggling to walk.

Malden and I found a spot right on the edge of the water outside the club. We squeezed in between the hordes of tourists.

"Do you want anything?"

"Can you just get me a couple of waters? I'm dehydrated."

"Sure."

I plopped my purse down and sat on the hot pavement. The burning sensation returned to my crotch. Oh, no–*please God no*! Make the pain stop. I wanted to grab my vagina and cradle it, but I was in the middle of a crowd of hundreds. The last thing I needed was to get arrested for public indecency. Malden returned with two bottles of ice-cold water.

"The Blue Angels should be going on in about a half hour," Malden said, handing me a bottle of water and pulling me off the pavement.

"I have to go to the bathroom," I told him, swiftly walking toward a line of about a dozen Porta-Potties I had seen earlier. A gate blocked the two on the end. I prayed that I'd get one on the end because I knew I'd be in there for a while. There were about two dozen people in line. I stood in line crouched over with my arms embracing my stomach and sweating. My crotch was on fire. It felt like flames were shooting out of my vagina. What had I done to deserve this?

The fifteen minutes in line felt like an eternity. I was next. Please God, please give me a Porta-Potty on the end. Please! Boom. An overweight lady wearing a visor and a cheesy T-shirt with the Golden Gate Bridge strolled out of the last Porta-Potty. I sprinted straight to it and thanked God for giving me that bathroom.

I stepped inside and immediately smelled the horrifically strong stench of pure shit.

"Ugh-fuck!" I shouted as I locked the door. My dizziness got worse. My head began to spin again. The foul smell made me feel ten times worse. There was urine splashed all over the plastic seat and I could see a ton of shit piled in the toilet. It was beyond disgusting. I wanted to run out, but I couldn't. I had to sit down. I quickly wiped all the piss off the seat and blanketed the seat with toilet paper. The last thing I needed was to pick up another disease from a filthy Porta-Potty. I sat on the pot and struggled to pee, holding my bare crotch in an attempt to relieve the stinging pain I felt.

"God no!" I shouted as the tears streamed down my face. The pain was worse than ever. I opened my purse and swallowed two more Vicodin. I also gobbled six cranberry AZO pills. Then, I sat with my head between my legs as I continued to hold my crotch with one hand. I rocked back and forth to relieve the pain a little. I prayed to God over and over again to make the pain go away.

It had been a solid thirty minutes. I couldn't move. I heard the first roaring jet engines speed overhead. There were ohhs and ahhs from the crowds. The Blue Angels had taken flight, and I was literally stuck in a plastic box sitting on top of a pile of shit. Sweating profusely from the pain, I popped more Vicodin like a crack head. I continued to rock back and forth. I used the last of my water to chug six more AZO pills. I sat in the Porta-Potty for another fifteen minutes. The pain slowly subsided. I felt well enough to stand. I pulled my jeans up and carefully exited. There was a line of dozens for the bathroom. I slowly walked past the people in line and I wondered if anyone noticed that I had been in there for over an hour.

When I got back to Malden, he gave me a deep look of concern. "Where have you been? The show started over fifteen minutes ago."

My eyes welled up with water. The tears began to fall. I bowed my head on his broad chest. "I don't know what's wrong with me–I feel so sick," I said, sobbing into his Polo shirt.

"You're going to be OK. Your body is in shock from that shot," he said, embracing me.

I wiped my eyes and looked up. The Blue Angels were above us in a diamond formation heading straight up into space. Even in my darkest hour of pain, I couldn't be prouder to be an American than I was in that moment. I was amazed at their precision. I always thought it was funny that people idolized celebrities so much. The guys flying these planes–and every service man and woman–those were my heroes.

"It's so beautiful," I mumbled as Malden held me tight.

"Aren't they magnificent?"

"They're unbelievable."

The jets scattered into six different directions. One headed toward Alcatraz, and another zipped right over our heads. The jet spiraled as it zoomed around the Golden Gate Bridge. The awesomeness of their performance temporarily distracted me from the pain.

The pain continued to fade. My crotch slowly stopped burning. I started to talk to Malden about the military and how much I loved our country. I realized I was high from the painkillers, and I was talking his ear off by the time the Blue Angels finished their performance. By the time the America's Cup started, my pain was almost completely gone. We headed back to Malden's motorcycle after the race. I was actually standing upright. Almost all the pain had disappeared. I still felt a little dizzy, but it was bearable.

"I know you wanted to go to the Buena Vista for an Irish

coffee, but if you're not up for it we'll just go home," Malden said, carefully placing the black helmet on my head and fastening the strap under my chin.

"You know what—I want to go," I boldly said. "I feel so much better. I think you're right—it was just that shot that made me so sick. I don't think being in the sun helped either."

"Are you sure?" Malden asked skeptically.

"Yeah!" I said with a smile. I thanked God for making me feel better and hopped on the back of Malden's bike.

We sped up the winding streets to the famed Irish bar. It was featured in my favorite romance film, *When a Man Loves a Woman*. I managed to snag two stools at the bar, even though it was packed with wall-to-wall people. I could see the entire Bay and the Golden Gate Bridge through the large windows lining the charming bar. The sun was beginning to set, and the orange light reflected all over the bay and inside the bar. I felt so fortunate to be in this beautiful city. We each drank two Irish coffees and headed back to Malden's house. We canceled our dinner plans with a couple of his brothers so I could go home and relax. We spent the night on his couch watching football. Malden cooked me steak and vegetables. I sipped a glass of wine, and continued to consume more Vicodin. We were both sound asleep, cozied up in each other's arms, before midnight.

I woke up to the smell of coffee and Malden rubbing my back. I opened my eyes and flipped over. He was intensely staring right at me with those deep blue eyes.

"Good morning, beautiful," he gently said. "I brought you some coffee."

I looked over and saw the white coffee mug on the nightstand.

"Thank you," I said in a haze. I had a slight pill hangover

from all the medication.

"Are you feeling better?"

"Yeah," I said slowly, as my mind quickly remembered the terrible amount of pain I was in less than twenty-four hours ago. "I do. I just feel a little foggy."

A shot of anxiety bolted through my body as I sat up in my bed. I realized that I had failed to check my phone even once the day before. I was so distracted by the tremendous pain—and just so out of it from all the meds—it slipped my mind. I wondered if Mick had tried to get hold of me and what the latest was with Celeste.

"Oh my God!" I exclaimed. "My phone. I didn't check it yesterday. Can you please grab it? I think it's in my purse in the kitchen."

"Sure," Malden said. "You just relax and enjoy your coffee."

I looked at the digital alarm clock on the other nightstand next to Malden's side of the bed. It was eleven in the morning. Holy shit—eleven! I had slept for twelve hours without waking once. I was in a full-blown coma. I couldn't believe it.

"Here you go," Malden said, handing me my iPhone.

I quickly grabbed it. The battery was on its last leg. I opened my messages and saw a missed call and text from Mick. I figured it was sent around the time I was taking up residency in the Porta-Potty. I cringed. I had never gone this long without looking at my phone for work—especially in the midst of a huge story. I opened his text.

Mick Madden: "Celeste is booked on a flight to LAX tomorrow night. We booked her to take a poly at two on Monday. Can you pick her up and take her to the poly? She'll be at the SLS Hotel."

Lana Burke: "Hi Mick, Yes, of course I'll take her to the poly test. I'm so sorry I was MIA yesterday. I came down with an infection and had to go to the emergency clinic, but I'm fine now."

I couldn't shoot off that text quick enough. Malden went into the bathroom and turned the shower on.

"Babe, we're going to meet my boys for lunch, and then we can head back to your place," he shouted from the bathroom.

"OK," I said as I slowly got out of bed. For once, I could stand up with no dizziness. I breathed a sigh of relief. Then I heard my phone beep. It was a text from Mick.

Mick Madden: "Jeez, I hope you're OK. We need you healthy to finish our big story! I'll text you after I get Celeste on the plane. I'm still worried she's going to flake."

Lana Burke: "Sounds good. Good luck!"

I joined Malden in the shower. He lovingly kissed me and washed my back and hair.

"I'm so happy you're feeling better," he said as he embraced me under the hot water. It was what I needed to hear from him. Despite everything, I loved him, and I felt safe in his arms. "I love you."

"I love you too," I said, rubbing my hands over his big chest. It dawned on me that this was probably the longest we had ever gone without having sex.

When we got out of the shower, we quickly got dressed, packed our bags and closed up his house. We picked up the boys from Bethenny's house and took them to a diner near the

Berkeley campus for a quick burger. His daughter claimed to be too busy with her schoolwork to join us.

Malden and I hit the I-5 highway around two in the afternoon. It was another beautiful day in Northern California. There were no clouds in the sky and it was as blue as the Pacific Ocean. The beautiful scenery of our route never got old. We passed rural hills for miles and miles. It didn't look like earth to me—I felt like I was on a yellow planet. Being from the Midwest, all the road trips I took as a child involved a backdrop of endless plains. Road trips in California are draped with snow-capped mountains, glistening lakes, rolling yellow hills and desert canyons. As beautiful as San Francisco is, I was happy we didn't spend the entire day there. I secretly wanted to get home in time for my new favorite show, *Revenge*. At the rate we were going, we'd arrive home just minutes before it aired.

Halfway through our drive, we stopped at a gas station to fill up. I was feeling so much better, but I took a couple Vicodin—just in case. I bought some snacks inside the gas station while Malden filled up the SUV. When I came out, he was getting his receipt from the machine.

"I'll drive," I said to him as I got in the driver's seat.

"Are you sure?"

"Yeah. We only have a couple more hours to go, and you've already driven the whole time."

There was no traffic on the I-5. We listened to a Billy Idol CD as we approached a patch of windmills. I was in the fast lane clutching the wheel tightly. The sun was setting fast and street lights were popping up everywhere I looked. The darker it got, the harder it was to focus. The headlights from the oncoming cars felt like daggers in my eyes. We passed a huge Costco. I recognized the logo, but the sign for the store was wrong.

"Why do you think that Costco sign says 'Coconuts'?" I asked Malden. "Do you think it's some sort of prank?"

"What are you talking about?" Malden asked, giving me a strange look.

"That sign," I said, pointing. "It says 'Coconuts.' How weird."

"Lana, no it doesn't," Malden said with a look of horror. "It says Costco."

"What?" I said as I looked at him.

"Lana, *watch out!*" Malden screamed, grabbing the wheel and swerving it to the right.

I sucked in my breath with a mix of panic and relief. I was a centimeter away from hitting the concrete barrier along the highway.

"Do you need me to drive?" Malden asked, concerned.

"I'm fine–I just spaced out."

I gripped the wheel tighter, but I struggled to stay in my lane. I could feel the car swerving in and out of the lines on the road. The oncoming car lights felt like nuclear missiles launching directly into my eyes.

"It's so magical," I stuttered. "It's like little pins of lights in the sky."

"What?" Malden shouted. "What are you talking about? Lana, pull over."

My head felt really light. The dizziness suddenly came back. The earth was spinning and all the car lights around me were fireflies.

"Did you collect fireflies? As a kid?" I slurred as the car accidentally slipped into the middle lane.

A huge semi, just feet behind our car, blared its horn.

"Lana, pull over–get off at this exit!"

My mind heard what Malden said, but I just couldn't process what he was saying. "What? I just don't understand," I cried.

"Lana, move over," Malden said, grabbing the wheel again. He swerved us into the slow lane.

"OK, OK, I'm trying," I said frantically. It started to dawn on me we could be in trouble. My palms began to sweat on the wheel.

"Pull onto this exit—and stop on the shoulder. We'll switch."

I slowly pulled the SUV to a stop, and Malden put it in park.

"Be careful getting out, Lana," Malden barked as he opened the passenger side door.

I stumbled out of the car and slowly walked to the passenger side. I opened the door and got in.

"Yeah, maybe I shouldn't drive," I said nonchalantly.

"Yeah, no shit!" Malden said. "You almost killed us."

"Ha, ha," I laughed hysterically. "You're so funny. You're a bear! You have bear paws."

I continued to laugh as I stared at Malden's hands. They looked exactly like the paws of a bear. I couldn't believe it. He was bear!

"I mean how do you even text with a bear paw?" I laughed. "Aren't your paws too big to type the keys?"

"Lana, maybe you should try to sleep," Malden said.

I looked at him and then tried to refocus on the road as I sat back in my seat.

"Oh, God!" I shouted. "No. Make the daggers stop!"

"What? Lana, what in the world are you talking about?"

I held my head and lowered it down toward my lap. My brain felt like it was going to explode. I felt faint and dizzy. I felt a sharp pain slowly develop from the top of my spine all the way down to my lower back. I could hardly breathe.

"I don't feel so good," I said, rocking back and forth, back and forth. I rocked the same way Dustin Hoffman had when he portrayed a man with a severe case of autism in *Rain Man*. I could not stop rocking. The pain I felt in my head, neck and spine was so severe that the only way I could relieve the pressure was to rock back and forth. Malden reached his bear paw over and placed it on my forehead.

"You feel warm," Malden said. "I think you have a fever."

"Ow, it hurts!" I cried.

"We'll be home soon. We'll put you straight to bed."

I continued to rock back and forth for the two hours left of our drive. Finally, we pulled into my apartment complex. When we arrived at my assigned parking spot, I immediately opened the door and got out. The second I put my legs on the ground, I could feel my knees buckle. Malden was pulling our luggage out from the trunk.

"I can't wait for you," I said breathlessly as I slowly walked to the elevator. "I can't walk well. Grab my stuff and meet me inside."

Each step felt like a marathon, but I walked toward the elevator as best as I could. The door opened immediately, and within seconds I was in my apartment. I threw my purse on the floor and ran to my bed and flopped straight in it. I could not stand for another second. I felt my body temperature soar. I was hot and sweating all over. I blacked out.

"Lana, Lana!" Malden loudly said as he turned me over. "Are you conscious?"

"What?" I said, slowly opening my eyes.

"You're all wet—this is good, your fever is breaking."

"I'm freezing," I said in tears. "I'm so cold, Malden."

I felt a chill go up and down my body. Goose bumps formed over my arms and chest. Malden ripped my clothes off and put a warm sweatshirt on over my head and tucked me snugly under my comforter.

"Are you warmer now?" he asked.

"Uh huh," I said, my eyes almost completely glazed over. The room continued to spin. My head, neck, eyes and brain all felt like they were being stabbed with a thousand knives. However, it didn't dawn on me how strange that was. All I could think about was *Revenge. Revenge. Revenge. Revenge. Revenge.* Thoughts of the hit ABC show repeated in my mind over and over again.

"Turn on the TV," I mumbled.

"What?" Malden shouted from my bedroom bathroom.

"*Revenge.* Channel seven, Malden. ABC!"

I heard Malden walk over to the TV and click it on. I heard the soothing female voice of the fictional character Emily Thorne talking during the show's introduction. I hadn't missed it. Ah, peace. I fought to keep my eyes opened past the intro. They were open by a sliver. I tried really hard to focus on the TV, but the light bolted through my eyes and stung my brain like a thousand bees. OK, OK, I thought. I don't need to watch the show. I can just listen to it.

I slowly faded in and out of consciousness. I could hear Malden rattling something plastic in my bathroom. I wondered what he could be doing, and then I smelled a strong, foul smell that I'm very familiar with. It was hair dye. I opened one eye just enough to peer into the bathroom. I could see Malden dying his gray hair brown as I lay frozen, in pain, on my bed. I lost consciousness after that.

I woke up the next day at noon. My head was pounding harder than ever. Malden had left for work. I got out of bed to go to the bathroom, and the entire room spun. I grabbed my phone off my nightstand and called my mom. I lay back down because it was too painful to stand. I told her that I was in too much pain to stand up, and she instructed me to go to the emergency room immediately. I knew Giselle would be at work and Malden worked an hour away – so I called French Rocker and had him drive me to the hospital.

CHAPTER 15

As I lay in the fetal position of my emergency room hospital bed at Cedars-Sinai Hospital in Los Angeles, I stared at the clock on the wall, with thoughts of death creeping into my mind. Time had appeared to stop. I heard the minute hand slowly turn – tick, tick, tick – each second felt like an hour. I slowly rocked back and forth, curled up like a helpless child in my cold bed. I've never felt such horrible pain in my entire life. My back, my neck, my head and my brain – oh my brain – even my eyes were all in excruciating pain.

So, this is what it feels like to want to die.

I had a revelation in my spinning head. I used to be against assisted suicide. I didn't understand how anyone could ever want to kill himself. Now I knew. I vowed that I would never judge others in pain again. I knew in my heart my medical condition was serious, possibly fatal. I saw the Grim

Reaper out of the corner of my eye. He was taunting me. He slowly curled his index finger toward himself, tempting me to join him.

The pain was so unbearable – I struggled to ignore him. I knew if my medical condition could not be fixed, I would not want to live anymore.

"Lana, Lana! Are you still with me?" Dr. David Peterson bellowed as he shook my arm. I slowly snapped out of my trancelike state.

"Uh-huh," was all I could muster.

"Look I can tell you're in a terrible amount of pain, but the morphine should be kicking in soon."

"Thank you, I don't know what's wrong with me. I've been in tremendous vaginal pain."

"I need to know about your sexual history. Would you like me to ask your friend to leave the room?"

I looked at French Rocker sitting in the corner of my hospital room, his hands clasped with concern and a look of sadness on his face. He had kindly driven me to the hospital and practically carried me into the emergency room.

"No. French Rocker can stay. I have nothing to hide. I don't care."

"OK, so how many sexual partners do you have?"

"One. My boyfriend."

"How long have you been seeing him?"

"Six months."

"Have you slept with anyone else?"

"No. He's the only person I've had sex with in a year," I said angrily.

"And you said that this past weekend your boyfriend took you to an emergency clinic in San Francisco, where you were treated for STDs?"

"Yes. Well, kind of," I stammered. "I woke up at three in the morning on Saturday in excruciating pain. My primary care doctor thought I had a yeast infection or a UTI so he wrote me a script for both. I didn't get better, obviously. My symptoms got so bad on Saturday morning that I couldn't sleep. I spent most of the night on the toilet holding my crotch in extreme pain. My boyfriend took me to a clinic in Marin County. The doctor there said he believed I could have gonorrhea or chlamydia—or both. He said the test results wouldn't come back for days. Since I don't live there or have health insurance right now, I told him to just treat me for both. So, the doctor gave me a shot that he said would wipe out most STDs. I don't know with certainty if I did or do have an STD."

"Was it a Rocephin shot the doctor gave you?"

"I think so. That sounds right."

"I need to ask again: are there any other sex partners that I should know about? This is important."

"No. I've been dating the same boyfriend for months. I love him – I'm devoted to him," I said in a panic. "I haven't slept with anyone else in almost a year."

"OK," the doctor said as he nodded and proceeded to walk out the door.

I knew in my gut I couldn't let the doctor leave without telling him what I had just recently uncovered about Malden.

"Wait, there's something else you should know," I called out to him. "I noticed the words were coming out a lot easier – maybe even a little too easy. My mouth went from a leaky faucet to a waterfall within minutes. I was feeling a little speedy now, like I had just ripped a line of cocaine and was ready to tell anyone who would listen my life story. The morphine was in full effect.

"Yes?"

"My boyfriend. Malden. I just found out that the bastard cheated on me."

"Do you know with whom?" Dr. Peterson asked as he raised his eyebrows in concern.

"He said it was an old friend. Some middle-aged single mom or something. I don't know. I'm not sure what to believe. I don't know if he's telling me the truth."

"Lana, this is serious. I'm afraid you may have a sexually transmitted disease – possibly HIV. It's crucial I get all the facts. Do you know if he leads a high-risk sexual lifestyle? Could he be sleeping with hookers, men or transsexuals?"

"What?" My stomach instantly went into a thousand knots.

"Lana, forgive me for asking, but this is Hollywood. I see it all the time. There's a high population of people with HIV here."

"Oh my God, no I don't think we have to worry about that. He's a fifty-six-year-old alpha male with five kids. I mean...no. That is crazy talk."

"Good," Dr. Peterson said as he let out a deep breath. "But I still will need his phone number to talk to him so I can confirm for myself."

I gave him Malden's cell phone number, and he left the room. More dark thoughts oozed into my brain. I envisioned my beloved boyfriend sleeping with prostitutes–or even male hookers. The thought made me sick to my stomach and I suddenly gagged.

Reacting swiftly, French Rocker moved the garbage can next to my bed. I threw up for the second time in one hour. I had flashbacks of my wild sexual lifestyle with Malden. We had a lot of sex everywhere and anywhere. The more I thought about it, the more I realized how abnormal our sexual lifestyle was. Could Malden be a sex addict?

Wait – I suddenly thought. Could he be gay? After all, you don't need a woman to have anal sex. I shuddered at the concept. His requests in the bedroom had slowly gone from lighthearted and fun to dark and outright creepy. The sexual deviancy. Who was this man I was dating? I had to ponder what he could be capable of, but I couldn't go there. I tried to shake the dark thoughts out of my mind and convince myself that the doctor was crazy for even suggesting any of the hooker and tranny nonsense. But, I couldn't stop thinking about the possibilities.

"Lana, your cell's beeping," French Rocker said as he pulled my cell out of my oversized Louis Vuitton purse on the floor. "A guy named Ari is texting you."

Oh shit – just what I needed. The big boss calling me. "Hand me the phone, please."

I opened my iPhone 5 and read the text from my boss.

Ari Davidson: "Lana, I need a status update on the lie detector test with the Celeste. We close in a few hours. It's two weeks before the election – we cannot afford to lose this story now. Please give me a call."

Oh, fuck. Everything was coming to a head. My relationship with my would-be wonderful boyfriend was deteriorating as well as the biggest story of my entire journalism career—and here I was, sitting in a hospital bed, sick as a dog with an unknown illness. And how ironic, hookers seemed to be a theme in both cases. This was not normal.

I responded to Ari's text immediately, as I usually do. Even a grave mystery illness and a trip to the emergency room couldn't stop my devotion to my job. I had called Mick earlier from the hospital to say I couldn't make it.

Lana Burke: "Ari, I'm so sorry, but I was unable to take Celeste to the lie detector test today. I assigned Mick to do it. I'm in the emergency room very sick. The doctors don't know what's wrong with me yet. I apologize for not being able to be there. I have put my heart and soul into this story for months."

Ari Davidson: "Thanks for the update. Take care of yourself and feel better. Please call me when you are up to it."

The ER doctor returned, and I immediately perked up. The pain had subsided greatly – I was feeling slightly normal again. Thank God for morphine.

"I talked to your boyfriend."

"And?"

"I asked him if he leads a high-risk sexual lifestyle and he said no."

"Did he admit to any cheating?"

"No," Dr. Peterson said as he shook his head. "He said he cheated on you once, like you said, and he claims he doesn't have any STDs."

"OK." I leaned back in my bed and exhaled a sigh of relief.

"Technically he could've contracted an STD and be asymptomatic so we can't rule anything out yet. However, after reviewing all your symptoms, I do believe there is a slight chance you could have meningitis. I'd say there's a one percent chance you have the disease. If you want, we can test for it."

"I don't see why not." I sighed. "What does it entail?"

"Well, we'd have to give you a spinal tap."

I immediately remembered a documentary I watched when I was a little girl about a young boy who had cancer. The child's mother narrated the piece. She talked about how her son had to get a painful spinal tap and how much it tortured her to watch her son undergo the awful procedure. The mother said that he screamed Bloody Mary so loud that the entire hospital floor could hear him. After I saw the movie, I prayed I would never have to receive a spinal tap. That documentary stuck with me my entire life.

"No, absolutely not!" I shrieked. "If you only think there's a one percent chance I have it, let's hold off on that. That seems a little extreme."

"OK," Dr. Peterson said with reluctance. "But..."

"But, what?" I panted.

"I was going to say that the worst thing you can do for meningitis is to not test for it."

My stomach dropped. "What does that mean?"

"It means, if you don't catch it early enough, you can die. So if we can't pinpoint your disease soon I may insist on the spinal tap." With that, he walked out of the room and I closed my eyes in defeat.

French Rocker had to leave for band practice. He assured me Giselle was on her way to stay with me. At this point – with the morphine kicking into high gear – I was feeling well enough to watch TV. I grabbed the remote on the stand next to my bed and switched on the KTLA five o'clock news.

"There's been a meningitis outbreak in California from a recalled steroid shot," a tan, blonde female newscaster reported gravely.

I couldn't believe it. I clicked to the next station, landing on another news broadcast reporting on the bacterial meningitis outbreak. I listened intently as the handsome male anchor reported that health officials believed the outbreak was caused by a bad batch of steroid shots. The shots were administered to patients in California within the past six months. I racked my brain – I was certain I had not received a steroid shot for several years. So, I flipped the channel, and yet again, a third news station covered the outbreak. I listened intently as if my life depended on it. And just maybe – it did.

Behind the reporter was a large graphic with a list of symptoms, including:

- Headache
- Stiff neck
- Back pain
- Fever & chills
- Vomiting
- Light sensitivity
- Confusion

I was shocked. Literally, I had every single symptom the newscaster listed. Panicked, I buzzed for a nurse, she came in, and I shouted to her that I needed my doctor immediately. About ten long minutes later, Dr. Peterson strolled back in.

"Do you know there's a meningitis outbreak?" I asked in a panic. "It's all over the news."

"No, I didn't," Dr. Peterson said in surprise. "I haven't watched the news all day."

"There is!" I shouted in a fury. "How could you not know? You work in the ER of the most famous hospital in California! Please – give me the damn spinal tap!"

Dr. Peterson rushed out of my room to prepare the spinal tap. My anxiety level skyrocketed. Then my phone buzzed again.

Mick Madden: "Celeste is a no-show to the lie detector test! I went to her hotel and she is nowhere to be found. We're running out of time. Please call immediately!"

All my hard work was going down the toilet fast, and I was lying in a hospital bed unable to do anything about it. Before I could even respond to Mick's message, Dr. Peterson and a nurse came back with some very unpleasant-looking medical equipment.

Oh dear God. Here we go.

Dr. Peterson was carrying a long metal apparatus that looked very scary. I turned away, not wanting to look at it. I knew in a few minutes he would be injecting that needle that looked like a medieval torture device into the bone marrow of my spine. God help me, I silently prayed.

"I'm going to apply numbing lotion to your lower back," the nurse calmly said. "Can you please lay on your stomach?" I slowly flipped over and felt her clammy, skinny hands unloosen the back of my hospital gown. She gently applied the cold lotion to my entire lower back in a slow circular motion. It probably could've put me to sleep if I didn't know what was about to happen next.

"Now I'm going to try to do this as quickly as possible but it's vital you lay still," Dr. Peterson said as he placed one hand on the middle of my back. "If you move at all it could screw up the test and leave you with paralysis."

"Oh good fucking Lord," I said as tears filled my eyes. "OK."

"On the count of three. One, two..."

"Fuck! Oh God!"

I could feel my body temperature rising and sweat forming at the top of my forehead. It felt like I had just been stabbed in the back with a stone cold ice pick. The doctor held the needle in my back for seconds. The seconds felt like hours.

"OK, breathe. We're all done," Dr. Peterson said.

I flipped over and leaned back in my hospital bed. I started to feel nauseated and exceptionally dizzy.

"Are you OK?" Dr. Peterson asked. "You're looking very pale."

"I just feel real dizzy."

"I'll have the nurse bring you some orange juice. Relax, the worst part is over."

I stared at him. The worst part is over? I wanted to shout: Not if I have fucking meningitis, you asshole! Something told me that the worst part was far from over. After all, I still needed to get several test results back – including an HIV test.

"Now, it will take about two hours before we get the results back from the spinal tap," Dr. Peterson sternly said. "So just please try to relax and watch TV or something."

Giselle, wearing Havaianas flip-flops, a Doors T-shirt over a black bikini top, and a pair of cutoff jeans, walked in shortly after the doctor left. I filled her in on everything.

"Meningitis? That doesn't make any sense," Giselle said with a look of deep concern in her eyes. "How on earth could you have contracted that?"

"I have no idea," I said in defeat. "All I know is that I've had all this vaginal pain for weeks and strange STD-like symptoms. I really thought I had your average UTI, but this won't go away. Since Malden just cheated on me, I'm scared he could've given me something. But then again, he seems fine – and he said he would get tested too – just to be safe. I'm so confused – I just don't know what's going on."

In my morphine haze, I could tell something was off with Giselle. She acted a little skittish.

"Is there something wrong?" I asked.

"With me?" Giselle asked.

"Yes, you seem off. Is there something going on with you?"

She cringed and gave me her classic guilty look. I had seen this look before. I instantly knew she had cheated. She hadn't been happy with her marriage for a while.

"Giselle no – tell me you didn't!" I said.

"Lana, things have gotten real bad – you don't understand," she pleaded. "I feel like we've fallen out of love. When we got married, he promised me the world and said that as soon as he got his visa he would start working full-time. It's been two years, and that's not happened!"

"Oh, Giselle." I sighed. "That's not a good reason to cheat. Marriage is work. Who is he?"

"Viper," she said as she looked down at the ground.

"Viper as in the rock star Viper?"

"Yep," she said.

"Oh my God Giselle – I can't believe this. Viper is the biggest train wreck in Hollywood. He's on TMZ every day. What are you thinking throwing away your marriage for a drug-addicted rock star?"

"I know, I know," Giselle said. "Please, Lana, you're sick. I don't want to make this about me. We'll talk about this more when you're better."

The nurse who assisted with my spinal tap entered the room. My attention shot straight back to my situation at hand.

"I'm getting a little anxious," I told the nurse. "My results from the spinal tap should be back by now. Do you know if they were positive for meningitis?"

"Um, I don't think so but you'll have to ask the doctor," she said turning her back and straightening the already organized medical equipment on the counter across from my bed.

"Well, could I talk to him?"

"I'll page him right now," she said and rushed out of my room.

Turning to Giselle, I said, "OK well that's a relief – I think. Something didn't seem right about her. She seemed nervous. Do you think she was lying?"

"I agree." Giselle nodded. "She definitely seemed nervous, but I don't think she's allowed to tell you your results. That would violate some kind of patients' rights."

Just then, Dr. Peterson strolled into my room. He leaned against the counter with papers in his hand and shook his head from left to right.

"So, what's going on? I don't have meningitis, right?" I eagerly asked.

"Unfortunately," he said. "You do have meningitis."

"Very funny. You're joking, right?"

"You have meningitis."

My breathing got heavy, and I was certain smoke was coming out of my nose like a raging bull. I was desperate. "I don't understand. I can't have it!"

"Yes, you do. I can't believe it. You're my first positive for meningitis ever."

I sat back in my hospital bed in total shock, unable to speak.

"Wait a second, are you fucking kidding me?" Giselle screamed at the ER doctor as she rose from her chair and threw her hands in the air. "How is that possible? This is insane!"

Dr. Peterson ignored Giselle and started talking with hospital security via a walkie talkie.

"Yes, we'll have to quarantine her. No one is allowed to go near her without a medical mask on. We will transfer her immediately," Dr. Peterson said. He rushed out of my room without looking at me or saying another word.

Looking at Giselle, I screamed at her to hand me my phone. I immediately called my mother. I knew she was anxiously waiting for an update.

My mom answered on the first ring.

"Mom. I have meningitis! The doctor just told me. I don't know what's going on," I cried, with tears streaming down my face.

"What? I can't believe this!" my mom gasped. "OK, calm down and try to relax. You are in the hospital getting good care. You're going to be OK. Is there anyone else there with you?"

"Giselle."

"Lana, put her on the phone."

I handed Giselle the phone to talk to my mom. The extreme dizziness was coming back and my head was spinning. I started having flashbacks of the recent events in my life. I was thinking about the night I found the condom in Malden's bathroom garbage can. The story he finally told me about the woman he had the affair with. I was having flashes of government vehicles following Celeste and me in Winnemucca. I thought about my conversation with Gov. Richards's lawyer, the strange events that happened to me at the Grand America in Salt Lake City and in Nevada. Someone broke into my hotel room, government agents followed me, my tape recorder went missing and now I had a potentially deadly illness. The reporter and conspiracy theorist in me couldn't help but wonder what the connection was. After all, I was supposed to be overseeing a polygraph test with a hooker for a story that ultimately could ruin the election for the Republican presidential nominee.

When Giselle got off the phone with my mom, I made

her hand me back my phone.

"Who are you calling?" Giselle asked.

"Malden," I replied.

There was no answer. I left a message for him to call me immediately and then shot him a text.

Lana Burke: "I'm in the ER, and I've just been told I have meningitis. Call me!"

Four residents walked into my room along with a security guard. They were all wearing medical masks.

"We have to transport you to a special wing right now in case you're contagious," one of the male nurses warned. "Please put on this mask."

The nurse handed me a medical mask as they all gathered around my bed to wheel me out. I felt like a total outcast. They were treating me like I had Ebola – what the hell was going on!

"Um, all right, can my best friend come too? I don't have anyone else here with me."

"Yes, but she needs to put on a mask immediately."

As they began to push my bed out of my room my phone beeped again.

Mick Madden: "I just spoke to a manager of the SLS hotel. Celeste's gone. The maid who cleaned her room told the manager that all of her stuff was gone. She's missing!"

My heart stopped. I knew the story wouldn't run without Celeste taking and passing the poly. Without a poly, the lawyers wouldn't clear the story for publication. Where in the hell was Celeste and was she in trouble? The story appeared to be dead, and I couldn't help but wonder if I was next.

CHAPTER 16

"Excuse me – nurse, nurse – please, you've got to help us out here," I said, giggling uncontrollably as I held out my iPhone. "We've got to capture this Kodak moment."

The nurse gave me a confused look as she straightened the IV tube wrapped around my bed.

"Lana, what in the world are you doing?" Giselle whispered with trepidation.

"Come on, come on. You've got to get over here, Giselle," I said, still laughing. I could feel the morphine pumping in and out of my veins. My hands trembled from the powerful painkillers, but I felt weightless. I didn't have a care in the world. "It's not every day you're quarantined at Cedars-Sinai. We've got to document this. I'm going to post this photo on Facebook. Nurse, are you ready? Giselle, is your medical mask still on? This is so great, so great!"

"Uh, are you sure you want to post a photo of yourself in the hospital?" Giselle asked, cringing in disbelief.

"Giselle, what the fuck – where's your sense of humor?" I snapped. "I wonder how many likes we'll get on Facebook. This is amazing!"

"OK ladies, are you ready?" the nurse asked softly, raising my iPhone with her bony hands.

"Cheese," I mugged, throwing up a peace symbol with my left hand. With zero reluctance, Giselle struck a sexy pose beside my hospital bed. She never passes up a photo op – even wearing a medical mask. It makes me wonder if she's the Kardashian Kris Jenner secretly put up for adoption.

"OK – here you go," the nurse said, handing me back my phone. "Dr. Peterson should be back in to see you soon, and I'll come back every hour to check on your vitals."

"This is so great! Just epic." I said, giggling at the photo of the two of us. "What should the caption be? Oh wait – I got it – how about laughter is the best medicine…."

"OK, Lana," Giselle said, smiling slightly in an attempt to appease me. "Whatever you want."

With one click on the upload button, a picture of possibly the worst day of my life – October, 8, 2012 – was forever embedded on the World Wide Web. Sadly, at that moment in time, I had no idea that the old Lana had just died. She would never return, and I would never be the same.

"Ms. Burke," Dr. Peterson said, gravely walking briskly with a team of four doctors, all wearing scrubs. "These are some of my residents," he announced without emotion as he shuffled a stack of papers. "They're here to assist me. We are still trying to get down to the bottom of your condition."

"Um, okay," I said with a crazy smile. "You know what

they say – the more the merrier!"

"Right," Dr. Peterson said flatly, ignoring my kooky behavior. "Now, I need to discuss some matters with you in private," he told me, looking at Giselle.

"Oh, she's cool…"

"You know what," Giselle interrupted. "I have a work event I really need to go to. I can come back after. Is that okay, Lana? I'm worried to leave you here alone."

"Please, please, please – I'm fine! Why you trippin' boo? Girl, you go do your thing! You go girl!"

"Excuse me -- are you a rap star now, Lana? You going to join R. Kelly on tour?" Giselle asked with a laugh.

"Sheeeeeet! Get out of here so I can hang with my resident peeps."

I stared at the ten eyes glaring at me above their medical masks. Dr. Peterson and the residents looked stunned.

"All right, Lana–try to behave yourself. I'll be back in a few hours."

"Lana, I hate to be the bearer of bad news, but we're still waiting for more test results," Dr. Peterson said.

"You're hilarious," I said. "I mean…what the fuck could be worse than a positive for a deadly disease like meningitis."

"Lana, you could have an STD-induced form of meningitis. For example, you're meningitis could stem from syphilis or herpes. Unfortunately, we won't know for sure for seven more days when we get those tests back."

"Wait, what?" I said, frazzled.

"You could have herpes or syphilis," he said flatly. "Now, do you have any blisters in or around your vagina?"

"Um, gross–no, not that I am aware of," I blurted, as it slowly began to occur to me how horrendous of a situation I was in.

"OK, we're going to need to double check to be safe. If you do have syphilis or HSV-meningitis, you will need serious medication to prevent any kind of brain damage. We'll need to examine your vagina with lights."

"Are you fucking kidding?" I said. "I'm so glad you brought in a slew of your medical students to witness this humiliation for me."

"This is just standard procedure, Ms. Burke," Dr. Peterson continued, unfazed.

"Well, my apologies in advance for not booking a bikini wax this morning. You know, if I would've known…well, you know. I just hope it's not a jungle down there. What is it Axl Rose says? Welcome to the jungle!"

I saw one of the male residents eyes crinkle from a smile. I was pleased to see that they weren't all made of stone.

"Ms. Burke can you please scoot down toward the end of the bed?" the female resident asked. She had beautiful eyes, which was all I could see since she was wearing a mask. Her strawberry blonde hair was pulled back in a low ponytail. I was grateful there was at least one other woman in the room.

I reluctantly slid down. I saw Dr. Peterson standing behind the resident, arms folded. I tried to avoid eye contact with Dr. Peterson and the residents at this point. I looked out the window, but my eyes were immediately met with pain from the headlights of dozens of cars zooming down Beverly Boulevard during rush hour. The lights seared into my eyes like swords – the pain was incredible.

"I'm going to look at your vagina now," the female resident announced as she turned on a flashlight. I couldn't believe it – was she searching for gold? Was she going to whip out an ax and a hard helmet next? God, this can't be my life. I closed my eyes. I could feel her cold hands inspect my entire crotch. The room fell silent. She continued to snoop around down there for several minutes.

"You know – I just don't see anything," she said, putting my gown back down. "I don't see one sore. She doesn't seem to have any signs of HSV."

"Let me have a look," a heavyset male resident said as he grabbed the flashlight.

"Excuse me – is this really necessary?" I said, agitated. "She said she couldn't see anything. I told you, I don't have any sores down there. I mean, it is my fucking vagina – don't you think I'd know?"

"Lana, please," Dr. Peterson pleaded. "This is important."

The clumsy male resident dug around in my vagina a little more aggressively than the blonde resident. I sat there silent in total frustration and embarrassment. I felt like a caged lab rat.

"Nothing," the resident said when he was finally done poking my genitals.

"Hmmmmm," Dr. Peterson said stroking his chin. "That's baffling because she has all the other signs for HSV-meningitis."

"But genital sores usually are the first symptom," the blonde resident said.

"What the fuck is this – a really bad episode of *House*?" I asked.

"Lana, please try to calm down." Dr. Peterson said. "We're still waiting on some tests. In the meantime, the nurse is going to give you an IV of Acyclovir on the chance you do have syphilis or HSV-meningitis."

"OK…what's Acyc, Acyclo," I stuttered as I struggled to remember what he said.

"Yes, Acyclovir. It's a strong drug that is necessary in case you do have syphilis or HSV-meningitis. We will get definitive tests back in seven days. However, we can't wait that long. If you don't take the medicine now you may die or end up with permanent brain damage."

"What!" I said. "So, if I do have syphilis or HSV-meningitis – what does that mean? How do I cure it?"

"If you have syphilis-induced meningitis, you'll have to have an IV in your arm for some time."

"An IV like this one?" I asked as I pointed to the needle in my wrist that was connected to the tube.

"Yes."

"For how long?"

"A few weeks – or maybe even a couple of months."

"Wait, so I'll have to stay in a hospital for months?"

"No, you can treat yourself at home with the IV."

"But what about work? I have a job."

"Some people with this condition go to their jobs with the IV."

"You've got to be fucking kidding me. You mean to tell me I'm going to have to drag this thing to work and tell my colleagues not to worry about the elephant in the room…that it's just there to, you know, treat the STD my scumbag boyfriend gave me?"

"Ms. Burke, you can explain it any way you'd like. Now, the nurse will be in shortly with an IV containing the Acyclovir drug – hang tight."

"Wait," I screeched before Dr. Peterson had a chance to exit. "When can I leave?"

"The hospital?" Dr. Peterson asked with confusion.

"Yeah – when can I go home?"

"Lana, you have meningitis. You'll need to stay here for at least one night and more likely two or three. Maybe a week."

I exhaled a deep breath as Dr. Peterson briskly left my

prison cell of a hospital room. I sat there sulking and envisioned myself walking into the *Los Angeles Post's* office every day with an IV. The thought horrified me. How the hell would I explain that to Ari and my peers? I could feel the effects of the morphine continue to fade and my grim reality coming back. My head pounded like a drum louder and louder each minute the drug dissipated in my bloodstream. Eventually, my sanity slowly returned to a small degree. I tried my best to get the idea of having to deal with an IV in my arm on a long-term basis out of my head. I actively pointed my mind in a different direction. I wondered what the latest was with Celeste. I grabbed my phone and shot Mick a quick text.

Lana Burke: "Any word from the Celeste yet?"

Mick Madden: "Found her! She spent the night with someone she met out last night. She's up to her tricks."

Lana Burke: "Jesus Christ! I'm glad you found her. When is the polygraph scheduled for now?"

Mick Madden: "Tomorrow morning…assuming we don't lose her again."

Lana Burke: "Jeez what a fucking nightmare! Good luck. Please let me know the poly results immediately!"

My phone beeped again.

Giselle Sprint: "I'm going to be stuck at this event for a while. I probably won't be able to get back until midnight. Are you OK?"

Lana Burke: "Don't worry about coming back. I'm

fine."

Before I had a chance to put my iPhone back down, it rang. Finally, it was Malden. "Hello," I said cautiously.

"Oh my God Lana – I've been at the doctor getting tests done all afternoon. My cell didn't get reception at the doctor's office. Are you OK?"

"No, I'm not fucking OK," I shouted. "I have meningitis! And they just told me I might have syphilis or herpes too. I won't know for sure if I have an STD for a week but I'm on medication for both syphilis and herpes."

"Wait, what," he said frazzled. "Syphilis or herpes? Are you serious?"

"I'm sitting quarantined in a hospital room at Cedars," I said, fuming. I swear I could feel smoke coming out of my ears. "Do you really think I'd be cracking a joke right now?"

"I just don't understand," he said dumbstruck. "My doctor told me I have no STD symptoms."

"Are you sure about that?" I asked sharply. "I have meningitis. Do you understand? That's a deadly disease often triggered by an STD. I won't know for sure for seven more days if I have an STD or not."

"OK, OK try to stay calm Lana," Malden softly said.

"Um…" I said, feeling skeptical. He was suspiciously calm.

"When are you going to leave the hospital?" he asked nonchalantly.

"Not until tomorrow at the earliest," I said, exasperated. "And it may be longer."

"You have to stay overnight?"

"Yes, and I'm sitting here trying to figure out why my boyfriend isn't here."

With the drugs and my disease, I certainly was confused

about a lot. However, one thing was becoming clear real fast: Malden was not the man I thought he was. I couldn't process how he wasn't hopping on his motorcycle that second and rushing up to my hospital bedside. I had mixed feelings of anger and utter sadness.

"Lana, I spent all afternoon at the doctor getting tests done so you wouldn't have to spend money out of your pocket to get them done."

His voice quivered. He didn't sound authentic; I wondered if he even went to the doctor. My journalist intuition spiked. I had a gut feeling he was lying to me.

"Yeah, well clearly the situation has changed," I said shocked, that he acted like he had done me a favor by going to the doctor. "Are you coming up here or not?"

"I can come up if you'd like, but I'll be in traffic for three hours." He grunted. "Won't visiting hours be over?"

I paused, not sure how to respond. How dare he bitch about traffic as I sit hooked up to an IV in the hospital? Isn't he supposed to be my knight in shining armor?

"I can take the bike, but it will take me at least two hours."

"You know what – forget it," I said.

"I can skip work or leave early tomorrow to come be with you," he said. He seemed distant and insincere.

"I'm tired, Malden." I sighed as tears filled my eyes. What. A. Fucking. Asshole. That's the only thought that came to my mind.

"Look, I'll talk to my boss tomorrow," he said sounding chipper. "I'll come down after I meet with him and spend the night with you. Hopefully, you'll be able to leave the hospital at some point tomorrow."

"OK," I sighed, holding back the tears.

"Hang in there. I love you."

"Good night," I said coldly, as I threw the phone down in defeat.

The tears slowly dripped down my face. I quickly wiped them away and tried to compose myself in case another doctor or nurse walked in. I had never felt so alone in my entire life. The man who had made me feel warm and fuzzy all summer long – who had claimed to love me – had just failed his biggest test yet. I couldn't believe that he didn't drop everything he was doing the second he found out I was sitting in the hospital with a potentially deadly disease. I thought about what I would do if the situation were reversed. I certainly would've moved mountains to be with someone I loved if they became ill. I sat in my bed in total shock and disbelief. I knew in my heart this was the beginning of the end. How could I ever walk down the aisle and exchange vows with a man who deserted me during my darkest hour? I was conscious enough to know that my brain was injured from the spread of the disease; however, my state wasn't so altered that I couldn't process the difference between right and wrong. It felt so wrong that I was sitting alone in my hospital bed as the man I loved chose to stay miles away from me.

My eyes fell heavy very quickly as the hours began to pass into night. I refused to eat the dinner the nurse brought to my bedside. I fell asleep by eight. I stayed in a deep sleep – with the exception of waking in what felt like a drunken haze every few hours when the nurse came in to check my vitals and change my IV bag.

I woke up around ten in the morning in a coma like state to my phone beeping. I had a text message.

Mick Madden: "She passed."

My heart stopped. I fell into shock.

Lana Burke: "Holy. Fucking. Shit."

Mick Madden: "I know. It's going to happen Lana. Our story is moving forward."

Lana Burke: "Speechless."

I felt a bag of mixed emotions: guilt, excitement, fear and worry. The story made me very anxious; I knew I couldn't put my real name in the byline. The story was bound to cause a shit storm that I certainly didn't want my conservative counterparts to know I was involved in.

Dr. Peterson showed up right before noon. He told me that I would need to stay in the hospital for the rest of the afternoon, as I needed to continue the Acyclovir treatment through an IV. After that, I could leave, but I'd have to continue the Acyclovir treatment at home for the next seven days with an oral prescription. He said that treatment through an IV is preferable but since they didn't know for sure if I had syphilis or herpes yet, I was allowed to treat myself through the oral prescription.

Malden called and said he'd leave work early to come spend the night with me. Giselle picked me up from the hospital at six in that evening. Before I left, I insisted that the nurse give me another dose of morphine so that I could hopefully deal with the pain better on my own.

Malden arrived at my apartment shortly after six in the evening. Despite everything, I couldn't wait to see him. I lay lifeless on the couch in silence when I heard my front door slam open.

"Are you here?" Malden shouted as he walked down the hall.

"I'm on the couch," I said weakly.

Malden walked over and stood above me. My stiff neck still hurt so bad that I was physically unable to lift my head up to look him in the eye. He wore his black leather jacket and held onto his black motorcycle helmet in his left hand. His face looked red – probably from the windburn from riding his motorcycle up on the 405 on such a chilly fall night.

"Traffic was fucking terrible!" Malden said.

"Oh…" I said with confusion, staring into the wall with my eyes half open. "I'm sorry."

"I tried to get here faster. It took me hours, even on the bike. And I had to go back to the doctor today. He said I have hypertension. He wrote me a prescription, and he recommended that I get a heart monitor."

"Oh no," I said with concern. "Are you OK?"

"No, I'm not. I'm a little freaked out."

I sat there baffled. My neck stiffened more and I felt pain shoot up, and down my spine. My neck still felt so stiff from the meningitis – even with the painkillers. My whole body ached. My eyes and brain throbbed. I could tell I had a fever again. I tried hard to look at him clearly, but my eyes could not focus. Everything continued to look blurry. It looked like there were three Maldens with black dots floating all around him. I couldn't figure out why I was seeing so many black dots. They appeared like a pack of flies that tend to swirl around farm animals.

"I'm sorry…" I started to say before stopping myself. I couldn't believe it. I just left the hospital with a diagnosis of meningitis and possibly syphilis – or herpes, too – and I'm sitting here, asking him if he's OK? Tears immediately began to stream down my face.

"What's wrong with you – are you crying?" Malden asked

as he moved to sit next to me.

"I can't believe this – is this a fucking joke!" I screamed. "I just got out of the fucking hospital, Malden, and I'm consoling you? And you have the gall to complain to me about fucking traffic? I wish I could sit in traffic for hours – I can't even sit upright in a chair without feeling unbearable pain! I have meningitis, and they think I have syphilis or herpes, too."

Malden sat down on the couch next to me, put his hand over his mouth and paused. I could tell he did not know how to respond to me. "Lana, I told you last night that I could come up to see you in the hospital, but you told me you were too tired."

My blood boiled. "Fuck you! If someone you love is in the hospital, you shouldn't have to ask him or her to come see you. Of course they fucking want you to! I shouldn't have had to ask you – you should've just come. What's wrong with you? How could you be so cold? I thought you loved me."

"Lana, I do love you – why do you think I'm sitting here with you now?"

"How could you not come to visit me in the hospital," I was sobbing now. "I would've moved mountains to come see you. This is just so fucked up."

"Look, we're both not feeling well. Let's just get into bed. We can eat dinner in bed and watch TV. I just want to get in bed and hold you. Can we do that? Can I just get into bed and hold you?"

I nodded. I slowly got up and strolled into my bedroom at a snail's pace. I threw on boxer shorts and a sweatshirt and moped into bed. Malden made soup for dinner, but I didn't have an appetite. He ate his dinner in bed next to me and we watched TV for a few hours. By the time he turned off the TV, I was almost sound asleep. I lay on my side facing away from him. I heard him rustle the blankets around as he got into bed for the night. He wrapped his arms around me tightly. I slowly drifted off into my drug-induced no-man's-land when a subtle thrust of his hips startled me. Oh my God, I thought. He has a boner!

Malden slowly rocked his pelvis back and forth in between my ass cheeks over my cotton boxers. I couldn't believe it – was he seriously trying to have sex with me? I was just diagnosed with meningitis and I possibly had syphilis or herpes and he was trying to fuck me? I couldn't believe it. He slowly flipped my body over so I was on my back. I was still so weak from the disease and the drugs that he easily handled me like a rag doll. He slowly ripped my boxers off as I stared at him through a tiny slit in my eyes. The room spun. I was still barely awake. I faded in and out of consciousness as he slowly inserted his hard cock in and out of my pussy. He kept spitting on his hand and rubbing it on my pussy. I was bone dry down there – I had never felt so unattractive and disinterested in having sex in my entire life. The whole act felt like a rape. How could he fuck me right now in the condition I was in?

My mind struggled to process the situation. As he delicately rode me back and forth, I drifted off into a dreamlike state. I didn't put any effort into our sexual encounter. I was lifeless. I had no energy to move any part of my body; plus, I was still extremely drugged up from the last morphine drip. The whole scenario felt out of body. I wasn't even sure if what was happening was real. Even with my fried brain, I couldn't process that my boyfriend was having unprotected sex with me in the weak and ill state I was in.

"My little girl," he whispered in my ear. "I could go to jail for you. I could go to jail for fucking you. This is our little secret. *Shhh…don't tell anybody!*"

312

My soul instantly popped back in my body. What did he just say? My entire body froze – I was completely paralyzed. I had a dark feeling Malden was reliving a horrible secret. I could feel his warm cum shoot into my insides. The sensation was heightened – I wondered if that had anything to do with the morphine I was on. He shook uncontrollably on top of me for a few minutes as he usually did. Then he slowly pulled himself off me. He couldn't remove himself fast enough. I turned over and closed my eyes. I was relieved it was over. I tried to ignore the monster next me. Why in the world would he whisper "I could go to jail for you" in my ear?

I woke up at noon in bed, alone. I figured Malden had left early that morning to drive back down to Orange County for work. I still needed to get my Acyclovir and painkillers. I struggled to get out of bed. My whole body ached, and my head continued to pound. However, I felt well enough to do something. I couldn't remember the last time I was home sick. I knew I wouldn't be able to return to work for a few more days. That's when a brilliant idea dawned on me. I had been eager to get a Brazilian blowout for a while now. However, you have to avoid washing your hair for a few days to let the chemicals sink in and straighten your hair. Since I couldn't work or hit the gym, I figured this would be the perfect time to get it done. I called 901 Salon to make an appointment. Luckily, Hailey had an opening midafternoon. I jumped on it.

I rested in bed and watched daytime talk shows for a few hours. I was feeling a lot better – so much better I figured I'd be able to go back to work sooner than I expected. I threw on Uggs, skinny jeans and a sweatshirt and headed to the West Hollywood salon. I still needed to pick up my medicine, but I figured I'd do that after my hair appointment.

I got in my X5 and pulled it out of my garage. It felt great to be back in my car. As I pulled out of the underground garage and headed west, bright rays from the California sun poured into my car.

"Holy fucking shit!" I shouted. "God fucking damn it!"

I immediately put my SUV in park in the middle of the ramp leading into my apartment complex driveway. I scrambled through my Louis Vuitton bag to find my Ray Bans. I could not believe the pain I felt in my eyes from the sun's UV rays. It gave me an instant headache and extreme vertigo. My eyes and brain literally throbbed. The light was unbearable. I didn't understand fully what was going on. I felt like a vampire. I couldn't cope with light – especially sunlight.

I exhaled a deep breath and headed west on Third Street to West Hollywood. The searing pain in my eyes continued, even with the sunglasses on. I held my breath and pushed forward. I kept telling myself I only had a ten-minute drive till I was at the salon. Once I was inside the salon and away from windows, I'd be safe.

I walked up the swanky steps to the trendy salon. A beautiful young brunette checked me in. She escorted me to the waiting area, where I sat on a black couch. There were two flamboyant guys in skinny jeans sitting on another black couch across from me. They were drinking champagne and giggling. There was a guy in the corner of the room playing a guitar and singing – not surprising for a Hollywood salon. The music killed my ears. I was next to a window with more sunlight beaming onto me. It was sensory overload. Every sound, every ray of light – everything in my surroundings made me sick. Suddenly, the room began to spin. I could barely see. I thought I heard one of the guys ask me if I was OK. Everything went black.

"Lana, Lana – are you OK?" Hailey asked as she pulled me upright on the couch.

"What?" I asked, barely conscious.

"You passed out," she said with a look of concern on her face.

I tried to sit upright, but I couldn't. I tipped over and lay back down on the couch. I couldn't sit up. I struggled to even speak. It seemed like the room was spinning at a hundred miles per hour. My head pounded more than ever and I couldn't keep my eyes open. The light hurt my eyes. I felt like I was dying. I was so embarrassed. I didn't know what to say. I struggled to form a sentence.

"I was…" I stumbled softly. "The hospital. I just got out."

"What? When were you in the hospital?"

"I, I, I have meningitis," I whispered. "I feel so sick." Tears streamed down my face. I felt worse than ever. I couldn't talk, I couldn't sit up and I couldn't comprehend what was happening to me.

"Do you want me to call an ambulance?"

"No," I whispered. "I, I – just give me a second."

I closed my eyes and fell asleep right there in the middle of a salon with a live band and basically a party going on. I wondered what everyone was thinking. What drugs is she on? Is she going crazy just like Britney Spears did back in the day? Did they actually believe me when I told them I'm sick?

At least a half hour passed before I awoke again. Hailey stood above me holding a glass of water. I drank it and mustered up enough energy to sit upright.

"Lana, I'm really worried about you – do you want me to call a car service for you?"

"No, it's okay. I shouldn't have come. I thought I was

315

better."

"Are you sure?"

"I just…" I stuttered. "I forgot to get my medicine. I just need to get my medicine. That's it. Then I'll feel better. I'll be fine."

"Are you sure?"

"Yes," I said, slowly rising to my feet. I was determined to get my medicine and go home and get back to bed. I was fine. I just forgot to get my medicine.

I got my car from the valet and told myself that I could be home in less than thirty minutes. I just needed to get my medicine first. I pulled my car onto Santa Monica Boulevard and immediately felt daggers from the sunlight dig into my eyes, even with my Ray Bans on.

"Mother fucker!" I shouted at the top of my lungs as I attempted to drive. "Please God Please! Make it stop."

The tears continued to run down my face. My neck, spine and back stiffened. I barely could feel my muscles in my arms to turn the wheel. All my reflexes were delayed – even driving five miles under the speed limit; I still came very close to colliding with several surrounding vehicles.

I finally made it to the Walgreen's drive-thru. When the pharmacist opened the window, I shoved all of my scripts at her.

"Please, please hurry," I pleaded. "I'm very sick. I'm in a lot of pain."

She gave me a look of horror and walked away. I wondered what I looked like. I didn't dare look in the mirror. I sat in the drive-thru of the Walgreen's facing west. The sun was dead ahead and it tortured me. I put my head down and my hand over my face so I wouldn't have to look at the sunlight. My pain was increasing throughout my body at an extremely rapid rate. I began to feel nauseated, too. It had been less than five minutes since I had arrived at the drug store, but I couldn't take the pain for one more second. I opened the drive-thru window with my left hand.

"Please fucking hurry – I can't fucking take this anymore!" I shouted into the drug store like a completely mad person. "Please!"

The pharmacist rushed over with the white paper bags filled with my medicine in hand.

"Miss, I'm working as fast as I can – I've got your medicine ready," she said.

I reached my hand out and aggressively whisked the meds out of her hand.

"I'm not a bitch – you just don't understand God damn!" I screeched. I made the mistake of lifting my head slightly, and a ray of light shot into my eyes like a bullet. "Oh my God, I'm in so much pain."

The tears streamed down my face again. The pharmacist stood there staring at me in shock. She was speechless.

"Ms. Burke, would you like me to charge this on your account?"

"Yes," I sharply said as I slammed my foot on the gas and sped off. I didn't even say goodbye.

I was less than a mile from my house, and I didn't know if I would survive the drive home. I sped throughout my posh L.A. neighborhood with no regard for other cars or pedestrians. I was a bat out of hell, and if someone was in my way – they were going to die.

When I got to my garage, I struggled as I attempted to walk up to my second floor apartment. I walked slouched over with my hands on my head in an attempt to alleviate the constant pounding I felt in my head, eyes and neck. Walking toward my door, I could feel a flood of liquid fill my mouth. I pulled the door open and rushed as quickly as I possibly could to my bathroom. I violently threw up an acidic yellow liquid. I hadn't been able to eat in days. I was throwing up pure stomach acids. It tasted and felt awful. Every time I attempted to stand up, I would projectile vomit again. I felt like I was living a scene from *The Exorcist*. I sat in front of the toilet for over two hours throwing up. I was so weak that once I was done puking, I had to crawl back into the kitchen to retrieve my phone from my purse. When I looked at it, I had seven missed calls. My phone immediately began to ring again. It was my mom.

"Lana, Lana," my mom anxiously said.

"Huh?" I said breathlessly.

"What's wrong with you? Where have you been? I've been worried sick about you. I have been calling you all day. Are you OK?"

"I-I-I…" I stammered. "No."

"Lana," she said with concern. "What's going on? Is Malden with you?"

"No." I sighed. "I-I-I threw up. I went to the salon and I fainted. Then I threw up."

"What? You went to a hair salon? What is wrong with you? You have meningitis – you can't go get your hair done right now. You have a serious illness. Why are you alone?"

"I don't know." I said, defeated.

"Lana, this is ridiculous. You need serious care right now. You can't take care of yourself. That's it; I'm booking you a plane ticket home. We'll get you to the best doctors and give you the care you need."

"OK," I conceded.

My mom told me she'd call me back with my flight information once she booked my ticket. I remained on the floor for hours. It slowly began to sink in how ill I was. I realized I probably wouldn't be returning to work for a long time. I was devastated.

CHAPTER 17

French Rocker and Giselle came to my rescue again by driving me to the airport. Meanwhile, Malden was carrying on with his life like business as usual.

"Lana, I know you're not going to want to hear what I'm about to say, but I'm having huge second thoughts about Malden," Giselle said, turning her head around from the passenger seat of French Rocker's Volkswagen Passat. We were headed to LAX on the 405 South.

"Huh?" I replied. In my haze, I was barely able to lift my head up to look at her. I crouched over in the backseat, leaning my head against the window with both my hands on my head. The vicious sun shined down on me like a laser beam. Even with my dark Chanel sunglasses on, the rays of light painfully seared through my eyeballs into my skull like bullets. I hated that the sun had become my biggest enemy – there's nothing I enjoy more than a sunny day. Every time a ray of sunlight flashed before my eyes, it felt like my brain immediately burned into a million dark ashes. And when the sunshine hit me – I huddled over in fear and pain – just as young Kirsten Dunst did in the her final scene in *Interview With A Vampire* before the sun burnt her little bloodsucking body to a crisp.

"Lana, he's a fucking asshole! I called him to explain how sick you were, and he brushed me off. He mocked the fact that you are flying home so that your family can take care of you," Giselle said.

"I don't understand," I whimpered. My energy level was at zero. I had taken a couple of Vicodin before I left for LAX airport, but my body was craving morphine. The Vicodin barely reduced the pain I felt all over my entire body.

"Lana, he said, 'Oh, of course she's running home to mommy!'" Giselle's voice sounded like thunder. "He's a fucking dick! You're sick as a dog, and he has not been there for you. His true colors are showing. You need to break up with him."

I heard the words come out of Giselle's mouth, but my brain struggled to process what she was saying. Didn't she just tell me she was having an affair with Viper? I knew she had my best interests at heart, but who was she to judge? My brain lacked communication skills, and I couldn't call her out anyway with French Rocker there. Every billboard we passed didn't make sense. The words were all jumbled and fuzzy. I could recognize a trademark such as McDonald's golden arches, but when I tried to make out the word "McDonald's," it didn't read correctly. The letters were misplaced. I had to stare at each sign I passed for seconds to make sense of the words. I had become dyslexic. Or maybe majorly dyslexic. I wasn't sure.

I had nothing to compare my illiteracy to. All I knew was that I wasn't reading correctly. I wondered how long this would last. My brain continued to throb. Fuck! I couldn't process exactly what was happening to me – or what Giselle was trying to tell me.

"He's not a dick, he just doesn't know...what to do to help me," I scrambled, attempting to come to Malden's defense.

"Lana, wake up! You're fucking dickmitized!"

"I'm what?"

"You're dickmitized! The sex you're having with him clearly is so good that it's blinding you from who this man really is. Plus, you're sick, so you're really not thinking straight. You know, everything is fine and great when you guys are running around on one vacation after another and fucking all over the state of California, but the second you guys are thrown a real life problem – or, should I say you are – Malden doesn't show up. Fuck that!"

My brain couldn't absorb the information. It was like trying to use a rock in place of a sponge to soak up water.

My phone rang. I slowly reached into my purse. It was Gunnar. "Hello," I said with a weak, raspy voice.

"Lana!" Gunnar said frantically. "Are you all right? I saw on Facebook you were in the hospital...or was that some kind of a joke? Were you on a TV set or something for work? What's going on?"

The rapid series of questions overwhelmed my injured brain. "Um...." I tried with extreme difficulty to compose a response. "Yeah – er, I mean no. No TV set. I was at Cedars-Sinai."

"What is wrong with you?"

"I have...men...meningitis." I struggled to say the word.

"What!" he shrieked. "How on earth did you get meningitis?"

"I don't know."

"Are you going to be OK?"

"I'm fine – it's just that…I was supposed to take the hooker to get the polygraph test and I just was too sick. I think…"

"Jesus Lana! I haven't spoken to the President in a few days. What is the latest with that? Is the story going to come out?"

"I don't know. I hope so."

"God, Lana, I can't believe this," he said softly. "I don't want to scare you or stir up your overzealous conspiracy theory mind, but you know that Gov. Richards has been linked to several meningitis outbreaks, right?"

My brain fog sharpened. "What do you mean?"

"Some of the companies he owns have been linked to meningitis outbreaks. You can Google it. Look, I'm really worried about you. What kind of care do you need? Do you need money?"

I was a little taken aback by Gunnar's offer. Even though he was a billionaire, he had never offered me a penny, and I had never asked him for one.

"No, I'll be fine. I'm headed to the airport now to fly back to Chicago. My parents will take care of me there."

"Are you sure? I could let you use my jet."

My heart fluttered. I couldn't believe the gravity of Gunnar's concern for me. He offered to help me more than Malden. Even though my brain was barely functioning it was still sharp enough to realize how backwards this was.

"Thank you, but it's OK. I got a flight on American."

"OK Lana. Well, please text me when you get to Chicago

– and if you need anything, you let me know right away."

"Thank you." I sighed, clicking off the call.

"Well it's official," I announced.

"Huh? Who was that?" Giselle asked.

"I should've married Gunnar."

"Oh, it was Gunnar," Giselle responded with surprise as she turned her head around from the front seat and raised her eyebrows.

"Wait, Gunnar – who's Gunnar?" French Rocker interjected. He was not a well versed on my extremely close relationship with the famous tycoon as Giselle was.

"What did he say?" Giselle asked, ignoring French Rocker's question.

"He told me to call him if I need anything. Oh, and he offered his jet."

"Wow!" French Rocker blurted out. "You should've taken it!"

I cocked my head back against the window and closed my eyes. I felt myself go in and out of consciousness. I picked up bits and pieces of the conversation Giselle and French Rocker were having about me in the front seat.

"Should we get her a wheelchair?" Giselle whispered to French Rocker. "She's so out of it – I'm worried she won't be able to make it to the gate on her own."

"That might not be a bad idea," French Rocker whispered back.

When we arrived at the American Airlines skycap, French Rocker quickly got out of the car and pulled out my suitcase. I couldn't remember what I packed, but I was pretty sure my packing job was a disaster. I was in too much pain to pack, and I struggled to organize my thoughts on what I would need to bring home. French Rocker grabbed my ID out of my wallet.

He checked my bag and got me my boarding pass. I felt so bad for him. He was so kind, and I knew he had no idea Giselle was cheating on him. Giselle helped me out of the car. I walked slower than my ninety-year-old grandma toward the airport entrance.

"Lana, we're going to get you a wheelchair," Giselle ordered.

"What? No, no, no. That's…God fucking damn it!"

"What is it?" Giselle asked, eyes widening.

"Just that sun – God, it's such a bitch!" I said, putting my hand up in the air to block the light from my view. "I'm fine. I don't need a wheelchair. I'm not a freak!" I didn't make that statement with much conviction, because I sure as hell was beginning to feel like a freak. A freak with a fucked up disease that I still knew very little about.

I said goodbye to Giselle and French Rocker. I slowly made my way through the security line. I felt the judgmental eyes of strangers staring at me – does everyone know that I have a crazy disease? It made me feel paranoid. Or was I paranoid? It was difficult to determine what was real and what was in my head – like a bad acid trip that won't end. I heard voices in my head shouting: "Freak! Freak! Freak!" Or was that the person behind me whispering in my ear? I didn't talk to anyone. The line kept moving, and I stood still. A middle-aged man in a gray suit with a maroon-colored tie tapped me on my left shoulder. His touch felt like a malicious attack. It startled me and made me jump.

"What the fuck?" I snapped at him and gave him an evil death glare.

"Sorry, ma'am, but the line is moving," the good-looking businessman meekly replied.

I was mortified. He was gorgeous. He looked like a hot

lobbyist I used to date in Washington D.C. I felt ashamed that I snapped at him. I softly apologized. This disease was turning me into a monster. I was frustrated and angry. Moreover, I couldn't understand why I didn't know to move with the crowd when the line moved forward. It seemed so basic, but my brain could not understand something so elementary.

When I found my gate, I was grateful it was right next to a bathroom. I saw the sign that read "men" with a male figure on it and walked right in without thinking twice. Inside I found a row of men with their pants down pissing at urinals. They all gave me strange looks. I stood there for a minute or two. I knew something was off, but I couldn't put my finger on it.

"Um, can we help you?" a heavyset lawyer-type with black thick glasses and a bad receding hairline asked.

"Oh," I said. "OK…now I get it. This is the men's bathroom."

"Um, yes miss — that would be correct," he said.

I giggled uncontrollably and slowly walked out. That was funny! I just walked into the men's room! I couldn't be more entertained with my actions. In college I had become a pro at sneaking backstage at concerts and into the men's room to pee when the line for the ladies room was too long. However, I had never walked into a men's room unintentionally in my life. I was proud of myself. I was simply hilarious. Move over, Kathy Griffin!

When I got to my gate, I sat in a chair four feet away from the entrance ramp. The sign clearly read, "Chicago Flight #454: On Time." I felt a sweet sense of accomplishment for arriving at the right spot with no wheelchair. I smiled. Passengers slowly got into line and boarded flight #454. I watched them all intently. I was like a toddler hypnotized by a cartoon. This was fun!

When all the passengers had boarded, the female flight attendant repeatedly announced over the speaker that it was the final boarding call. No one was left at the gate besides me. I found the entire series of events utterly amusing. Finally, a male flight attendant slowly began to close the door as the female flight attendant approached me. I was fascinated. I could do this all day. I felt relaxed and momentarily had forgotten about the extraordinary pain I felt.

"Miss, you aren't on this flight, are you?" she inquired.

"Yeah," I said nonchalantly.

"Wait, you are?" she asked in shock.

"Yes," I said proudly and with the same distorted confidence Zach Galifianakis exuded in all of *The Hangover* movies.

"Ma'am we are closing the gate – do you have your boarding pass?"

"Yeah, I do," I said, nodding my head with delusional pride. I slowly reached into my purse and found my pass. I handed it to her with no urgency.

"Miss, you need to board now," she said, gently grabbing my arm and guiding me to the gate. "You almost missed your plane."

"That sounds good," I said, still unfazed.

She gave me a confused look as she scanned my boarding pass. I slowly strolled down the walkway to the plane. It wasn't until I walked on the plane and saw that everyone had already stowed their bags and strapped themselves into their seats, that it began to sink in that I had just come extremely close to missing my plane. My drug-induced and brain-fogged confidence slowly evaporated. I couldn't understand why I was just sitting at the gate, watching everyone board as I remained seated, void of any emotion or awareness of what was happening.

When I sat down and buckled up, the booming headache returned. As the plane took flight and rose higher and higher into the atmosphere, the pressure in my head increased simultaneously. As we continued to soar to an increasingly higher elevation, I felt the beat of a loud drum hit my inner skull over and over again. I downed four Vicodin in a row like a druggie, and I placed my head between my knees. I tried to hold my head with both of my hands in an attempt to alleviate some of the unbearable pressure I felt in the core of my brain. I rocked back and forth again like Dustin Hoffman in *Rain Man*, only pausing every few minutes to let out a subtle moan. I could feel pairs of eyes glaring at me from every direction. I occasionally looked up to glance at the people around me. Everyone appeared like a wide-eyed abstract human figure, straight out of a Picasso. Their distorted faces and oversized almond shaped alien eyes chastised me. I tried hard to ignore them, but it was difficult. The whispers I heard in my head while I was in the security line at the airport returned. Or was it in my head? Was I becoming possessed by the devil? Is this what it's like to see demons? It reminded me of Charlize Theron's character in *Devil's Advocate*. She could see demons, but no one else could. Does this happen in real life? What was I seeing? I closed my eyes and prayed to God the voices and demons would go away. I tried my best to look normal and kept to myself as I sat huddled in a ball in my seat. After an hour of searing pain, I finally dozed off into a partially conscious dream state, but it felt more like a nightmare. I remained hunched over in my miserable state for the entire four-hour flight.

When I landed at Chicago's O'Hare International Airport, I somehow managed to find my bag. My mom waited outside at arrivals in her cream-colored VW station wagon. Sitting in the front seat was our family dog, Snuggle Bear, a West Highland Terrier. I felt the brisk, bitter cold as I exited the airport, wearing nothing but a Rolling Stones T-shirt, ripped jeans and flip-flops. I couldn't understand why it didn't occur to me to bring a jacket. Or did I? What did I pack? I wanted to punch a wall. Why can't I remember anything!

I threw the suitcase in the trunk and sat in the front in a catatonic-like state. Snuggle Bear immediately leaped into my lap and began to lick my face. I didn't even look at my mom – I looked straight ahead in a daze.

"Oh my God, I am so glad you're here," my mom gushed.

"Huh?" I said. My eyes were closed as I tried to cope with the pressure in my head. The relatively short flight and the walk from the gate to arrivals had utterly exhausted me. I hadn't seen my mother in months, and all I could say to her was "Huh."

"Lana," my mom said, flashing me a sad look. "Are you OK?"

My head immediately started pounding again. I threw my head back in my hands. It was unbearable. I needed to lie down, but I was in the front seat of the car so that was impossible. Plus, I did not have the energy to move to the backseat.

"My head – it's unbearable!" I screeched as I rocked back and forth. The tears streamed down my face. Snuggle Bear became frantic and quickly licked my face and hands.

"It's going to be OK. We'll be home soon and you can relax. I'll take you to Dr. Johnson tomorrow. You're going to get through this," my mom said, trying to reassure me as she pulled away from the curb.

I sat in silence the entire car ride home. Snuggle Bear usually strokes my arms with his paw for tummy rubs whenever he's in my lap, but he didn't bug me once. He's never done that before. It was as if he could sense how ill I was. My brain raced. Strange images popped into my head. Rainbows, elephants, Celeste, donkeys, Gov. Richards, Malden's complaining about traffic and our strange sexual encounter the night I got out of the hospital. My head spun. What was it Gunnar told me? What was Gov. Richards's link to meningitis? I tried to string thoughts together, but they were shattered fragments. My thoughts formed like single puzzle pieces that were ripped in two. No matter how hard you tried to put the puzzle together you couldn't – because you didn't have whole pieces. I was pretty sure I could think like a normal person, but I couldn't connect thoughts, ideas and concepts.

When we got home in the North Shore suburb of Glenview, I quickly said hello to my father before crashing in my old bedroom. Snuggle Bear curled up right next to me like the loyal best friend he is. I spent the next eighteen hours sleeping. I only got out of bed to go to the bathroom or to take a Vicodin or a Xanax.

I went to see Dr. Johnson, my primary care doctor since I was a teenager, the next day. He gave me the grim news that aside from Acyclovir and the painkillers, there was not much I could do for my meningitis.

"You just have to rest," Dr. Johnson instructed.

"OK, but I'm working on a big story right now. When do you think I can get back to work?" I said with deep concern.

"Lana," Dr. Johnson said, alarmed. "I don't think you understand the severity of your disease. You could bounce back in a few weeks, but most patients I've seen with meningitis, it takes them several months – even years – to recover."

"But, I don't understand," I said, shaking my head. "That doesn't make sense. There's no way it will take me that long. I'll be fine."

Dr. Johnson repeatedly told me to take it easy and asked that I not rush back to work before I left his office. He never had struck me as an alarmist before, but he seemed to be a little overcautious with me. I couldn't understand why. I was certain I'd be back to work in no time – probably in a week, tops.

As my mom drove us back home from the doctor's office, I put in a call to Ari. I wanted to reassure him that I'd be back to work in a few days, give or take.

Ari answered promptly after one ring. "Lana – are you OK?"

"Hi, Ari," I said. "I just wanted to check in with you. I'm at home in Chicago so my parents can take care of me for a few days, but I'm fine. I should be back to work in a week or so."

"That's great news," Ari said. "We need you. I actually was just going to call you. I'm going to send you the copy of your story with Gov. Richards's and Celeste. I need you to fact-check it."

"OK," I said.

"Also, do you want a byline for the story?" Ari asked.

"Uh, I don't think so," I said.

"Lana, you worked so hard on it. Are you sure?" he asked. "How about we use your alias?"

"OK," I agreed. "Use Ruby Ghostfire."

"Love it." Ari laughed. "You're the modern day female Deep Throat."

"Thank you."

"I want you to know that we stand by you, Lana," Ari said reassuringly. "I don't want you to worry about work. You take as much time as you need to get better. Your job will be here waiting for you once you're well enough to return to work."

"I appreciate that," I said with a sigh.

I hung up and wanted to cry. My mom sensed my frustration.

"What's wrong?" she asked.

"My story on Gov. Richards – it breaks this Wednesday. What if he loses the election because of me?" I sobbed.

"Oh wow!" she said. "Lana, all you did was your job to the best of your ability. If he loses the election it'll be because of the choices he made not the choices you made."

"I don't know." I sighed, unconvinced.

I could hear Mary's voice echoing the words "trust in God" over and over again in my head. Trust in God.

Ari e-mailed me my *Los Angeles Post* cover story so I could fact-check it. The cover had a sexy photo of Celeste smiling, cropped next to a photo of a stunned-looking Gov. Richards. The headline read: "World Exclusive: Gov. Richards Romps With This Hooker!"

The taglines were:

- "His Fetish For Golden Showers!"
- "Oral Sex In His Sacred Mormon Underwear!"
- "Booze & Cocaine Wild Nights!"
- "Secret Meetings At Posh Hotel!"

I cringed at the cover! It was so outrageous, and it made Gov. Richards look awful. I read Celeste's interview that they structured in a Q and A format. They uplifted many of her quotes such as:

"He asked me to pee in a martini glass, and then he drank

it!"

"He never took his Temple garments off, but he gave me the best oral sex I've ever had!"

"He made me drink alcohol and snort cocaine!"

The article at the top read in bold print: "She passed a polygraph test!" The article featured tons of photos of Celeste, most that she supplied us with. One was of her in a bikini washing a car. Another photo featured her in a floral dress with a more conservative look. Another photo featured her drinking straight out of a bottle of whiskey. The more I read, the more ill I felt. What had I done? However, everything was accurate. I e-mailed Ari to let him know the story looked good.

I spent the next day few days in bed with Snuggle Bear. I tried to watch TV, but the light from the flat screen TV hurt my eyes too much. Instead, I would listen to the TV, but not watch it. Malden called every day to check in on me. He had softened since I arrived in Chicago and apologized that he did not take work off to stay with me after I got out of the hospital. Despite his turnaround, Giselle's statements about Malden plagued me as deeply as my disease. My memory had turned very hazy, but Giselle's thoughts on Malden were engraved in my brain like a tattoo – even though I tried to ignore them.

On my fourth day in Chicago, my longtime friend Sasha picked me up to take me to get a mani-pedi. I figured that I was well enough to sit in a chair for an hour or two. I was feeling a little better, and my spirit lifted when I saw her. This was my first outing since my appointment with Dr. Johnson. I was excited to go out and do something that I had taken for granted so often when I was healthy.

"So, what exactly is meningitis?" Sasha asked from the spa table across from me as we both got gel manicures.

"It's a disease that inflames the meninges of your spine and affects the soft tissue surrounding your brain. That's why my head hurts so much," I said as my head almost fell into my hands

"You OK?" the Vietnamese nail technician softly asked me.

"Yeah," I struggled to say, attempting to lift my head out of her nail file.

"Uh, are you sure you're okay?" Sasha asked. "No offense – you're not looking so good."

"I just need a pill. I'm sorry – hold on," I motioned to my nail technician as I reached in my bag to grab another Vicodin. I quickly snuck it in my mouth.

"What was that?" Sasha asked.

"Vicodin."

"Nice – can I have one?" Sasha asked with a laugh.

"Um…"

"I'm just kidding."

After the women finished our nails, we moved over to the spa pedicure chairs. My nail technician turned on my massage chair – it felt like pure ecstasy on my sore and tortured spine.

"So, when do you think you'll be better?" Sasha asked.

"I'll be fine in a few days," I said, slowly slumping over in my chair. My body dramatically leaned left. I soon found myself hanging over the side of the spa chair like Bernie Lomax's corpse from *Weekend at Bernie's*.

"Ugh," I moaned, putting my hand on my forehead. *Boom. Boom. Boom.* There was that beat of the drum. It pounded in my head as loudly as it had the day I had flown home. I couldn't believe the pain was still so prominent after spending days in bed. I struggled to sit upright in my spa chair. It felt impossible, like I was attempting to climb Mount Everest.

"Lana, Lana – what's wrong?" Sasha asked, visibly concerned.

"God! My fucking head. I need another Vicodin."

"Here, I'll get it for you," Sasha said, quickly jumping off her spa chair and grabbing the bottle from my purse. My nail technician looked distraught as she looked at me, her pathetic rag doll of a client. I quickly swallowed the Vicodin in total desperation. I closed my eyes and rested over the side of the chair. I prayed the pain would go away. Come on Lana – you can do this, I said to myself in my head.

The pain increased – even with the Vicodin. I couldn't bear sitting in a chair for another second. I needed to go home and lie in a bed. I saw the nail technician reach for the red Esse nail polish I had picked out. I was coherent enough to know that polishing my toenails would require me to sit in this chair for at least another ten minutes. The thought was unbearable.

"Stop!" I shouted as tears began to fill my eyes. "I'm sorry – I can't. Sasha, I need to go home. I'm so sorry."

"No, no – don't worry," Sasha said with concern but reassuringly. "We'll go. That's fine."

When I got home, I went straight to bed. Between the constant beating drum in my head, I couldn't help but think about what had just happened. Was I so sick and pathetic that I could not even tolerate sitting in a fucking chair for a half hour to get a pedicure? I felt so lost and hopeless. When would this pain and torture end? Was Dr. Johnson right? Was I going to be stuck in this medical purgatory for a year? The concept pained me like a black dart through my chest. My dark reality seemed to get worse with time – not better.

On my fifth day in Chicago, my ringing cell phone awakened me. It had been a full week since my October 8 diagnosis of meningitis at Cedars-Sinai. It was the call I had been dreading. Was I positive for syphilis-meningitis?

"Hello," I answered, worried.

"Is this Lana?" a frantic voice snapped back on the other end.

"Yes," I said.

"Lana, Lana, it's Dr. Peterson. I got your test results back. You have HSV-meningitis. You need to go to the emergency room immediately!"

"Wait, what?"

"Lana, you have HSV-meningitis. That's herpes-meningitis. It's one of the kinds of meningitis that can cause the most damage to the brain – like I explained to you at the hospital. I hope you've been keeping up with your Acyclovir treatment, but you need to go to the hospital and get treatment through an IV."

"What!" I shouted in despair. I immediately began to comprehend what I had just been told. "I have herpes – like the STD?"

"Yes – now, can someone rush you over here right away?"

"What, no? I don't know."

"Lana, you need to get to the hospital."

"But I'm in Chicago. I don't understand."

"Then go to a hospital in Chicago."

"Wait, I'm so confused," I said. "Will you talk to my mom? I don't understand."

"Yes, I'd be glad to."

"Mom! Mom!" I frantically shouted from upstairs. I could hear my mom fidgeting in our kitchen downstairs.

"What?" she shouted back.

"My emergency room doctor is on the phone – he said I need to go to the hospital immediately.'

"What!" she shouted back as I heard her gallop up the stairs.

"He wants to talk to you," I said in a distressed fog.

My mom plowed into my bedroom and grabbed my iPhone faster than a hawk snags its prey.

I sat down on the bed and felt my soul leave my body again. I blankly stared at my alarmed mother as she spoke to Dr. Peterson. One thought repeated through my head over and over: Malden. What had this man done to me? Will I need an IV for the next six months? How will I be able to do my job? Who will ever date a woman who has fucking herpes? I had become a public outcast in one phone call. I'd go back to Hollywood wearing a Scarlet Letter across my chest like Hester Prynne – except I'd be wearing an H instead of an A.

When my mom got off the phone with my doctor, she calmly looked at me and told me we needed to head to Glenbrook South Hospital immediately.

"That bastard – he gave me an STD, Mom! I might have brain damage! He ruined my life!" I said as the tears poured down my face.

My mom embraced me. "You will get through this, Lana, but we need to go to the hospital immediately!"

My mom rushed me to the remodeled hospital in Chicago's North Shore suburb. She has a tendency to speed, but that day she hit a new record. When we got to the turnaround at the hospital a few miles away from our home she quickly pulled into the ER driveway.

"You check in while I park," she said hurriedly.

Panicked, I walked in as fast as I could. Each step I took

fell in sync with the drumbeats that continued to pound in my head. The pain felt more amplified than the day before. I wondered if it was due to the stress of my current situation.

"May I help you?" an African-American nurse, who was sitting at the check-in, asked warmly.

"I have meningitis!" I said in a psychotic panic. "I have herpes-meningitis. My doc – my doctor from L.A. I live in L.A. – I need help fast! He just called and told me…"

"OK, I'm going to need you to fill out some forms," she said, grabbing a clipboard.

"No, I don't have time!" I said as tears began to fill my eyes again. "You don't understand. I'm going to die! He said I'm going to have brain damage. I need to get in there now!" I said as I pounded my fist on the table. There was that tiger inside me that always got me what I wanted when I found myself in a tough situation – especially when I was working on a big story.

"Okay, okay miss – let me get a doctor for you," she said as she got up from her chair.

I walked to the nearest chair and sat down. I stared blankly at the TV airing *The Price is Right*. I noticed only one elderly man in the waiting room. I quietly thanked God that there wasn't a huge wait. Within seconds, an Asian doctor quickly walked out, but the second she laid eyes on me, her step stalled.

"Hi – I'm Dr. Lee." She seemed exceptionally serious. "The nurse said you have HSV-meningitis?"

She looked at me apprehensively – why?

"Yes," I shouted back breathlessly. "My doctor, he, he just called. I was in the hospital in L.A. a week ago with meningitis. He just called and said I now have herpes-meningitis. He said I need treatment through an IV immediately, so that I don't get brain damage."

OK," she said. "Why don't you follow me into the emergency room and we'll get you checked out."

Dr. Lee had no urgency in her tone and talked to me as if I were a child. She slowly guided me to a bed in the ER. I was confused by her demureness and was still in shock from Dr. Peterson's phone call.

"So, I'm going to need your name and some information from you. What hospital were you at in Los Angeles?"

"Cedars-Sinai," I snapped back quickly. Why wasn't she rushing to get me the drug IV?

"What's your name?"

"Lana – Lana Burke," I panted.

"I'm going to need to see some ID," she said leisurely, as if I were a teen at a liquor store trying to buy alcohol.

"That's fine – it's in my purse on the table," I said as I pointed to my bag. "It's in my Louis Vuitton wallet."

"I'm going to need to get your test results faxed over from Cedars-Sinai before we can treat you with anything, so please just hang tight," she said, grabbing my ID. She exited and closed the curtain behind her. I got out of the bed and grabbed my phone.

My mom entered seconds later. "What did they say?"

"They are getting all my medical records faxed over from Cedars-Sinai. I can't believe he did this to me, mom! How am I supposed to live with an STD? This is horrible!"

"Everything is going to be OK, Lana. I promise," my mom said gently.

"No, it's not mom! It's not!"

I unlocked my phone.

"Who are you calling?"

"I'm calling the bastard who gave me herpes."

339

Malden answered his phone after two rings. "How are you feeling?" he cooed on the other end.

"You son of a fucking bitch!" I shot back.

"Wha-at?" He sounded genuinely shocked.

"You gave me fucking herpes!"

"What are you talking about, Lana?"

"I'm in the emergency room in Chicago! My doctor from Cedars called – he said I have fucking herpes! You gave me fucking herpes! You're a lying, cheating, disease-infected scumbag!"

"I don't know what you're talking about. I don't have herpes!"

"Bullshit," I screamed. "Bull –fucking – shit!"

"Lana, I don't," he said with agitation. "I got tested the day you were at Cedars, remember? I had a full battery of tests done. Everything came back negative. Stop with the accusations."

"You're a fucking liar," I growled. "You're the only person I've slept with this entire year. You're the only person who could've given this to me. You fucking asshole!"

"You're wrong," he said defensively. "I did not give you anything, and I'm not going to sit on the phone and take this abuse."

"Fuck you!" I shouted, tears streaming down my face.

The line went dead. Malden had hung up. I fumbled with my phone in an attempt to call him back immediately.

"Lana, I know you're upset, but you need to keep your voice down. We're in a hospital," my mom said as she approached my bedside. I ignored her.

Malden's phone rang and rang. I got his voicemail.

"That mother fucking scumbag!" I shouted as I threw my phone on the hospital floor and wept.

My mom picked up my iPhone. I could see a crack in the screen as she handed it back to me. She grabbed a tissue and gave that to me, too.

"I just can't believe he did this to me," I cried. "And he won't even admit he has herpes. He's a fucking liar!"

I bawled for minutes. My mom tried to make me feel better by telling me that if I did have the STD – I could become an advocate for women's health. She said I could go around to schools lecturing about safe sex. I wanted to throw my purse at her. As I sat in yet another hospital bed with a fried brain and the reality that I had just contracted an STD from the man I was madly in love with – the absolute last fucking thing I wanted to hear was how I could become the poster girl for herpes! Was she on crack? I mean really – and I'm supposed to be the one with the fried brain?

"Ms. Burke..." Dr. Lee said as she entered the room with a pile of papers. "We got your medical records faxed over from Cedars-Sinai. I'm going to have to apologize to you. To be quite honest, when you walked in here and said you had meningitis, I didn't believe you."

"Wait, what!" I said in confusion. My brain struggled to process her statements. Why in the world did she not believe me at first?

"You're an extraordinary case, Ms. Burke. I've seen many meningitis patients and to be honest, I've never seen a patient as coherent as you with your diagnosis."

"I don't understand – what do you mean?"

"Most people who come in with meningitis are so out of their minds, they don't even know their own name. We've had to wrestle other meningitis patients down like wild animals. Some of them have walked in stripping off all their clothes. Others repeat themselves over and over again – it's like the movie *Groundhog Day*."

"Are you being serious?" I asked, still confused.

"Yes. It's quite remarkable that you're able to answer questions intelligently and your memory seems to be intact."

"Good Lord, that's really scary," my mom interjected. "Lana, thank God you're not like that."

I sat back in my hospital bed, still frazzled. Other people with meningitis can't even remember their own names? They walk around in public naked? The thought of acting in that manner horrified me. I felt momentarily humbled. But then I recalled my herpes diagnosis.

"Well, what about the herpes – Dr. Peterson said I have herpes?"

"Yes, you have HSV-meningitis."

"So my boyfriend gave me the STD?"

"No, you don't have an STD," Dr. Lee calmly said.

"Wait, what do you mean? Dr. Peterson told me I have herpes-meningitis. He said I have the STD kind."

"No, you don't have an STD. You have a form of viral meningitis. The strand of herpes you have is the same strand that causes chickenpox in children."

"So wait, are you saying I don't have an STD?"

"No, you have the strand of HSV that causes shingles and chickenpox."

"I don't understand. My boyfriend cheated on me. I just yelled at him over the phone. Dr. Peterson said I have an STD. So I'm not going to have herpes outbreaks?"

"No, you're going to be just fine. We're going to treat you with an IV of Valtrex here for a few hours, and then you will be able to go home. I'll just need you to take an oral prescription for Valtrex for the next few weeks."

"I'm still confused – isn't herpes permanent? Won't I

have it for the rest of my life?"

"No, not this strand."

"So, then how the hell did I get this?"

"You could've caught this any number of ways. Have you been in any big public crowds recently?"

"Well, I flew home to Chicago a few days ago and before I went to Cedars-Sinai I was in San Francisco for Fleet Weekend."

"Well, there's a good chance you could've contracted the disease from the large crowds I imagine you found yourself in during Fleet Weekend."

I sat back speechless in my hospital bed as the doctor stuck the IV needle into my right wrist. The pain of the needle digging into the prominent thick blue vein under my right palm did not faze me at this point. My head spun. I found myself more confused than ever. When I walked into Glenbrook South Hospital I was certain Malden had given me an STD that caused my meningitis, but this doctor assured me that wasn't the case. Nothing made sense. I began to feel horrible for reaming Malden out. Gunnar's words about Gov. Richards's ties to meningitis shot back into my disease-infected brain. Could Gov. Richards be behind my illness? I felt like I was living in a parallel universe or some kind of a twilight zone. I didn't know what the hell was going on, but I was damn sure I didn't pick up meningitis from attending an air and water show in San Francisco. I already had vaginal pain and symptoms at the show. My gut told me there was much more to the story.

My mom took me straight home after I spent a few hours at the hospital receiving the Valtrex treatment intravenously. She graciously offered to pick up my new prescriptions so I could get back into bed. I actually felt pretty good, but I knew that had everything to do with the fact that I had insisted the doctors pump me with morphine through an IV before I left. I got into bed and whipped out my phone. I felt horrible about my altercation with Malden. He must have been telling me the truth – all of his STD results must have been negative like he said. This whole mess was a series of really unfortunate events. Although Malden had not been there for me when I initially got ill, I did still love him. I knew I needed to salvage whatever I could of our relationship. I called him. No answer. I quickly typed him a text message.

Lana Burke: "Please pick up the phone. The doctors misdiagnosed me."

Malden Murphy: "Are you going to yell at me?"

Lana Burke: "No. I want to apologize."

Seconds later my phone rang. It was Malden.
"Hello," I softly answered.
Silence.
"Hello…are you there?" I asked.
"Yep," Malden grunted.
"Look – I'm sorry I yelled at you. The Cedars-Sinai doctor told me I have herpes and you're the only person who could've given it to me."
"I told you I went and got tested for everything the day you were in the hospital," Malden chided. "That's why I wasn't in the hospital with you. I was getting my own tests done."
"I know. And you got all the results back?"
"Yes! I told you they were all negative. I'm clean! I've been tested for everything under the sun. I got a full battery of tests done and I'm totally clean."

"OK, well, the doctors at the Chicago hospital told me that there was a mistake. I do have herpes but I don't have the STD kind of herpes. I have a form of herpes that causes chickenpox in children. The doctor said I could've picked up my meningitis in San Francisco when we were watching the Blue Angels or something. But I did experience all those painful vaginal symptoms before the show."

"I love you, Lana, but you can't keep jumping down my throat. I don't deserve to be talked to like that."

My stomach sank. Was I the bad person in this relationship?

"I'm sorry, Malden, but what was I supposed to think?" I attempted to reason with him. "The doctor told me I had herpes, and you're the only person I've been with for almost a year now. Plus, you cheated on me. Anyone else in my shoes would have reacted in the same way."

"All right, look – let's just move on from this," Malden said. "There's a mortgage conference in Chicago in a few days I was thinking of attending. I'm going to get a room downtown. I know you can't do much, but maybe you could come down and stay with me?"

"OK," I agreed without thinking.

I hadn't seen Malden in days, and despite everything that had happened, I still got butterflies in my stomach at the thought of seeing him.

I spent the next few days in anticipation of Malden's arrival feeling like a tortured prisoner in my parents' home. I so badly wanted to move around, work out, go out and do something, but the pressure I continued to feel in my head whenever I would stand or even sit up in a chair for too long was still pretty unbearable. However, I was improving. The progress I made was shockingly slow, but I was making small strides. I began to watch TV for a few minutes here and there instead of just listening. When the light from the TV hurt my eyes too much, I just shut them and continued to listen. I couldn't read books. It was too painful. The task of reading pages of words was too tedious for my corrupted vision and it was still difficult for me to make out words on paper. I still suffered from some kind of dyslexia. However, I could skim social media and articles. It hurt to do so, but I couldn't resist because I was so bored out of my mind. I endured the pain to momentarily free myself from my chains of boredom. When I went online it served as an escape. I obsessively Googled "meningitis." The horror stories I attempted to read from other people touched by the disease were terrifying. Many people end up dead, blind, deaf or locked up in a mental institution for the rest of their lives. The stories were too much for me to handle, and they literally made me feel even more ill.

One day, I ventured into my old closet with Snuggle Bear following closely behind. I spent hours digging through old pictures. I found dozens of photos of me with different politicians from my days campaigning, including Governor George W. Bush before he became President. I had at least a dozen photos of myself with GW from different rallies on the campaign trail. There were also photos of me with Senator John McCain, Congressman John Kasich, President George H. Bush, and many others. I had attended the 1999 Republican Straw Poll, the Iowa Caucuses and countless presidential debates when I worked for Bush. Then, I found the photos of me in the White House after Bush won the 2000 election. I was on the road to a bright future in political journalism. I interned with the White House press corps working alongside some of Washington's top journalists including David

Gregory, Helen Thomas, Wendell Goler, Terry Moran and Major Garrett. At the age of twenty-one I worked alongside the country's elite journalists; yet, I somehow ended up working for the *Los Angeles Post* as a tabloid reporter. I still struggled to wrap my brain around the idea that the one diehard Republican in all of Hollywood was handpicked to be the journalist to take down the Republican Presidential nominee. I still couldn't process this. Now, the election was only two weeks away, and I was sitting in a closet at my parents' house in pajamas. How did I get here?

I grabbed Snuggle Bear and got back into bed with him. I reached for my MacBook Air laptop from my nightstand and opened it. I typed "Prescott Richards" and "meningitis" into Google. In seconds, the search engine came up with over a hundred thousand results. I was floored. I slowly scanned over all the headlines on various news sites:

• "Richards's lax regulation may have fueled meningitis outbreak"

• "Blaming Richards for deadly meningitis and other wild liberal media claims"

• "The meningitis that Richards's deregulation built"

• "Richards's lack of action had a hand in meningitis outbreak"

• "Richards and meningitis outbreak"

• "Left-wing writer blames Richards for deadly meningitis"

I opened the first article and tried my best to read and comprehend it.

The fatal meningitis epidemic sweeping the United States can now be traced to the failure of Gov. Richards to adequately regulate the Utah pharmaceutical company that is being blamed for the deaths.

At least 344 people in 18 states have been infected by the growing public health crisis and 25 have died so far.

But the epidemic may also play a role in the presidential campaign, now that state records reveal that a Utah regulatory agency found that the Utah Conserve Co., the pharmaceutical company tied to the epidemic, repeatedly failed to meet accepted standards in 2004 — but a reprimand was withdrawn by Gov. Richards administration in apparent deference to the company's business interests.

I skimmed the rest of the articles. The more conservative news sites stated that it was ridiculous to link Gov. Richards to any of the meningitis outbreaks. I typed in other combinations with meningitis such as "meningitis conspiracy theory" and "meningitis biological warfare." My searches led me to information about conspiracy theories surrounding Plum Island Animal Disease Center. I had heard a little about the New York island that was owned and run by the government. According to Wikipedia:

Since 1954, the center has had the goal of protecting America's livestock from animal diseases. During the Cold War a secret biological weapons program targeting livestock was conducted at the site. This program has been the subject of controversy.

The center is located on Plum Island near the northeast coast of Long Island in New York State. During the Spanish-American War, the island was purchased by the government for the construction of Fort Terry, which was later deactivated after World War II and then reactivated in 1952 for the Army Chemical Corps. The center comprises 70 buildings (many of them dilapidated) on 840 acres (3.4 km²).

Plum Island has its own fire department, power plant, water treatment plant and security. Any wild mammal seen on the island is killed to prevent the possible outbreak of hoof and mouth disease. However, as Plum Island was named an important bird area by the New York Audubon Society, it has successfully attracted different birds. Plum Island had placed osprey nests and bluebird boxes throughout the island and will now add kestrel houses.

I scrolled down to the conspiracy theories related to the island:

On July 12, 2008, a creature dubbed the Montauk Monster washed ashore at Ditch Plains Beach near the business district of Montauk, New York. The creature, a quadruped of indeterminate size, was dead when discovered, and was assumed by some to have come from Plum Island due to the currents and proximity to the mainland. Palaeozoologist Darren Naish studied the photograph and concluded from visible dentition and the front paws that the creature may have been a raccoon. This was also the opinion of Larry Penny, the East Hampton Natural Resources Director, though others claim that this is unlikely and interpret the fleshless part of the upper jaw, visible in the photo with empty tooth sockets, as a beak, implying that the creature was a kind of hybrid monster, an extremely implausible and unlikely circumstance.

I opened a new window and typed "Montauk Monster" into Google images. I was shocked at what I saw. The creature looked like a pink pig with the beak of an eagle and claws like a bird too. Was this for real? I went back to the Wikipedia page on Plum Island and read on:

> Some say Plum Island opened under Project Paperclip. This was a top-secret government program to recruit Nazi scientists who were working on animal diseases during WWII. It has been suspected that more than 2000 scientists were brought here and offered employment contracts and US citizenship. One of the areas of expertise they had was experiments with disease-infected ticks. It is suspected that Dr. Erich Traub, a physician once in charge of the Third Reich's virological and bacteriological warfare program in World War II, was involved with the biological warfare research at Plum Island.

> From the Belarus Secret it states: Even more

disturbing are the records of the Nazi germ warfare scientists who came to America. They experimented with poison ticks dropped from planes to spread rare diseases. I have received some information suggesting that the US tested some of these poison ticks on the Plum Island artillery range off the coast of Connecticut during the early 1950's...

I opened another window and searched for more sites with information on Plum Island. I found several websites tying Plum Island to the first case of Lyme disease. The pain from staring at the computer screen for so long felt like swords slicing into my eyeballs, but I couldn't stop. I muscled through the web of information despite the searing pain. One article in particular struck me:

Plum Island is coincidentally within miles of the place where Lyme disease originated, the epicenter of Lyme, Connecticut.

People who blame Plum Island for Lyme disease clearly demonstrate that infected ticks from Plum Island could have easily been transported to the mainland via the hundreds of different birds that would nest there.

After years of denial that Lyme disease is a biowarfare agent, the Centers of Disease Control admitted when opening Margaret Batts Tobin Laboratory Building in Texas that the facility would be used to study diseases as anthrax, tularemia, cholera, Lyme disease, desert valley fever and other parasitic and fungal diseases. The Centers for Disease Control and Prevention identified these diseases as potential bioterrorism agents.

My eyes widened as I read about the origins of these diseases and their ties to biological warfare. I found a ton of information tying Lyme disease to bioterrorism; however, I wasn't able to find as many links to meningitis. I knew there was something about Lyme disease that hit home for me but I struggled to remember what it was. As I read on and on, I tried to jog my memory. I knew there was some relevance to Lyme disease – something! Come on, Lana, think! What is it? I closed my eyes for minutes and focused as hard as I could on my thoughts. I said out loud: "Lyme disease – where have I heard this before?" It hit me hard – that's what Malden's daughter has! I quickly Googled "Lyme disease symptoms."

I clicked on the list of symptoms that appeared on the Mayo Clinic's website:

> The signs and symptoms of Lyme disease vary and usually affect more than one system. The skin, joints and nervous system are affected most often.
> Early signs and symptoms
>
> These signs and symptoms may occur within a month after you've been infected:
>
> • Rash. A small, red bump may appear at the site of the tick bite. This small bump is normal after a tick bite and doesn't indicate Lyme disease. However, over the next few days, the redness may expand, forming a rash in a bull's-eye pattern, with a red outer ring surrounding a clear area. The rash, called

erythema migrans, is one of the hallmarks of Lyme disease. Some people develop this rash at more than one place on their bodies.

• Flu-like symptoms. Fever, chills, fatigue, body aches and a headache may accompany the rash.

Later signs and symptoms

In some people, the rash may spread to other parts of the body and, several weeks to months after you've been infected, you may experience:

• Joint pain. You may develop bouts of severe joint pain and swelling. Your knees are especially likely to be affected, but the pain can shift from one joint to another.

• Neurological problems. Weeks, months or even years after you were infected, you may experience inflammation of the membranes surrounding your brain (meningitis), temporary paralysis of one side of your face (Bell's palsy), numbness or weakness in your limbs, and impaired muscle movement.

Less common signs and symptoms several weeks after infection, some people develop:

• Heart problems, such as an irregular heartbeat. Heart problems rarely last more than a few days or weeks.

• Eye inflammation.

353

- Liver inflammation (hepatitis).

- Severe fatigue.

I was stunned by how similar Lyme disease symptoms were to meningitis symptoms. I read the line that explained that a patient may "experience inflammation of the membranes surrounding the brain (meningitis)" over and over again. My swollen brain tried to process all the information that came at me. What were the odds that I contracted a disease so similar to the one Malden's daughter has? Were both diseases created in a government lab in this country as some form of biological weapon? Even though it was so hard for me to string thoughts and information together, the reporter in me knew there must be a connection. My intuition began to kick in. I felt sick. I closed my laptop and lay in the fetal position holding my head and closed my eyes. I knew something was terribly wrong. I knew biological warfare was a real thing. Meningitis is a disease that if it doesn't kill you, it will damage your brain enough so you cannot function for months. If Gov. Richards wanted to get rid of me or at least impair my brain enough so I couldn't finish my story, meningitis truly was the perfect biological weapon to poison me.

CHAPTER 18

Against Dr. Johnson's orders, I flew back to L.A. the morning my story broke. I was anxious to get back to work, even though I was still ill and very weak. I didn't let that stop me. Ari assured me that my job would be waiting for me, no matter how long it took for me to get well. But I knew better. In this business, you're only as good as your last story.

At both Chicago's O'Hare Airport and Los Angeles's LAX airport I spotted dozens of people walking around carrying or reading an *L.A. Post* with my cover story on it. It was all over and everywhere people were talking about the scandal.

As soon as I got to my Weho apartment, I flipped on Rox News Channel. *The O'Malley Factor* with Shamus O'Malley was on. Shamus, nicknamed Shameless for his aggressive reporting style, interviewed Gov. Richards's spokesperson George Carson.

"The *L.A. Post* has a bombshell story on your candidate with an on-the-record interview with an escort who allegedly passed a polygraph test and makes outrageous claims of a sexual affair with Gov. Richards. What say you, Mr. Carson?" Shamus asked.

"We one hundred percent deny these outrageous and offensive accusations, and Gov. Richards is pursuing his legal options to clear his name." George said.

"So he's suing the *L.A. Post*?" Shamus asked.

"Our attorneys have been in contact," George said. "That's all I can comment on the legal matter."

Gov. Richards's attorneys had sent the *L.A. Post* a legal letter and threatened to sue. Ari and I expected this. We do not anticipate that Gov. Richards will actually follow through with filing the suit. Once a lawsuit is filed, the *L.A. Post* can subpoena evidence during the discovery process that Gov. Richards would most likely prefer to keep private. However, Gov. Richards's attorneys were obligated to at least threaten a lawsuit to diffuse the situation. Silence from their side could make him look guilty.

"Any idea who the reporters are?" Shamus asked. "They have used pen names for their bylines. Who is this Ruby Ghostfire?"

"We do not know who these reporters are," George said.

"Liar!" I shouted at the TV. They knew exactly who I was — they practically killed me!

"We do know that the *L.A. Post* is notorious for making up outrageous stories," George said. "They've been sued for libel numerous times in the past and have lost. The publication, and their quote end quote 'journalists', have no credibility whatsoever."

I flipped to LMCH and *The Sarah Storm Show* was on.

"So look at what we have here," Sarah snickered. "The Republican's Mormon conservative Republican candidate whose entire candidacy is based on faith and family values appears to be having a sexual affair with a hooker."

I cringed and turned off the TV. My stomach sank. What had I done?

There was a media frenzy with my story on Gov. Richards, but thankfully no one knew I was Ruby Ghostfire. Malden and I smoothed things over during the few days we spent together in Chicago. He would go to his conference in the morning, and come back to the hotel with food during a break so we could eat lunch together. I was even well enough to go out with him for a nice steak dinner at Chicago's famous Gibsons restaurant. But that week, I spent most of my time sleeping at the hotel while he attended the conference. He was attentive and loving during our time together. I told myself that if we could make it through this nightmare situation – we could get through anything.

However, I still had so many questions about my disease and I couldn't shake the feeling that there had to be a tie to Gov. Richards. I knew there were several mysteries surrounding my illness waiting to be unlocked. I temporarily compartmentalized those questions so that I could focus on returning to work and improving my health – for now. The toll the disease took on my brain made it difficult to focus on multiple endeavors. I used to be a pro at multitasking; now I struggled to juggle multiple objectives. I tried my best to operate on a one-track mind.

***

My first day back at work felt like another out-of-body experience. I still walked slowly and had severe head and neck pain. I thought I could function close to normal with the help of the painkillers my doctors had prescribed for me. When I arrived at the office, the same whispers and the distorted faces I saw on the plane to Chicago returned. As I navigated my way through the sea of cubicles anchored by low to mid-level gossip journalists, I felt eerily self-conscious. Some of my colleagues gave me a warm "hello" or asked how I was feeling. I tried my best to smile and continued to walk back to my office at a fast pace. I felt like an outcast. Everyone appeared uncomfortable talking to me. I confronted a dozen uneasy stares. You would have thought I had walked into work with a third leg. Once I got into my office, I closed the door behind me and sat at my computer. I felt my anxiety level rise. I quickly popped a Vicodin. Within seconds, Nigel burst in the door.

"Oh my God Lana – I can't believe you're back!" Nigel, with his petite frame and spiky dark hair, gushed. He was wearing white skinny jeans and a hot pink shirt decorated with sequins. With my blurred vision, he literally looked like a flamingo. My mouth dropped, and I looked at him in shock.

"Lana – hello? Are you OK? I've been so worried about you. I knew you were sick, but I didn't know you had meningitis until the other day when Mick told me."

"I'm fine." I giggled.

"Lana, what are you laughing at?" Nigel asked as he looked curiously around the room.

"No, no it's nothing…"

"Um, okay – are you sure you're okay?"

"It's just your shirt." I said with a giggle.

"You don't like the pink? I thought you loved my outfits!"

"No, I do. It's just…you look like a flamingo!" I said as I laughed uncontrollably. "A pink flamingo!"

"Excuse me, honey," Nigel said in his bitchy gay voice.

"No, Nigel, don't be offended. Look, I think I'm high right now. I'm still taking some major pills for all my headaches and neurological issues."

"OK, I get it." Nigel sighed. "I was going to say you look a little loopy."

"Really? Is it that obvious?"

"Well, maybe just to me. It's not just that you seem loopy, though. You look really peaked."

"I do?" I asked in shock.

"Yeah, Lana – you look sick," Nigel insisted. "Are you sure you're okay to be back at work this soon?"

I couldn't believe that after three weeks away from work, I still appeared to be ill. Dr. Johnson's suggestion to stay home for at least a few more weeks haunted me. Was I back too soon?

"I'm fine," I said, glaring at Nigel. The room spun around him, and pesky black dots that looked like horseflies spun around his head. It was hard to focus on him and our conversation.

"So how did you end up with meningitis? Do the doctors have any idea how you got it?"

"The doctors don't know – they're all kind of scratching their heads about my disease. It's really weird."

"That's crazy. How do you think you got it?"

"I'm not sure," I said, anxiously beginning to bite the nail on the index finger of my right hand. "It keeps me up at night."

"Well, if anyone can solve a mystery it's you. I've got to get back to the desk. Let me know if you need anything. I'm glad you're back – but you take it easy today."

"Thanks, Nigel," I said with a loving smile as I turned on my desktop computer.

Ari held the morning meeting in his corner office. Everyone warmly welcomed me back. I did my best to smile and act normal. Secretly, I was a nervous wreck. I hoped that they wouldn't pick up on the fact that I was high as a hippie at a Phish concert from the painkillers.

Ari began the meeting by holding up the newest issue of our biggest competitor and my former employer *Celebrity Weekly*. There was a photo of Celeste on the cover wearing her Nazi costume, holding a beer in one hand with a Confederate flag in the background. I gasped. The headline read: "Gov. Richards's Hooker Is A White Supremacist Nazi Lover!" The taglines read:

- "She Married This Sex Offender!" (It read next to an arrow pointed toward a photo of Billie.)

- "Her Criminal Past!"

- "Her Madame Tells-All: 'She's A Pathological Liar!'" (The tagline read next to a circled photo of a heavy redheaded woman in her forties with arms covered in tattoos. I presumed it was Madame Victoria.)

"I want you all to see *Celebrity's* cover," Ari said. "They're trying to ride off our wave. I want you all to work hard on follow-up stories this week on Gov. Richards. Mick and Lana, please put in calls to Celeste."

Mick and I nodded. Ari read through the other top stories of the day.

I tried to concentrate during the meeting, but it was hard to focus. Besides, the effects from the Vicodin were driving me crazy. My entire body itched. I scratched my arms, nose, and head, back – I even wanted to scratch my crotch, but I refrained. I was trying to be subtle about my scratching, but I feared that everyone was picking up on my obsessive scratching. I know it must've looked crazy, but I couldn't control myself. I felt so unbearably itchy I had to scratch myself every few minutes. Ari's words became inaudible like the schoolteacher from the *Peanuts* comic strip. All I heard was: "Wah, wah, wah, wah, wah, wah, wah, wah…"

"Lana – hello?" Ari asked, agitated

"I'm sorry, what?" I said as I snapped out of my haze of brain-fried boredom.

"Does that sound good – can you write up the story on Lamar Odom cheating on Khloe Kardashian?" Ari asked, still irritated.

"Yes, yes of course. No problem."

"Do you have anything else to pitch, Lana?"

"Um…not right now," I explained. "I'm just getting situated back at work, but once I get in touch with my sources I'll send in some leads, and I'll be sure to contact Celeste."

My anxiety level went up a notch. It was my first morning back, and Ari was already grilling me for leads. When the meeting was over, I rushed back to my office as fast as I could. I tried calling Celeste. Her phone had been disconnected again. I wasn't shocked. I tried to access her Facebook page to message her, but it was gone. I had an easy story to write on the Lamar's roving eye. I figured it would only take me an hour to write. I normally could report and write up at least half a dozen stories in a day. I began to search the blogs to catch myself up on the details of Lamar and Khloe's marital woes. However, within minutes of online digging, my photophobia started to get the best of me. The lights of my desktop computer killed my sensitive eyes, and it still was extremely difficult to read. I had to read slowly and some sentences two or three times to really comprehend what I read. I struggled at basic work tasks that used to come so easy to me. After working for a half hour on the story, I had to put my head down on my desk and close my eyes.

I fell sound asleep. My cell phone woke me up. It was Malden. I had been out for an hour. I thanked God no one had walked into my office before I picked up the phone.

"Hello," I said with a raspy voice from my catnap.

"Were you sleeping?"

"What? No," I lied. "I told you I was going back to work today."

"I know it's just that your voice cracked when you answered the phone."

"What's going on?"

"Well, how's your first day back?"

"It's fine," I continued to lie. "Back to the old grind."

"That's great news. See...I knew you'd bounce back quickly," Malden said with pride.

"Yep..." I said, unconvinced.

"This weekend some of my family is coming to stay with me for an impromptu family reunion of sorts at my beach house. I want to make sure you can come."

"Um..." I paused, trying to process Malden's offer.

"Do you have plans?"

"No…" I said reluctantly.

"Do you not want to go?"

"No– it's not that. It's just that I haven't been back in L.A. for weeks. I need to get my life back in order."

"You have all the time in the world to do that, Lana – this is my family. My brother, Max, from Tennessee, will be there. He's the one brother you've never met. I'd really like you to meet him and his family."

"OK – I'll go," I conceded, feeling the pressure from Malden. "I'm working from home on Friday, but I can probably head down early afternoon."

"That's perfect," he said. "I'll go to the office for a few hours before I pick Max and his family up from the OC airport. I have business dinners and other things going on the next few nights, so I can't come up to see you."

"That's fine." I sighed. "I need my rest anyway."

I turned the flat screen TV on in my office, hoping to help keep me awake. Megan Riley's show *The Riley File* was on Rox News Channel. The bombshell blonde conservative talk show host grilled George Carson. He was back on Rox defending Gov. Richards.

"Celeste Homan is a White Supremacist Nazi sympathizer with an extensive criminal past, which is outlined in detail in this week's *Celebrity*," George said. "She is a proven liar and criminal, and she has no credibility and no facts or evidence to support her claims."

I wondered where *Celebrity* got the info on Celeste's Nazi ties. I kept thinking about the break-in at her house and how the photos of her in the Nazi costume, the Confederate flag and other items were stolen from her house. I was convinced it was Gov. Richards's people – the Danites. They were preparing to shoot down Celeste's credibility if the story did break. I bet they had hand fed *Celebrity* all the info for their cover. I muscled through the day as best as I could. At a quarter to five, Ari came into my office.

"Lana, did you file the Lamar Odom story?"

"Um what?" I said in an aching fog. I glared at my computer and had only typed two hundred words for the story.

"The cheating story," Ari sternly said.

"Oh right...I'm almost done."

"Lana, you've been working on it all day. Usually it takes you less than an hour to pump out a story like this. Are you sure you're well enough to be back working full-time?"

"Um....yeah."

"Well, you're not functioning at one hundred percent."

"It's just that I have these bad headaches," I said as I rested my head on my right hand. "It makes it difficult for me to read and write, but I can still work."

"So what percentage would you say you're at in terms of your recovery...eighty percent?"

"Ummm...probably," I continued to hesitate. "You know...probably sixty percent."

That was a flat out lie. I knew that my brain was barely functioning. I was probably only functioning at twenty percent – thirty percent tops. I began to sweat. Did Ari know I was lying?

"What about Celeste?"

"Her phone is out of service, and her Facebook profile is down."

"That doesn't surprise me. Well, go home after you file the story and get some rest. I hope you're back at one hundred percent soon. Please keep trying Celeste."

I spent the next few days at work absolutely struggling. Basic skills I took for granted such as reading, writing, typing and even brainstorming story pitches had become strenuous feats. I had grossly overestimated my ability to function at work. It was showing, and it made me a nervous wreck.

On Thursday night, Ari e-mailed me and asked me to come into the office on Friday instead of working from home. I knew this was a bad sign. Within minutes of my arrival, he called me into his office. When I walked in and saw him sitting in his chair, tapping his fingers together rapidly with a grim look on his face, I knew he was about to give me bad news.

"Lana...I have some bad news for you," Ari said, straightening his posture in his chair as he looked down. I knew immediately he was going to lay me off. The CEO of National Publishing had a horrible reputation for spontaneous mass layoffs.

"OK," I said as I slowly eased into the chair across from his desk.

"Despite our big coup with the Gov. Richards story, overall the magazine isn't doing well. Our numbers have been down for a while, and quite frankly, the entire company's numbers are down. The CEO ordered more layoffs today, and I have no choice but to let you go. I feel horrible with your illness and everything. I can promise to give you as much freelance work as possible with the holidays coming up..."

"But I don't understand," I said as a stared at him in shock. "I just risked my life and nailed the biggest story of the year for you bastards! You sent two reporters to get info out of Celeste over the course of a year with zero luck. I was the one who found her! I was the one who got her talking twenty-four hours after you assigned me the story. Christ, Ari – I even had a sleepover with that bitch! I practically died for this story -- she stole my underwear for God's sake!"

"I know, I know, Lana," Ari said, rapidly nodding his head. "You're a fantastic reporter. No one doubts that. This has nothing to do with your skills. You're getting laid off due to cutbacks."

Ari was using some fancy footwork to rationalize the situation, but I was smart enough to know what was really going on. "So...who else is getting laid off in this office?" I asked, fishing for any kind of reassurance that the layoff truly had nothing to do with my quality of work.

"You're not the only one..."

"Who else, then?" I asked desperately.

"You know...some freelancers in other cities."

I immediately knew he was bullshitting. I burst into tears. First I lose my health and now my job! I was mortified and devastated. Deep down I knew my layoff was due to the brain damage I struggled with from the meningitis. "I can't believe this," I sobbed. "I know I'm getting laid off because I'm not able to function like I used to with my disability. I know that's why."

"Lana, I'm sorry you're still not feeling better – I truly am."

"I know I can't function the same way I used to." I continued to cry. "I'm trying my best, and I'm getting better every day. I'm just not recovering as quickly as I expected. I never should've come back to work so soon. My doctor warned me, but I was afraid I would lose my job if I didn't come back soon. I just can't win."

"Lana, I promise I will give you plenty of freelance work, and once you're back to one hundred percent maybe the company will be in a better position and we can chat."

Ari gave me a hug before I left his office. Thank God I didn't have much to clean out from my office. There's nothing worse than the layoff walk of shame. I rushed out of the building without saying goodbye to anyone. I was humiliated. The disease had been humiliating enough – and here I was, humiliated again. I had never felt like such a loser in my entire life. The career I had worked so hard to build for over a decade had just crumbled like the Berlin Wall under Reagan's administration right before my very eyes. I called Malden for comfort on my way home.

"Hi, babe!" he joyfully said from the other end. "What's up?"

"Well, I'll be able to head down to Orange Country a lot earlier than planned."

"That's great news! What time can you leave?"

"Um....now, pretty much. I just need to pack a bag," I darkly said.

"I thought you had to work this morning?"

"So did I."

"What do you mean, Lana?"

"I just got fired," I said, my voice breaking, and tears falling down my face.

"You what? How is this possible? I don't understand. You're the best reporter."

"Ari blamed it on layoffs, but I'm the only person who got laid off in the L.A. office. I told him I know it's because I can still barely function with all of my neurological problems."

"I can't believe this. Well, you did take all that time off this summer," Malden said.

"Excuse me?" I snapped back as my tears froze.

"No, I didn't mean it like that," Malden stumbled. "It's just – you've been traveling a lot."

"You mean *we* traveled a lot this summer," I snarled. "Any vacation days I took off this summer were to be with you, Malden."

"No – I know, I know," he groveled. "That came off wrong. Look, we'll figure something out. Don't worry, Lana, it will work out. I've got to go pick up my brother and his family from the airport. Head down as soon as you can. Let's try to have a nice weekend and not worry about your job. Can you do that for me?"

"OK," I conceded, letting out a deep breath.

I didn't hit the road till almost four in the afternoon. – prime traffic time in L.A. I went straight home and cried myself to sleep. I slept for hours. My head hurt worse than ever. The stress of my new unemployment status heightened the pain I felt in my head and eyes. Aside from my medical problems and lack of a job, I also knew that I'd be hit with outrageous uninsured hospital bills in the days to come.

As I sat in traffic down to OC, the setting sun's rays compounded with the oncoming car headlights blinded my eyes and sliced through my brain like needles. I hadn't attempted to drive for more than a few minutes since I got sick. I was not prepared for the challenge. I drove in the fast lane, and I could feel myself swerve in and out of the lane whenever traffic sped up. The oncoming headlights made my vision painful and blurry – it was as if I'd thrown down seven shots of Patron before hitting the road. The lights intoxicated me. I suffered the same physical symptoms I did when I attempted to drive home from San Francisco the night before I entered the emergency room. As I swerved in and out of the lanes, my sweaty palms held the wheel tight. I prayed to God out loud: "Please God, please have me arrive at Malden's safely!" I repeated my prayer over and over again.

I made it to Malden's home safely by the grace of God. I felt guardian angels or some higher force protected me my entire trip down. With all the horrible events I had been handed these past few weeks, God couldn't be so cruel as to throw a car accident into the mix. When I arrived at Malden's home later, I immediately met his brother, his wife and their two teenage boys. The adults were sitting on Malden's couch, drinking red wine, and the boys were playing pool.

His brother, Max, was not what I had expected. Malden had told me stories about how they toured Europe and worked on Wall Street together. Malden said Max was the one brother most like him. However, all I saw was an overweight drunk man with a receding hairline. His wife, Mary, struck me as a very soft-spoken and submissive housewife.

"So, I hear you work for the *L.A. Post*," Max announced after Malden introduced us. "Are you Ruby Ghostfire?"

"No," I quickly said.

I didn't know what else to say. I wanted to shout, 'Yeah, I'm Ruby Ghostfire, and I did work there up until a few hours ago, asshole!' I bit my lip. I was at a loss for words. What do I say? I was so embarrassed. Talk about rubbing salt in the wound. Fortunately, Malden was quick on his feet and threw me a lifeline.

"Yes, she's freelancing for them," Malden said. "She got sick a few months ago, and her doctors instructed her to lighten her workload till she's back to one hundred percent."

I breathed a sigh of relief.

"Yeah...I freelance for them," I said with zero confidence.

"Well, you should come down to Nashville. I could tell you a ton of stories involving all the country stars that live down there. They're all having affairs – you'd have a field day."

Malden grilled chicken skewers for us for dinner. Max dominated the conversation as we dined on Malden's patio table. He went on and on about all the country stars he knew. He didn't have Malden's looks, but he sure had his ego. I found it strange, though, that Max made references to his "AA" meetings as he downed one glass of red wine after the next. Were the AA references a joke? I didn't get it. I ate quietly and tried my best not to sulk about my unemployment and mental impairment woes. I graciously chatted with them and tried my best to act the part of a perfect girlfriend. Meanwhile, I was secretly popping Vicodin in between glasses of wine. I wouldn't have been able to keep my eyes open without the painkillers.

After we wrapped up dinner, I walked to the powder room next to the kitchen and noticed a bottle of Adderall sitting inside Mary's purse. I had taken Adderall a few times in college for all-night studying marathons to pass the final exams for the early morning classes I had slept through most of the semester. I sharply recalled the huge surge of energy the drug gave me for hours on end. It was around eight at night, and all I could think of was how desperately I needed that drug to keep me functioning for the next few hours. Before I knew what I was doing, I found my hand reaching for the bottle inside Mary's purse.

"Lana, what are you doing?" Malden asked, grabbing my arm.

"Huh?" I gasped sheepishly. "You startled me."

"Isn't that Mary's purse?"

"I don't know...I think so."

"Then, what are you doing?" Malden asked with a lighthearted laugh.

"I saw the Adderall and I just…I don't know what happened. I'm in so much pain, even with all these painkillers. I want to stay up and hang with you guys, but I'm dying over here. I know the Adderall will help me."

"You want Adderall?"

"Yes, I do."

"Well, I can just give you some of mine."

"What?" I said in shock. "You have a prescription for Adderall?"

"Yeah…for my ADD." Malden shrugged. "Follow me."

Malden headed to his master bedroom, and I raced behind him. He went straight toward his black leather briefcase on the floor next to the bed. He reached in and pulled out bottles of prescriptions. I was floored.

"What are all those for?" I asked. "I thought the only prescription you took was for your heart condition."

"There's that and some pills for my back condition," Malden casually said.

I was speechless. We had been together for months, and I had never once seen him take a pill. As he fumbled through the bottles, I noticed a glass on both his nightstand and the nightstand on my side of the bed. Malden's OCD caused him to be overly clean. He never left items out for more than a day. My radar immediately went up.

"Why is there a glass on both of your nightstands?" I spouted at him.

"Huh?"

"The nightstand on my side of the bed — why is there a glass there? Did you have someone stay over last night?"

"Um…" Malden paused. "Is that an accusation?"

"It's a question," I coldly snapped.

"My son slept here," Malden shot back.

"Your sons are in school in San Francisco!"

"No my young one, Lana. The scud missile."

"He lives in Dallas!"

"Well, his mother came to town for work and asked me to watch him for a few days," he continued.

369

"You have a five-bedroom home – why the hell would he sleep in bed with you?"

"It's a bad habit his mom started him on," Malden said. "I'm trying to break it, but I'm never with him, so it's difficult."

"Malden, we talked on the phone last night. How in the world did you fail to mention that your toddler son was in town from Dallas? You told me you had business dinners this week."

"Lana, do you trust me or not?" Malden asked, standing up and putting his hands on my shoulders. I stood there, pouting, with my arms crossed over my chest. "Do you want to call his mother so she can confirm that he was here? I'd be happy to do that so we can get on with our night with my family – who flew all the way across the country to spend time with   us."

I glared at him waiting for him to break.

"Do you want me to call her?"

I looked up at him in disdain. I didn't buy his bullshit for one second, but I didn't have the physical capacity to challenge him. "No, forget it." I shrugged. "Give me the pill."

"OK," Malden said, as if everything was fine. He grabbed my hand and guided me to the bathroom.

Malden opened the orange prescription bottle and pulled out a pill. It was a huge yellow capsule. It looked much bigger and different than the few Adderall pills I had taken in college.

"Are you sure that's Adderall?" I cautiously asked.

"Yeah." Malden grabbed a short, clear glass on the sink and filled it with water. He filled the glass halfway with water. He cracked the pill open and poured the contents into the glass.

"It's better if you drink it," Malden instructed.

"Really? In the past I've just taken the pill," I hesitated. "Are you going to take one too?"

"Sure." Malden stared intently and handed me the glass.

I peered down and saw yellow particles floating around in the water. I was so miserable. Would this make the pain I felt go away?

"Fuck it," I said, chugging the concoction as fast as the Irish girl in me can throw down a Jameson shot.

Malden took out another pill and filled the same glass, presumably for his own use. I walked out of the bathroom before he downed his Adderall cocktail. I glanced at his infamous bathroom garbage can as I walked out. Empty.

Back in his bedroom, I surveyed the surroundings like a hawk. Nothing else appeared to be out of place. Malden brushed me aside and exited the room. I immediately went into his briefcase. I looked through all his prescription bottles. There were over a dozen. I quickly read the labels and wasn't familiar with any of the drugs. Then I found one bottle of Cialis. I knew it! He had been taking performance enhancement drugs. I wondered if that was the explanation for his post-ejaculation spasms.

I felt nothing from the pill so I headed to the kitchen to pour myself another glass of wine. When I walked back into the family room, I found Max and Mary on the couch sipping their wine. They appeared to be bored – the environment was dull.

"How about some music?" I suggested, walking over to Malden's dated sound system.

"Sounds great," Max said.

I opened the 3-disk CD tray. Inside I found Florence & the Machine, Adele and Norah Jones CDs. Norah fucking Jones? I couldn't believe it. Malden doesn't even own these CDs. I turned around and saw Malden in the kitchen, opening a new bottle of wine.

"Malden," I said, creeping up behind him. "When did you last use your stereo?"

"I don't know – is there a problem with it?" He shrugged.

"When was it? Was it last night with your son?"

"Ahhh…no," he said, looking confused. "It probably was the other night when I had John over for dinner."

"Oh really. You expect me to fucking believe the chairman and you had dinner together and listened to Norah Jones, Florence & the Machine, and fucking Adele? Are you kidding me right now?" I asked, raising my voice. "You're cheating on me again, aren't you?"

"Lana, stop this now! I'm not cheating on you. I told you I'm done with that."

"Then where the fuck did those CDs come from Malden – you don't own those CDs. I've gone through your collection a bunch of times."

"You know I like to listen to all kinds of music, Lana."

"Those are the CDs you chose to play for your pit bull boss you had over for dinner? You're unbelievable!"

"Is everything OK in here?" Mary asked cautiously, as she slowly walked into the kitchen.

"It's fine," Malden calmly said.

"OK." she sighed. "I'm really jetlagged from traveling all day. The kids are in their room playing video games in bed, and I think I'm going to hit the sack too. Good night."

"Good night," Malden said as she left the kitchen. "Let me know if you need anything."

Malden walked up to me and wrapped his arms around me. I began to cry. I had lost my job. I was still so sick, and I was certain my boyfriend was cheating on me again.

"Lana, you've had a bad day, and you're taking it out on me," Malden pleaded. "I told you that I would never cheat on you again. You're jumping to conclusions – you know I listen to all kinds of music. You need to stop this."

"How am I supposed to believe you after everything you've put me through?" I sobbed. "You broke my trust. That's something you need to earn back."

I couldn't stand being in his embrace for one more second. I wiped my eyes, put myself together and walked back into the living room. I sat next to Max and continued to chat him up as if everything were normal. I felt speedy, and I was talking way faster than normal. Enter my Adderall high.

"So…you're not bad," Max said, giving me a mysterious dark stare.

"Well, I'm glad you approve," I said, unimpressed, taking another sip of wine.

"No, I mean, I think you're hot," he said, glaring at me intently.

"Um…OK," I said dumbfounded. "Thanks – I think?"

"I think you and I should get together," he said without hesitating.

"What in the world are you talking about?"

"You know, I think we should go in the other room and get naked."

My buzz from the drugs intensified, but even so I still knew exactly what I heard. Was he kidding?

"Oh, yeah," I answered sarcastically, unsure how to handle the situation. "I'm sure your wife and my boyfriend would love that."

"Well, Malden can join us," Max said, with no change in the tone of his voice.

"What?" I asked sharply.

"You know, the three of us can go in his bedroom and have some fun."

"Like a threesome?"

"Yeah."

"Are you being serious?"

"Yeah."

"Is this something you guys have done before?"

"Yeah."

"What whore would actually agree to fuck two brothers?"

"A hooker." He never cracked a smile. He was serious.

"I don't get it." I laughed nervously.

"So what, one of you fucks me in the ass while the other is fucking me in the pussy? You know, Malden loves to fuck in the ass. He just can't get enough of the back door."

"Yeah, that's exactly what we should do," Max said with a straight face.

He was so intent and controlled. I couldn't believe what he was saying. How could he possibly be trying to fuck me with his family, including his two children, in the next room? I'm aware of the fact that it's most guys dream to have a threesome – but with your own brother? Who does that? This is fucking hillbilly shit. When did my relationship become a chapter from *Flowers in the Attic*?

"OK, Max – great idea. I'm sure Malden will love it," I said snarkily as Malden walked back in the room. "Why don't you tell him about your brilliant idea?"

"What's going on?" Malden asked, as he sat down on the couch.

"Go on – tell him," I ordered.

"Well, I was just telling Lana that, you know, we should all go into your bedroom and, you know, get into bed together…"

I glared, waiting for Malden's reaction. He sat there speechless for a few seconds.

"You know Malden, have a threesome like he says you guys do all the time!" I shouted in a fury.

"What's wrong with you, man?" Malden snapped at his brother, as he stood up and walked away toward his bedroom. I stormed in right after him. After I walked in his bedroom, I slammed the door and exploded.

"What the fuck is wrong with you and your twisted fucking family! You guys have threesomes together with hookers? That's incest! You guys disgust me. You're like a bunch of inbred drunken hillbilly losers!"

"That's not true, Lana," Malden pleaded. "We've never done that. He's wasted – he doesn't know what he's talking about. He's an addict – he's in AA."

"I thought that was a joke. Who talks about their AA meetings all night as they chug bottle after bottle of wine? Does he think he's Edward Norton from fucking *Fight Club*? What is wrong with you guys!"

"You're the one who was sitting so close to him and flirting with him. You led him on."

374

The hair on my neck stood straight up. There he goes manipulating me once again, but it wasn't going to work this time.

"Are you fucking kidding me? How dare you turn this around on me!"

The room started to spin as I launched accusation after accusation at Malden. I began to feel dizzy. Malden's face became distorted. I struggled to form the words I so badly wanted to say. I knew I was slurring. The rest of the night fell into a black dark abyss.

I woke up in bed the next morning totally naked with Malden standing above me in sweatpants holding a Bloody Mary.

"Here, drink this," he instructed.

I looked at him in total confusion. Why was he waking me up with a Bloody Mary? He had never done that before. He brings me coffee some mornings, but never a cocktail. My head pounded. I soon remembered the disgusting offer Max made to me the night before.

"Are you mad at me?" Malden asked.

"Your brother tried to have sex with me last night!"

"I talked to him this morning, and he feels terrible – he's going to apologize to you."

"Where are my clothes?"

"I think they're out on the deck – by the hot tub."

"We went in the hot tub last night?"

"Yeah."

"Whoa, wait – why don't I remember anything after your brother hit on me?"

"Lana, you drank a lot."

"I always drink a lot. I'm Irish, I have a high tolerance."

"But you took that pill."

"I took Adderall. It's an upper. If anything, it should've sobered me up. It's like cocaine."

I felt ill. Something was deeply wrong. I had that horrible dark, gut feeling I get whenever something terrible has happened, except I had no memory of anything. Why did I have no memory? Did Malden really slip me a date rape drug? Malden got back into bed and attempted to kiss me. I pulled back, and as I did – I felt my feet roll over something at the end of the bed. I reached down and grabbed it. It was a white woman's sock with a pink heel, and it wasn't mine.

"Are you fucking kidding me?" I shouted, throwing the sock at him. "This isn't my sock, you asshole! What's your excuse going to be now – your son wears women's socks?" I jumped out of bed and stormed into the closet. I grabbed Malden's Squaw Valley sweatshirt and threw it on.

"Lana, it's my sock," Malden pleaded. "Like a dumbass I bought women's socks instead of men's."

My relationship had become an episode of *The Jerry Springer Show*. At this point, Malden's excuses were so ridiculous it was laughable. "Do you really think I'm that fucking dumb? Go get my stuff from the deck," I ordered.

I stormed into the bathroom and slammed the door. I quickly peed and brushed my teeth. When I walked out of the bathroom, I grabbed my Louis Vuitton purse and started throwing everything that I kept at Malden's into it: workout clothes, makeup remover, a brush, etc.

As I packed up my stuff, I noticed scribbles on the cover of the *Maxim* magazine sitting on Malden's nightstand. I looked closer and made out the writing: "You make me want to fuck!"

In a rage, I seized the magazine and looked closer at another scrawl, accented with doodled hearts: "Pay dem' dues!"

It certainly wasn't Malden's handwriting. When Malden walked back into the room, I chucked the magazine at him. It fell to the floor.

"You're fucking a hooker, aren't you?"

"What!"

"She scribbled all over your magazine, you idiot! I don't even need to search for evidence of you cheating on me, because you are so dumb and sloppy it literally hits me in the fucking face! You're worse than fucking Charlie Sheen. Now that I'm unemployed, I should work as a writer for *Two and a Half Men*. I wouldn't even have to think – you've given me plenty of content to write an entire season!"

"What in the world are you talking about?"

"Read the cover, you idiot," I screeched, picking up the magazine and approaching him with it. My eyes fell inches away from his. I held up the magazine and pointed at the scribbles: "'You make me want to fuck?' 'Pay dem dues?' I knew it. Your brother told me last night. You're both fucking hookers – aren't you?"

With that, Malden took his right bear paw, the one that had touched me so lovingly before – and smacked me hard across the face. It stung like a bitch! I stumbled backwards and fell on my ass. I immediately raised my left hand to my cheek to apply pressure. It didn't ease the pain. It stung and tingled. I sat there with my eyes wide, glaring at Malden in shock. I had no words.

"You hit me," I cried, my eyes filling with tears. My thoughts flashed back to the fateful night that Malden had raised his arm to me at dinner with Giselle and French Rocker. I knew then that he was a wife beater. That inner voice that Oprah tells you to always listen to, I chose to ignore. Deep down, I had always known the smack was coming, but I had turned a blind eye to the signs. I was disgusted with Malden, but even more disgusted with myself for falling for his façade. He wasn't the person I thought he was – it was all smoke and mirrors.

"I told myself I would never do that again after I hit my ex-wife – now I have to break up with you," Malden said coldly said as he glared at me.

"Excuse me – not so fast," I shouted in a blood-boiling rage. "I'm breaking up with you – you wife-beating scumbag! And this time, I'm never coming back. I should call the fucking cops on you."

Malden retreated and stormed out of his room. I quickly gathered my stuff and raced out of his house without running into any of his houseguests. I was bawling hysterically as I threw my stuff in the trunk, then hopped into my car and sped off.

I cried the entire drive home. My vision was so blurred from my photophobia and tears that I could barely see. My eyes fogged up like a car windshield in an intense downpour with no wipers or dehumidifier. I listened to Muse's rock opera song *Eurasia* on repeat the entire way home. My drive felt like a bad dramatic movie scene happening in slow motion.

I had hit rock bottom.

CHAPTER 19

It was mid-morning the day of the election, and the buzzing of my doorbell woke me up. I hadn't heard from Malden in days, and I had spent most the weekend hibernating in my apartment in shame. I was jobless, boyfriend-less – and my big, bombshell story on Gov. Richards had become a distant memory.

I opened my door wearing a thong and a KISS T-shirt. It didn't even cross my mind to put more clothes on. No one was there. I looked down and saw a tall glass that held some kind of floral arrangement wrapped in brown paper and green cellophane. I quickly brought the flowers into my kitchen and tore off the paper to find the card. There, imbedded in two dozen beautiful red roses spaced with baby's breath, sat a tiny white card. It read:

> To Lana:
> I miss you.
> Love, Malden

That's it? The motherfucker hits me across the face and it doesn't occur to him that an apology is in order? My emotions had been on an up and down roller coaster for days. I didn't have the heart to tell my parents that Malden had hit me – I was too embarrassed. However, I did tell Giselle. She made me promise that I'd never go back to him, because she said the abuse would only get worse. Deep down, I knew she was right. The second he hit me, I knew our relationship was over. Our dreamlike, fairytale summer was over. However, a gnawing feeling inside me told me – in fact, demanded – that I get more information from him. I knew that I needed to find out the truth about the cheating and all of his dark secrets. There was some kind of gravitational force pulling me back to Malden, and it would not stop until I got all the answers I needed.

I spent the next few hours surfing from LMCH, BNN and Rox News Channel for the early election results. Just as I was about to head out the door to cast my vote for Gov. Richards, my phone beeped. It was Malden.

Malden Murphy: "Did you get anything from me today?"

I caved. I felt there was no purpose in delaying the inevitable.

Lana Burke: "Yes, I did."

Malden Murphy: "Will you please talk to me?"

Lana Burke: "I have no interest in talking to you unless you plan on telling me the truth. I know you were cheating on me again."

Malden Murphy: "I'm ready to tell you the truth."

I waited a few minutes to process Malden's statement. I had serious doubts that he planned on telling me the truth. Two seconds later, my phone rang. It was Malden. I didn't pick up.

Malden Murphy: "Are you there?"

Lana Burke: "I'm only willing to talk to you in person. I want you to look me in the eye."

Malden Murphy: "Can I come up tonight?"

Lana Burke: "OK."

After I voted, I went to an afternoon spin class at SoulCycle in West Hollywood. I had slowly worked toward getting back into my fitness routine. I could muscle through a class, but it was still difficult for me to do all the exercises on the bike. My hand and eye coordination and balance were still off from the meningitis. So, I sat in the last row and did my best to keep up with the rest of the class. I zoned out during the class and planned how I was going to manipulate Malden into telling me the truth about his double life. I knew he had way more skeletons in his closet than I could ever imagine, but regardless, I felt well prepared for the task at hand. I had become a pro at persuading people to disclose information about themselves that they did not want to reveal. I decided that I would play the sweet and sympathetic card with Malden to get him to admit he cheated. I would even go so far as to tell him that if he wanted to have sex with other women, I'd be OK with having another party join us in bed. I'd get him to think that I was so open to this kind of a sexual lifestyle, that I'd get him to tell me everything.

I got home from spin just in enough time to freshen up. I took a long, hot shower and spent extra time shaving my legs and crotch. As angry as I was at Malden, I still wanted to fuck him. We had never gone this long without sex. I knew his sexual appetite was abnormal, and the constant sex made me hunger for more and more sex. Even though our relationship was pretty much over, I didn't see a reason why I shouldn't at least get one more orgasm out of him. I wasn't sure if that was rational thinking. I still salivated at the idea of fucking him like a wild animal, despite all the pain he had caused me. This reminded me of my discovery of his Cialis pills. I quickly researched the side effects for the drug on my iPhone. Seizures and convulsions were listed as side effects. Could that explain his spasms after sex?

I threw on my ripped Flying Monkey skinny jeans, black Uggs and a wife beater tee. I couldn't think of a more appropriate shirt to wear for Malden. I blow dried my hair and put on minimal makeup. I didn't care to look great for him. I was emotionally and physically exhausted from the horrible sequence of events that had recently occurred in my life, and I was still weak from my illness.

As promised, Malden walked in at six that night. I forgot he had a key. I was sitting on the couch watching Rox News Channel. The polls were closing on the East Coast. Early exit polls projected that President Oyama would win key states New York, Florida, Pennsylvania and Ohio. I stood up and crossed my arms when I saw him. He immediately walked over to me, with his head and shoulders down. He looked weak. He was wearing jeans and a black Patagonia fleece vest with a black shirt underneath. He attempted to wrap his arms around me for a hug. I kept my arms folded across my chest, and I refused to hug back.

"Lana, I'm so sorry," Malden said, rubbing my back.

I pulled back and sat on my couch, motioning him to do the same. "Sit down," I ordered. He conceded and sat next to me on the couch.

"I'm only going to say this once, Malden. I need to know what happened. I know you have continued to cheat on me. I need to know who else you were sleeping with and why. If you're not prepared to tell me the truth tonight, then there's no point in you being here. You're wasting both of our time."

"I understand," he said, nervously fidgeting with his hands. He attempted, and failed, to keep them clasped together. "If I tell you everything, would you be willing to work on our relationship?"

"What do you mean?" I asked.

"Would you agree to stay with me and maybe go to couples therapy?"

I knew deep in my heart that the only person in this relationship who needed therapy was Malden. I knew that he was fucked up past the point of no return. I also knew that I had to make him think I still had every intention of staying with him in order to get him to tell me the truth – even though I was afraid of what that was. I had so many questions. Who was he cheating with? Was he fucking hookers? Did he really have threesomes with his brothers? Who were those "monsters"? Was he a sex addict? Why in the world did he get off by pretending I was his daughter during sex? I was no psychologist, but there were a lot of signs that he had been a victim of some kind of abuse, possibly sexual. His deviancy was not sexy anymore; it was very disturbing.

"Yes, I will do what it takes to save this relationship if you're honest with me," I lied.

"OK." He bowed his head.

"So let's not waste any time – tell me about the cheating," I said, glaring straight into his deep, blue eyes.

"There've been a couple of gals I've been seeing for years now…."

"Like girlfriends? Do they think they are in a relationship with you?"

"No. It's not like that. We go out every once in a blue moon. They're not my girlfriends. You're my girlfriend."

"So there are only two?"

"Yes."

"And you've continued to see them our entire relationship?"

"Not our entire relationship. We've had so many ups and downs and fights. When we were on breaks, I'd see them."

"We've never taken a break, Malden."

"You know, when we've fought."

My heart felt crushed. "You told me we were in a committed relationship. I introduced you to my family. I loved your children!"

"I know. You have to understand I've been single for ten years. I've never committed to anyone in over a decade. My feelings for you scare me. I've never been in love like this. I had given up on love. I figured I'd be a bachelor the rest of my life and that I'd never get married again. But I'm in love with you, Lana. I want to spend the rest of my life with you. I'd like to marry you."

I wanted to roll my eyes, but I knew I needed to get more info. "What about hookers?"

"What?"

"Are you sleeping with hookers?"

"No."

I wasn't convinced.

"Malden, it hurts me so much that you don't love me enough to want to be with just me," I cooed as I began to plan in my head what manipulative line I would say next. "That's devastating to me. But you know, I love you so much that if you truly felt the need to be with someone else sexually, I'd be open to inviting someone else into bed with us. If that's what you felt you needed."

"You mean, like a threesome?" he asked, raising his eyebrows in shock.

"Yes. If you need to have sex with another woman that badly – I'd rather be involved than have you do it behind my back. I love you that much," I said as convincingly as possible. It killed me to give him such a pass, but I knew it had to be done.

"You would really do that for me?" Malden asked as his eyes filled with tears. Wait, tears?

"Yes."

"That's the most beautiful thing anyone has ever said to me," Malden said genuinely, as a tear dripped down his left cheek.

I wanted to throw up. Is this guy for real? That's the most beautiful thing anyone has ever said to him? What is wrong with him! Who is this sick monster I've dated for months? What planet is he on? My mind immediately went back to his creepy brother Max's talk of threesomes.

"You know, Max told me that it's what you like. You're my man. I want to do whatever it takes to pleasure and satisfy you. Is that something you'd still be interested in?"

"You'd really do that for me?"

"Yes, if that's what you felt like you needed. Who did you and Max do a threesome with?"

Malden leaned back on my couch. He appeared more relaxed and comfortable. My strategy was working. "We did it a few times in our twenties."

Gotcha! He was confirming all my dark suspicions about his secret life.

"With whom?"

"We were in D.C. this one time," he said casually. "We were out drinking in Georgetown, and we met a woman who worked for the government. She invited us both back to her condo. She was interested in me, not Max. She took me back to the bedroom while we were at her place. I started to fuck her in the ass. Max walked in on us, and she asked him to join us."

"So you fucked her in the ass and Max did what?"

"He fucked her in the pussy," Malden said as he stared blankly into space.

"He fucked her in the pussy the same time you were fucking her in the ass," I repeated.

"Yeah," Malden said with a monotone voice.

I was disgusted. With all the crazy Hollywood stories I've covered in my career, I had never in my entire life heard of two brothers having a threesome together. It struck me as sexually

385

disgraceful, trashy and disturbing. Malden momentarily broke out of his trance.

"Would you ever let two guys fuck you at the same time?"

"Um, no. That I would not do. That's degrading. It sounds like a gang rape to me."

"Yeah, it is degrading," Malden said, back in his trance. I could feel a dark presence come over the room. I could see his mind had wandered to an evil place.

"Malden, who are the monsters?"

"The what?"

"You've mentioned monsters before from your childhood. Did someone hurt you when you were a child? Were you molested?"

"I didn't like my stepdad…"

"Did he molest you?"

"He was verbally abusive."

"Just verbally?"

"Lana, I really want to make this relationship work," Malden said. "I want you to know that I have told the other girls that it's totally over. That I'm in a committed relationship with you and I want to make it work."

I wasn't buying his bullshit for one second. "When did you tell them this?"

"The other day. I'm not seeing or talking to anyone else."

Malden and I went back and forth for hours. I continued to humor him to wring more info out of him. I told him I would consider couples therapy. However, I told him I wanted the key he had to my place back until he had proven to me he was faithful. As much as I was beginning to loathe this sexual freak I had fallen so blindly and deeply in love with, I still was so attracted to him. I was horny, and the JFK Jr. smile was still irresistible. I felt like a dog in heat. When was the last time we had sex? I wanted nothing more than to hump him all night – and I knew he felt the same. After hours of talking, tears and basically getting nowhere, we went into my bedroom.

Malden slowly ripped all my clothes off and began to fuck me in the pussy. I forgot how perfect his penis felt inside me. I knew he was a much worse person than I had ever realized. As he glided back and forth on top of me, I got aroused at how evil he was. He was a dark and deviant sexual predator. I felt like I was kissing the enemy – or worse – the devil. I envisioned him and his brother fucking that woman in D.C. together. It made me disgusted and angry but eerily turned me on at the same time. I dug my nails deep into Malden's perfect ass and pulled him closer to me as I moaned out loud.

"Harder," I shouted to him. "Fuck me like you fucked that bitch in D.C."

"Oh yeah," Malden panted as he started to thrust his cock deeper and deeper into my soaking wet pussy. "You like that?"

"Faster and harder!" I demanded as I slapped my hand on his ass cheek as hard as I could. The sex felt so good, but I hated him so much.

Malden paused, leaned into my ear and whispered those dreadful, creepy words: "You're my naughty little girl. I could go to jail for you. Don't tell any of your friends at school."

His words were chilling. I felt ice go through all my veins. He couldn't help himself. He couldn't resist the daddy-daughter role-playing, and it was disgusting. It made me ill. I squeezed his ass harder and moaned in ecstasy and horror.

I stopped him from gliding back and forth for a moment. "Don't you think it's strange you pretend I'm your daughter during sex especially since you have a daughter?" I asked him as I glared into his deep blue eyes.

"No." He shrugged without hesitation and continued to fuck me. I couldn't believe it. It didn't even faze him. He saw nothing wrong with the sick fantasy.

I paused, my body motionless. "You're like the Big Bad Wolf," I said as I glared into his eyes.

He momentarily stopped riding me and looked straight back into my eyes. I felt a shroud of dark energy come over me. The man I had fallen in love with was gone. I could see his soul through the windows of his eyes. It was pure evil. Malden didn't exist. It dawned on me that the man I had fallen in love with was nothing but an illusion.

"Yeah…I am," Malden said boldly as he continued to rock his hard cock in and out of my wet pussy. "I'm the Big Bad Wolf."

I felt my heart skip a beat as I lay underneath him frozen. I closed my eyes, hoping my reality would disappear. I took a deep breath, counted to three in my head and opened my eyes. Malden's eyes had turned into bright red bloody flames. He grew fangs and thick layers of fur within seconds. I was no longer cupping his perfectly masculine ass in my hands – I was grasping huge chunks of thick, black and gray fur. He had turned into a ferocious wolf. The furry, giant penis of a wild animal thrusted inside me. It scared me, but it turned me on too. It made me go wild. It reminded me of Mina's twisted love affair with her dark prince in Bram Stoker's *Dracula*. I was eating forbidden fruit, and it electrified my entire body. The wolf growled and continued to thrust his cock inside me, harder and faster. With his mouth open, his saliva dripped off his fangs onto my hard perky nipples. I panted louder and louder. He leaned in, put his big paws around my neck and dug his claws deep into my skin as he began to bite my ear. The pain from the nails and the bite hurt and aroused me. I couldn't contain myself anymore.

"Oh, oh, oh, oh fuck," I screamed at the top of my lungs. The wolf lifted his head in the air and growled as I moaned. I could feel the wolf's penis throb and explode in my pussy filling it with his warm foreign cum before he collapsed on me. The wolf breathed heavily with his chest contracting rapidly for minutes. His tongue escaped his mouth as he panted, but he kept his paws wrapped tightly around my neck. I closed my eyes again and temporarily dozed off from exhaustion and distress.

When I awoke a few minutes later, Malden was back on top of me. The wolf was gone. I immediately pushed him off and struggled to catch my breath. After my breathing slowed, I looked over at Malden. He was stroking his penis – it was erect again!

He was ready for round two. I knew in my heart that after round two, it would be the last time I'd ever fuck him. I wanted to make it mind-blowing for him so that he would regret destroying our relationship that much more. Malden flipped me over so that he could fuck me in the ass. Here we go again.

"No, you flip over," I instructed as I got up and pushed his shoulders around so that he was on his stomach.

I racked my brain to try to come up with something I could do to pleasure him that the hundreds of other women had never done. I straddled my legs over his ass and planted my dripping wet pussy on his ass cheeks. I rubbed my wet pussy slowly all over his ass. I massaged his butt with my pussy as slowly and seductively as possible. Malden moaned.

I leaned forward and stuck my tongue inside Malden's right ear. I swirled it around in there for minutes. He continued to moan. I scratched my long nails all over his scalp and slowly made my way down his back. I licked my tongue slowly down his back. I took my time. Minutes had passed before I was kissing the small of his back. I was at the top of his ass. I kissed and licked both ass cheeks. I marveled at his perfect ass. I would miss it. Then, I slowly began to spread his ass cheeks apart.

"What are you doing?" Malden asked as he slowly pulled his head up from my bed.

"Relax," I said as I pushed his head back down. "Don't say anything."

I could tell he was uneasy, so I continued to lick the top of his butt crack for a few minutes. When I felt his muscles relax more, I spread his ass cheeks further apart and began to lick his asshole. His legs tightened immediately, and he began to moan like crazy.

"Oh, oh, oh – oh my God," Malden shouted. "Oh God. That feels so good. No one's ever done that before."

"Relax," I quietly said.

I continued to stick my tongue in his asshole. It was disgusting and hot. He had fucked me in the ass so many

389

times. I had had a love-hate relationship with anal sex. Now it was my turn to fuck him in the ass. I slowly raised my right hand and stuck my index and middle fingers up his butthole.

"Oh God," Malden shouted. "Oh my God that feels weird. I dunno…"

"Be quiet." I sternly commanded as I continued to move my fingers in and out of his butt.

I continued to lick his ass for a half hour. Malden moaned like he never had moaned before. When I felt like he was satisfied enough, I pulled him up and positioned him standing on the ground next to the edge of the bed. I crawled to the end of the bed and lifted my legs in the air.

"Now you can fuck me in the ass," I said as I pushed Malden to get in a better position.

He stood up with his erect penis. He pulled me closer to him, spread my legs and spit in his hand. He wiped his saliva all over my ass and immediately thrust his hard cock into my anus. I knew it wouldn't take long for him to climax at this point.

"Oh, oh, oh – that feels so good, Lana," Malden said as he glided his wet cock in and out of my anus. I gripped the side of my mattress and clenched my teeth.

"You like being fucked in the ass, too – don't you daddy?" I asked darkly.

"You're my naughty little girl. Oh oh oh God, Lana, I'm going to come," Malden shouted. "Oh fuck!"

As his warm cum filled my ass I momentarily saw the wolf return with his fiery red eyes. I had to blink multiple times before I could see Malden again. Was my mind playing tricks on me? Were the illusions caused by the painkillers and the damage the meningitis had done to my brain? I couldn't understand why I was seeing things. Or was I? Perhaps I was seeing clearly for the first time in my life.

"No one has ever licked me in the ass before," Malden panted. "Wow, that was amazing."

I couldn't help but feel a slight sense of pride. I had accomplished my mission.

Malden passed out cold minutes after we finished fucking. All my lights were on and the TV was still on the Rox News Channel. The polls were all closed on the East Coast and the early election results were coming in.

"President Oyama's won states Florida, Ohio, Iowa, Wisconsin and Illinois so far," Scott Shepard announced on live TV. "Things aren't looking good for Gov. Richards – there's a lot of blue here on our map."

Fuck! I was devastated. Gov. Richards had been up in the polls even after my bombshell story came out. The night was still young, though. I took a quick shower to rinse off the filth that was Malden Murphy.

When I got out of the shower, I put my wife beater back on and put on a pair of gray cotton short-shorts. I walked over to the bed and glared at Malden. He was snoring heavily. I could tell he was in a deep sleep. I knew he wouldn't wake for hours. I knew this was my chance to uncover the truth.

I quietly walked over to his pile of clothes on the leather chair next to my bed. I reached into the pocket of his fleece vest and found his smart phone. He had told me earlier he had just recently gotten a new one. I prayed it wouldn't have a lock on it.

Bingo! It was unlocked.

I quickly scrambled to figure out the logistics of a phone that I was completely unfamiliar with. Within seconds, I was scrolling through his text messages. I could not believe what I saw. One text was worse than the next from what seemed like an endless stream of women. First there was Tracy.

Malden Murphy: "You make me so hard…especially before I explode."

Tracy Real Estate Agent: "Wow, and then you shake forever. Very hot."

Malden Murphy: "I want you to cum in my mouth too. And taste your cum."

And then there was Bonnie…

Bonnie Balboa Cafe: "I can't stop thinking about you. Last night was the best sex I've ever had."

Kim Quiet Woman Bar: "Sometimes I'm not sure about our relationship. We have a deep connection."

Excuse me, a relationship?

Karyn Pelican Inn: "I really like you, but sometimes I feel like you're just using me for sex. Are you?"

Malden Murphy: "Yep!"

Karyn Pelican Inn: "You're a fucking jerk! I knew about you since the moment I met you."

Nick The Abbey: "It was great spending the night with you too last weekend. Are we still on for tomorrow?"

Wait Nick? From West Hollywood's most popular gay bar? Was that short for Nicole or was Malden fucking dudes too? My heart raced and my stomach sank.

Michele Rebound: "Miss you!"

Wait, Michele Rebound? What the hell does that mean? Is she Malden's backup plan chick? Is she waiting in the wings in case things don't work out with me? I couldn't believe how desperate these women came off. It was very clear on social media that Malden was in a serious relationship with me; however, clearly none of these pariahs had any problem playing the role of one of his many other women on the side. It disgusted me. I read on.

Josie Double D: "Are we still on for this weekend? You still owe me a payment for the last time I came over."

Wait, what! A payment? I knew it – he was fucking hookers too! My worst fears had become reality. I was horrified beyond belief. Each text I read got worse, but one message popped out more than the others.

Judy Vinalli: "Can't wait to see you in Tahoe again this weekend."

Malden Murphy: "You too. Will you bring your little schoolgirl skirt like last time?"

Judy Vinalli: "Yes. I'll put my hair in pigtails. I love when you grab my pigtails and thrust your cock inside me."

Malden Murphy: "We'll drink wine by the fireplace while the kids play and I'll fuck my little girl all night in her schoolgirl skirt."

I felt more ice-cold chills go up and down my weakened spine. I clearly wasn't the only woman he pretended was his daughter during sex as he had claimed. I felt so sick and dirty. The man I had fallen in love with was totally deranged. My mind raced – is he capable of hurting the most innocent kind of a victim out there? My reporter's intuition told me to hop online immediately and research Judy. I looked over at Malden. He was still sound asleep. I needed him to stay asleep a little longer so that I could continue to access his phone before he woke up. I grabbed my phone and took photos of all the text messages between Malden and the women. I also snapped photos of all their names and phone numbers.

I grabbed my laptop and went to Safari. I typed in "Judy Vinalli." My jaw dropped as I read the fourth headline that appeared in the search engine:

REAL ESTATE AGENT ACCUSED OF MOLESTATION SLAIN

There was a mug shot of a man with deep blue eyes and brown hair. He resembled Malden. It was Judy's slain husband who was charged with molesting a child. The story read:

> A man found shot to death in his San Francisco home last week was a 40-year-banker who had been facing child molestation charges, according to police.
>
> The body of Derrick Vinalli was found Oct. 2 in his condominium. Vinalli's sister reported him missing after he didn't return calls for several days.
>
> "The house was dark for days," a neighbor said.
> Vinalli's body was found in a bathroom. He had been shot in the head once. Police classified the death as a homicide. There are no suspects in custody.
>
> San Francisco police arrested Vinalli on July 22 on suspicion of committing lewd and lascivious acts with a child. Vinalli leaves behind wife, Judy, and two young daughters.

I couldn't read further. I was beside myself. I didn't want to know anymore. I didn't want to look at Malden's phone for one more second. How could a woman – whose husband was most likely murdered for molesting a child, who has young daughters – pretend to be a little girl, going so far as to put her hair in pigtails, while she fucked my boyfriend? There were too many ties to child molestation. Was Malden part of some sort of pedophile ring? I was horrified. I thought my worst fears about Malden involved sex with hookers of legal age, but the more I dug, the more the circumstantial evidence pointed to sins that went way farther than sex with a hooker. I felt so foolish and devastated. I had fallen under his satanic spell. I couldn't wait another second to get the Big Bad Wolf out of my house. I was convinced he was the devil in the flesh.

In a rage, I texted all the bitches on his phone and told them that Malden had a serious girlfriend and if he told them otherwise they had been misinformed. Then, I stormed into my bedroom and began to hit him on the back.

"Wake up! Wake the fuck up, you mother fucker!" I screamed as I hit him repeatedly.

"What?" Malden said in a haze.

"You want to tell me about Bonnie from the Balboa fucking Cafe? Or Tracy? Michele the rebound? What about Josie and her double D tits? Or Karyn? Or how about Nick? The chick you met at a gay bar or was it a dude? Or do you even know! Or how about my favorite, your little girl Judy – you know, the one who was married to a child molester and dresses up in pigtails and a little schoolgirl outfit when she fucks you!"

"What are you talking about?" Malden asked, still half-asleep.

"I broke into your phone, you idiot! You haven't ended things with any of the other women. You're fucking hookers and women who apparently have no problem with pedophiles. You're a sick fuck – get the fuck out of my house!"

"How dare you go into my phone," Malden shouted angrily as he jumped out of my bed, still naked. He quickly threw on his jeans, shirt and shoes, "Where's my fucking phone?"

"I texted all your bitches, by the way, and informed them that you had a girlfriend," I said, chucking his phone at his chest as hard as I could.

"How dare you text them!" he shouted at me as he caught his phone.

"How dare you cheat on me, you lowlife scumbag!"

The rage and adrenaline I felt got the best of me. He slapped me when I last accused him of cheating. He tried to make me feel like the bad guy when all along I knew I was right. I couldn't restrain myself any longer. With all my might, I took my right hand and socked him in the face as hard as I possibly could. The tiger in me had been unleashed.

He stepped back and stared at me in shock. I took both my hands and pounded them on his chest and shouted, "Now you know what it feels like to be punched, you piece of shit!"

He glared at me with his fiery red wolf eyes then stormed into the bathroom. He locked the door. I could hear him lift the toilet seat.

"Get the fuck out of my house or I'll call the police!" I shouted as loud as I could while pounding on the door. I was certain my neighbors could hear my screams – and I wanted them to. I knew that Malden was capable of more serious violence than a slap in the face.

A minute later, Malden swung open the bathroom door and stormed out.

Before he exited my apartment, he shouted, "Never contact anybody I know ever again, you bitch!" He slammed the door behind him. I sat on my bed, threw my head in my hands and sobbed. Within seconds, my phone beeped. Malden was sending me texts filled with rage.

Malden Murphy: "Fuck off! You will get violated."

Lana Burke: "What do you mean I will get violated?"

Malden Murphy: "Sleep on it."

Lana Burke: "If you try to hurt me I will involve the police. Not sure why you would do this to me, but I will do what is necessary to protect myself."

Malden Murphy: "A simple warning. Unfriend everyone you know through me now on Facebook. I will be watching."

Lana Burke: "Fine."

Malden Murphy: "You know all the tricks. You're a dirty girl. Down and dirty."

Lana Burke: "Stop bullying me."

Then like the bipolar freak he is, Malden changed his tune.

Malden Murphy: "No one's ever done to me what you did to me in bed tonight. That felt amazing."

A second later, the wolf was back.

Malden Murphy: "My life is none of your business. You're a professional trash digger. Get a job with some social value. Take a shot, dirty girl. Messing with you is gonna be fun. I'm monitoring your e-mail."

Lana Burke: "You hacked into my e-mail? That's illegal!"

Malden Murphy: "Be careful. You are forewarned."

Lana Burke: "Just please leave me alone. I want you out of my life forever."

The TV was still on. The President was about to make his acceptance speech. Gov. Richards had conceded to the loss. I felt ill. I couldn't bear to watch the country crumble as my life continued to fall apart. Was this my karma for exposing Gov. Richards? I felt tremendous shame and guilt. I popped two Xanax to put myself in a self-induced coma and went to bed, miserable.

CHAPTER 20

I woke up at ten the next morning in a panic. The gnawing feeling in my stomach had returned. My gut now told me that there had to be a tie between my illness and Malden instead of Gov. Richards. That had become the more plausible explanation for my illness. After all, he had told my doctors and me that he didn't have any STDs or lead a high-risk sexual lifestyle. I had just proven that he did, in fact, lead a high-risk sexual lifestyle. But I needed proof there was a connection. I frantically threw on a black Lululemon yoga outfit, jumped in my X5 and sped down Third Street to Cedars-Sinai Hospital.

I raced into the emergency room, walked up to the counter at the entrance and demanded my medical records. The heavyset Hispanic woman at the desk informed me that I needed to go to the Cedars-Sinai library to retrieve my records. She directed me to the second floor of the building across the street.

I ran across the street, entered the building and rushed into an elevator. Just as the door was closing, two medical interns were discussing where to go for happy hour after work. I caught my breath, punched the second floor button and pulled down my yoga sweatshirt. They gave me a strange look. I did my best to flash them a friendly smile, but my lips barely moved. When I got to the second floor, I saw a sign with two arrows on the wall. One arrow read "maternity ward" and the other read "library." I briskly walked in the direction toward the library. It had glass doors at the entrance, and there were sky-high bookshelves filled with files. An elderly redhead with short, curly hair was sitting at the desk, reading a book. I quickly walked right up to her desk.

"Hi, I was in the hospital recently, and I need my medical records," I said in a rush.

"OK," she said, grabbing a clipboard from behind her desk. "I'll need you to fill out these forms, dear, and I'll need to see your driver's license."

I quickly reached in my purse and grabbed my ID from my wallet. I handed it to her and then sat down on a plastic chair in a waiting area. As fast as I could, I filled out the forms. I wrote my name, birth date, address, and the dates of my hospital stay.

When I finished the forms, I handed them back to the redhead.

"Just give me a few minutes," she said as she got up and disappeared behind the tall bookshelves.

She came back five minutes later with a manila envelope. I was surprised by the envelope's heavy weight. I quickly ripped my medical records out of the envelope as I headed back to the same seat in the waiting area. My medical records were fifty-six pages long! I couldn't believe it. I had only stayed at Cedars-Sinai for one night! I sat down and began to dissect all the papers at a high-speed pace. I read:

Emergency Treatment Record 10/08/2012

History of Present Illness: This is a 32-year-old female who states she recently found out that her boyfriend cheated on her. She has had two weeks of symptoms that started out like a yeast infection with itching but more of a liquid discharge than normal. She took Bactrim and MetroGel. The itch went away pretty rapidly but it took longer for the discharge to go away. Currently, she does not have any pelvic pain and she was mostly better but then two days ago she developed dysuria and an odor. She went to an urgent care, they gave her medicine for possible STD exposure. They gave her prescriptions, and they told her she might have a UTI. She did get a shot of Rocephin at the time. She started to feel better, but she started feeling worse again in the last two days. She has bilateral flank pain, pain up and down her spine, headache which is similar to her back pain, subjective fevers, nausea and vomiting. She feels lightheaded. Headache is much worse on standing. Triage notes reviewed.

I scrolled down further and continued to read:

Procedure Note: Lumbar puncture. Given the clinical presentation, I thought the patient probably had a partially treated pyelonephritis but partially treated meningitis was also in the differential. Patient decided to proceed with lumbar puncture. Risks and benefits were discussed.

My heart began to race, and a pit began to form in my stomach. I had flashbacks of the silvery medieval torture device that pierced my spine. My stomach churned, and I felt faint. The room spun. I felt like I might throw up or pass out – or both. I took a deep breath and read on:

She was placed in a right lateral decubitus position. Clear fluid was obtained on the first pass and sent to the laboratory. Patient tolerated the procedure well. Emergency Department Course and Treatment/Discussion: Results of the lumbar puncture were positive, showing protein of 240 and 330 white cells, mostly lymphocytes. Based on this, I was concerned the patient could have viral meningitis even herpes encephalitis. I started her on Acyclovir. I have discussed the case with Med Teaching. Plan is for admission.

Diagnostic Impression: Partially treated meningitis.

The tears began to roll down my face. I couldn't believe what I was reading. I had forgotten the horrible trauma I had been through. It was as if my mind had intentionally blocked it out to protect me from remembering the truth, since it was so awful. I began to dry heave as I cried. I tried my best to cry quietly. Thank God no one else was in there other than the kind redheaded lady who had her nose too deep in a book to notice my breakdown.

I continued to read the fifty plus pages of medical records. Dozens of doctors had evaluated me, and many tests were performed on me. All my final test results concluded that I had HSV-meningitis. However, from all the research I had done online, I had learned there were only two kinds of herpes. There's HSV1, herpes of the mouth, or HSV2, genital herpes. HSV2 is transmitted through sex. The ER doctor from the Chicago hospital told me I had a strand of herpes that causes chickenpox in children and it was not an STD. I imagined that had to be HSV1; however, nowhere in any of my records did it read that I had HSV1. I couldn't figure out why. My sadness turned to angry motivation. Why didn't my records specify what kind of HSV I had? I put the records back in the manila envelope and paid the librarian to make copies for me. When she finished, I stuffed my medical records in my purse and raced out of the library just as quickly as I had raced in.

As I crossed the street and headed back to the emergency room, strong rays from the sun pierced through a row of palm trees. The light instantly pinched my eyes. "Fuck me!" I shouted as I squinted and cringed in pain. As I briskly walked across the street, I frantically searched for my Ray Bans with my right hand in my purse. I found them and threw them on right before I walked back into the emergency room. Ah, relief! The sunglasses instantly eased the pain I felt. The same heavyset woman was still behind the desk fumbling through some papers.

"Excuse me   Miss, excuse me! I need help!" I sharply said.

"I see you're back. What can I do for you now?"

"I need to see Dr. Peterson immediately. I have a question about my medical records from a recent visit here and it's an emergency!" I said in a panic.

"He's an emergency room doctor," she explained. "You can't just waltz in and see him. You can't even make an appointment with him."

"OK, then I need his phone number," I demanded.

"I'm sorry, but we can't give out phone numbers for the ER doctors," she said.

"No, you don't understand. My medical records don't make sense. I need to find out what happened to me!"

"Miss, I'm sorry, but I can't let you see him. The emergency room is for emergencies only."

"This is a fucking emergency, God damn it!" I growled as I slammed my hand down on the counter. I looked up and through the tiny window in the door leading into the emergency room I saw Dr. Peterson walk by. I bolted.

"Dr. Peterson!" I shouted as I ran toward the door and thrust it open.

"Ma'am you can't go in there," the desk nurse shouted after me. "Security, security – I need help over here!"

When I got in the emergency room, I saw Dr. Peterson just a few feet away from me, talking to another doctor.

"Dr. Peterson – do you remember me?" I said as I waved my right hand at him. "You treated me for meningitis."

As Dr. Peterson looked up, a black muscular security guard burst through the door and grabbed my arm.

"Ma'am, I'm sorry, but you need to go," the security guard said as he grabbed my right arm and pulled me toward the exit.

"No wait, please, Dr. Peterson – I need to talk to you. It's about my health. It's an emergency!"

Tears filled my eyes, and my Ray Bans instantly fogged up. I ripped them off and put them on the counter in the middle of the room where two nurses sat. I quickly wiped the tears from my eyes.

Dr. Peterson raised both his hands, "It's OK. I know her. Please let her go."

I exhaled a sigh of relief.

"Are you sure?" the security guard asked warily.

"Yes." Dr. Peterson nodded.

"Thank you," I said as I looked at the doctor, tears rolling down my face.

"I'll be over here by the exit if you need me," the security guard said as he walked away.

"How are you doing?" Dr. Peterson asked, gently putting his right hand on my left shoulder.

"Not well," I explained. "I don't understand what happened to me...how I got meningitis. Some doctors said I could've picked it up at the air & water show in San Francisco but it doesn't make sense! I don't understand how an STD didn't trigger my disease. When I was here, several of my symptoms were, you know, they were vaginal. Do you remember asking my boyfriend if he led a high-risk sexual lifestyle?"

"Yes," Dr. Peterson nodded.

"Well, I just confirmed that he's cheated on me with dozens of women. I think hookers too! I just left the hospital library. I got all my medical records. In the dozens of pages it reads over and over again that I had HSV-meningitis.

403

However, nowhere does it specify if I had HSV1 or HSV2. The ER doctor I saw in Chicago told me with certainty I had no STDs. She said the kind of herpes I had is the same kind of herpes that causes chickenpox in kids. However, my records don't cite what specific strand of herpes I had. So what does it all mean? Did I have an STD or not? Nothing makes sense."

"Let me see these," Dr. Peterson said as he grabbed my records and quickly scanned them. "OK, I see why you're confused. The doctor in Chicago never should've told you that you had the kind of herpes that causes chickenpox in children. That's clearly a misdiagnosis, because if you review your records, you'll see that the antibodies you had for herpes then were so new that they hadn't formed yet. Since they hadn't fully formed, the tests were unable to determine what strand of herpes you have. However, since it's been weeks, the tests will now conclusively show what kind you have."

"Then will you please test me now?" I begged. "Please, Dr. Peterson."

Dr. Peterson exhaled a deep breath and gave me a sympathetic smile.

"I will walk you to the front desk and tell them to admit you," he said as he directed me toward the door. "You'll have to get in line with all the other patients, but as soon as you get back in here I'll administer the test. Plus, I don't think it would be a bad idea to test you for all STDs again since we now know your ex-boyfriend does seem to lead a high-risk sexual lifestyle. It will take about an hour or so to get your results back."

"Thank you so much, Dr. Peterson," I said.

I sat in the waiting room for an excruciating hour before they allowed me back in the emergency room. Once inside, I was escorted to the same bed in the cordoned off area I was in the first time I visited the ER. A nurse promptly stuck a needle into my left arm to draw blood for the STD tests. She reiterated that the results would be back in about an hour. I lay my head down, closed my eyes and attempted to doze off.

"Excuse me," I heard a deep man's voice from behind the hospital curtain that bordered my bed for privacy. "Can I come in?"

"Um…sure." I said sitting up, baffled.

The man's right hand grabbed the curtain just a few feet away from me. Although my vision was still blurred from the meningitis, I could tell the mystery man's fingers were long, slender and appeared to be perfectly manicured. His hand had faint wrinkles, and I could slightly see veins. The man had to be in his forties judging by my quick assessment of his hand. He slowly pulled the curtain to the side. There stood a six foot, one inch slender man in a navy suit with a white-collared shirt underneath and a red tie. His outfit was perfectly coordinated. He looked the way one of the many politicians I had worked for did on the day of an important political event. The man had lush, short brown hair and large brown eyes. He looked at me and gave me a huge smile. He had bright white piano teeth, and his smile brightened up the entire room. He was gorgeous! I blushed. Who the fuck is this dude, and why is he in my hospital room?

"Hi," he said energetically.

"Hi," I responded, embarrassed. I looked like crap – my makeup had smeared off from the tears, and my hair was a disaster. I was in no mood to meet a good-looking stranger. "Um, is there something I can do for you?"

"I think you left something behind." He said, eyes piercing at me, still flashing his bright smile as he held up my Ray Bans.

"Oh my Ray Bans," I said, gratefully. "Of course. Thank you. I'm always losing them."

"No problem," he said as he approached my bed and handed me my sunglasses. "I heard you talking to the ER doctor. I was in a room close by. I'm here with my father who is having heart problems. I went to get some coffee, and I noticed you left your sunglasses on the counter."

"Well, thanks for grabbing them. I'm sorry to hear about your father."

"No, it's OK," he said. "He's going to be fine. He's a tough dude, a war veteran. Anyway, I overheard what you told

405

the doctor. I apologize for eavesdropping, but I feel compelled to tell you that if your ex-boyfriend did infect you with a venereal disease – you do have legal rights. You know that, right?"

"Excuse me?" I asked.

"In California, it's a crime simply to expose someone to an STD without full disclosure, and in civil court you can sue for a lot of money for contracting an STD from a deceitful partner."

"Wow…I don't know what to say. I guess thanks for the information." I said, trying to collect my thoughts. "I appreciate the tip, but I don't think…hopefully I don't have any STDs. So I won't need to pursue any legal avenues."

"Right," the man said, reaching into his back right pants pocket. "I hope that too. However, if that doesn't turn out to be the case, I can help you. My name's Bruce Davis."

He opened his brown leather wallet and pulled out a business card and handed it to me. It read: Bruce W. Davis. He worked as a partner at BLD Law firm on Flower Street in downtown Los Angeles.

"Um," I said as I stared at the card. "Thanks. I'm Lana."

He stuck out his right hand. I slowly reached out my right hand and shook his. He had a strong and confident grip.

He smiled warmly and said, "It's really good to meet you, Lana. You take care now."

"You too," I said after he had already turned his back to me. I looked at his card for a couple of moments. "Bruce Davis," I said aloud. I reached for my purse on the stand next to my hospital bed and put the card in a sleeve in my wallet.

I prayed to God Bruce's appearance wasn't a sign for what was about to come. I lay back in my bed and grabbed the TV remote. I flipped on the TV. The last time I had turned on this TV I caught news reports on a meningitis outbreak. Now, it was on BNN. I watched a montage of clips from the President's acceptance speech. I cringed.

As I lay in the ER hospital bed, I got an awful, sinking

feeling. I picked up my iPhone and jumped on Facebook. Something inside of me was telling me to reach out to Malden's ex-wife. I didn't have her number, so I found her profile and shot her a quick message. Oddly, she still used Malden's last name.

Lana Burke: "Hi Bethenny, I'm sorry to bug you, but there's something important I need to talk to you about and it involves some serious health problems I'm having. I'd really appreciate it if you'd chat with me on the phone. I don't have your number, though. Best, Lana"

Twenty minutes later, I was surprised to get a response.

Bethenny Murphy: "Hi, Lana, I can chat in an hour. The kids won't be home then. My number is 415-555-7780. Thanks, Bethenny"

My anxiety level rose. I felt anxious to chat with her. The way Malden had talked about Bethenny you'd think she was the devil. I wasn't sure how the conversation would go or how she would react to me.

I killed another half hour by flipping back and forth from BNN to Rox News Channel watching their election recaps. I felt like I was living out a real life Greek tragedy. I was one of the few Republicans in Hollywood, and I was responsible for Gov. Richards's demise. I had tremendous guilt. Dr. Peterson walked back in the room. He had a grim look on his face that I recognized from the first time he had bad news to report.

"Well, your suspicions were correct," he began. "You're positive for HSV2."

"Herpes 2, so that's…" I wondered out loud.

"Genital herpes," Dr. Peterson explained. "You have genital herpes. It's an STD you only get through sexual intercourse."

"So I had HSV2-meningitis?" I asked in defeat.

"Correct," Dr. Peterson said. "So, your first day in the

hospital you were negative for both kinds of herpes. That means that you had been clean your entire life up until then. A week later, you had a positive result for herpes, but since you had been so recently exposed the antibodies had not formed enough to narrow down what kind of herpes you had. Were you sleeping with anyone else besides your boyfriend?"

"No, he's the only person I've slept with in over a year," I stated.

"If that's true, that means scientifically he's the only person who could've given this to you," Dr. Peterson said, shaking his head. "Lana, this is not only disturbing because he told both of us he was clean – it's a crime."

"Yeah, so I've heard."

"It's illegal to knowingly expose a sexual partner to an STD without disclosing that you have one. Not only did he expose you to an STD, he lied, which prevented you from getting the proper healthcare that you so desperately needed immediately. If I would've known you were exposed to herpes, I would've kept you in the hospital for a week on an Acyclovir IV drip to avoid serious brain damage. The drip is way more effective than the pills."

The tears returned to my eyes, and I felt my heart crack into thousands of tiny pieces.

"I just..." I said, trembling. "I can't believe this man I was so in love with would lie to me as I'm sitting in a hospital bed dying!"

"It's very disturbing behavior, Lana," Dr. Peterson said. "I'm not a lawyer or a police officer, but I strongly suggest you look into your legal rights."

"I can't believe it," I said, tears rolling down my cheeks. "I was so in love with him. How could he do this to me? I mean, maybe he doesn't know he has it?"

"That's possible, but not likely." Dr. Peterson sighed. "Now is there anything else I can do for you?"

"No," I said as I wiped the tears off my cheeks. "Thank you so much for helping me today."

"Of course," Dr. Peterson said with a stoic smile. "I wish

you the best of luck."

I slowly walked back to my car with my shoulders completely hunched over in defeat. I felt destroyed. It had been an hour though, and it was time to call Bethenny. I waited until I got into my car, so I was in a quiet space. I reluctantly dialed her number. Knots formed in my stomach as the phone rang. After three rings, a soft woman's voice answered on the other end.

"Hi, is this Bethenny?" I nervously asked.

"Yes, it is," she said.

"Hi Bethenny – it's Lana," I said as I cleared my throat.

"Hi, Lana."

"First of all, I want to thank you for taking my call. I realize this is a little awkward, but it's very important that I talk to you. I think you might be able to help me."

"Well, I'm happy to help," she said. Her friendliness surprised me. It was a relief. I felt at ease with her on the phone.

"I'm calling you because I've had some serious health issues. I recently came down with a bad case of meningitis…"

"Oh my God – I had no idea," she exclaimed. "Can't you die from that?"

"Yes," I said. "When my doctors first diagnosed me with meningitis, they were all scratching their heads, unsure how in the world I could've contracted the disease. They thought there was a possibility my meningitis could've been caused by an STD; however, all my STD results came back negative at first. Well, long story short, I found out today that I had HSV2-meningitis. My meningitis was caused by genital herpes, and the doctors have concluded that scientifically there's no other person who could've infected me with this besides Malden."

"Wow – I…I didn't know herpes could cause meningitis," Bethenny said.

"Neither did I." I sighed. "Malden told all my doctors and me that he does not have any form of herpes or any STDs. My doctor suspects he's been lying to me."

"Oh yeah – he has that. He didn't tell you?" she asked.

"Wait, so he does have genital herpes?" I asked. My jaw dropped.

"Oh yeah!" she said. "He's had it for over twenty years. He gave it to me too, and he gave it to a mistress he had in London. She called me after they had a long affair that went on for a couple years. She told me he gave her herpes, too."

"Oh my God!" I said in shock. "I just, I-I can't believe it! I don't understand how he could lie to all of my doctors when my life depended on this information and I was so in love with him. I trusted him!"

"I've been there," she said sympathetically. "He did the exact same thing to me. I found out he had herpes because I found his prescription for Valtrax. When I finally confronted him about it, he tried to turn it around on me and accused me of giving herpes to him."

"What?" I asked.

"Then he had an affair with this woman in London. He was doing business there regularly – I had no idea he was cheating on me. I was here struggling to raise our children alone while he was in Europe. He told this woman that he was going to divorce me and that they'd be together. That never happened. The woman called me hysterical. She wasted years of her life with him, and she contracted herpes from him, too. He destroyed both of our lives."

"I'm speechless," I said shaking my head, trying to process everything she was telling me.

"He's a sociopath. I get phone calls from women he's slept with all the time. He's a sex addict and a womanizer. When our daughter got sick with Lyme disease, he totally abandoned her. She wants nothing to do with him. I worry that our boys will grow up to be womanizers just like him. I'm trying my best to raise them right, but it's hard to shield them from their father's bad behavior. He was cheating on you too right in front of our children. There were many weekends that they'd come home upset because they knew you had no idea their dad was cheating on you. They love you, and they've been hoping things would work out between you guys."

My stomach tightened in a hundred more knots. I felt pressure on my chest as if someone had placed a cement block on it. I gasped for air. I couldn't believe Malden gave his children the burden of maintaining his lies and sins. I loved those kids. The idea of him cheating on me in front of them was too much.

"I'm sorry, I'm just in total shock," I said breathlessly. "I knew he was hiding things from me, but I had no idea it was on this level. There's something else that's been bugging me. I know this is a weird question, but did he ever drug you?"

"Oh yeah. He slipped ecstasy in my drink a few times while we were married. Who does that? Who drugs their wife?"

"Are you serious?"

"Oh, yeah. Lana, you have no idea."

My brain was shrouded in a cloud of disbelief and despair. However, I also felt relief and a sense of accomplishment for finally unlocking the truth.

"There was one night he put something in my drink, but I don't think it was what he said it was. I've had this sinking feeling for weeks that something happened to me that night. His brother made advances toward me while his wife and children were in the next room. And - "

"Which one? Max?"

"Yes."

"That doesn't surprise me. He's a creep."

"He is creepy."

"Yes, the entire family is messed up. Malden has serious issues. I think he's suffered some kind of abuse when he was little."

"I've suspected that, too."

"I always thought that Malden is secretly gay, but since he's such a macho guy, he just can't go there. So, he suppresses everything and deals with his demons through drugs and alcohol."

So the Nick in his phone probably was a gay dude. I

couldn't believe it. Had I fallen in love with a gay man?

"What about hookers? I found evidence that he may have been cheating on me with hookers…"

"Oh yeah, for sure," she said nonchalantly. "I hired a private investigator during our divorce, and you wouldn't believe the stuff the investigator uncovered. It got to be so sickening, I had to tell the PI to only tell me the bare minimum that I needed to know to win our divorce battle."

The journalist in me wondered how she could resist hearing every detail of Malden's double life. "So you were able to prove he was sleeping with hookers?"

"Yes, he was sleeping with hookers – and even minors. He was having sex with one of his old bosses' daughters. She was seventeen."

Did I hear her correctly? Did she just tell me he slept with a minor? I wanted to puke. "Are you kidding me?" I asked as I threw my left hand in the air. "Hookers and a minor? I feel ill."

"Yes. The PI found records of him hiring hookers all over the place. He even managed to find hookers in Mormon Salt Lake City of all places."

"Wait, Salt Lake City?"

"Yeah," she said calmly. "He does business there too – so he claims."

"Didn't he stop there and Winnemucca, Nevada, during that cross-country road trip he took with the boys?" I asked.

"I'm not sure – I can't remember where they went," Bethenny said.

That's when the light bulb went off. I knew I had to get off the phone immediately. I had heard enough. "Thanks so much for talking to me," I hurriedly told Bethenny. "I really appreciate it, but I've got to run."

"You know – you should sue him. I read that a woman sued Robin Williams for giving her herpes and she got millions. I bet you'd win. I got very little justice out of taking Malden to court for our divorce. Maybe you can get the justice I never got. I can help you."

"Um, I don't know. I'm trying to process all this information," I said, flustered. "I really appreciate you taking the time to talk to me. Please give the kids my best," I said before clicking off my phone.

I turned on the engine of my car like a complete and total mad woman. I sped out of the parking garage and took a right on Beverly Boulevard. I flew down the L.A. street thirty miles per hour over the speed limit. I felt sweat form under my armpits and on the brim of my forehead. All the pieces were coming together. I had finally unlocked the mystery behind my illness, and my worst nightmare had become a reality. I didn't know how the tables had turned. My life as a tabloid journalist had just turned into the most horrendous tabloid story of all time.

When I got to my luxury apartment complex, I raced my car into the front entrance, almost hitting a young mother pushing her newborn in a stroller. I cringed and waved to her and mouthed "sorry." I saw my favorite guard at the entrance. I didn't even wave to him to say hi as the gate opened. I could not get home soon enough. I drove into the underground garage so fast my tires screeched. I quickly parked my car. The left wheel spilled over the white line on the ground into my neighbor's spot. I didn't even consider taking the two seconds it would take to reposition my car. I sprinted out and raced to the elevator. Luckily, the elevator door opened right away. Once I got to the second floor, I bolted to my apartment. At the door, I fumbled through my purse for a few seconds before I found my keys. I flung open the door and ran into the kitchen. I threw my purse on the counter and opened the main kitchen cabinet. I pulled out a basket filled with notebooks, checks, cameras, photos, a flip cam and other tools I used for reporting. I threw almost everything out on the counter, and there in the middle of all the crap was Celeste's dated cell phone. I opened it quickly. It was dead. I grabbed the charger I had purchased for it in Winnemucca and waited an excruciating five minutes before it turned on. I stood in my kitchen with the cell phone in my hand and stared at it intently as if I were waiting to get results back from a pregnancy test.

As soon as the phone lit up, I went straight to the phone directory. I had a gut-wrenching feeling that I had missed something. I scrolled down the list of all Celeste's contacts until I got to the M section. The first name on the list was Mac, the second Mark, and the third name was Mal. I skipped past Mal, looking for Malden. There was no Malden. I went back to the name Mal. Before I tapped the appropriate key to pull up the details of the contact, I had a flashback from journalism school. One of my first days in Journalism 101, I remember the college professor spontaneously calling on me. I was half-awake and hung over from drinking with my friends the night before.

"Lana, are you with us?" the professor chastised me.

"Yeah."

"Please tell me – what is the definition of the Latin root word mal?" he asked.

"Bad or evil." I said.

"Good," the professor said. "I'm glad you're still awake."

With that thought, I clicked on the name Mal. The contact opened on Celeste's phone. I scrolled down to see the number. It began with a 949 area code -- Orange County's area code. My heart stopped. It was Malden's cell phone number! I scrolled down a littler further. Under "title", Celeste had listed him as "Client Number Twenty-Eight".

Not only did Malden fuck hookers, he had fucked my subject! My boyfriend was just as much of a scumbag as Gov. Richards; however, my theory that Gov. Richards used biological warfare to infect me with a brain-altering deadly disease was wrong. The wacky conspiracy theory was all in my crazy mind. The true enemy had been right under my nose and in my bed this entire time.

I felt weak and dizzy. My meningitis symptoms instantly came back: vertigo, photophobia, back and neck pain and nausea. My knees buckled, I fell to my kitchen floor and sobbed for several minutes. The things that were most important to me in my life – my career, health and boyfriend – had been completely stripped from me. I felt naked, raw and completely defeated. I felt unbearable anger too. A fire began to rage in the epicenter of my soul.

I lifted my head, still sitting on the kitchen floor and reached my arm up and grabbed my purse off the counter. I pulled my phone and wallet out. In my darkest and weakest hour, I could still feel the tiger inside me. She lengthened her spine as I removed the card out of my wallet. I read the cell phone number listed on the card and carefully dialed the numbers on my cell phone as my hands trembled. The phone rang. No answer. I didn't pay attention to the generic recorded greeting. My tiger rolled her shoulders back, stretched her neck high and sat proudly. I heard the beep to leave a message.

"Hi, Bruce, It's Lana. We met in the emergency room today. Please give me a call back when you get this. I'm at 310-555-7405. Thanks."

I hung up the phone, took a deep breath and my tiger let out a thunderous roar.

Made in the USA
San Bernardino, CA
08 December 2018